THE PARAGON HOTEL

ALSO BY LYNDSAY FAYE

Dust and Shadow
The Gods of Gotham
Seven for a Secret
The Fatal Flame
Jane Steele
The Whole Art of Detection

G. P. PUTNAM'S SONS
NEW YORK

THE PARAGON HOTEL

Lyndsay Faye

PUTNAM

G. P. PUTNAM'S SONS
Publishers Since 1838
An imprint of Penguin Random House LLC
penguinrandomhouse.com

Library of Congress Cataloging-in-Publication Data

Names: Faye, Lyndsay, author.
Title: The paragon hotel / Lyndsay Faye.
Description: New York : G. P. Putnam's Sons, 2019.
Identifiers: LCCN 2018012903 | ISBN 9780735210752 (hardcover) | ISBN 9780735210769 (epub)
Subjects: | GSAFD: Historical fiction. | Suspense fiction.
Classification: LCC PS3606.A96 P37 2019 | DDC 813/.6—dc23
LC record available at https://lccn.loc.gov/2018012903
p. cm.

Printed in the United States of America
1 3 5 7 9 10 8 6 4 2

Book design by Amanda Dewey

For Bethy

No free Negro, or Mulatto, not residing in this state at the time of the adoption of this constitution, shall come, reside, or be within this state, or hold any real estate, or make any contracts, or maintain any suit therein; and the Legislative Assembly shall provide by penal laws, for the removal, by public officers, of all such Negroes, and Mulattos, and for their effectual exclusion from the state, and for the punishment of the persons who shall bring them into the state, or employ, or harbor them.

—Oregon State Constitution, Article 1, Section 35, 1857

The "Negro and Mulatto" section of Oregon's constitution was technically repealed in 1926 but was only later amended to remove all antiquated racial language in November of the year 2002. The vote was 867,901 in favor of modernizing it and 352,027 against.

PROLOGUE

You're supposing that you hold in your hands a manuscript. A true story I knitted into a fable, tinted with my own brushes, chiseled *tappity-tap* until its rough edges were erased and nothing but clean, smooth autobiography remained.

You're entirely wrong, dearest. This isn't a book at all.

I'm scratching out this first bit last, and you just shuffled past me into the kitchen, yawning, giving me the gimlet-eye routine. You're ever so good at it, but it doesn't work on yours very truly; and after you've poured yourself some coffee and refilled my chipped brown cup, you'll ghost your hands over my shoulders and try craftier means of wheedling it out of me. What exactly I've been working on all this while.

Well, you may proverbially put up your shoes and kick off your heels and save yourself the botheration—I'm giving this to you tied up with a pretty twine bow later tonight.

I stepped outside very early, while you were still sleeping. Sprawled out and snoring and safe, or as safe as we can ever be again, in the tidy little home we've made together. There was enough wind sliding down the brown hills to ruffle my hair, and a scrub jay flashed its wings, pure blue against California porcelain dawn, high above my head, and for the first time, I allowed myself to believe that we can actually get away with it. We can live like this. Not *here* necessarily, Christ knows I'm well aware the need to skedaddle could descend at any time, but this morning I knew . . . we'll figure it out.

The pair of us.

Parts of this will disturb you. Whether it'll be the parts you were a part of, so to speak, or the parts that are new—well, I suppose I'll just ask after you're finished reading. I can imagine your mug as you devour this, impatiently turning pages, orderly at first, because you're awfully orderly, and then papers scattered higgledy-piggledy all over the hardwood.

I might leave, for most of that. Walk to the equestrian-supply store a few miles down the road, the one we discovered lightning fast, remember, with its little door behind the racks of leather chaps, and the speakeasy beyond with the barkeep whose mustache makes him look so wonderfully tragic. Like he lost his one true soul mate years ago, and that soul mate was a devoted sheepdog. I'll sip whiskey—it's good here in San José, the contraband, I know you agree—and try to get him to admit he's wrestled grizzlies. Leaving you to yourself while you read this story that isn't exactly a story. Because you mustn't think of it that way. Promise me you won't?

It's not a book. This was never a book.

This is a love letter.

· One ·

NOW

New York probably is infested with as savage a horde of cut-throats, rats, treacherous gunmen and racketeers as ever swarmed upon a rich and supine principality.

—STANLEY WALKER, *The Night Club Era*, 1933

Sitting against the pillows of a Pullman sleeper, bones clacking like the pistons of the metal beast speeding me westward, I wonder if I'm going to die.

The walls of my vibrating coffin are polished mahogany, windows spotless, reflecting onyx midnight presently. I've been watching them for several days. When I wasn't switching trains, which was its own jostling hell and doesn't bear repeating.

Does Salt Lake City ever bear repeating, really?

I don't even suppose I took the fastest route cross-country. So long as I was always moving. I remember fleeing New York, still adrift with the shock. Battling sucking currents of lost love and lost city dragging me under. Changing at Chicago I remember—the hustle, the weight of all that metal, the sheer rank sweat of making the connection. I recall prim forests, sloping hills. Downy wheat tufts, crops we tore through like an iron bomb, and desolate empty skies. Big burgs, shabby shacks, towns undeserving of the word, all blurring into *America.*

But at night it's been the black window, the white alcove curtain, smells of cigarettes and pot roast and cold cream, and the fever slick coating my brow confirming that I'm going to die.

I'm in shock, possibly. Despair, certainly.

Now it hits me in a crack of panic that I'd prefer death drop by when I'm ninety and not twenty-five, supposing it's all the same to the Harding administration.

Panting, I tug at my hair. The sudden flare momentarily douses the fire in other locales. I wonder when my bunkmate will return to torment me. I wouldn't have taken a sleeping car if I hadn't been forced—acquaintances are dangerous. They pore over your mug out of sheer boredom, make remarks like *God, isn't our porter just dreadful, these sheets are barely tucked in.* They don't give a knotted cherry stem what you think of the porter, they can't really see him anyhow. No, they hanker to watch you *react* to them. Then they can journal it, whether you're haughty or humble or hateful. Whether you're all right.

Whether you're not all right, which is ever so much more interesting.

Dangerous, what with death and dismemberment potentially in hot pursuit. I couldn't go full-scale deluxe, though. A private car would have been checked first by someone searching this train, any cadet axman would chart the same course. Private cars, sleeping cars, then public seating. Maybe I ought to lend a hand to the brakeman, trade a few dirty jokes in exchange for a hiding place.

If only I could dangle from the undercarriage like a bat.

The bullet wound deposited in Harlem started reaping interest in Chicago, and now we're well past Walla Walla and it's aiming to make me a swell payout. Last time I staggered to the facilities, it looked like a volcano had erupted, crusted reds and blacks. Now it's eating me alive. I can't sit up in a public car. Has to be a sleeper, has to be *this* one; I leaped on this connecting train in Denver like an outlaw onto the town's last nag.

My heart isn't beating, it's clenching its fist at me.

Clamp-clinch. Clutch-grip.

Beastly. Tears keep welling up and my throat keeps closing, and *no,* I say.

You're called Nobody for a reason. Just be yourself. Be Nobody.

Be Nobody, and breathe.

Having died before, I ought to be more sanguine over the prospect. I first died six days ago at the Murder Stable when Officer Harry Chipchase hustled me out of that gruesome dungeon, snapping, "Run, kid!"

"But I—"

"Damn it, Nobody, hitch a ride to the moon. You're dead to this town now, you hear?" Harry was always dour, but I'd never seen his face turned the color of molding cheese previous. "I swear to you, I'll find a body somewheres. Trust me, kid. You died today. Now, *run.*"

Portland, Oregon, is as far as I can think of from New York, New York. Still. It might not be far enough. If I can get to Portland, he can track me there. In 1921, you can get practically anywhere with a little jack jingling in your pocket.

I identify a faint, floating nausea not confined to just my belly. My skin is actually queasy. Tiny ripples pass along it as if my body is a river. That's new. I don't much care for new things just now.

Rat-a-tat-tat.

Terror gushes, but I choke out a "Come in?"

The paneled door slides, and I exhale. It isn't my forced

companion—she must still be gossiping in the dining car. She retires around one a.m., is up with the dawn. It's only Max, our Pullman porter. Real warmth seeps into my skin again.

Max. He's not the blackest of the lot, he's a sweet rum color, but plenty black enough to play this godforsaken gig. His eyes are wide set, an amber tone below philosophical brows, and he has large hands I figure ought to be playing music someplace daylight never visits. Maybe thirty years old. He sells phonograph records on the side to the travelers, and I bought one. "Crazy Blues" by Mamie Smith and her Jazz Hounds. Max was tickled to pieces—hell, he'd have put on a parade if I'd admitted I'd seen Mamie play live. But the purchase was enough. Small things like that make people cotton to you.

"Miss James?"

I'm tempted to say, *Call me Alice,* but they don't do that sort of thing on Pullman trains. In fact, I'm meant to call him *George,* after George Pullman, because George Pullman is the type so steeped in Christian humility that he orders all the Negroes on his trains renamed George. Bet he could charm the skin off a tomato in person.

"Hullo, Max. Here for the trapeze act?"

Then I wink at him. It feels a bit less like dying on a train car.

Anyway, Max is safe. He has a purebred Brooklyn accent, and we picked him up in Chicago at the transfer, which is how I figure he's so musical. Hell of a sideline record stock he displayed for a fellow who fluffs pillows. I like the version of Nobody I can be with Max. She claims to be an easygoing flapper on the run from a dreadfully cruel gentleman caller, Yonkers born, midlevel typist, interested in jazz but doesn't know much yet. Likes the Greenwich speakeasies that look like tearooms. Terribly droll those, likes to chew the fat about the latest plays over Darjeeling spiked with bootleg rum. Likes cats. That sort.

"'Scuse me for saying so, but you're looking real poorly, Miss James." Max glances behind himself.

"Well, I'm in Oregon, you see."

He exposes the glint of a flask in his pocket.

"Oh God," I gasp. The pain flares up again, rich and real. "Name your price."

"Take it easy," he says quietly. "Settle down and have a snort on the house."

Angels sing faint arias. I don't dawdle over finding out what it is before I guzzle the stuff. Good corn liquor, not the best but not cheap hooch either, small-batch operation. Pure Midwestern moonshine. The drink cuts a rug through my veins.

"Beg pardon, but this louse hurt you real bad, didn't he, Miss James?" Max's genuine frown sticks me right in the chest.

Well, yes, Nicolo Benenati shot a small-caliber bullet that grazed my torso like a neat little sewing stitch, out the other side, so it was more of a lark than it could have been, and I got the wound to stop bleeding a few hours afterward, happy day.

Hissing, I force my eyes shut until I'm less set on weeping all over Max, because it simply will not do. I like him. I like him awfully. I like his smooth brown lips and his wise-guy jabs and the way his eyelashes fan. I like his quiet magnetism. I like how he reminds me of someone.

Your nickname is Nobody, remember. Nobody at all.

"The trapeze act isn't very cheery tonight," I admit.

"Aw, look, there's a doctor over in car three, and we can—"

"No doctor."

"Why's that, miss?"

"Because this is very silly nonsense, just an attack of nerves, probably, touch of stomachache, and I'm being a wretched little idiot. How long until Portland?"

"We'll be there before dawn."

"You're a dear."

"When we pull in," I think Max says, his vowels thick and strong as big city blocks, "you're coming with me, all right? I know a girl what don't fancy a regular-type doctor when I see one. You'll be just fine, Miss James. I'm gonna make sure."

Nobody the sweet flapper would answer him, I think, but by now I live in a different world than he does, a seasick haze of nothing at all.

When I wake up, my bunkmate has returned. Looking dreadfully hopeful of conversation, and here I'm fresh out of the stuff. And probably about to lose consciousness again.

"Oh, Miss James, you *are* pale. Should I fetch you some ginger ale?"

Hearing Mrs. Muriel Snider speak, I reflect, is better than being shot. But not by a terribly wide margin.

"You're so kind, but I couldn't possibly put you to the trouble." I offer her a shy smile.

Really, I've been doing a crackerjack job at not looking agonized.

Mrs. Muriel Snider has a face that makes me figure God took His inspiration from a potato. She's sedately dressed in a brown traveling suit when she isn't sedately dressed in a nightgown, and I'd wager that she's sedately dressed in a bathing costume when taking a bath. The Nobody I am with her is fluttery and inexperienced, hinted she met with an embarrassing riding accident, devoutly Protestant, anxious whether she's authoritative enough when giving her piano lessons, thinks grape juice should be served at all religious services including the Jewish ones, embarrassed to be unmarried. Knitter. That sort.

Thankfully, after stanching the bleeding left by the slug, I wore my most invisible duds. So she can't fault this Nobody for being in the wrong clothes. It's a below-the-knee skirt and a belted jacket in quiet shepherd check. And my honey-blond hair is bobbed, but long enough I can pin it so no one notices.

"Anyhow, we're almost there, I hope?"

She checks her watch. "Oh, yes, dear. Are you sure you don't want me to bring you some hot milk, perhaps? I wouldn't trust this George of ours to get the temperature right."

Smiling again, I picture round after round from a tommy gun shattering her skull, *smash-crack*, blood soaring like a startled flock of redbirds.

It isn't like me. I'm not violent. But I'm in an awfully bad mood.

"This late, it'll only upset my digestion, I fear."

"Heavens, yes, I never noticed how long I was gone, for the kindest Presbyterian minister and his new wife were in the dining car—she's already expecting just before their first anniversary, and I was fit to bursting with happiness for them! And with the amount of advice I have to offer, having raised six of my own alongside Fred? The poor young dear simply peppered me with questions."

She removes her jewelry, puts it carefully in her handbag, and sniffs as she locks the satchel, placing it behind her pillow. The lengths I go to ignore her are positively transcontinental.

"You're such a comfort, you know, Miss James. Forgive me for being this direct, but so many young women have abandoned the ideals of motherhood and child-rearing. Anyhow, I wanted to tell you that I trust in you, truly, to find a proper mate. It's nothing to be ashamed of, dear, being a tad plain, a bit forgettable. That requires moral courage, you know, and someday the right man will take notice. Just you trust in God and in His timing."

The genuine smile that pools over my face pleases her. I'm recalling sitting at the Tobacco Club with Mr. Salvatici, wearing a House of Worth gown. It plunged in great V's down my chest and my back, neckline bordered in a thick stripe of golden beadwork that made my carefully curled hair gleam like Broadway at midnight. The loose bodice fell in pale sea-breeze greens and blues, dripping sequined bubbles into an underskirt of aqua tulle, and when I threw back my head and laughed from heavily rouged lips, only six or seven hundred people that night looked at me at all.

If I'd wanted to get storked, I could have done it when I was seventeen. I wear a rubber womb veil, thank you—all the fast girls do, and the careless ones have been more than once to the lady doctor who solves their problems. She takes a vacation every Christmas to shore up her energies for the post–New Year's stampede. No kidding. A lot has changed since the War. Since Prohibition.

Since six days ago.

If I must die, let it be in a city. Nobody dead nowhere is too much punishment. So let it be in Portland, I decide, wondering how far I can make it until dissolving into ocean foam like some mermaids of note who weren't loved in return either.

When we arrive, it's still dark.

Clash-ring. Grate-scrape. Whistle blast.

Now my head is pounding, and I dread what happens next with all that's left of my heart.

Here's mud in your eye.

Sitting up, I use my arms mainly, and I don't shriek over the sensation. Markedly unpleasant though it is.

"Well, you simply must contact me when you're feeling better, Miss James," Mrs. Snider fusses. "I think we could be great friends despite the difference in our ages. My husband, Fred, is a member of the Arlington Club, and you seem of such good stock, I imagine he must know your parents already. Which is their congregation?"

"Oh . . . my parents are poor farmers some sixty miles outside the city. I send them whatever I can from my own income as a music teacher. In fact, I'm still very new to Portland. I miss them, and the farm, just . . . just terribly."

When she raises her eyebrows, it's as if a cardboard box lifted its lid. "You dear, sweet soul. Please look me up—the right connections mean everything. And there are a great many young bachelor gentlemen of our acquaintance with sober and pleasing ways! Here is my card—"

As I'm taking it, resenting the extra weight of carrying so much as her printed name, a polite knock sounds.

By now my pulse is too feeble to blaze up into genuine panic and gives a flicker of dismay instead. But it's Max again. He's wearing a chocolate-brown hat that suits his lighter complexion and a beige trench that matches the pale leather of his luggage. His eyes dart, identify the olive coat I'd hung and forgotten, and he snatches it up, draping it respectfully over my shoulders.

Mrs. Snider looks as if someone just slapped her on the ass. It's dreadfully unfair I haven't the energy to be amused.

"Aw, Miss James, I can't tell you how much I appreciate this here favor you're doing me." Max's grin is blinding. "You're a model Christian, I tells you. I'll carry your bags like they was my own firstborn."

"You—I—whatever is the meaning of this, George?" Mrs. Snider splutters.

Max whisks off his hat and rests it over his heart. "It's like this, see. I was looking sorta down as we passed in the corridor earlier, yeah? And Miss James asks what's wrong, and I own up that my mum's been sick, and times is hard. Not feeling too jake herself, Miss James here offers to pay me to carry her things. She a genuine example of piety and charitableness, says I."

Max is fibbing like a born grifter.

That means Nobody the sweet flapper can fib too.

"Oh yes—I do feel so weak, and George here needs everything he can scrape together for his family."

Mrs. Snider's brows lock. "My dear, this is—"

"No time, Mrs. Snider," I insist, knowing Max can't. He picks up my flowered carpetbag and valise. "I'm expected by my roommate, and she worries over the smallest delays. I'll go much faster with George's help. Thank you for your kindness. I just know we'll see each other again when I'm better!"

With my last reserves, I follow Max's deliberately slow strides. Not used to being abandoned like an empty tuna tin, Mrs. Snider doesn't yammer over it. Which might be proof of the existence of a Higher Deity after all.

Every step is torture. The aisles fill with strangers squeezing past one another, pinstripe suits, fedoras, silk skirts under wool cloaks, flat cloth caps. I concentrate on Max's broad back until we reach the exit and I falter at the handrail, eyeing the steps as if they're Niagara and I donned a barrel this morning.

Max turns. "Right this way, Miss James, steady as she goes."

A red-hot railroad tie is lodged in my side, and this time I can't help it. A pleading noise escapes my nose as I descend, and Max takes my arm. Quickly releasing it, he hovers. Not touching me, wouldn't that be simply scandalous, but ready to catch me should I go the way of the high pop fly ball. A chill April breeze brushes my damp skin.

People are probably staring now.

Well, if watching me die is their brand of flea circus, I'm not giving them a curtain call.

"Miss James, you gotta get through the station, and then I'll help," Max says under his breath. "Ready?"

I don't answer.

I walk.

Union Station is bigger than I thought it would be, more elegant. In fact, it's altogether jazzy. Marble walls the color of sand with pretty etched arches, a high coffered ceiling painted a warmer yellow, stone floors in the same beach-bright tones. Dignified metal chandeliers hang over the benches stretching *away, away, away* as my vision tunnels. It's no Penn Station, but it'll serve.

Concentrate on the floor.

Concentrate on your shoes.

Max's hand is three inches from my left elbow.

Concentrate on that.

When we emerge into star-spangled night, my jaw unhinges. There are so *many* galaxies strewn like fistfuls of seed pearls behind the station's clock tower with its pointed peak. Shockingly, achingly beautiful. I wouldn't mind its being the last thing I see.

"You ain't used to the light."

"The what?"

"One thing I've learned from trains is the less city you're in, the more stars there is. That there's science, Miss James."

As we step away from the glow of the station, I stumble, Max says, "Easy now, scrapper," and his hand wraps around my forearm, warm and comforting, and tears are making fast tracks down my cheeks because I can't hold down the fort any longer.

"Where are we going?" I choke.

Max looks down. "Aw, none of the waterworks, Miss James. A tough bird like you? Put a dab of mustard on it. On our way, you can tell me where you're from, 'cause it sure as hell is summery ain't Yonkers."

If I weren't so compromised, I'd be flabbergasted. It's impossible to see through Nobody's personas.

She isn't there.

"Harlem. But don't bother sending back my remains, the river will do. I presume you have a river here—any city that's of any consequence simply must have a river. Crooked police department and working sewers likewise impressive features."

"Speakeasies. A good deli."

"Maybe even a fountain, if you're terribly posh."

"Sure, we got a river. There's even a fountain."

"Max, you amaze me."

"I'll show 'em to you."

"Some other time."

"That'll be swell. Harlem, you say. Born and raised?"

"Bred too. Established eighteen ninety-six."

"Well, that explains it," he mutters.

"Please say where you're taking me, the suspense is altogether too decadent for five a.m."

"I'da thought you'd have that much figured by now. We're going to see the doctor."

I fight him, wild with terror, until he folds me up using his coat like a straitjacket.

Sucking in air despite the burning hurt it causes, I nestle there with my head on his chest. Rain starts to fall, a cool *pitter-pat* of moisture mingling with the tears on my cheeks, gathering on Max's shoulders. I like the sensation, feel as if I'm being washed away someplace cleaner. Someplace new that God just slapped the serial number on. Maybe that's what Portland is like, I can't tell yet from inside this lovely cave where I gasp and shiver. Max smells of sweet cigar smoke and something like cinnamon and the clean starch in his pressed shirt.

"Hush now, hush," I think he's saying, "I've got you. You need to hush."

We're in an alleyway, streetlight from draperies of electric bulbs bathing us and the rain glistening on the pavement, Max and his coat and me inside it. Because Max isn't an idiot, and this is the sort of thing, in every place in the slow-spinning world except for Harlem, that could get him killed, and why he's decided to risk his life for nobody at all, I haven't the faintest idea.

I only calm after Max starts singing "Avalon." His voice is a low purr.

I found my love in Avalon
Beside the bay.
I left my love in Avalon and sailed away.
I dream of her and Avalon
From dusk 'til dawn.
And so I think I'll travel on
To Avalon.

· *Two* ·

Oregon is a land for the white man, and refusing the toleration of negroes in our midst as slaves, we rightly and for a yet stronger reason, prohibit them from coming to us as free negro vagabonds.

—"ALL HAIL! THE STATE OF OREGON,"
Oregon Weekly Times, Portland, Oregon,
November 14, 1857

The road is muddy. Puddles swell and shimmer. The crying jag left me hollow as a shell casing. Max navigates roads I can't see save for rain scattering like shattered crystal, humming with his hat pulled low. Finally, he guides me into a side street littered with broken bottles and cracked bricks. A featureless door confronts us, as does the happy stink of fry grease.

"Miss James, welcome to the Paragon Hotel."

Max pushes his way through.

We're in a clean, spacious kitchen with a white-and-black tiled floor and copper pots hanging from the ceiling. An extraordinarily thin colored woman with biceps like braided rope and a red kerchief tied 'round her hair marvels at us.

"Maximilian Burton, who do you got there, and what are you doing in my kitchen with her?" she demands.

"Miss Christina." Max makes a little bow without letting go of me. "Don't you look swell this morning? I'd stay and chat, but I needs to get Miss James here to a room."

Thunking a spoon against the pot she tends, Miss Christina crosses her arms over her chest, hunching as if to see me better. She must be well over thirty, but her small size lends her a youthful quality. She's lean jawed and plain but very lively—the sort who make out spectacularly as flappers, with a few spangles and an artful smear of lipstick—and she appears to suppose I'm some kind of cheap floozy when really I'm an awfully expensive thug.

The fried fish I smell sits on a wire rack, a staff meal for the maids and the doormen. It's so familiar, it's heartbreaking—I've lived in hotels for my entire life, I know how they operate just before dawn. Bread rises in the oven and beans bubble in the pot with some sort of pork oozing into them. I wonder when I last ate and can't recall.

"Oh, she needs a room, does she?" Miss Christina's face screws up. "And whoever done heard of a stray cat, not to mention a white one, following you home, Max?"

"There's this type of situation known as an emergency," he hisses.

"Oh, you figure?"

"Yeah, I figure."

"Your emergency, is it, personally?"

"How many crises you suppose you've handled without a direct stake, Miss Christina?"

"My share. But you ain't right in the head if you figure we can take her in, things bad as they are. She's unlucky."

"So's a white girl's corpse in one of my sleeper cars. What's your opinion on broken mirrors?"

Her eyes widen. She shouts out the kitchen door for help.

Rainbow spots dart to and fro across my vision. Before I can be so bold as to request a chair, a sturdy blue-black matron charges in with a prim, pretty maid and a pair of half-dressed bellhops who gape at me with varying levels of astonishment.

Then every eye flies to the older woman. As if she's a high priestess or a queen, possibly both.

"Max, child, there had better be an explanation forthcoming, and I mean at this very moment," the woman drawls with a peach-dripping Georgia accent.

"I done found her in Chicago and was with her on the Denver leg, barely able to move from her bunk. She's from Harlem. We can't let her die alone on a train platform," Max bites out. "Someone hurt her, bad. I can't tell if it's lady troubles or—"

A storm of activity interrupts him. People call out instructions, feet vibrating through the tiles of the kitchen floor. I can feel this with marvelous accuracy because I'm on the kitchen floor. The back of my head is cold. There isn't one place that hurts any longer, there are only vibrating waves of *please stop*, and I've lost the reason this is happening to me.

Probably for the best.

When the bellhops get back and a flat half-assembled cot is wedged under my back, I do finally scream. And figure I'll keep at it even though the matron is trying to hush me.

Next thing I know, I am indeed in a hotel room.

The chandelier is thick with metal leaves, the walls neatly papered. Petite cobalt flowers on a grey trellis. Squinting, I see a basin and pitcher, a desk, a sapphire chintz bench with a cushioned armrest, carved posts at the end of my bed.

My coat is gone, shoes missing, and my dress half shrugged off me. A man's unsteady hands are setting the coverlet over my lower half.

Then they're lifting my chemise and I push them away.

"No!" I snarl.

If you ever must see a doctor in an emergency, you see one in our pay, or who knows how fast you would be in the Hudson, my dear young lady, a well-remembered voice that can't protect me anymore says in my head.

"Miss James, I think is your name?" a gravelly rasp inquires. "Or so Max tells us. I don't really give a damn what your name is, but I am a physician and must adjust your underthings."

Blinking, I try to understand what sort of fellow I'm looking at. It's not exactly duck soup. His face is pale mulatto and as blanketed in freckles as New York summers are populated with mosquitoes. His irises are green, peering from behind what some would call spectacles and I'd call a set of awfully sturdy beer steins. Wire-brush grey hair bristles from his pate. I smell cheap whiskey, a sweet-sour cloud, which may or may not be emanating from him. Since he wears only a robe and pajamas, he either resides at the hotel or else doesn't plan on running for public office.

"All right, I'm Miss James, then."

"Dr. Doddridge B. Pendleton. Whether or not you are in fact Miss James—as I said, I don't give a damn."

"I'm awfully sorry to be so much trouble."

"Trouble is the nature of my profession."

"Where's Max?"

"Sugar, this ain't the time for a wide audience, agreed?" The matron sits on the end of the bed. Her thick hair is braided in proud hulking coils, upswept, and streaked with pewter. An upside-down tornado. "I calculate you're wary of strangers, but so are we, and I can vouch for the doctor's character. Now. Is it lady trouble?"

A pause. Recalling I'm going to die, I lift my chemise myself.

"It's twenty-five-caliber trouble."

The twin wounds have turned monstrous. Fire-breathing dragons guarding a horde.

Dr. Pendleton slides his glasses up and down his nose like a trombone. He exchanges a grim look with the matron, who shakes her head.

Tension spreads in spider-silk patterns, fans weblike throughout the room. The vote against my being here seems unanimous so far, saving only Max. I'm not brainless enough to think we're in Harlem, but from their faces, this is the moss-draped heart of Jim Crow Missouri with a right jolly banjo strumming in the distance. Not a Northern port city.

"Miss James, was this done by accident?"

Animal fear parches my throat at the slightest reference to Nicolo Benenati.

"Of course it was an accident," I grate. "This is what happens when a silly girl takes up with a real rat, and I'm paying the piper now. He was drunk, he's always drunk, *God*, and he'd spilled me enough times before that I hated the thought of visiting the carpet again. So I ran, and I think he meant to scare me. He always says he loves me when it's over, but after this—can't you see? I could have died."

That's an old story, and a good one.

Dr. Pendleton blows air past his lips, and yes, the liquor perfume is definitely his brand. "Is this man likely to follow you here? Truthfully, now."

I force a laugh. "Not in his state—he passed out cold as an icebox. Missed me playing Red Cross, me packing, the whole onion. Doc, I never meant to get Max in hot water. He rescued me, and I didn't have a vote. He seems dreadfully headstrong."

"Does he now?" the matron drawls. The woman owns about as much gravitas as a mountain, and is roughly the same shape.

"Yes. I think his friends should watch out for that tendency in his character. Now, are you going to toss me street side, or patch the old girl up? When he said I was dying, I'm . . . pretty sure he had the right idea."

This evaluation is made through the last of my exhausted tears.

Dr. Pendleton whisks his glasses off. "Oh, I was always going to patch you up. It doesn't matter whether I like a patient or not, or what race they are—I've taken a sacred oath. Which is lucky for you, since I don't like you being here at all."

"Um . . . thank you?"

He produces a vial and pours a smidge of liquid into a kerchief.

"Miss James, I aim to close these apertures. Your blood has been severely poisoned, but you are not yet fully in the grip of sepsis. It's my belief that you cannot stay still for such a painful procedure. If I give you this chloroform, I admit there is a minor chance you may not wake up—but if you do not allow me to treat you, you certainly will not survive. It would be unethical for me not to mention it."

My lips part as I absorb this.

But there's only the ceiling above me and a chandelier to address. I'd say goodbye to the hotel room, but it's unfamiliar. I'd say goodbye to Max, but he's done enough already, so much that it lodges in my throat like a sweet thorn.

I'd say goodbye to myself, but we lost touch a very long time ago.

"When you put it like that," I reply, and reach up to pull his handkerchief down to my nose.

At first, there is only afternoon light gilding my blond lashes. It's pleasant. I take care not to stir.

Calm. Stay calm.

Something chemical is happening, something familiar. It's not laudanum, I'm fairly certain. If it were heroin, I wouldn't recognize it. The hurt radiating from my side feels like it's locked in a display case. Not gone, not even hidden, just trapped. Therefore, probably morphine.

Same as the other time I was shot.

I keep very still. The cotton clouds in my ears slowly dissolve.

". . . gone more days than he's here, but he ought to have considerably more sense in that head, you ask me. Or maybe all those miles of tracks shake the sense clean out of Max soon as he gathers any."

It's the matron speaking, tense as a high-wire act. A cool compress replaces the skin-warm one I hadn't realized was on my brow and I can smell her, a welcoming orange oil aroma harking of cleaning products rather than vanity.

They're keeping vigil.

Which means I'm still dying.

"Why, Mavereen, you'd not ask a cow to lay an egg, surely, no matter how fast friends you were or how many favors the cow owed you," says a new voice. "Whatever makes it reasonable to expect Maximilian to have any *sense*?"

This woman's voice is altogether remarkable. Medium high, breathy as a debutante's. The accent is indeterminate enough to mean *touring company* decisively. You hear the same glib, almost self-conscious pitch in song-and-dance girls from Santa Fe to Atlantic City. The flat-morning-champagne and washed-off-glitter sound of viciously quashed twangs. Ruthlessly annihilated lisps. The midtown clubs I frequented had those girls going for ten a penny, ready to hop in a cab with the first swain who lit their cigarette.

But I check myself. Not so with this woman—hoofer, chanteuse, or comedienne, she's performed in more cabarets, slapped more suitors, and then calmly reached for her brandy and soda. My best friend, Sadie, and I would have adopted her for the evening, floating her tab solely to hear her commentary on the menfolk. She's not just an artist.

She's a critic, and an awfully good one.

"Blossom, you're always after excusing that boy," the one called Mavereen chides.

"Max isn't a boy any more than I'm a strawberry farmer, honey. He's thirty-one."

"Thirty-one and too purblind foolish to let white people take care of white people! And it's half for this little lost mouse's sake I say that too. Do you pretend her own folks would approve?"

"Well, *several* points to make now." Blossom's tone is dry as a Bowery martini. "First, we both got her into that nightdress, and she isn't a mouse. She's been shot before, unless you think that scar on her arm means she walked into a hot steel poker, which *I* don't."

If it weren't for the morphine, I'd be crawling out of my skin.

They know you aren't who you're pretending, and it's been all of eight hours, maybe. Grand. Suppose you send an at-home card pinpointing the Paragon Hotel back to Nicolo Benenati, tell him you prefer Tuesdays to have your heart cut out and left in your mouth, remember—wasn't that a sight, his eyes still open and his jaw forced cavernously wide and the scarlet lump of muscle not beating inside it?

And then to finish bringing trouble to these perfectly decent people, why not send a slug through your skull without paying your room bill.

"Next," Blossom continues, "Max having full-white half sisters and all, it's hardly the shock of the season he helped someone desperate who probably reminded him of a sibling."

Oh.

"And lastly," she concludes as a cool, vanilla-perfumed hand tucks a piece of my hair back, "she made it from New York to Portland in this state. *Alone.* I'd bet you my pearl choker you like so well that this one doesn't have her own folks to disapprove of anything."

"Fine, Blossom, there's no denying a word of that logic, so you've got me pinned up against a wall as usual—"

"Honey, you know I never *try* to show anyone up, I'm just observing a few facts."

"Your facts are all well and good, right till the time when either someone comes looking for this stray, or this town finds out we have us a white lodger!" Mavereen hisses. "We ain't running a charity hospital. Think of the risk, for once in your life."

"I do, Mavereen," Blossom rebukes coldly, outrage coloring her tone. "I think about risk *constantly.* I think about it more than I think about money, and I am forced to think about money *a great deal.* Anyway, if I *didn't* take precautions, I imagine you'd call down lightning and zap me to cinders."

"Lord have mercy. Blossom, why do you always have to rile me up so? It ain't hardly decent." Mavereen slides the window open and lights a cigarette. The rain must have stopped, the breeze curling into the crannies of my bedsheets like a teasing lover.

"Why, I could give out that the devil put me up to it, but it's *entirely* for my own pleasure." Worriedly, Blossom adds, "You're distraught over more than our signing up for the Samaritan act. Anything . . . untoward today?"

"Depends on what you call untoward. Seen the newspaper I left out in the meeting room this morning? Had a wire from my cousin to go with it. They strung up another Georgia Negro back home, left him for the crows and the ants. Wasn't much skin left on his back in the first place, seemed like, and the critters made plenty quick work with the rest. He was a local shopkeeper's boy. Eighteen."

"Oh, Mavereen, honey." Blossom sounds aghast. "But surely we read that sort of thing more often than we read, 'and the black fellow cast his vote entirely without incident and went home to a hot roast.' What happened *here*, and I ask again—was it untoward?"

Mavereen sucks in an angry mouthful of smoke. "If cats die natural from slitting their own throats and curling up in hotel doorways with their guts spilled, then no."

"Oh, Mav," Blossom gasps. "Well, no, I don't suppose I've ever heard of a cat in such a depressed state. Did Rooster find it?"

"No, Wednesday Joe did, when he arrived for his shift. Poor sweet angel, you know how he loves anything with fur. Cried and cried before I managed to wrestle him into uniform. Brought tears to my own eyes."

"Did . . ." She pauses. "Did Davy see?"

"No. But it's sheer luck and God's grace that he didn't. Whatever nasty piece of trash did this wanted it public, didn't want us to have time to notice they'd defiled our home again. I tell you, I can't hardly think on it. Recollecting an honest-to-God exodus, sugar, the wilderness I traveled to be someplace better, and for what? So I could scrape cat guts off our . . ."

Blossom seems to traverse the room and I hear a muffled sniffle followed by a soothing hum.

"Mavereen, if you had these cowards in front of you, why, they'd piss themselves over the licking they were in for."

"Blossom, language, I've told you a thousand times."

"Have you any idea how difficult it is to *forget* words once you know them?" her friend teases.

"Gracious, what am I doing? Blubbering over some cast-off white girl's sickbed when there must be a dozen or more rooms to check, and my maids running wild. Don't tell anyone you saw your Mavereen in this state."

"Oh, *death* first," Blossom vows.

"Stay with her until Dr. Pendleton gets back? I'm tired witless, and I just know the linens for the dinner service need ironing. The new downstairs girl has been plenty distracted over . . . well. All this nonsense."

"Don't say another word. I'm not due at the club till eight tonight, and the getup is as easy as rolling over in bed. Go on—I can handle the likes of Miss James."

You really can't, I think, though the brag endears her to me.

The door shutting behind Mavereen provides me with the perfect opportunity to awaken. Twitching, I fuss with the coverlet, set free a tiny moan.

Because I want to see what Blossom is like about as much as I want to see what she makes of Nobody.

The Nobody I am around Blossom will be a slightly jaded version of the sweet flapper Max knows. More like the desperate woman Mavereen and Dr. Pendleton met last night. Doesn't do dope but doesn't mind when someone else does, may have been kept as a banker's baby doll but thought she was in love, cut her bare foot on broken glass in the street once when her dancing shoes had pinched her. Never pays for her own cigarettes. That sort.

"Miss James? Are you all right?"

The curtain rises.

Whatever I expected Blossom to look like, I've fallen short.

She smiles. She's dark, dark as any African. These things matter in places where we've dumped pink, white, yellow, red, black people into the same paint can. Her skin is burnished, as if she's aglow. Blossom's lips and eyes are delicate, pretty watercolor strokes of peach and umber. But her cheekbones and her brow prove positively architectural. If you left a Grecian temple alone for around thirty-five years, a bit older than they'd mentioned Max was, and then you lacquered it, that would be Blossom. She wears artful cosmetics and loose fabrics in dragonfly hues, a gold-threaded scarf draped at her neck.

I cough. "If there's water, please . . ."

Blossom sweeps away and returns with the substance, which never tasted quite so much like pure, icy gin. A side effect of either the morphine or the pine forests hereabouts, doubtless. She resettles herself in the bedside chair.

"Who are you?" I ask. "Oh heavens, that sounded so coarse. I mean, thank you. I'm all in shreds."

"You certainly are, honey." Blossom tilts her stone-carved chin, evaluating. "Now, let me see. Some might say that I ought to send you straight back to dreamland, and some might say I should ask you *every* little thing about yourself. But I think presently—your being in God's lap and all, and thinking terribly lengthy thoughts—you must want to ask *me* a few things. Well, I am always disposed to talk to interesting people, and you, Miss James, interest me *unnaturally*. Who am I, you inquired? My name is Miss Blossom Fontaine, I live down the hall, and I am a cabaret singer. Next?"

My answering smile gushes like a spill of blood. Oh, I know how one gets into the knack of reading people well. A few hard years, some harder knocks, and human beings come into clearer focus. And Blossom just read me like a front-page headline.

"I was always dreadfully fond of the *W* questions," I rasp.

She laughs, a musical sound. "Yes, because *how* can be too complex to even contemplate. As to *when,* you are Tuesday, April the nineteenth, of nineteen twenty-one."

A quick calculation tells me that means I've spent seven days shooting myself cross-country like a rocket with a pair of festering bullet wounds in my side. No wonder Max was forced to hoist sleeve and mop me up.

"What happened to me after Dr. Pendleton knocked me for six?"

"Nothing you could call very active on your part, honey. Dr. Pendleton worked his medical magic, how I am not aware, but he's *terribly* thorough. Cranky as an elderly weasel, but never mind that. Then we found this nightdress for you and changed your bandaging once. That shaft someone drilled through your person already looks *much* better. You continued to do very little, which brings us to the present. You're *overwhelming* me with liveliness. Please reduce the throttle a bit."

I'd gladly laugh—it's the fastest-drying glue for friendships, and for some uncanny reason I instantly want to exchange intimacies with this person—but I haven't the strength.

"Whose nightdress is this?"

"Gracious, what a cordial and unexpected *W* that was. Mine. It's only cotton, and I lost the ribbon for the eyelets, I'm *tragically* careless, but there was no way of knowing whether you'd bleed all over it, you understand. You can see it when I allow you mirrors, which is *not* today." One side of her mouth slides up, and the opposite side of her granite brow swoops down, and I know she has as many comedic patter songs in her repertoire as lost love ballads. "And I'm ever so much taller than you, Miss James, so don't take any constitutionals, or you'll be flat on your ass."

"Duly noted. Um, regarding one that particularly concerns me . . . where am I?"

"You're at the Paragon Hotel," she declares, the tightness from earlier returning to her voice.

"If you'd care to continue?"

"Oh, *gladly.* But let us make this a bedtime story, for I'm marvelous at those and you look worn threadbare, all right? Let me see, the Paragon opened in nineteen-oh-six, and is full to bursting of decent citizens and lunatic nomads. I admit to being of the latter variety. It is one of the busiest hotels in the city of Portland, and profoundly well-appointed. We've six or seven business ventures in the building, so practically anything you like, just ask me to fetch it for you, and you shall have it in a *trice.*"

"Truly?"

"Of course, honey. And I'll take you for a tour once you've resumed your normal complexion. A complexion which, I must add with regret, is a cause of some concern for us, as the Paragon is simply the only Portland hotel where both the most aristocratic and most hardworking of Negroes are all invited to rest their weary heads. Oh you're smiling—I mean the *only* Portland hotel, quite literally," Blossom adds with a hard glint in her eye. "When it comes to segregation, you may consider yourself free to whistle 'Dixie' where the great state of Oregon is concerned. So you present a moral enigma to the establishment, you see, and I *always* adore those. Better than fresh coffee."

"Oh." I meditate on this. "What a shame. You'll have to chuck me out, and I like it here ever so much."

The naked truth in my words is audible.

"Gracious, but you *are* from Harlem, aren't you? Max was right, the dear lunk of a man. You could be from literally nowhere else in America! How marvelous. Are there any other questions you'd care to pose before you rest?"

Don't think of it, Nobody.

I disobey myself. I do think of it, and though I'm too dry souled to weep by now, it must show in my face, for Blossom swiftly shifts closer.

"Why did this happen to me?" I ask in a cracked whisper.

"Oh, honey." She brushes the backs of her fingers over my cheek. "I haven't the slightest idea. I never do, you know. Not about that."

Three

THEN

Only on feast days does Little Italy, in Harlem, recall the Bend when it put on its holiday attire. Anything more desolate and disheartening than the unending rows of tenements, all alike and all equally repellent, of the up-town streets, it is hard to imagine.

—JACOB A. RIIS, *The Battle with the Slum*, 1902

So. Where to begin?

I'll start from the start, I suppose, that being the traditional technique: I was born on March 23rd of 1896, on the day the Raines law was passed. And thus for the first ten years of my life, I was raised in a so-called Raines law hotel, one called the Step Right Inn.

That still dings my pride. If only the owner had prognosticated all the days when he might be tempted to make a joke, and stayed in bed accordingly.

The Raines law was a liquor tax then, in the same way that

Prohibition agents are defenders of justice now. Itchy to curb drinking among the huddled masses and clever enough to notice that the immigrants were only let out of harness on Sundays, the law stated that no one save hotels could serve the giggle juice on the Lord's day of rest.

Everyone thought that was dreadfully cute.

Sometimes the way to solve a thorny problem is to whack straight through. The saloonkeepers—who were plenty often landlords—bought some used furniture, swept the back staircase, and demanded their hotel licenses. Dandy! The stevedores and carpenters and bricklayers could continue spending their Sundays getting soused while the dearly beloved polished the children and scrubbed the lampshades as ever.

A collective sigh of relief was heard as far off as Florida.

The snag to this seemingly crackerjack idea was that now the saloonkeepers had rooms but no kitchens. The second part of this thorny dilemma was solved quicker than a New York springtime: serve pretzels. As the French would parley it, *voilà*. Now, I don't mean to imply that *only* pretzels were served. Sometimes pickles or peanuts or in the awfully tongue-in-cheek Irish establishment operating eight blocks from where I grew up, the cabbage leaves that were too brown to go in the stew pot. If there are browner cabbage leaves than ones the Irish won't touch, may God have mercy on those who eat them.

The solution to the first part of the problem, the empty rooms, did not cause a single head to be scratched: fill them with whores.

About Catrin James, then. My mum was Welsh, from Glamorganshire. Probably still is, I suppose. In any case, she emigrated to New York in 1893 with nothing but a scalawag husband. After a week, she misplaced him, and she wasn't too sore. Everything was jake. Realizing women always, while alive, have certain salable assets, she took to vending them along the East River, which amounts to finding an Ohio homestead plot and saying, "This'll do."

Along came an Italian one day whose name she refused to tell me despite my insatiable curiosity. He was handsome and charming, even in his severely limited English, English my Welsh mum could barely understand. Relevant to this anecdote: my mum was still unreasonably beautiful. She still laughed a great deal. She always has. Her snout was a splendid snub button and her cheeks juicy fruit. A bluenose would have called her a trollop, and the faster sort of flapper would have hailed her as sister.

And the Italian—he called her *bella. Bella, bella, bella,* all through the cold, starry night. Occasionally he wanted to expound beyond that word, and paid a Columbia student to translate his sentiments into the American vernacular.

Come away with me, my bella!

Or:

I have found us a place already—it is very far uptown, but all I can afford if we are to live alone together, motherfuck these dripping basements with their twelve pairs of eyes. Only I will see them in our bedroom—yes, the way you are looking at me now, mia dolce.

And for good measure:

You will forget that this money-changing ever happened to you and forget your cock-gobbling husband, and one day when he is stabbed in the gullet, he will think of you as he dies and regret only that he did not spend every second devoted to your happiness.

Catrin said yes. The hind leg of a donkey would have parted ways with its owner.

They moved to Harlem, my mum and the amorous Italian, and lived as husband and wife, and introduced themselves to everyone as the same. They were happy.

What a simply marvelous thing to say. I'll say it twice: they were happy. And they had a year together. My father the Italian did not die for any romantic reason—rescuing Mum, or even holding his own in a fight. He was bitten on 134th Street by a vicious stray mutt, and the wound quickly became diseased. Fatally so. After the funeral, my mother decided that there were no new places she wanted to see terribly much without him.

So Mum got back to work.

Two weeks before the Raines law would go into effect, she was reekingly pregnant, and still more odoriferously poor. Two days before the Raines law would go into effect, my mum, as she was absolutely splendid at planning when not fried off her tits, marched into the newly renovated Step Right Inn on 107th Street and demanded a job. Seeing as she knew what the proprietor knew about the empty rooms' future use.

But no one else had yet been in the dire straits to say.

I was born there with the assistance of two of my mum's hooker friends. When I was still small enough to ask featherbrained questions, and demanded to know who my dad might be, I can still hear her replying, "He's gone from us now, and there is nothing to be done about it anyway. Nobody . . . let it go."

Silly enough in retrospect, I'll admit. But I thought she was saying my name.

The first step on my journey to becoming a ruthless criminal happened on July 24, 1906, and wouldn't have occurred at all if it hadn't been so goddamned hot that day.

Malevolent mists rose from 107th Street. Leek trimmings chucked from windows sizzled as they perished on the paving stones. Mustachioed men cursed, lifting the brims of bowlers to smear sweat from their swarthy brows. Skies positively leered with blue as birds swooned from fire escapes. Hard-faced women with fleshy elbows slapped their children for the fun of it, hissing, *Bambino stupido!* The very air was mean.

And Mr. Mangiapane was meaner.

At ten years old and living in a Raines law whorehouse—pardon, hotel—small acts of defiance were precious rubies in mine eyes, and nothing pleased me better than riling the proprietor of the Step Right Inn. He was a short, squat Sicilian who brought to mind a horse turd, and his name was Mr. Mangiapane.

"Get her the hell out of here!" he spat at my mother, pointing a trembling sausage finger at me. "Get that nasty little rat of yours out of my saloon during business hours, or I will raise my cut!"

Catrin sat at the oak bar, nursing her first beer of the day with decorous inattention. She adjusted the corset she wore under an open blouse that made her look like a creamy moth flitting about. Still funny, and still sanguine about her life despite the fact some would have found it positively heinous.

I did. Which was the reason I enjoyed driving off her customers.

"And what is it this time, Mr. Mangiapane, that has yer balls in such a tight knot?" she asked in her Welsh brogue.

"Stupid bitch!" he squealed. "I send to you your first customer fifteen minutes ago, your disgusting creature offers to carry up his *colazione*, and five minutes later he is raging at me because the beautiful fried cutlet I sent had been replaced with a fried *dishrag*."

Mum giggled. "I've naught in the way of medals to award, but that were a bloody good one, my lovely."

My mother never minded my driving away loose-limbed, lantern-jawed suitors. Partly because hijinks amused her, and partly because she'd become one of the most popular ladybirds north of 90th Street. So there was jack to spend—we were always warm and always fed. I could attend desultory classes at the Catholic school up the street or play truant, just as I pleased. Meanwhile, the reason

Mr. Mangiapane was so upset over a harmless prank was that he was awfully proud the Step Right Inn served actual food, food cooked by a Roman known only as Crispy Ezio. He could fry anything, and by God, did he take strange pleasure in the task. Ezio also happened to be fond of me, forever sneaking me fried whitefish and chucking me amiably on the jaw.

And by the by, breaded and fried rags do indeed look identical to breaded and fried chicken. Bit tougher on the old nutcracker, however.

"He was bad news anyway," I scoffed. My only clothing that god-awful sweltering day was a cast-off shift so short that Mum had supplemented it with a pair of boys' trousers, and I already felt as if I'd sweated out the entire Hudson. "It was counterfeit coin he tipped me with."

Their faces fell with the speed of meteors.

"Get her *out*!" Mr. Mangiapane shrieked. "Out! Nobody is deadly luck!"

Mr. Mangiapane called me Nobody because Mum sometimes did, and Mum did because I'd told her the story. It was a ridiculous nickname because I was so *visible*—laughing, hooting, racing, whistling. Still. The moniker began with love, as so many twisted things do. I think many a trouble begins with love, and it's important to remember that when life feels like the shit scraped off Death's boot sole.

"Please calm yerself, Mr. Mangia—" Mum attempted, flying off her barstool.

"Nobody even living under this roof is more than I care to bear! *Ma vai a quel paese!*"*

He threw me out of the hotel as Mum stared in dismay. I sailed like a kite before gravity took me to task, my arm struck an empty

* Get out of here—literally "go to that country."

tomato crate, and I nearly rolled into a bay-colored draft horse tethered outside.

It hurt. My body and my pride. I lay there, wincing as blood bloomed. But by age ten, I'd decided the hell reserved for sissies was of the grimmest, so I lurched for the saloon's door only to find that it had been locked.

"Bastardo!" I raged.

When I stumbled to the window, cupping my hands to peer in, Mr. Mangiapane and Catrin James were in a torrent of conversation, hands gesticulating like banners in a gale. All the blooms in Mum's hothouse cheeks were pale with frost. Her boss resembled a dew-speckled red apple, if apples were capable of frothing rage.

Disturbed, I stepped away, fingertips leaving tear tracks on the glass. I believed in omens—both good and bad. We all did in Little Italy. We lit our candles at Mass and wished on pennies in fountains. But there had been no portents of late. I'd spilled neither salt nor olive oil. Been careful to eat lentils at New Year's.

My guts quivered. Clearly, I'd miscalculated the import of bad currency.

But how?

Sun searing into my scalp, I surveyed my options. I could walk to the river to watch the giant vessels with their masts like spreading oaks, the squat steamers with their barnacle skins, the jolly tugs. Or I could steal cherries from Mr. Campo's grocery, since he was foolish enough to situate their box on the street-corner side (I ask you). Maybe I could press my nose against the pawnshop windows over on Broadway, salivating over sparkles? A lonesome sniffle threatened when I struck upon richer ore.

I'll find my best friend, and we'll visit the armies of the cats!

So I set off in search of Nicolo Benenati with great gusto, after stopping to buy a cured-meat stick from the corner store.

Next task was locating him. Nicolo wasn't playing baseball with his cousins outside his apartment on 106th Street. Neither was he at his dad's cigar shop beneath their home, though Mr. Benenati scraped my cheek with his wire-brush mustache and told me to inform his son that if he didn't turn up to work his hours soon, he'd catch hell. He wasn't tending his beloved tomato plants in the incinerated tenement death trap we loved so passionately.

Sweat trickling down my sternum, I finally caught sight of Nicolo across the deafening river rush of Lexington Avenue. My closest friend stood at a pushcart buying pickles from one of the Yiddisher vendors. I slipped past drays drifting like so many lumbering barges, squeezed happily between a truck loaded with bricks and a wizened farmer delivering fresh-baked manure.

"Alicia!" Nicolo exclaimed, giving my name four syllables as usual. His grin dimmed. "Jesus, *topolina*,* who the hell have you been boxing with this time?"

Kicking the pavement, I shrugged, which was my form of bragging. Because I felt the usual indefinable surge of *yes, you* that I always did in Nicolo's company.

On the day everything changed, he was two years my elder, and therefore twelve. He wasn't cleverer than all the other scamps bubbling out of the boiling vat called Harlem—but he was intensely focused. He wasn't stronger either—but he was quick as a wasp. He wasn't handsome—but he owned a striking hatchet face, a straight black hairline without a trace of peak, and a pair of weirdly slanting brows hitching a tent over his stake of a nose. And he was savagely dynamic. It didn't matter a hatpin if Nicolo was rooting in his secret vegetable garden so he could bring Mrs. Benenati gifts she forever accused him of having stolen, or knocking a baseball through the window of a Broadway tenement, whooping with laughter as his

* Little mouse.

gang took to their heels. Everything about him was honed to a sharper edge.

As for me, I was simply different, and he liked that. No, I may not want to write this, but I owe it to my old friend: he loved it. Love in the fire-gutted sense of the word.

Small wonder that I stood out from the other girls: I was a street brawler before I turned into Nobody. Like Nicolo, I was alone, as Mum had decided one pregnancy was quite enough, please pass the coffee. So there I was: half Welsh and half Italian, with chocolate eyes and wispy blond hair. Is it any wonder that I was often, shall we say, accosted? Everybody wanted the spare dough I cadged out of my generous and forgetful parent. Neither of we Jameses had ropes of pearls, but when we actually wanted something, it was ours for the purchasing. And we wanted so little to be happy—or Mum did, and I knew no better. Witness! Hot chestnuts, juicy oysters, sticky lemon drops, the amaro she had grown to love. When the local delinquents tried to take my coin, I fought like a wet cat, twisting, biting, clawing.

And usually winning.

"I boxed with Mr. Mangiapane," I answered when Nicolo pressed me.

"No kidding!" he exclaimed. "Taken to bearbaiting?"

Considering whether to tell my friend about the counterfeit coin, I hesitated. "He thought the breakfast I delivered to a guest upstairs wasn't funny."

Nicolo's brows twitched. "And?"

"Replacing a fried cutlet with a fried dishrag was plenty funny."

Nicolo roared with laughter, canine face tipped to the simmering skies. "Did he try to beat you?"

"Nah, not him. He chucked me out and I made speed."

"But what will they do when you get back?"

"Non mi interessa," I answered—although in fact I did care, and was fretting over it dreadfully. "Where is everyone?"

"What, Nazario, Renzo, Piero, those strapping young criminals? There's supposed to be a new cockfighting ring on Lenox and they wanted to find it." Nicolo shrugged. "I have to go to work anyhow, so—"

"No! No, the cats!" I cried. "We must visit the armies! *Viva i gatti, viva!*"

"But yesterday I didn't set foot in the shop, and—"

"You can make up the time. Today's only Tuesday. Please?"

Nicolo's father was a gentle fellow and a generous employer. And getting what I wanted from Nicolo with *please*, in those days, was like wishing on a genie's lamp.

So he yowled like a tom. *"Viva i gatti! Chi i gatti vivere per sempre!"*

Off we strode, munching pickles. The cat armies waged war in one of the many empty city blocks to the west, between 109th and 110th streets, just south of Morningside Park. We trudged up the hill, grasses tickling our knees, until we were at the scoop in the earth where the sheltering stones made fortresses for our troops.

Here the boulders punched through the earth, and everywhere—in grass, under rock, and up oak—the feral cat community dozed. A one-eared tortoiseshell we called Umberto glowered happily at us from his stone perch. Sherbet, the orange tabby, rolled to soak up more sun. One ever-so-filthy specimen called Attila self-administered a futile bath. There were dozens of them, and the cat armies made joyful marching songs play in our hearts.

"Damn it," Nicolo lamented, "we didn't stop to—"

"Nessun problema. Come on, Nicolo, as if I'd forget the start signal." I produced the dried sausage, broke it in two, and raised my half like a battle standard.

It remains one of my happiest memories. Despite its overture, and its finale.

"Ready the troops!" I cried.

"Load the muskets!" Nicolo shouted.

"Feed the horses!"

"Clean the cannonballs!"

"Polish the buttons!"

"Dry the socks!"

"Ready . . . aim . . . *fire!*"

As the two chunks of meat soared, we settled in to watch the heady pageantry of some threescore cats fighting over *salsiccia*. A chorus of hissing, growling, and shrieking commenced.

"Go, Napoleon, go!"

"Lucrezia, *puttana*, get him, get him, get him!"

We didn't hear the footsteps behind us. Weren't even listening for them. A shiver still goes down my spine when I remember the high giggle.

We turned around.

Dario Palma waved. Smiled in his brutal manner, showing crooked teeth. "Nicolo, glad to finally catch you. There's business to discuss. Alice, you're unnecessary. Goodbye."

Dario spat. Every passing day, he seemed more ape than man. Long arms trailing knuckles through the streets, scruff sprouting from his chin. With Dario were the other two neighborhood psychopaths, Doctor Vinnie and Cleto the Crow. Doctor Vinnie liked to catch mice and blind them with an ice pick before setting them loose in the pen where his dog, Caesar, was chained. Cleto the Crow gained his moniker from empty, staring black eyes. All three were fourteen. It was usually easy enough to avoid them—plunge into a crowd, slide into an alleyway, slip through a bodega.

We had no such options in upper Manhattan's woodlands. A

tingling in my fingers told me to curl them into weapons even as a tremor in my knees told me to *run*.

Nicolo, always so suave, tensed. "Come on, Alicia, I have to be at the shop."

Vinnie and Cleto fanned out.

Dario giggled again, an unnaturally sharp sound. It ought to have slit his throat. "You're not going anywhere until you settle up. You owe us a dime, Benenati. Like I told you. We know that your old man pays you these days."

"He pays me chicken feed."

"Listen, we've had this conversation. The likes of us patrol your street, and the likes of you pays a small fee. You're grateful for our protection, yeah?"

"We protect you," Vinnie emphasized.

"We protect you plenty," Cleto parroted idiotically.

"Never asked for that, did I?"

"It would hurt me to think you were ungrateful, Benenati. I have a tender heart," Dario sneered.

"You'll have a tender face after I beat the shit out of it."

His lip spasmed into a fishhook. "Pay up, or we're learning you a lesson, *cazzo*."

"Leave him alone," I growled.

"Alicia, you keep out of this," Nicolo ordered.

"Why? Come to think of it, she can pay up too," Dario decided with dark glee. "Give me a kiss, Alice. Make it good enough, and I won't charge you again for, say, a month?"

"All right then, you stupid peasant," Nicolo snapped, widening his feet. "Better make it count. You'll only have the one chance."

Before I knew what was coming, Cleto the Crow had swooped down with his dead eyes and tossed me aside. I heard through the broken bells in my ears shouts in Italian and English, the crushed-cabbage thudding of fists. Scrambling up, I threw myself at the maelstrom. Again and again I launched my body and was repelled, and again and again Nicolo dodged, darted, head sunk like an ox as he landed clever hornet stings on the bigger boys.

Dario, Doctor Vinnie, and Cleto the Crow beat my dearest friend like a carpet. They kicked him with heavy boots when he fell. Doctor Vinnie kneed him in the groin. Cleto held his face in the dirt. Dario giggled throughout. They blacked Nicolo's eyes, knocked his proud nose off-kilter.

Nicolo yelled for me to run. Refusing, but too weak to fight any longer, I screamed my lungs out, threw rocks.

It didn't matter.

When they were finished, they went through his pockets and extracted the ten cents they wanted. Dario, his gorilla's face flushed with sweat and triumph, took his pecker out and giddily pissed in Nicolo's face.

Slapping each other's shoulders over a job well executed, the trio walked away.

Losing a safe space—and the vale of the cat armies was one of ours—carves a canyon through a person. It had been the site of so much innocent ridiculousness. There was love there, and there was peace, lying on our backs as the blue skies above us ignited into scalding pink, then orange, then an ash-flecked black. When you lose a place that once was safe, the hole remains, and you can never get that piece of yourself back again.

Not for all the rum in Canada.

Crawling, I reached Nicolo. His young body shook like a cowering field mouse's. He didn't want me to see that, but the shock had shorted a circuit. Helpless and sick, I balled my fists in my already torn sleeves and wiped at his face, his hair, tried to erase the mingled blood and piss. Tried to remake Nicolo as he'd been before. I was only ten, mind—I still thought you could remake people.

"I'm all right," he gasped when he saw I was crying. He caught my hands. "Alicia. It's all right, *topolina.* They're gone, the pricks. It was only ten cents. Shh. Only a dime, don't cry."

"I couldn't stop them."

"I know. It was too goddamn hot this afternoon, that's all, an angry day."

"An unlucky one," I agreed raggedly.

"Exactly. The sun will go down, and it was only a dime. It'll be over soon."

Nicolo was wrong. We had just entered *malavita.*

The bad life.

A world in which the monsters were the monarchs.

After we'd limped back to our neighborhood, we parted ways—my friend to tend to his nose and me to pour my heart out to my mum. My sweat had turned sour with dread, and the tears despite Nicolo's repeated pleas hadn't stopped. When I reached home, desperate for kisses, my chin dropped.

All the windows of the Step Right Inn were broken. Glass everywhere, a sadly glittering ocean. Mr. Mangiapane clutched a broom to his chest, his fat hands shaking. He spoke with the customer whose cutlet I'd switched out for a dishrag, ducking his head like a penitent. Bobbing his jowls against the folds of his neck. The john looked stern but attentive. Sort of paternal, as if aware mortals made lug-brained errors. As the acid in my stomach turned to lead, I realized precisely what counterfeit currency signaled, and felt a hot rush of shame over my own thoughtlessness.

The Corleonesi dealt in fake currency—in fake currency, and in dread. The concept of "protection" wasn't unique to youthful bullying. Dario and his ilk learned from their fathers. Their uncles. Their elder brothers. So it didn't matter that there weren't yet Five Families.

There was one Family. And one was enough for Alice to begin to disappear.

• Four •

NOW

The government is spending millions to enforce the Eighteenth Amendment. Isn't it right to spend a few millions to enforce the Fourteenth? One says a man shall not drink and the other says he shall vote. I would rather spend a million to enforce the Fourteenth Amendment than 14 to enforce the Eighteenth!

—CONGRESSMAN OSCAR DE PRIEST,
The Advocate, Portland, Oregon, September 28, 1929

I tumble from dream to dream as if I'm the Alice who encountered a rabbit with a timekeeping fetish. I'm standing before a mirror in a gilt scalloped frame, pinning a netted cap of copper sequins over my hair, deciding which Nobody is called for. Trying on souls for Mr. Salvatici and tossing them aside like scarves. I'm at the edge of the Hudson in denim trousers and a man's cap pulled low, the moon a wicked smirk, clenching and unclenching my hands in my pockets. I'm at the Tobacco Club, heart going like a hi-hat, and—

Whimpering as I snap awake, I discover I'm still not alone.

There's a child in my sickroom. Blinking against wit-dulling pain, I examine the creature.

"Who are you?" he asks in a piping voice.

"The Queen of France," I manage.

"Oh. You must have been in the War, then. 'Cause you sure look terrible," he notes.

Well, this is fixing to cheer me up any old amount.

"We all look this way in France. We're ever so strong for invalids—romantic, don't you know. See here, good sir, just who am I addressing?"

"Davy Lee. I'm six."

"Ah."

"I just finished class at Mrs. Evelina's Weekly Betterments downstairs. She lets me draw knights and dragons."

"She sounds a peach."

"She is. Do you live here now?"

"That's a topic for further study."

"I live here, just down the hall. In a fortress."

"No kidding."

Davy sits in the chair Blossom vacated, swinging energetic legs as if remaining still is an affront to personal freedoms. He's a hazelnut shade with eyes painted in woodland colors, catlike, and he'll be handsome as anything once the baby chub dissolves. Delicate bee-stung lips, lashes unnaturally long. Any self-respecting flapper would cast about for the shears and swipe them straight off his peepers.

"I get to meet you now, because Mavereen is checking the dining room before supper and Blossom is out singing." He studies me hungrily. "If you start to look *too* sick, I can run for Dr. Pendleton and rescue you, the way the Yanks saved the world from the Hun. Boy, do you look sick. Are you fixing to die?"

"I'm none too keen, no."

"I've never seen a person die before. It'd be awful interesting. If you *nearly* die, I can save you, though. Wouldn't that be even better?"

"Short man, you are impertinent."

"Sorry. Have you ever seen a dead body?"

"Oh, acres of them. Simply dozens," I confess.

"Gosh."

"Yes, *quelque* luck."

"You don't seem much like a queen. Who are you, really?"

"Nobody." I sigh. "Davy, could you be a dear and fetch water from that pitcher? I'm expiring."

He complies with the strangely rolling motion some children possess. As if they were spinning hoops or tumbleweeds. Croquet balls. He pours the water, *splish-splosh*, and returns radiating civic pride.

Sitting up, I grind my teeth against the firebrand on my side. By the time my whistle has been wetted, I'm ill with the effort. A clatter sounds when I return the glass to the nightstand.

Ain't we got fun.

"Maybe even if you do start to die, I won't need Dr. Pendleton. Maybe I can save you myself. Then I'd deserve medals, I figure. At least two." Davy gives me a grin, rubbing at unruly curls.

"Two medals is the going rate?"

"Yeah. But I'd settle for cookies if there aren't any medals downstairs. There are cookies downstairs for sure."

"Really? That's some strategic intelligence you've spied out."

"Miss Christina makes the *best* cookies. But she never eats any herself. It's awful peculiar."

"Miss Christina sounds a few whiskers shy of a rabbit, in that case."

"You're the wrong color to be here."

Biting my lip, I consider the word *segregation* and all the dreadfully droll rules of conduct it entails. The bizarre lad has identified a problem, all right. But I'm exhausted, and strung together with fishing line for all I know, and attempting to ignore a shattered heart.

God help me. Supposing God is inclined to help liquor peddlers and gun molls.

"It's mighty funny, you being here. I'm not allowed to play with white kids anymore." A distressed line beetles Davy's brows. "Not even the ones a few blocks away, who have the best kites. Ever since they whupped me something awful."

I frown. "Somebody gave you a licking?"

He nods, touchingly sobered. "I thought they were my friends, but they changed their minds. Six months ago. They called me all sorts of names. And I needed stitches. Right here, on my eyebrow."

"That alone merits a medal," I say with deeply personal sympathy.

He brightens, then the cloud returns. "I'm not even allowed to leave the Paragon anymore without somebody grown. It's awful dull not to go outside to play. We could be cowboys and Indians much better down at the park. Me and Wednesday Joe, I mean. Here we have to use the hallways. And we aren't allowed to do that on account of guests, so we have to sneak."

Muzzy headed, I recollect reports of felines dying untimely. And I am concerned.

The door clicks open and Mavereen's face pokes in. I'm even more impressed by her now I'm not dying quite so quickly. The empress appears thoughtful. Ruthlessly pressed square-necked dress, swirling cone of coffee-and-soot braids artfully arranged. Midnight skin of the silent type refusing to give up whether she's forty or sixty. She'd make an equally fine church board directress or cathouse madam, and her dark eyes are molten.

"Davy Lee, did I or did I not tell you that Miss James was sure enough off-limits? What on earth you think you're doing disobeying me?"

Davy's excusing himself before Mavereen even finishes. "But, see, no, what happened was—"

The door swings wide as Mavereen's finger rises to point down the hallway. It's an inexorable gesture. A sunrise. There is no arguing with it.

"I ain't having none of your lip tonight, Davy Lee. If you don't march on out of here and get to polishing the candlesticks for Miss Christina and finish afore dinner service, I'm putting one of her spoons to good use, and you'd *better* not think I mean making cookies."

Davy makes such speed as if he had never been present. I deem this wisdom. Mavereen steps into the room.

"I'm so sorry. It wasn't much of a gabfest—he brought me water, and I was grateful, Miss . . . ?" I attempt a weak smear of a smile.

"Mrs. Mavereen Meader." Her tone is full of cordial but tightly bottled. "Mr. Richard Meader long ago passed into Christ's fold. I'm the head housekeeper here, which is as much as to say as I run the Paragon. Maids, cooks, laundry, porters, elevators, top to toe and then some extra in the middle—even surgery now, seems like! Dr. Pendleton, who done stitched you up proper, he owns the deed to this place. Made some sharp investments years back. But I operate it. Saints alive, you must be feeling all but turned inside out, Miss James. Think you could see your way to managing somc soup?"

My stomach roars a basso profundo agreement.

"I could try. I'd be ever so grateful. And don't think I'm ignorant of the risk you're taking—I've been far too much trouble already."

"Well, there's some powerful truth there, Miss James, but if I don't keep you fed, that there's on *my* conscience." She nods. "Soup it is, then. You hankering for anything else, particular like?"

About a dozen glasses of gin, with yellow ribbon lemon curls, lined up before me like penitents awaiting forgiveness or slaughter.

"Maybe some tea, if it's not putting you out too much?"

"Tea isn't any botheration at all, sugar. Now, *you*? You might be a botheration. But tea's as easy as standing in the rain. I'm after a token in return, though."

"Name it, do."

"Keep yourself to this floor? It'd rest my mind considerable over what folks might say."

"Of course." My palm covers my heart. "Anything I can do. And more to come."

"Well, never you mind offering favors on credit, now." Despite the rebuke, she sounds relieved. "Your tray shouldn't be more than a quarter hour."

She shuts the door behind her. Meditating on the furry corpse laid at their doorstep, I try to recall the look Mavereen Meader exchanged with Dr. Pendleton the day before. That silent debate hadn't been over segregation alone—I've seen entire populations ruthlessly shoved under thumbs before. Something awfully queer is going on.

You might be out of the frying pan, Nobody, but this bears a remarkable resemblance to a fire.

I doze until a gentle knock at the door sounds.

Rat-a-tat-tat.

A smile from out of nowhere tugs at my lips when I recognize the familiar rhythm.

"Come in."

And there's Max. Nobody the sweet flapper makes sure to look startled. Fuss with the bedclothes, smooth her hair back. No matter what healed battle scars Blossom and Mavereen lamped on my person, they may well have kept mum about them—women often do, we're ever so skilled at secrets—and appearances must be maintained.

Anyway, I'm only half kidding. The laddie makes my heart do pony tricks.

"I'll be damned. She's a scrapper after all." A grin creeps onto Max's affable face.

"Entirely thanks to you. I'd take the usual line and say you're a prince, but you seem more of a knight, don't you? Oh, I simply can't tell you how grateful I am."

He jerks a thumb at a rolling cart in the corridor. "You mind me playing George, Miss James?"

"My schedule is elastic." I wave him inside. "But I do mind your playing George."

Max whisks the lid off the tray with all the natural showmanship of a midtown Manhattan maître d'. Or a Pullman porter, I suppose. In any case, it's a dandy maneuver and my chapeau is off to the fellow. He adjusts the angle of a tiny pink moss rose in a bud vase. It's all so cheering I think I could weep for joy, and then tears actually spring into my eyes and I glance out the window.

Stop it this instant. Nobody the sniffling milksop is the worst goddamn version of you yet.

"Why do you mind my playing George?" Max slides a friendly paw behind my back, supporting me with another pillow. After all that time on the train together I don't mind him touching me, mind even less than if it were Blossom or Mavereen.

"Oh, how could you ask me that? After rescuing me in such a fashion? Your Pullman porter routine is top of the line, but you're not really George, you're Max. What's the use in playacting?"

"Dunno, Miss James." Stretching a crick in his neck, Max pulls a cigarette case from his pocket. "If your name really is Miss James, which I kinda figure it might be, and then again it might not. What's the use in *your* playacting?"

"Why, Max!" I exclaim. "I can't imagine—whatever do you mean? No, wait, I see. Oh, Max, I'm so dreadfully sorry, really I am. Of course I fibbed about being from Yonkers back on the train, but surely they've told you that I had a hole in my belly? The lowlife I was hotfooting it away from made a pincushion of me, and I was awfully frightened."

"Not the frightened angle—that part there I believe." Max takes a shrewd drag. "Somebody or other made a tunnel in you, probably in Harlem, you made tracks, and we made acquaintances, like, at the Chicago station."

There is a pause.

"Nice to meet you?" I whisper.

"Aw, likewise." He raises expressive eyebrows as if doffing a cap. "But I ain't talking about the Yonkers line you put out neither, see, I'm talking about the whole picture. 'Scuse my bluntness, but you want me to believe you're a dumb kid with bad luck what got smacked around and hit the road when it was once too often. That kinda yarn is easy to spin. But it ain't never happened to *you.* You ain't a dumb kid."

"Why, Max, you wound me. I'm only twenty-five."

"That's as may be. But you're also something else, I figure."

I'm several something elses, but you aren't meant to find that out.

The air in my throat solidifies. "What am I, then?"

Max shrugs. "You're gonna tell me."

"Is that so?"

"Sure. Right after you eat that there soup. That's Miss Christina's specialty. Tea should be steeped too, I'm betting." Max pulls the infuser out. "Outstanding. Cream? Sugar?"

"Yes, please," I answer faintly.

Max, with dining-car finesse, pours my tea. Then he pours a second cup I hadn't noticed behind the bud vase. Produces his flask and adds a generous dollop of John Barleycorn to each. He sets his drink on the nightstand, lifting the tray ever so carefully over my outstretched legs. Performance having drawn to a close, he seats himself and takes a civilized sip of spiked tea.

And the crowd showers roses at his feet.

When I draw a shuddering breath, Max says cheerily, "If you needs help with the spoon, just holler. But s'posing I've only caught you wrong ended, then start with the tea, I figure. That's just the tonic. And I got all night, Miss James."

"What an awfully happy coincidence."

"Ain't it the truth?"

Carefully, I lift the teacup and inhale. Saliva pools instantly. I sip.

What kind of monster, what soulless breed of cur, would take alcohol away from everyone and suggest replacing it with milk?

"Aw, now that's better, ain't it?" Max chuckles. I've never seen him laugh before, and it's a spill of light, crowding everything else from his face. "Nothing like the first swallow."

"It isn't very sportsmanlike to try to get a lady drunk to cadge her secrets from her bosom."

"Nah, I don't need no hooch for us to converse. You already done bought 'Crazy Blues,' remember? Can't talk music with a stranger and agree on so much and not end up chummy, that's science. Now, I'll sit here real quiet like while you eat that soup and drink that tea. Do my best lamppost impression, honest to God. After that, you're gonna warble like a canary."

"And if I decline this invitation?"

One shoulder lifts in what seems—incredibly—commiseration. "Then we sit here awhile. I ain't obliged to fill my four hundred hours for the month, Miss James, on account of I capped out eleven thousand miles first. That there's the trick—distance, not time, and you're outta harness for longer. Or you are if you're cracked like yours truly, and willing to take nothing but cross-country runs. We hit pay dirt at eleven thousand and thirty-six miles here in Portland. Shoulda congratulated me on another stint finished, but you was under the weather, so I'll forgive that you didn't bake a cake. Today's Tuesday, and I got till Friday to warm this chair. Eat."

I'm raising a spoon before I even know the white flag is in hand. Believing this is due to hunger alone would be an unwise astigmatism—that was an awfully authoritative tone.

You clearly understand this fellow about as well as you understand Hindustani. Pay attention.

Silence seems a fair proposal, so I allow it to permeate the room like Max's cigarette smoke, testing its quality. *Friendly. Wary.* If Max were any other fellow, I'd be terrified enough to dangle out the window like a set of drying stockings by now.

The soup is surprisingly decadent. Fish and clams and oysters, rich and bloodred. Cioppino, we'd have called it in Harlem. You could ladle this stuff in gilt-edged china, drop it on a white tablecloth, and charge six bits for it in Manhattan and no one would say boo. There are stories in this soup—Miss Christina's stories. I wonder where she learned them, and why they taste this complicated.

As I eat, a stronger breeze tickles the muslin curtains. It's different from anything I've ever smelled before—cedar sap and river sludge, yes, but those are faint bass notes against the high chord of rain-washed sky. As I eat, I sneak glances at the cheery cobalt chintz bench beneath the window, its color fading in the expiring light, and wonder what sort of Nobody might sit there listening to a new jazz record or writing a letter. Since I'm dead, and thus can't scratch out notes to any cherished correspondents anyhow, the idea is quickly soaked with rich romance.

I wonder if Maximilian would ever pay me a call. Walk slowly up behind me in the mirror, trace his fingers over my neck as I'm brushing my hair.

The drugs are winning by three lengths, as drugs are wont, and you're done with your soup.

Glancing over, I discover Max regards me as doth the archaeologist the pot shard. Cigarette dangling, lids at three-quarter mast. As if he's listening to "Beale Street Blues" at four o'clock in the morning instead of just contemplating a girl.

I set my spoon down with decision. I survived my previous life by keeping staunch allies—the loyal-unto-demise variety, and I delivered the goods despite certain fatal errors in judgment. Fatal, seeing as I am now postmortem. Anyhow, I had, if you will, a "family." The only thing I'm better at than vanishing is loyalty, and Max seems a worthy candidate. Time to peel off the sweet flapper like the second skin she is.

Here goes nothing—or rather, here goes Nobody.

"Thanks for the chow, Max. It was awfully big of you. May I have a cigarette, please?"

Grinning, Max slouches messily. "Aw, hell. There you are. I ain't much educated, but I can find a trumpet in a teacup, wouldn't you say?"

"Speaking of teacups, mine sprung a leak."

Shaking his head in amusement, Max clears away both tray and cart. He tops us up again and adds a second cigarette to the one between his lips. Lighting it, he hands it over.

I take a drag. It's asphalt and moonlight, better than the soup. Not quite as good as the liquor. If you're wondering, this is the Nobody I was around Mr. Salvatici. Sees everything and everyone, comments with unflinching candor, wears couture Lanvin crinolines and oilskin hip waders with equal aplomb, can talk jazz for hours, drinks like a trench laddie, and follows orders. Burrows into closets for people's skeletons. That sort.

"So," I posit. "We're pals, you say."

Max angles his jaw, appraising. "Yeah. So about the time you got yourself keyholed . . . we should converse about that. These lunatics are my second family away from Brooklyn, and I done brung you here."

"You didn't have a gun to that clever noggin of yours, Max. You didn't have to do that."

"Oh, yeah." He says it musically, on a fall. "Yeah, I did."

While this is fascinating, I don't admire to antagonize my new brother-in-arms. Thus, I table the question, though I burn to know why I was dropped here the way a cat drops a dead bird for under-appreciative human associates.

"My name really is Alice James. And I really did grow up in Harlem. But you knew that already. I'm half Welsh and half Italian, if it matters to you."

Max smiles with his lips, eyes abstaining. "I'm half German and half Negro. You ain't shocking no one in this room, Miss James."

"Well, it's a sight different for you."

"Yep. I'm aware," he reports with steel in his tone.

Blood rises in my cheeks. "Of course you are. What a dreadful buffoon you must—"

"Let's keep to the topic." Max shakes out another smoke. "This injury what we're discussing—you done told Mavereen and Dr. Pendleton it was thanks to a rotten beau. Was that true?"

"Not to a literalist."

"Were you in hot water, or was it purely accidental?"

"Sure, supposing you call the invasion of France an accident."

"How amusing you make that sound, Miss James. Maybe I shoulda said Second Lieutenant Maximilian Burton when we was first acquainted."

I open my mouth and shut it again. This . . . this explains a great deal.

The daring rescue, the forcefulness, and the way he moves under that moss-green shirt, just for starters.

"That wouldn't have been very bright, George," I tease.

He shrugs. "Well, now you know. I can learn you some French, if you'd care to. Like how you said, your time is elastic."

"Teach me some French, I suppose you to mean."

"No, I meant 'loin ya.'" Max winks. "I parleys Brooklyn and French—for an English lesson, you wanna talk to Blossom."

"Yes, I suspected she was a student of the Queen's tongue." Tapping ash into my saucer, I hesitate. "Sorry. Um, I promise I'm not pulling the damsel stuff again. Haven't yet broached this topic with anyone living, we two met a few fleeting days hence, you understand."

"How's about I'll help? The shot was aimed square at you, then, and the trigger was pulled by I s'pose a pretty dangerous guy?"

"Thankfully, it was his backup Pocket shooter, just a pellet gun, really, which is the reason we're having this tea party."

"And why did he decide you needed a gap in the midsection, then, Miss James?"

"Please call me Alice." The smoke must be stinging my eyes. I pass my thumb under both, edging away salt water. "I actually meant to say that on the train, believe it or not. Not, I suppose."

"Damn straight I believe you. There's more than just one reason why you're at the Paragon Hotel, Miss—Alice."

Nobody, I correct him in my head. I take a rib-cracking breath and start hacking away again. When my eyes open, a water glass rests on the table and Max is standing there radiating bonfire levels of concern.

"Thanks." After several cool swallows, I'm as recovered as possible. "Sit down, for God's sake, you'll wake the children."

Max returns to smoking with his elbows on his knees, unthreatening and round-shouldered.

Steady as she goes.

"Right, here's a general line on the situation." I address the wall, watching a film from long, long ago and the other side of the continent. "I was born dirt poor, *quelque* surprise, everyone in Harlem is. The fellow who shot me was my bosom associate from the cradle. As we advanced in years, we both fell victim to shall we say unfortunate events, and shall we also say unwholesome influences. You might as well know that I belong to a gang of shameless bootleggers who often find their business interests at cross-purposes with other hoodlums. I found myself in the crosshairs of those same cross-purposes. Undeclared war."

"Declared or undeclared, it don't make a dame any less croaked."

"Precisely so. When I was hit, a policeman on the graft named Harry Chipchase—I always have to say both names, his moniker is too precious—promised to conjure up an Alice James-ish corpse for me. I vanished and presume Alice James is already buried, so obviously writing love notes to the boys back home is nixed. Probably I got away clean. *Probably* no one is looking for me. So here we are. Prohibition, my poor choices, and your good graces brought me to the Paragon Hotel to do with as you see fit. I mean that literally, Maximilian. You're a second lieutenant, you said—your freshest recruit, reporting for duty, sir. I'll be up for anything you ask within the fortnight but at the moment ought to refrain from ballet."

I make a flourish with my hand in lieu of bowing. My nerves sing like a teakettle left to burst, but that doesn't make any sense. My luck is holding. I haven't walked under any ladders or touched a lightning-struck tree. And I didn't even jinx myself by saying *Nicolo Benenati.* Max's spine hits the back of the chair as he ruminates, both of us finishing our cigarettes while the sky turns vacant and black as any corpse.

Max remarks, "So you're mixed up in the liquor racket. So's half the damn country. I dabble too. You ever kill anybody yourself, like?"

I shake my head. "Never."

How many people died on your account, though? Have you even any idea?

Dust motes of pure silence sprinkle through the air.

"Here's what I'm gonna propose." Max's voice rings, no longer speculative. "You care to share any of this here yarn with the others, that's your business. I for one won't say peep. You had some bad breaks and then some worse ones. Similar to the picture you painted me before, but this one I can look at without squinting."

"Ever so pleased my tale of woe passes muster."

"It don't go very far. But it keeps to the roads, like."

"I've poured out to you just about all I can," I protest, exhausted. "I am as putty in your hands, Max. You're safer not knowing the whole encyclopedia, but I'll keep at it if you want me to."

"Yeah, I got that part. We're good."

"You're not tossing me through the window? Truly?"

"We're on the fifth floor, Alice—I ain't never been keen on smashing music lovers. Thanks for playing straight with me."

He stands and stretches. I feel wrung out, altogether drained. If only I could trust this magnanimity—we aren't the same race, the same sort, aren't even pals. Not the way he says we are. Not until I've guarded his armor chinks, bled a bit for him. Every circus charges an entrance fee. Mr. Salvatici's sure as hell did. By rights, I ought to be put through my paces. We're just a pair of people who talked music before Nobody's masks started cracking. And instead of leaving this suspicious dame to shuffle off the old coil, Max half carried me home to his nearest and dearest.

Why, for God's sake?

"Am I at all like your sisters?" I blurt as he drapes linen over the spent cart.

"Beg pardon?"

"Forgive me, but. I overheard Blossom mention that you had white siblings. Is that . . . is that why you're going so far out on a limb?" I gesture helplessly between us. "This pledge to keep my secrets, it's an awfully nifty thing, but as for your part. Christ, Max. I need it to be real. Not just decency or politeness, things no one gives a damn about. Do I remind you of your sisters?"

Max's deep-set eyes narrow. They're darker than gold, lighter than bronze. The color of an elegant brass rail in a speakeasy. Or, better still, of a pocket watch that's been taken out and consulted over a few generations.

"No, you don't remind me of my sisters," Max concludes. "You ain't nothing at all like my sisters."

"But I do remind you of someone?"

"Yeah, sure you do."

"Because you remind me dreadfully of someone, you see."

"Is that so."

"Yes."

"Well, I'll be. Did you like the guy?"

"Not always," I admit, and my heart beats in ragtime. "Did you like the person I remind you of, Max?"

"No," he says, not even having to think it over. "Not one little bit. Good night, Miss James. You keep safe and warm, you got me? Sleep well."

Five

From this study I agree that the Negro ought to be educated and helped but I would not want to associate very much with them. I guess there are Negroes better than I even, but to me a Negro is a Negro.

—"A NEGRO IS JUST A NEGRO,"
The Advocate, Portland, Oregon, May 1, 1926

When I wake again, all is velvet darkness, and barely audible footsteps *brush-scuff* past my door.

Mind cavernous with dread, I spring from the mattress.

Twin wounds shriek. Light paints a stripe under the door and my shaking hand hits cool metal. I tug, clutching the frame as I struggle. There isn't another way out of this room, so I must duck through the assassin's arms and escape, over river and under skies, find a slow boat to Shanghai or someplace more remote before—

"Jesus! Are you—no, no, don't struggle like that. I've *got* you, honey. It's only me."

Blinking away the nightmare, I'm in an ordinary corridor. The carpet is a whirlpool of sage and maroon, the walls above the chair rail a pale melon tone. Strong hands have me by both elbows, and subtle vanilla perfume caresses my nose. Blossom's artfully manicured brows twist with alarm.

"Oh God. I'm sorry." A sting at the crook of my elbow registers. Another tiny puncture wound—two where previously only one winked up at me. "I think Dr. Pendleton gave me more morphine. How could I have missed that? I was afraid that you might be . . . I was half sleepwalking."

"Well, you *certainly* aren't operating at peak efficiency."

"That's a swell understatement. I'm so embarrassed."

Her eyes are amused at their corners. "Can you stand?"

"I can do any amount of dandy tricks. That one—yes, that seems to be back in the repertoire. I'm sorry."

"Oh, it's far from the first time a near stranger has flown into my arms, and should I lose my natural magnetism, I assure you I'd simply *die* of boredom."

Adjusting the low-scoop collar of my borrowed nightdress, I shiver. A shadowy figure appears down the hall. I barely stifle a gasp before I realize it's only a maid, neatly uniformed and capped, with a pair of pillows in her arms. Her eyes slice to me, lingering.

"That's one of Mavereen's minions," Blossom whispers teasingly. "Don't attempt any late-night debauches around here, your sins *will* find you out. Well. Treat your debauches with due moderation, anyhow. Our dear Mavereen is a monument to virtue, rather of the antique variety."

I nod. My attention cuts back to the yawning shadow of my bedchamber. My crackling nerves want nothing to do with it. The dim behind me is fume dense, paralyzing.

Night is for knife thrusts and the powder flare of gun muzzles. Night is for reports to Mr. Salvatici, when you play the Angel of Death.

Night is for the last time you were shot.

Before you knew what brand of evil you were mixed up in.

"Seeing as I'm just back from the Rose's Thorn and still

indecently sober, why don't you keep me company?" Blossom's china-doll lips are rouged crimson and puckered in sympathy. "Oh, the Rose's Thorn is a club where I perform. Portlanders are *lunatic* over roses—it's absurd, they're everywhere. Come along to my room? It's a ghastly prospect to contemplate sleep directly after finishing a set, so I never attempt it. Saves me time I would otherwise have spent studying the ceiling."

"Saves it for what?"

"Why, for leisure, of course, which is a *sight* preferable to insomnia. There is a great deal on my mind of late."

"Would I be intruding awfully much?"

"Gracious no, honey, if you don't come, I'll only end up having a conversation with Medea. And I'm *considerably* too young and alluring to talk to cats."

A smile lands on my face, as welcome as an unexpected kiss.

"A sightseeing trip sounds swell. It hasn't been the jazziest of times in there," I own as I shut my door.

Blossom offers an arm draped in an eggplant-colored cloak. A fine mist dusts it, as if she were coated in cloud, and I wonder whether anything in Portland is ever entirely dry.

"Lift the hem of that shift before you get a mouthful of carpet. There's a good girl. You're in room five fifteen, and I'm five twenty-three, just this way. Do you think you can walk so far? There's a robe I can lend you as incentive, it's the most alarming shade of green and would be simply *decadent* with your coloring. Wherever did you come by onyx eyes with such fair hair, by the way? If that blond is from a bottle, I'm Cleopatra."

"Dad was Italian."

"Oh, marvelous. Tell me at once how to insult someone in Italian."

"Puttana della miseria." I note that she was correct to claim superiority of height—five foot nine, at the least. Her fashionably

short hair is parted on the side and arranged in shining finger waves, topped with a spray of billowing purple feathers.

"And what does that oh-so-lively phrase mean?"

"The 'most dreadfully miserable whore of all the world's many unhappy whores' comes closest."

Blossom emits a regular pipe organ of a guffaw. Then she claps a hand over her mouth murmuring, "Honey, don't do that to me in the hallway, it's three o'clock in the damn morning and one of the maids will scold. Hush now till we reach headquarters."

Travel is painful and the carpet eddies like a wind-churned lake. But I mind less than I ought to. Blossom is clearly the sort who, when inclined to pal around, can make one feel like a coconspirator in under sixty seconds. Such women are generally equally deft at freezing a gal out blizzard quick, and I feel disproportionately glad to have qualified.

Particularly after Max said he didn't like the person you reminded him of. Not one little bit.

Letting go of Blossom as she produces a key from a jet-beaded reticule, I contemplate my bare toes. Whether or not Max is strong for the duplicitous criminal type is irrelevant. Really, who in his right mind would be? Max saved my life and brought me supper and poured me booze and is keeping my secret and what did I expect, bonus compliments?

"Welcome to my sanctuary," Blossom trills as we enter. "Do not under threat of certain disfigurement even *contemplate* touching the demon in cat guise reposing on the divan. Medea, what atrocities have you been committing this evening?"

A ball of ivory fur with electric-yellow eyes glowers at me from the identical divan as in my room, though this one hosts maybe sixty or seventy tasseled pillows. Medea, having confirmed that I'm beneath her notice, stretches her front legs and returns to dreamland.

"I found her at a theater in New Orleans, meowing to raise hell in the orchestra pit. In retrospect, I think she really *was* attempting to contact her cohorts in Hades. She was only a kitten, and I a lonesome chorus girl far from home. A sap, in other words. I took her to my bosom, and she instantly drew blood. Literally."

"Must've been a lawyer in a past life."

"Or a producer, perhaps. Since that day, she has *plagued* my existence without relent."

Blossom is practically cooing, scratching the elderly mop behind its ears. I see a young Nicolo, his sweetness with favorite warriors of the cat armies, and swallow something that sits in my belly like cement.

"Oh, Miss James, you're looking peaky enough without added exercise. Take the bedside chair."

"It's Alice," I say, adjusting yet another velvet pillow. "Thanks ever so."

My neighbor's room hardly resembles my own save the layout. Framed pictures of famous black singers and actresses adorn the walls—Abbie Mitchell, Evelyn Preer, Ma Rainey. The headboard and coverlet match mine, but a length of Chinese-patterned silk adorns the end of the bed. A screen printed with a pagoda and some conceited-looking herons creates a dressing room. Birds in the house are beastly luck, so I trace the sign of the cross on the chair cushion. Still, I'm terribly strong for the place. Blossom's abode isn't a neutral room for a stranger to wax horizontal and then depart, all trace of her vanished like footprints along the shoreline.

This room is her home.

"Where were you homesick for, way back when you were a sap?" I tuck my feet into the chair, resting my temple on my fist. The planet is still keen to buck me off.

"Chicago. I'd just left home for the first time. But I must warn you, I remain something of a sap, I'm afraid. I still miss places, just different ones."

"Where is that, then?"

"This evening? San Francisco. I suffered like anything leaving there, *exquisite* suffering. It's a marvelous place, very European, all the candy-colored houses and the salt winds and the Bohemians. I used to perform at the Palace Hotel in the Pied Piper Bar, right under that simply *stunning* painting, dreaming of singing so beautifully I could bewitch all the town's children and lead them off into the mist like I did with the rats. I haven't managed it yet, by the way. With rats or children."

"Bad luck," I commiserate.

Blossom winks at me. Removes her cloak and lays it over her vanity chair, turns to look in the mirror, and I can't help myself. All telegraph lines between my brain and my face are felled. I stare.

And stare.

She wears the most dramatic gown I've ever seen, and I am well versed in the garment trade. Its structure is vaguely Grecian, supposing Grecian means "stunning." All depends upon a thick choker collar covered entirely in paste diamonds, from which the spill of violet silk falls over her small breasts and lean legs. In the back, the same piece of fabric's more tightly gathered drape cascades down her spine, but the sides are entirely open—her arms, her shoulders, her whole torso from the waist up is bare. A matching crystal belt fastens the front panel to her midriff. How a single piece of cloth attached on either side of a glorified necklace could look this glamorous, I know not, but it suits Blossom's svelte form so perfectly that I realize I'm not breathing.

"Do you like this old rag?" She preens in the mirror as she removes her earrings. "I found it in Paris many moons ago, for, oh, I'd estimate eight fortunes. No, eight and a half."

"I think that witchcraft was employed and your dressmaker is in danger of some light roasting."

Chuckling, Blossom deposits her hair plumage in a vanity drawer.

"It *is* rather fine, isn't it? What's your preference, gin or scotch? I assume you imbibe, and you must consider that a compliment."

"Oh. Whichever you're having, thank you."

My hostess unscrews the top of a perfume atomizer made of lovely yellow-green vaseline glass and pours two whiskeys into cut-glass tumblers.

"A toast!" she proclaims. "To the survival of the fittest."

"And the terribly unfit, come to that."

"Oh, well *done*. Hear, hear."

Glasses clink. Blossom glides away, flips the lid of a record player resting on a low table, and the opening strains of Verdi's *Don Carlos* reach my ears. She vanishes behind her screen. I can just make out the finial of a wardrobe behind it.

"Now, tell me *every* little thing that happened today, and don't skimp on detail, gossip, or unsubstantiated rumor," she orders. "If you don't have any, do feel free to invent some. And if you can't remember names, make them up."

The scotch is, to my delight, real. None of the swill steeped in tree bark for room 523, apparently. "There's not much to tell. Imagine a deceased beetle with its legs in the air and make it a bit less sprightly."

"Beetle shaped, but a mere husk?"

"That's the ticket."

"Goodness, what an inauspicious beginning. *Such* luck! You can only improve from here, you see. But surely we looked in on you since I left?"

"Oh, yes. But for obvious reasons, I'm not the belle of the ball."

"There isn't much demand for strange white invalids at the Paragon Hotel, I'll admit. But as far as I'm concerned, you're terribly intriguing."

"That's awfully decent of you."

"*Indecent,* I think you'll find. I'm a contrary person."

Reappearing, Blossom ties a blush-pink robe over matching silk pajamas. She lobs me a wadded ball of poison-emerald cloth that unfurls midair to become a second dressing gown of equally exquisite manufacture. As in not manufactured, but sewn. Medea eyes its flight with malicious interest and hops from the sofa to the bed.

"No, I couldn't possibly—"

"Put it on—you're ruining the high tone of my boudoir something *tragic*," she insists happily as she lowers herself sideways into the vanity chair. "So. Who paid you court today?"

"Max, for one." The words are carefully casual. I don't know who palavers with whom in these parts.

"Darling man, I could simply eat him with a spoon."

But do you? I can't help but wonder. Given my new loyalties to the chap.

"He's a decorated war hero, I'll have you know, since he won't spill a *word* about it otherwise," Blossom continues breezily. "The French had no sooner dropped the Croix de Guerre round his neck than the British had mentioned him in dispatches and added a Victory medal—if not for segregation, the man would resemble a game of ring toss. Our country won't so much as shine his shoes, naturally."

The discomfort that has been worming its way through my innards since Max declared himself a second lieutenant gives a twisting reminder. Not that I'm any stranger to battles, of a sort. Likewise have hardship and I clasped hands and called each other cousin. But when FATS ARE FUEL FOR FIGHTERS and SAVE A LOAF A WEEK TO WIN THE WAR and FOOD IS A WEAPON: DON'T WASTE IT posters covered New York City like a second skin, I was supping on caviar washed down with champagne, or conversely champagne supplemented by nourishing caviar. Mr. Salvatici kept us all in the fine sort of fettle, and if the money before the Volstead Act happened to come from brothels, dice joints, pool parlors, craps houses, and establishments dedicated to ponies running in a circle? Well, we didn't think twice over it. I hadn't remotely understood anyone who put his name down to sleep in trench sewage, freeze to death, and be shot at.

"Max has been so good to me," I confess. "What sort of stationery does one use to say, 'Smashing that I continue to exist, you are hereby thanked for it liberally'?"

"Oh, ecru, I think."

Another smile bubbles to the surface. "Are you very close friends?"

Blossom's eyes pucker charmingly. "He isn't my sort, honey. But yes, we're thick as thieves. Most of the permanent residents at the Paragon are."

If Max isn't your sort, who on the earth's surface is? I wonder. Then I picture an older black gentleman—taller than she, richer than Solomon, with a cinder-brush mustache and a shirt with French cuffs. There aren't many. But they do exist, and they probably lodge at the Paragon. And enjoy genuine scotch.

"Two medals," I muse. "So that's why Davy Lee wants his own pair. A touch of Max worship. He's willing to trade them in for cookies, of course. Awfully sensible."

A grin mounts an offensive and soon conquers Blossom's entire face. "Christ no, he's the very *least* sensible child ever born. Tell him half a story and he'll make a world to live in. Truth and fiction are blurred where that one's concerned. However did you meet Davy?" Her expression shifts. "*Please* don't tell me he was running loose again. We all take turns keeping the beautiful scatterbrain intact."

"Davy admired to either watch me die or save my life, it was dreadfully muddled. Either way, it made a roaring smashup for the esteemed youth. I suppose he's seen Max's medals?"

The glad look Blossom adopted has staying power. It's making her eyes jig above the steep planes of her cheekbones. "Oh, *rather.*

Only about six times a day does he show an interest—when Max is here, you understand. He's all too often on trains, or back in Brooklyn. How was Davy faring today?"

"Very jazzed over drawing in a class with, um . . . sorry, my mind isn't quite—"

"My dear friend, Mrs. Evelina Vaughan. Weekly Betterment? Yes, she collects causes like they're postage stamps. Evy tutors a pack of colored youth thirsting for knowledge—teaches toddlers clay molding and aspiring teens proper French, that sort of thing. She's mad as a hatter. And what did Davy make of you?"

"I'm the wrong color. Apparently I look ill. *Quelque* shock. Who does the kid belong to?"

Swiveling round to face her mirror, Blossom samples the spirits and then dips a cloth in a porcelain pot of cream, which she applies to her kohl. "Not a soul."

"Come again?"

"I mean simply no one, honey, he's a foundling. A foundling I found, not unlike this terrible animal before you but with a *much* better disposition."

Medea is kneading at a pillow, pricking tufts into the fabric with sadistic glee.

"However did that come about? They aren't like pennies you can just pick up wherever you happen upon them."

"Gracious no, but I've a certain yen for lost things. You're as lost as can be, Alice James, just *terribly* misplaced, and look where you find yourself," she adds with a warm glance. "And come to mention it, he was rather like a penny. Davy was left in a bassinet in Seattle, Washington, adjacent to the trash behind the nightclub where I was ending a two-month headlining contract. Simply *horrific* screams led me outside after curtain call."

Since she knows I'm from Harlem, I decide shock would be overacting. "How old?"

"Two months."

"Healthy?"

"In full voice, anyhow."

"Was his name in a note?"

"No note, the poor dear mite. I named him Davy, and he was in the *lee* of the bin, you understand. It has a ring, doesn't it?"

"It has the whole jewelry box. What about accommodations? He said he lives here in a real fortress."

"Yes, that would be in Christina's suite across the way. Max made a castle out of scrap wood and installed a bed inside after she complained the child was perennially building battlements out of her sheets. As head chef, she's hardly ever in her rooms, you see, so he's less bother there. But she *dotes* on him, we all do. At the time of his discovery, the hotel was already to be my permanent sanctuary, and when I waltzed in with Davy, we all decided he was ours for the keeping. Dr. Pendleton tutors him and the other boy who works here, Wednesday Joe. Mavereen instills morals, Max shows them how to throw a punch or a baseball, as you please, Christina feeds them, and I spoil them senseless. It's *grand.*"

Blossom ducks into her bathroom, wets a towel, and scrubs her face clean of lotion. Either the hard stuff is making me dizzy or she's even more striking when the brazen planes of her skull are uninterrupted by lip stain and eye glitter.

"But it must have been difficult, when he was a baby," I argue. "A local orphanage didn't occur?"

"Honey, as bad as you'll find the weather here is, Seattle is worse. I'm indecent, I'm not *cruel.*"

"You're a regular saint," I marvel.

"Well, aren't you the sweetest thing, but no, I'm a sap. I *told* you. A mere ninety-five percent of the Paragon's tenancy would agree, and the rest have just now checked in."

"Saps lose their wallets to pickpockets and leave safes open for yeggmen. You gave Davy a new life."

Blossom angles the edge of her drink at me meaningfully. "I've needed those myself, you see. So I collect spares and pass them out whenever—Medea, *honestly*!"

Medea, with a half-chewed tassel hanging out of her mouth, slinks back to the divan.

"Why did you leave San Francisco?" As soon as they're past my teeth, I want the words back. "Please don't answer that if you're vexed by it. You mentioned suffering."

Perching on the edge of the bed, Blossom rests her glass in her lap. "It was a very old story. The one that causes all these endless reams of song lyrics and sonnet penning. My true love left. My heart was broken. And what in the wide world was I to do?"

I will my eyes to stay dry. This is Blossom's tale. Or it's everyone's, and therefore still not mine to wallow in.

"Were you always a performer?"

"All my life. *Lives*, I suppose. And what did you do when you were in Harlem?"

Not wanting to contradict what I told Max, I answer, "This and that. It was always changing."

Correction: who you were targeting was always changing, and Nobody changed with them.

"Honey, even if your career was to take ten-dollar bills so you could go to the powder room, I *promise* you that I find no fault with the choice. If you were a choir girl, you wouldn't have been shot at. If I were a choir girl, I wouldn't be in Portland."

Pausing, I consider.

Surviving through loyalty to your rescuer is not enough.

Particularly when Max seems likely to be gone the lion's share of each month. Mrs. Meader appears not to like the idea of me, while Miss Christina and Dr. Pendleton take exception to the corporeal me, and Davy is a mere sprout.

Blossom, though—I could be loyal to her too, and that would be like family a little, and I wouldn't feel as if I'm the last woman in the wide, cold world.

I clear my throat. "When you said I was lost . . . you saw the other bullet scar, didn't you?"

My hostess peers at her glass as if it's a scrying ball. "If you want to know how observant a sap I am, the answer is exceedingly."

"Do you enjoy cautionary tales? Shilly-shallying children eaten by wolves, that stuff?"

"Alice, I am *gone* on them," Blossom breathes.

Repeating what I told Max takes less than two minutes. Blossom listens with rapt attention. I've never met anyone with a more manufactured accent matched to artless sincerity. She must be a simply smashing actress. If she told me head colds cured heartache, I'd sleep with the window open. When I'm through, she whistles.

"My *word.* It's too tragic. You were faced with certain death and forced into exile."

"Like the very dickens."

"And have been delivered into an ever-so-strange land."

"The old bird is in the market for fresh feathers."

"Oh, the *agony* of displacement. I know *just* how it feels. How can I help?"

"When I'm grateful to people, I'm loyal to them. It's—I need that, need the, um, purpose. So whatever you want from me, in thanks for your kindness? Just ask. I'll see it through."

Her tongue touches her upper lip in puzzlement. "Why do I sense that you're entirely in earnest?"

"Possibly because I'm half Italian. We're the sort who either throw ourselves weeping upon your grave or help you into it."

A knock interrupts us. Startling, I grip my half-empty glass, ready to test it against the assailant's temple. But a young woman's voice says, "Blossom, I've been checking here every half hour, I need you to—oh."

I evaluate the newcomer. She's short, pleasingly plump enough to be ten years out of style, a garden of youthful bloom. Though she's dark, where Blossom's skin reflects ocean glints and cobalt dusk, hers has a red-brick undertone. Her long hair undulates, glossy and black as piano keys, and her shockingly full lips part company in dismay. A sheet of lined paper suffers between her fingers, crumpling.

"Blossom, what in God's name are you doing?" she exclaims.

"Miss James, may I introduce to you Miss Kiona." Blossom sweeps to her feet. "Refreshment, Jenny? Whatever's the matter? You look sixteen shades of furious and it's just the *tiniest* bit unsettling at . . ." She glances at a pretty mother-of-pearl desk clock. "Three twenty-seven a.m."

Medea yowls her agreement, glaring.

"How could you ask such a thing?" Jenny Kiona's cheeks are aglow. "We have to plan, we have to fight, we can't just take this like—like animals, they already think we're animals, and I wait for you all night long to show you what I've come up with and now I find you with this *invader*?"

"Alice is fine," I suggest humbly.

Blossom barks a laugh. "There, you see? Come along now and be friends."

"Jenny, was it?" I extend my hand.

She doesn't take it. "Yes, Jenny. Or you can call me that, anyway. Ka'ktsama seems to elude people. Listen, Blossom, send her away at once. We need to—"

"Politics before breakfast or after supper is never wisdom, honey."

"This isn't politics! It's our lives! You have to take this seriously."

Blossom pours another scotch, her face a stark mask. "I am taking it very fucking seriously, and *you* are taking a drink."

Steam billows from Jenny's ears. "You'd truly prefer to booze and socialize with . . . with her than strategize with me?"

"Strategies require mascara, and as you can see, we're past that landmark for the night."

"You always do this." Jenny vibrates dangerously. "Trust people. Just . . . without any thought whatsoever. It worked out all right with Evelina Vaughan, but this time? We don't know her, what her views are, whether she's at all respectable herself. We *have* to present a civilized image right now, it's essential. And here comes a white woman with a mysterious bullet wound and you're chattering away with her over backwoods moonshine—"

"*Hardly* that, honey," Blossom demurs.

"She could be an arsonist for all you know!"

"Put me down for medium rare, in that case, I can't abide overdone meat."

Jenny blinks. "You're sick."

"Yes, that's *very* likely." Shrugging at Jenny's glass, Blossom downs the grog herself like a brine-crusted privateer. The fissures around her tender mouth aren't just from laughter, and within all the straight contours, gentle purple shadows semicircle her eyes.

"This is dangerous," Jenny pleads. "It's not the same as the Weekly Betterment classes, you know, in broad daylight so all can see it's for a good cause. She isn't like us!"

"Of course she isn't like us, *look* at her," Blossom snaps, making a balletic orbit with her empty hand. "That doesn't mean she's like *them.* Think for a moment, if you can. A frog isn't like a flamingo. That doesn't make it a hippopotamus."

"I do think." Jenny's full lips quiver like a fly caught in a web. "I . . . just don't always think what you do. But whenever we argue, you make me feel like an idiot."

"Honey, please don't—"

The door slams. *Don Carlos* must have soured in Blossom's estimation, because she leans to disengage the needle.

"Jenny is the loveliest girl, monstrously bright, hot as tropics for reform, but she thinks she can change the world," my hostess exhaustedly volunteers. "She's mistaken. She also thinks you're nothing like us. Well, she's right about that, but *I'm* nothing like *her*, and here we find ourselves."

Downing the rest of my nightcap, I consider my course. The past twelve years of my life were devoted to service; defending someone again is like having air.

Break the champagne over the mermaid's bosom.

"This is about the trouble Davy mentioned earlier. Isn't it?" I wobble toward the door and Blossom springs up with a small alarmed exclamation. "I want to help. You must know that I've no intention of siphoning hospitality until you're all dry, and I have proof in my room."

The trek back along the Sahara hallway is exhausting sans camel. When we switch on the lights, I fold myself into my bedclothes and point at the valise sitting next to my carpetbag and jut my chin suggestively.

When Blossom opens the luggage, she takes a quick breath and flattens her fingers over her prominent collarbone.

"I know," I commiserate. "The first time I saw fifty thousand dollars in cash, it took me the same way."

· *Six* ·

THEN

Mafia ***can objectively be defined as the mysterious sense of fear which a man notorious for his crimes or brutal use of force arouses in the weak, the meek, and the cowardly.***

—THE PREFECT OF GIRGENTI TO THE MINISTER OF THE INTERIOR, June 30, 1874

M*alavita* may have planted the seed of my criminal career, but I'd a plethora of sunny days and watering cans to speed its growth. And all this steady nurturing of my corruption burst into full flower at last on the night I met Mr. Salvatici.

I own a taste for devotion the way some own a taste for narcotics. Young Alice didn't fling herself at every pedestrian in upper Manhattan swearing fealty—but some girls dream of wedding dresses and fashion veils from day-old newspaper.

I dreamed of standing in front of a bullet for a friend.

After our immersion in *malavita*, I stopped playing pranks on my mother's johns. They could be Family—they could kill us.

Stopped walking with my head up, eyes on the second stories of the crumbling brick tenements, the fourth, the rooftop, sky-high. Who knew what lurked there—it might stare back.

Stopped talking. Started listening.

"You're vanishing, Nobody," Mum said to my twelve-year-old self, two years after Nicolo's beating and the massacre of Mr. Mangiapane's windows. We had fought many battles in the interim. I was sick of the crunch of fists landing. "That nickname were meant fer a joke—I can barely see you anymore."

*"Nun essiri duci sinno ti mancianu, nun essiri amarusinno ti futtinu,"** I replied.

So there I was: slipping into the shadowlands while still burning to be of use to someone. And three years later, I was given one fiery hell of an opportunity.

On Friday, October 27 of 1911, when I was fifteen, the rain drenched our neighborhood with zesty vim. The windows of the Step Right Inn wept at the advent of winter, and along 107th Street expired leaves and potato peelings bobbed downriver like so many shrieking shipwreck victims.

Pressing one hand to my lower back, I surveyed the dining room, wielding a beer-soiled dishrag.

There wasn't much doing. Everyone was bobbing for apples or whittling at pumpkins in anticipation of All Hallows' Eve. A trio of scarlet-fingered wet-washwomen nursed pints. Two Sicilians shared a bottle of Chianti. One was unknown—the other was Dario Palma's uncle, Tommaso Palma, and therefore an object of loathing. And a regular customer with a hat pulled low over his temples read *The New York Times* while he awaited my mother. Who was already occupied in every sense of the word.

---

* Sicilian phrase meaning everything in moderation: "Don't be too sweet lest you be eaten, don't be too sour lest you be shunned."

"Poor Nobody, scrubbing day and night," Mr. Mangiapane slurred from behind the bar. "What a Cinderella."

I polished the empty table before me.

"Never fear, *mia dolce.* Your drudgery can't last long."

Here comes your daily prognostication.

"You'll be keeping somebody warm soon." He appraised me with revolting enthusiasm. "Plenty of somebodies."

This brings us to another reason I'd been right merrily courting invisibility: I needed a profession and was unfit for any save human slot machine. Whether by marriage or rental hardly mattered to me. Without the safety afforded by obvious disease, or better yet a Siamese twin, I was one living parent away from a stranger paying me to dip his wick in my wax.

A tinny bell chimed. "Go on, to the kitchen with you! It'll keep that ass firm while I hold my dick waiting for you to accept *amor fati.*"* Mr. Mangiapane scratched at his belly swell.

To this day, I believe Mr. Mangiapane ought to have been orphaned before conception. I edged silent as a cat's tail through the swinging door, wondering how best to curse him with the evil eye, since Halloween was such a ripe occasion. The familiar blast of cornmeal and animal fat aromas hailed me.

"Ah, here she is! *I carciofini fritti sono pronti.*"

Crispy Ezio, black locks writhing like eels under his hairnet, nodded at the fried baby artichokes on the prep counter. Our esteemed chef presided over a deep copper skillet of sizzling lamb sweetbreads. I once asked Ezio whether any food was actually better off sans hot lard bath. He asked me whether any mortals were better off unbaptized in the blood of Christ.

Popping a morsel in my mouth, I lingered.

---

* "Love of one's fate," or contentment with the inevitable.

"Didn't you eat yet, *passerotta*?* Here, I have for you fried chickpeas."

Crispy Ezio elbowed the snack in my direction. He was the only one in the hotel who hadn't noticed the small breasts spurting from my lean frame. I adored him for it. Even Mum pinched them teasingly.

"Mr. Mangiapane is itching to try me out as a *puttana*," I whispered. "All he needs is a starting pistol."

Ezio snorted. *"Impossibile."*

"It's pretty likely, actually. How else am I meant to live?"

My companion shook his head, clucking. "You see before you, Nobody, one lucky *bastardo*. When I landed here, I had nothing. To live, as you say—this occupied all of my many brains. For survival a man is supposed to sacrifice something, give up *un poco di* spirit. For me, Mr. Mangiapane needed a chef. And I fry things. Holy mothershit! What a match! So fortunate. Perhaps the same, for *tua madre*. Making men happy? A match. For you? Not a match. What do you want to do?"

"I've never wanted to do anything. Not the way you fry things, anyhow."

"Who do you want to be, then?"

"I want to be the Apostle Peter except that I wouldn't deny Christ, I'd rescue Him and we'd run Pilate's soldiers through with our spears." My heart drummed. I'd never told this to anyone before. "I want to be a knight serving a noble king, like King Arthur. I want to be Doc Holliday and save Wyatt Earp's life during a saloon standoff. That sort."

Through the door, Mr. Mangiapane bellowed something crude. I was taking too long.

---

* Little sparrow.

"Then you must do this very much strange thing." Crispy Ezio shrugged fondly. "You must succeed. It is required."

"Why?"

"You are *American*. Half-breed, born in New York! It is your birthright, *passerotta*. Go—I have more coming. *Vai, vai!*"

I went. My mother's regular had removed his hat, revealing a face I always found pleasant save a mouth like an afterthought. Maybe it occurred to the doctor that the newborn would need to eat and simply slit a line. Who knew? But apart from the paper-thin lips, the *Times* reader was just a quiet Italian with philosophical blue eyes. I delivered him one of the *carciofini* bowls, keeping to his periphery as ever. Then I ghosted over to the Sicilians with fried tokens of the Step Right Inn's esteem.

The stranger was tall, with a loose-jowled hound's face. Dario's uncle Tommaso was older, with grey hair combed forward over his bald egg. Both wore dark, expensive suits. Both spoke their native dialect, which meant my mind glossed over words that weren't Italian—Greek, Hebrew, all the bits thrown into the stew called Sicilian.

But I grew up here. I could understand them perfectly.

"It's too soon after the last time," the hulking fellow muttered.

Dario's kin drew a finger along the rim of his glass. "Old Benenati has been operating on credit, as far as the Boss of Bosses is concerned. So he won't pay with money? Time settles all debts."

The two names nearly froze me. But freezing is noticeable, so I pretended to scratch barmaid notes, ears straining outward like Victrola horns. Old Benenati, of course, meant Nicolo's father. But Boss of Bosses? We considered that position Satan's local deputy.

Known to every Italian on Manhattan Island only as the *Clutch Hand.*

"A lot of work for us, to off Old Benenati over hen feed," the stranger complained.

Uncle Tommaso smiled. “It could be a fortune. It could be a penny. His life is worth less than a penny, you see. You must understand that, even if you’re new to this country.”

The other ducked, his apologetic reply too colloquial to catch.

“No, I don’t think you do. This is about order. Heaven and earth and hell below.”

Swallowing, I affected to dust the piano.

“There’s a saying about us back home,” Tommaso Palma continued in a gentle, sickening tone. “You probably know it. At the head of everything is God, Lord of Heaven. After him comes Prince Torlonia, lord of the earth. Then come Prince Torlonia’s armed guards. Then come Prince Torlonia’s armed guards’ dogs. Then nothing at all. Then nothing at all. Then nothing at all. Then come the peasants. And that’s all.”

The hangdog fellow grimaced.

“In Italy, we are the peasants. Not so in America. We’ve redrawn the map, rearranged the system. Rehung the stars. Who is the Boss of Bosses in this parable I’ve just told you?”

“I’m sorry, I shouldn’t have said—”

“Anything, very true, but who is he?”

“The Clutch Hand is like Prince Torlonia.” Hand shaking, the stranger drained his wine.

“And I am an armed guard of Prince Torlonia. *You* are a dog, a dog I’ll put down if I need to. Benenati is a peasant who isn’t paying his tribute, and he will burn for it. The letter was very clear.”

“How was it signed?”

“‘All of Corleone.’”

The big man shivered and then went still.

“We must be on our way.” Uncle Tommaso stood. “The sun has set enough, and the weather is clear.”

They dropped coins and turned to retrieve their coats. Exited with their collars tugged high against the wind, the older carrying a black leather bag.

My feet as they made measured progress toward the kitchen burned to run. I resisted. When I'd cleared the swinging door, I touched the back of Ezio's shirt.

"I have to go out. Can you serve the rest of the food?"

"*Ovviamente*, not a worry." Ezio's attention darted my way, snagged there. "Good Lord. What's happened now?"

"No time." My fingers fumbled over my apron tie.

"Did cockshitting Mangiapane insult you again?"

"He's only a pig, Ezio. It's *cagnolazzi** trouble this time."

Ezio produced a string of colorful Italian swear words. "Put that back on. You are not mixing yourself up with Family!"

Tossing the apron on a rack holding dried tomatoes and pickled peppers, I stood on tiptoe to peck Ezio on the cheek. "Pray to St. Jude for me."

"Nobody—"

"I have to," I said.

The kitchen door *snicked* shut. A blade of wind scraped my throat. I shoved my hands in the pockets of my thin cotton dress, not wanting to feel them shake. Uncle Tommaso had said *burn for it*. Arson was a common punishment, from the Jewish firebugs preying on Jewish peasants to Italian incendiaries preying on Italian ones. Half a block from Nicolo's house, the electric streetlamps fizzed to life, glowing firefly yellow. A skittish horse whinnied. An omen or just a poorly broken mare? Teeth tightly locked, I wondered what the contents of the Family man's bag was. Alcohol? Kerosene?

Saving the cigar shop might be impossible, but the Benenatis lived above it.

I can at least get them out. They can run.

---

* "Wild dogs," or Mafioso in training required to prove themselves with violence.

Vanish.

I turned onto 106th Street, its stoops littered with festive straw bales and sagging gourds. Nicolo sat on his chipped front steps smoking cigarettes with his friend Nazario, a curly-headed rascal with soulful eyes that had been hardening lately. Cooling like a spill of wax.

At the time, though, Nicolo's were still warm as summer whenever he spied me.

"What you want to woo her with is cannoli, not roses." Nicolo grinned rakishly. "Antonia is fat in *all* the right places. She'll make a dozen sons and get so huge you'll have to buy a metal bed frame."

"*Non è un problema.* I know steelworkers. God, she makes me crazy," Nazario admitted sheepishly.

"Maybe you're in luck and she loves tiny dicks. Oh, shit. Shut it, there's a lady present." Nicolo spread his arms to me in greeting. "*Buonasera!*"

I caught him by the wrist. "Come inside."

"Good Lord, Alicia, what the hell is—"

Dragging him up the front stairs didn't take much effort, since Nicolo would have followed me anywhere. Nazario waved a puzzled goodbye as I shut the front door.

"Jesus, *topolina*, you're trembling." Nicolo extricated himself, but only to hold my hands. "Whose face do I need to mash this time?"

"I overheard Dario's uncle Tommaso saying they mean to torch your cigar shop."

"What?" he exclaimed. "Is this about those thugs from the new tobacconist's three blocks south?"

"No! This isn't some petty cigar store rivalry, they said your dad hasn't paid his protection money. This is the Boss of Bosses. They said the order was signed 'All of Corleone.'"

The frown on Nicolo's face turned thunderous. He didn't bother with lights, and I nearly tripped in his wake as he clattered up the shabby stairs to their apartment. When we plunged inside, he turned up one small lamp, its glow sickly in the stifling dim. I stood on the braided carpet with blood pounding in my ears.

"Where—"

"Mom and Dad are at Enrico's. His pork chop is back on the menu this week."

"Then what the hell are we doing?" I demanded shrilly. "You all have to run for it!"

"No. We don't."

A shadow shaped like my friend Nicolo turned away from the bookshelf. Only this wasn't Nicolo. It was a seventeen-year-old man with muscled arms, eyes glowing like the cherry at the end of one of his father's cigars.

The silhouette had a gun in its hand.

"No," I gasped. "Nicolo—"

"The Clutch Hand can suck my cock."

I crossed myself. "Please don't say his name. And that isn't how this works."

"It is now." Nicolo pushed the window curtain a few inches aside. I heard him inhale.

"What?"

"There's something moving. Down in the rear yard. Is it them, you figure?"

"Probably, they just left. Don't confront a pair of Corleonesi. Please. It'll be a closed-casket ceremony and I don't even have a black veil." My stomach had relocated to my shoes.

My friend approached me, thin and taut as a riding crop. The gun gleamed as he slowly lifted it to his lips, kissing the barrel with strange reverence. Finger resting gently on the trigger, he then pressed the side of the weapon over my heart.

"They frightened you," he whispered. "And they're attacking my home, my business. This is all *mine*. The Corleonesi can rot in hell."

I chased him out of the parlor and down the stairs. Surely Nicolo meant to open the till and pay the men off, holding the gun only as a precaution. Surely he would run down the street to 102nd and the police station house with its green beacon blazing and get help.

Not that they could help. But surely, he knew he was no match for the Family.

Surely.

"Head to the café at the end of the block and wait," Nicolo ordered as we burst outside into smoke-thick dusk. "I'm going around through the alley. Safer than being pinned in the doorway at the back of the shop. I'll have the advantage."

"Don't do this," I begged.

You've always listened to me. You love me, I think, though I'm not sure what that looks like.

"Get two orders of the bruschetta for us and don't eat it all."

"Nicolo—"

"Trust me, *topolina*."

He dashed away.

Of course I trusted him. And of course, I followed after anyhow. He didn't see me as I floated behind, a drab afterthought of a person. When he entered the alley between the town houses, I hung back. Ears straining for a gunshot, a curse, a masculine cry of pain. My breath was sulfurous in my lungs, which I chalked up to terror before I realized it was a real smell.

Crude oil and chemical bite and shoe leather.

I had to stop him. I was nearly to Nicolo's gate, which he'd left swinging, when a hand closed around my mouth.

I thrashed like a seizure victim. Then the edge of a knife rose before my eyes, and I went numb.

It was already crusted with blood.

"Your friend is about to make a curious discovery," said an even baritone. "It will doubtless startle him, but he isn't my concern. You are my concern, Miss Alice James. Now, walk in front of me, in that lovely unnoticeable way you have, into Central Park."

Too terrified to protest, and too perplexed to ask questions, puppet Nobody simply complied. The brief journey west to the Park was nightmarish, and not just thanks to my circumstances. A haze of guttering lanterns lit my path, decorative paper-mache skulls swinging from the brownstones' gaslights, punctuated by the violent blasts of early holiday firecrackers and revelers cackling like devils.

That lovely unnoticeable way you have.

Had this killer—for a killer he surely was—been watching me?

We entered the Park at 106th Street. After sunfall, the northernmost acres were dusk etched over gloom, though before us I could see, beyond the weeping trees, the hill where old rebel army fortifications decayed. Rotting for lack of redcoats. I'd frolicked there with Nicolo before *malavita*, searching for Revolutionary bullets. Now any second I could be joining the soldiers' ghosts.

The knife met my spine, and my throat seized.

"This bench will do nicely, Miss James. Please sit down."

Obedience was my only option. But when I turned to view my captor, my mouth fell open. Here was the sedate regular with the newspaper. The one who liked my mother, the one whose penciled-in mouth was edging up in an unreadable smile.

"What do you want?" I managed through a wire-thin throat.

"Oh, nearly everything." His voice was smooth as an untouched pool, with the distant specter of an accent. "But nothing I think you'd be unwilling to give."

Run, said the rustling of the trees.

Run where?

"My name is Mauro Salvatici." His knife rested concealed behind his angled thigh. "I'm an acquaintance of your mother's, as you surely know. A fine woman, charming. But I confess I often return to observe you rather than to dally with her."

"Observe me?"

"Why, yes. You, Miss James, have mastered the art of hiding in plain sight. No easy trick. You float from table to table like a moth, and when I've followed you—yes, and I do beg your pardon—you accomplish the same in the busy streets. If sufficiently roused, however, you burst into violent action. You have deeply impressed me."

"Who *are* you?"

"I'm the man who wants to stand up to the Corleonesi."

Speechless, I gawked at him. His high brow and his liquid eyes and his mouth like a scar.

"There's no standing up to the Corleonesi. They piss in your face and slaughter your kin."

"Nevertheless, you just *did* stand up to the Corleonesi. As did I. Nicolo Benenati has by now discovered two warm corpses behind his house."

I'd no response to this, sick with fear as I was. He might as well have already cut out my tongue. For all the good it was doing.

"You imagine me dangerous. Good—I am dangerous. But I am also, you will find, sane. Which compliment cannot be paid to the Clutch Hand. Now. Why do you suppose he sent assassins to your friend's door?"

A shudder rocked me. Embarrassed, I clasped interlaced fingers between my knees.

"Mr. Benenati didn't pay his protection money," I answered. "Old Benenati's a good man, and people like him. So . . . it would be an example. To hurt him."

"Very good, my dear young lady."

"Nicolo will inherit that shop." I shook my head, eyes tearing. "They wanted to destroy it. Destroying things is all the bastards ever do."

Mr. Salvatici pulled out a white kerchief, casually wiping his blade. "Yes, but that did not in fact happen, and here is what will happen next. Doubtless your friend will drag them into the rear alley and attempt to remove the blood from his own backyard. Police will discover that the dead men are Family—they will then shrug and walk away like always. My gang is large and well-connected downtown. No, don't fret, I promise you that we mean you no personal harm. I require a willing ally for this task, not an indentured servant."

"Task?"

"Miss James, I own a hotel, the Arcadia. It's just there." My eye followed his long index finger to glowing lights. "On a Hundred and Tenth and Fifth Avenue. Nothing like your Raines law monstrosity. A real hotel, with amenities. I propose that you live there as my ward. Your room, your board, your training, your comforts—I'll see to everything."

I found this proposal astonishing. Just not astonishing enough, as it turned out.

"But *why*?"

"Because what I need are eyes and ears in Harlem. Here, I am alien, in a way I'm not in Hell's Kitchen. And you detest the Family."

"Everyone does."

He lifted a shoulder, folding his gore-smeared handkerchief. "Granted. But prolonged tyranny dulls the wits and weakens the blood of the citizens under it. They grow lazy. Inured to suffering and thus greedy of the smallest favors. Tyranny is water over a sandbank, wearing all resistance away. You are a rebel—despite your outward timidity. There are two types of rulers, Miss James: commanders and parasites. The Corleonesi feed off of the likes of you. I'm likewise a criminal, Miss James, I put it to you frankly, but I dislike monopolies. They're stifling. And I dislike parasites still more."

"I don't understand. I only know you just murdered two Mafia fire starters."

He laughed softly, thin mouth stretching. "Indeed—I solved a problem you could not. An efficient means of proving I want you by my side."

Questions picked at my skull like buzzards. Nevertheless, ten minutes ago, I had one option as regards career.

Now I had two, and Nicolo was alive.

"But why me?" I insisted.

"People take no more notice of you than the breeze. You speak Italian and Sicilian. You're young enough for me to train as I please. In fact, you are brimming with untapped potential, so much that it's already spilling onto the ground, and I detest seeing potential wasted. It infuriates me. You're desperate for a way out, and I can give it to you. That will inspire loyalty. And I'll prove loyal in return."

I ought to have realized that this explanation held about a thimbleful of water.

Ain't hindsight a peach?

"And if I say no?" I questioned, every limb tingling.

"You won't." Mr. Salvatici rose. "I'll give you a week to consider, however, and if you do say no, nothing will happen. But I won't be there to protect you five years from now. Ten years from now. Twenty. Good night, my dear young lady, and give my best to your mother."

He walked away. Left me with the squirrels and the willows and the lonesome frogs, trying to glue my world back together.

When I think of my father, the love-addled romantic who called Catrin James *bella, bella, bella,* I know he was a man of strong ambition. Mum took life as it came. Like a particularly intelligent sheep. But Dad, oh, Dad must have been a regular roarer. It must mean something that, while my skin is milky and my hair honey hued, my eyes are so dark as to nearly be black. They must be his eyes. Because that night, I could see my future if I chose to remain at the Step Right Inn. Ten percent of this sack of organs would be of value to anyone.

The rest? So much garbage. The older, the rottener.

• *Seven* •

NOW

As soon as one nigger is allowed to stay in these parts, this community ceases to be a white man's country, and in as much as it doesn't take very long for a family of niggers to increase into a "buck town" of large population, the coming of one nigger is the beginning of future trouble.

—WILLIAM H. GREEN, "Let's Keep Grant's Pass a White Man's Town," *Southern Oregon Spokesman*, Grant's Pass, Oregon, May 24, 1924

By Thursday, the day before Max returns to life at sixty miles per hour, I'm recovered enough to tour the Paragon Hotel.

This ought to elicit sturdy cheers. But tension hereabouts crackles like late-March ice over a pond. When Davy barrel-rolls—the boy's unstoppably curious—into my sanctuary to find me scouring the New York newspapers for familiar names, it's to deliver wild tales of monsters in the sewers and snakes in the vegetable patch, and to ask why I'm still here. As if I'm a countdown to an awfully grim foray into No Man's Land.

"It's 'cause of the ghosts who are after us," he tells me gravely. "The ones haunting the woods. Miss Christina says they'll sure get us good if you stay on much longer."

"Miss Christina ought to eat more cookies," I inform him, puzzled.

But it lacks all conviction.

Mavereen drops by once daily, gracious and stern, gladdened my color is now offending pinkish rather than offending death-white. Frowning whenever I compliment the fineness of the china, the softness of the linens, the marvelous flatness of the walls. By now I've paid her in full, same as Dr. Pendleton, which only amplifies their enthusiasm over becoming less acquainted.

As for my new friend, we sit on her bed gabbing like sisters, poring over fashion rags and listening to opera and jazz records. Blossom doesn't seem to give a Bronx cheer in a moratorium that I'm a hoodlum. But while she bestows easy smiles and peat-smoke whiskey, she refuses to discuss the film of worry clouding her eyes.

"When you're well again, honey," she soothes. "It's not that I don't trust you. I did from day one—I'm a sap, remember?"

But her attention wanders to empty corners and her buffed nails drift between her teeth. And I can no more force a confidence than I can repeal Prohibition.

Mornings are endless, a sea of broken clocks. Everyone I love is lost to me. I haven't a clue whether half of them are dead or alive and it's maddening, not knowing if their names are being called from across a crowded nightclub or etched in unrelenting stone.

Max stays away, and I force myself not to notice.

The knock at the door still sends a pulse through me, but I recover when my eyes flick to the clock. Four thirty on a lush, wet afternoon. My escort is punctual to the minute.

"Do come in!"

Blossom steps through, wearing a voile handkerchief tunic

frock ending in four dramatic points, the pattern on the georgette overblouse done in cobalt and dull gold. The woman is a veritable ode to triangles. She laughs at my own costume, fanning her fingertips over her cheek.

"Honey, what in the name of Sam Hill can you *possibly* be wearing?"

"Perfect, isn't it?" I demonstrate my newly recovered ability to pivot without plummeting like a Sopwith Camel. "Mrs. Meader is apt to stick a bulb in my mug and a lampshade on my head to help me blend in downstairs otherwise. This'll prove how smashing I am at disappearance."

"Yes, I need to talk with you about Mavereen." Blossom makes a dainty fish face. "Christ almighty, you're a beauty of a bluestocking."

"I told you—I'm not always tearing around blocking lead pellets."

"Naturally, such a life would be *exhausting*. But I never pictured the transformation would be quite this complete."

The Nobody I am to explore the hotel wears a slipover crêpe de chine blouse in a grey like our mornings, with a black wool skirt. The accessories are the corker: a businesslike silver head scarf erases every wisp of blond, powder dulls my lips, and I've both a notebook and an unapologetically spinsterish pair of reading glasses. Studied classics but likes the library's solitude better than its stories, reluctant suffragette disgusted by actual politics, idolizes Nellie Bly. Believes in cold baths and strong coffee. Never quite grew into her elbows. That sort.

"What about Mavereen?" I don a Votes for Women pin, the final touch. "Anyone lamps me, I'll take a shorthand note and say I'm writing about the most dreadfully curious hotel on the West Coast."

"Ah, yes, Mavereen. Mavereen is something of the—how shall I put this?—the goddess supreme."

"I gathered. Her decrees absolute and her nail clippings holy relics?"

"Precisely. And there's to be a meeting tonight. The established residents make up a board of directors of sorts, *terribly* official, the endless discussions, are we doing enough? What about doing something else altogether? Or not doing a thing in the world? *Riveting.* Your name has arisen, you see. Often."

My hackles tingle. "Give me the straight stuff."

Blossom twitches a regretful shrug. "You didn't think that paying the rent would change your spots to stripes, did you? Oh, don't look like that, honey. I'm on the side of the misfits. If they vote to torpedo you, I'll give them what for. But I don't have a *flawless* success rate."

"You told them, didn't you?" I question, hurt. "About the money. You supposed I was hot to quit New York and swiped it."

Blossom raises slender hands in protest. "*Perish* the thought."

"It's entirely mine, and I never got it by loafing either."

"Alice, I *know*, and I also know what sort of take a girl can swing these days considering the state of national aridity. But this has nothing to do with filthy lucre. Maybe . . . maybe you can stay a few weeks, get your sea legs under you, and find a place that better suits."

This place suits.

The truth is, I've been shoving thoughts underwater like unwanted puppies. When your world is emptied, you cling to strangers, clutch straws so as not to fall off entirely. I feel beholden to them, but they owe me nothing. I want to help them, but they haven't asked me to.

They remind me of home, but that isn't their fault.

"Display for me the wonders of the Paragon," I announce with an effort. "Maybe I'll write a real story instead of a pretend one."

"Now, *there's* the spirit." Blossom takes my arm. "We'll work it out, won't we? The two of us. You'll be set up happy as a clam at high tide."

I realize, fighting tears, that Blossom is not nearly as fine an actress as I supposed her to be. Or maybe the subject of belonging nowhere is near enough to her heart that acting doesn't enter the picture.

We make a goodly number of stops before the afternoon unravels like a sweater knit by a maiden auntie.

The elevator is a swank one, its pretty floral brass frozen in weatherproof bloom. Blossom squeezes my elbow like an overgrown schoolgirl when it arrives at the fifth floor.

"You're about to be subjected to the most *delicious* nonsense," she confides.

"*Quelque* fun. By whom?"

"Wednesday Joe, our young elevator operator. Lord above, but he's a treat. Mavereen has been trying to knock Christianity into him for simply ages. Dr. Pendleton has been making equal efforts in the direction of sound science, but nature is working against both."

"Why so?"

"Because he's Jenny Kiona's little brother, and every scrap of good sense was squandered on the elder sibling."

When the grate opens, I meet the eyes of Wednesday Joe Kiona. Like his sister, his dark skin owns a mahogany hue. This, then, is Davy Lee's comrade, and I place his age at thirteen or thereabouts. He wears a smart navy uniform, and where Jenny is all plush curves, he is clearly sprouting as doth the summer weed, because his wrists are visible and I can divine the color of his socks.

"The Queen of France!" he exclaims, bowing. "Your Majesty, I'm mighty pleased to make your acquaintance."

"I suppose Davy told you that," I surmise.

"What sort of day can we expect, young soothsayer?" Blossom questions. "Spare us *nothing*, I beg, we are better off duly forewarned."

Soberly, the lad locks the grate. "It's pretty tough to say, Miss Fontaine. Seeing as it's Thursday and there's always luck leftover from Wednesday, of course."

"Wednesday is the most fortuitous day of the week." A laugh lurks at the edges of Blossom's stark cheekbones. "On account of its balance, its equidistance from both Saturday and Sunday, it is the *pinnacle* of happy circumstance."

"But earlier a fella didn't close his umbrella when he came into the lobby, so we might be in for it."

"Shocking barbarism," I aver. "What steps did you take?"

"Stopped off at the restaurant to throw salt over my shoulder. You'd best do the same, Miss James."

"Oh, trust in it, my good man."

My notebook emerges from my pocket when we arrive downstairs. Blossom, expansive as a peacock with tail feathers sky-high, sweeps forward and I follow. A paler version of her shadow, silent as a secret heartache. The lobby of the Paragon is a bustling hive, blacks from warm beige to pitch blue arriving and departing and complaining about the weather as they shake droplets from elaborately coiffed hair. From the double glass doors I surmise lead to Miss Christina's dining room wafts a friendly perfume of celery soup and baked clams.

Blossom laughs explosively when I sneak a dash of salt from a passing busboy's tray and actually do toss it to the carpet, and then for nearly an hour, I drift through the Paragon's ground floor behind her. When I'm occasionally noted by a towel-laden chambermaid, she nods and promptly disappears. Blossom is a born entertainer, wry and immensely proud regarding her home. The swirls of lollies at A. G. Green's Ice Cream Parlor are "Only the best sweets outside of Paris, and you know you can trust a woman of my figure—I'm *cruelly* particular." The haircuts to be had at Waldo Bogle's Physiognomical Hairdressers, Facial Operators, and Cranium Manipulators are "Perfectly serviceable, but add the absolute *cream* of gossip to the mix and you could be freshly shorn and elected mayor all in one stop." George Moore's Athletic Club and Turkish Bathhouse is too risky for longer than "Just a peep, honey, I don't care how enthusiastic you are about marble and steam and scantily dressed men."

We're sipping coffees in a discreet alcove, Blossom in sprawling glory and myself practically inside a fern, when the trouble starts. Dr. Pendleton comes charging down the corridor. His freckles are a swarm of fire ants, the portholes he uses as glasses fogged.

"You!" He lurches to a stop.

My first thought is that he means me. He doesn't, of course. He doesn't even see me.

"Dr. Pendleton." Blossom's tone is as measured as a ruler. "What are you getting up to in this fine establishment of yours, other than the usual light refreshment?"

"Certainly not practicing my profession, since you've forgotten our appointment, Miss Fontaine!"

Blossom, to my bewilderment, seems entirely taken aback.

"I'm so *terribly* sorry, doctor." She adjusts a delicate gold bracelet. "I—that's inexcusable."

"Just because I don't give a damn about your health doesn't absolve me of responsibility for it," he snarls.

I study the thinness of my companion's wrists and feel a shockingly strong pang.

"Well . . . what a curious and yet appropriate way of encouraging me to be mindful."

"Don't mix it up with any notions of tender feelings."

"I'd say 'may death come first,' but I do actually hope to avoid that final curtain call." A growl like the trilling of a jungle cat enters her tone.

"Especially when you're apparently traipsing all over my hotel with that white woman you're so inexplicably fond of! I had it out of Wednesday Joe."

"If you're going to call Miss James 'that white woman,' you might choose to do it *internally* since she's two feet away, you ridiculous man," Blossom drawls.

Teetering like a top, Dr. Pendleton glares. It's not surprising he failed to notice me. I'm very good at this, and he's been imbibing with red paintbrush firmly in hand.

"It's good to see you, Dr. Pendleton," I state.

A finger approaches Blossom's nose. "You! Less of the catting around and more paying attention to your calendar. And you! Make better haste out of my hotel!"

"My goodness, what have we here?" comes a new male voice.

The ice pick of alarm spears my heart. Two fresh arrivals stand before us, arrivals who cause Dr. Pendleton to mop his mottled brow and Blossom to offer her hand as if suavely leaning to grasp the stand of a microphone. It's a performance suddenly, and it doesn't take any professional thinker of thoughts to parse why.

"Officer Overton, well if it isn't our champion of justice," Blossom breathes. "And Officer Taffy at his side. To what do we owe the pleasure?"

Officers Taffy and Overton are verily apples and iguanas. Taffy is the apple—significant beer paunch, Irish complexion, the vaguest border between chin and neck. The happy, daft expression he wears reminds me of nothing so much as Mr. Salvatici's pigeons.

Officer Overton wears the shoe on altogether the opposite foot. He's shorter and much thinner, with razor cording in his throat and sun-stained farmer's skin. Dark hair, dark eyes. Dark thoughts behind the polite smile. I've met people who want power and importance—people like my former associates. And I've also met people who like to breathe fear in like a draft of Eau Impériale. If you've been hurt by enough humans, you learn which ones admire to rattle the bars of the cages and watch the animals cower.

Welcome to the monkey house.

Both wear long blue woolen sack coats, brass buttoned, with matching trousers and five-pointed silver star badges. Overton has his rounded helmet neatly tucked under one arm. Taffy wears his still, and Portland's atmospheric peculiarity drips onto his slumped shoulders.

Blossom flourishes at me as if I'm a prize greyhound. "May I present the simply *divine* Miss Alice James, my friends? Miss James is a reformer, here working on an article about the Paragon. She's vowed to do us *full* justice in print, which I need hardly tell you would be a nifty bit of fanfare."

I shake hands with both as I realize that Dr. Pendleton just vanished into thinnest air.

Officer Overton bows, giving the helmet in the crook of his elbow a military air. "Miss James, how do you do? I hope you're enjoying your visit from . . . ?"

"Connecticut," I supply, aloof and prickly.

"A reformer, you say? We have plenty of those in Portland. You'll be right at home! Why, this state was built on utopian ideals."

"Is that the case?"

"Oh, it is," Blossom gushes. "The families who settled here wanted absolutely everything *just so.*"

"Quite right, quite right! America first, that's the motto hereabouts. A more God-fearing society than you'll find in this land . . . I just can't imagine it." He peers at my pin. "Votes for women, eh,

Miss James? A radical, then. You'll have been celebrating liberally over your victory last year, no doubt?"

"Certainly not. I believe that female votes must be accompanied by feminine sobriety." I fiddle with my glasses.

"That's good to hear. Always nice to meet a *reasonable* suffragette. But how about marriage? Children? Pardon me for saying so, but there's those who take female independence pretty far, pretty far indeed," he counters.

"Not every fond hope can come true at once, Officer Overton."

"Of course, of course. So you round out your days over shedding light on the Negro problem. Very admirable. Miss Fontaine here is quite the character in these parts. I can't imagine anyone could give you a more thorough tour—she's shown you everything, I trust?"

"Oh gracious, not yet." She laughs. "We were just sitting down to a spot of refreshment. But—"

"Well, that's all to the good." His smile is a cake with too much icing. It sticks in the throat. "Taffy and I are here for a routine inspection, and she can come along. Surely she'll want to know about whatever we find. Won't you, Miss James?"

I brandish the notebook. "Naturally."

Blossom is already in motion, having eagerly linked arms with Officer Taffy. He regards her with simple joy, eyes as bright and as aware as lamp glow. Officer Overton's shoulder kisses mine, informing me that he has just taken a pair of hostages as we set off for whatever portion of the Paragon he admires to inspect.

I give myself three guesses as to what sort of business venture that might be. Then I subtract two of them.

"Are you planning to stay with us long, Miss James?" I detest cops like this, the ones with mouths like traps tenderly clicking.

Waiting for you to make the smallest mistake, and then *snap-crunch.* "The Paragon is a ripe subject for newspaper coverage, a very ripe subject, in fact. Are you familiar with the plight of the coloreds hereabouts? And the unique situation of this establishment?"

"What do you mean, precisely?"

He laughs the laugh of a man who expects others to flinch rather than join. "Oregonians are dedicated idealists, Miss James. As I said, utopians. Historically, Negroes are not allowed in this fair state at all. We wanted to avoid the misery, the degradation, that plagued our sister states below the Mason-Dixon."

"There were never plantations here," I realize.

"No slavery for the untouched West, oh no!" He's warming to his subject, eyes trailing down Blossom's spine. "The Negroes here today came by way of the railroads. It remains illegal for them to reside and work in the state. Oh yes, very illegal indeed! But the necessity of treating all of God's creatures as they deserve no matter how lowly . . . it ties our hands. There were Portlanders of the previous generation who could claim never to have set eyes on a colored person, let alone disputed with one. Sadly, those days are past, Miss James, but we do what we can."

I can't tell whether my nausea is due to the chitchat or my injury. Meanwhile, Blossom, ever since being instructed by Dr. Pendleton to practice better timekeeping, decayed along all her sleek architecture, a rusting iron girder. And if she's happy to see Officer Overton, I will dine on Raines law cabbage. Taffy she's treating like a pale puppy, but Overton devours her energy like a gash left to fester.

"Peacekeeping in the Wild West must require considerable fortitude," I encourage him. "Do tell me more?"

"Oh, no, no, I had best show you. Please do the honors, Miss Fontaine," Overton calls.

We arrive at a corridor behind the central elevator. Without hesitation, Blossom approaches the only unmarked door in the hallway. Officer Taffy—as if unaware human males were capable of doing otherwise—opens it for her.

"Aren't you always *simply* the sweetest?" she coos. "Well, other than your friend Officer Overton here."

Overton blinks like a priest eyeing a roast.

Blossom descends a sharply inclined staircase lined with orange glass lights. It's a particular portal in a particular hotel, yes. But it's also every corridor leading to all the secret lairs in America. This is Omaha, Detroit, Fort Lauderdale. This is the resistance. This part I know how to do. If you've heard rumors that being a hoodlum is a dangerous hobby, don't discount 'em.

But I'm absolute aces at it.

Below, the walls are largely bare. I spy a second door, a countertop where prices for ginger ale and soda are displayed. Max sits at an upright piano dragging out a Creole tune. Mavereen Meader, Dr. Pendleton—who seems more alert and whose hair is noticeably drenched—and Davy Lee conduct a Bible study. Always a quaint touch. The atmosphere pulses, cigar-dank and gritty. I can practically hear the rushed calls of *Next time, old sport* as the rats scattered. It's identical to every other gin and faro joint in these United States of Nonsense with a single exception.

This is now *my* gin joint.

"Well, I never!" I exclaim.

"Miss James, this is the Paragon's *very* own event space for every jazz hound and balloon lungs traveling through our beautiful city," Blossom declares, spinning. "We've hosted artists hailing from St. Louis to Cincinnati, and they *never* fail to throw a concert. It's just rotten luck that no one's passing through. Davy, you run along. Upstairs with you *now*. Miss James's article about our hotel is coming along swimmingly, Mav, isn't that fine?"

Mavereen turns a page of the New Testament with a single finger. "Why, just as fine a thing as I ever done heard."

"Congrats from the natives," Max agrees warmly.

"Officers." Mavereen's smile is honey drenched, her eyes bee-stings. "I been meaning to visit the station house again. Aren't you that sweet to save an old woman the trip? There's been another of what y'all are calling *incidents*."

"Incidents, you say?" Officer Overton taps his fingernails against his helmet. "Why, they seem like harmless pranks to us professionals. No one here was hurt, were they?"

"No." Mavereen presses her hands together. Hard. "But we sure enough fret over vandalism. Seeing how many other Negroes been roughed up. Why, ten in East Portland so far, as I recollect. Three more nearabout. One of them hurt bad, real bad. Broken ribs, broken arm, and a busted head, sir."

"And if anything of that sort actually does happen, you'll come straight to me, won't you?"

"Yes, indeed I will." Mavereen stands regally. "You yearning after any early supper? Compliments of the establishment."

"Actually, we're hoping to clear up that regrettable problem we had last time we were here." Officer Overton's attention arrows to Max. "Miss James, I'm sorry to report that we've had to tell this boy to mend his ways. On multiple occasions."

"Oh, my word."

"Deplorable, I agree. But no self-respecting reformer would want to publish an article without knowing the whole truth, would they?" Officer Overton is happy as an ant at a picnic. "Have you mended your ways, Mr. Burton?"

"Sure thing." Max blinks, guarded and calm. "I mends 'em all the time. Daily. As a hobby, like."

"Are you mocking me, Mr. Burton?" Officer Overton inquires through his teeth.

Max whistles. "I ain't in the habit of mocking police."

"But are you right now?"

"Hell, I s'pose you'd have to tell me."

There's blood in the air. Twitching my jaw *no* at Max, I lift my eyes from the page.

The second lieutenant reaches behind him and tickles the treble clef.

"I'll ask the same question once more, expecting a civil answer. Have you mended your ways, son?"

"Davy, run on up to the kitchen," Blossom snaps. "Whatever are you doing down here? Miss Christina is looking for you."

Davy, who has shrunk mouse size, stands.

"Answer me," Officer Overton commands Max with obvious glee. "Give me firm evidence you haven't got any moonshine in this roach nest or I'll find it myself."

"What kinda evidence do you figure proves something *isn't* there?" Max questions.

Several predictable but startling things happen.

Dr. Pendleton explodes, "Go to hell, pigs!" as he produces a nearly full liquor bottle. Mavereen lurches to keep him from swinging it, protesting that she thought he'd been at the cooking wine again, that she'd no idea what he was truly up to. Officer Taffy goes to restrain the offender, a frantic Blossom snatches Davy up quick as pick pocketing, Max rises with his open hands in the air, and thunderclap quick there's a truncheon in Officer Overton's fist and Max is on the hardwood, blood oozing.

This is my signal to shriek.

"Do you want this cockeyed old coon in the drunk tank again, or do you want to cooperate?" Overton hisses, his hat still wedged against his body as if he's a five-star general.

Max holds his palms up from the floor. "Yeah, yeah, Jesus, I'll be your best pal. I knows where he keeps it. You want I should get up?"

"What the fuck do you think?" Overton snarls.

A whimper sounds. Bizarrely, it emerges from Taffy, whose mouth dangles open.

"We don't have to hurt them again, do we?" His simple face is flushed berry pink. "You said we didn't have to this time."

"That was assuming this boy minded his manners, which was foolishness, unadulterated foolishness," Overton repeats in his singsong fashion.

Max, knowing better than to stanch the bleeding, trudges into the supply room and emerges with an armful of liquor. Not all of it, heavens no. But enough. Some cops—the good sort—just want to sit down and yarn over a free whiskey. Harry Chipchase wanted a steady paycheck, and he deserved it too. Overton wants the whole goddamn parade, and Mavereen is wringing her hands, giving it to him. I'm half swooning in a chair, giving it to him. Dr. Pendleton is restrained by Taffy and no longer nearly as drunk as he's making out, giving it to him. Max is half-concussed, giving it to him.

In the meantime, in between time.

Transaction complete, Officer Overton waves the truncheon. "Do you see what you're dealing with now, Miss James? What level of people these are?"

"Yes, it's not at all what I expected," I answer timidly.

"Well, it's a fine thing that you're writing an article about the place, then, isn't it?" he scrapes, towering over me. "You can expose the sickness that lives inside every one of these animals."

"That isn't—"

"What a little nigger lover like you wanted to write? You wanted to say they were perfect angels, didn't you? Rough around the edges, but the intentions, God, the noble intentions. Or did you want to make a name for yourself, poking your nose into speakeasies and dice joints? If you so much as dream of crawling away from this hotel without an article to your name, a *real* one, I'll see that every single one of these mongrels pays for it."

"Officer Overton," I state with harsh spinster clarity, "you can rest assured that there will be an article forthcoming. As to whether or not the Portland police department comes off well in it, I likewise assure you that I am extremely fair-minded and not given to flights of fancy. You will be treated precisely as you deserve."

"That'll be nice, then. You'll be writing about how I saved a pack of degenerates from the ruination of alcohol." Overton finally settles his helmet where it belongs, on his head, producing a blinding grin. "Afternoon, everyone. Oh, and Mrs. Meader? You can bet I'll be checking into these 'incidents' of yours again. Soon."

· *Eight* ·

Klansman Brentneau, who hails from Denver, Colorado Klan, was a visitor in our klavern and he gave a wonderful account of the trials that his Klan were passing through and finished by telling us he thought Oregon just about the livest state in the Union.

—MINUTES FROM THE MEETING OF THE LA GRANDE, OREGON, KU KLUX KLAN, February 27, 1923

We've gathered in a snug parlor with dark-paneled walls and a club-style table. The sun is probably setting as Dr. Pendleton stitches Max's head wound, but the skies still wear a grey blindfold.

"What the hell were you thinking, having Davy down there?" Blossom demands. She's been pacing for ten minutes, skinny arms ferociously akimbo.

"Language, child!" Mavereen chides.

"I don't give a single flying fuck about my language, and I *certainly* have no intention of tempering it—there are circumstances requiring heightened speech and I'm not so *very* keen on putting this one into blank verse, so kindly answer the goddamned question!" she cries.

"You watch yourself, miss," Mavereen breathes.

"Aw, hey, calm down there, crackerjack," Max says soothingly to Blossom. "Davy's fine. He was down there on account of he was delivering more peanuts. Rooster was on guard duty, warned Mavereen, she came running like a Kentucky Derby favorite, we cleared out the joint with Doc, and when we turned around Davy was still there, like. It was an accident."

"An *accident* is misspelling *psychology* or nicking yourself shaving," the singer growls.

"And just what did y'all think *you* were doing parading Miss James here over every inch of God's creation?" Mavereen counters icily.

"Showing our guest a bit of Southern hospitality. I'd be *ever* so consternated to learn you've never heard of the practice."

"Again, we don't need your sarcasm, Blossom," Jenny Kiona objects. She sits with her pretty chestnut face framed by her fingertips, staring down at a jumble of notes.

"No, we need another one of your *delightfully* effective lectures or sermons or mixed-race ice-cream socials, or articles for *The Advocate.*"

"I am not the enemy here!" Jenny cries, slamming her fists on either side of her paperwork.

"Jenny's right," says Rooster. He turns out to be an enormous charcoal-colored fellow, with a bald head and a rhino's posture and a voice that makes you think God just dropped by for a stern word. His button-down is scarlet, his expensive suit black. He speaks slowly but with tremendous authority. "Who's the enemy, Blossom?"

Blossom's remarkable face corkscrews into an expression of profound disgust.

"The Ku Klux Klan."

She sinks into an armchair in the corner.

"Enough said," Rooster pronounces.

"The *Ku Klux Klan*?" I marvel from my uncertain position hovering before the fireplace.

The silence roars. Dr. Pendleton snips off the thread holding Max's brow together, and Max claps him on the shoulder.

"Come and sit, sugar. You're turning green."

Mavereen pulls out a chair and I take it. Head full of flaming crosses and the silhouettes of lynching trees.

"I'll tell you a story, Miss James." She lights a cigarette. "I was born Mavereen Johnson in Moultrie, Georgia. Them's some of the biggest former slaveholders in Colquitt County—the Johnsons, I mean. Plenty of their livestock took the name, just like Ezekiel Johnson, my daddy. Now, some Negroes back then could have told you tales about bondage that would nigh about peel your mind clean. Time as a house slave was horsewhipped for not noticing the hall clock had stopped running. Time as a buck was told if he didn't pick himself a 'wife,' they'd sell his frail old mamma, and the only girl available was all of twelve. Not my daddy, though. The Johnson slaves worked up a sweat, but they were kept in ham and fresh butter, clothed like quality, and after the war, there's many a one stayed and toiled for good wages. Like my pa."

"Give me a crust with my freedom instead of a feast with shackles," Jenny murmurs.

"It's Mavereen's life," Rooster intones. "Let her tell it."

"I was born free in eighteen sixty-seven, married lucky in eighteen eighty-five to a good man name of Richard Meader what supplied a fair amount of the local produce." Mavereen studies a smoke wisp. "I knew every soul in that town and every Christmas, I sang carols up at the Johnson estate and they treated me like family, and still I wasn't content. Time came when the itch got too strong—Richard and me, we sold the farm and headed for a land where we'd never been slaves. Richard applied for fifty-six jobs in Portland, finally ended up cleaning toilets at the courthouse. Accidentally crossed shadows with a white man and got slapped in the face for it once. He died of pneumonia in a fever sweat after two years here, dreaming of sunshine."

Blossom bites her fist. Dr. Pendleton polishes his glasses. Rooster regards the ceiling, while Jenny Kiona chews the end of her pen and Max takes long pulls on a cigarette. I wonder at the practice of abusing anybody different from you, Italians so strongly preferring to abuse each other.

"They were well used to coloreds in Georgia," Mavereen continues. "But I thought there was someplace different. Someplace pure."

"What could be purer than the virgin West?" Blossom mutters.

Mavereen swivels to face us. "There's noplace pure on God's earth. And the difference here is that they don't even know how to speak to a colored. Our kind don't *exist* except as a stain on the community. And that is where the KKK comes into it."

"There are plenty of crusaders in Portland who don't feel that way," Jenny counters, chin landing on her palm.

"True enough. And plenty more who do."

"To describe us as a stain is oversimplifying white rhetoric," Jenny insists. "The KKK purports to uphold standards of sobriety, Protestantism, and civic prosperity. There are far more disadvantaged blacks here than well-to-do ones, so when they picture us, they see poverty and struggle."

"You aren't black," Rooster observes. His specialty seems to be the statement of facts.

"No, I'm red, which is worse. By elevating our economic situation, thereby proving our social worth, we can begin to build more bridges."

"You build the bridges, I'll bury the cats," Blossom drawls.

Jenny flushes. "Intermingling between the races will help to break down the walls between us. Colored people comprise less than one percent of the Portland population. Ask Max about Brooklyn."

"Not gonna lie, I'm about as intermingled as they come. That don't mean I can take my sisters for tea at the Ritz," Max notes.

"I'm talking about gradual enlightenment."

"When in human history has that ever worked?" Dr. Pendleton demands.

"I'm making actual efforts. What are you doing?"

"Hey, hey, efforts might mean something different to the doc," Max objects.

"Like what? Getting drunk earlier than we do?"

"Like patching people back together while bullets whiz over your noggin and then seeing it every night in your sleep for the rest of your life, kid," Max snaps. "We ain't sitting on our thumbs here."

Quiet settles among them, seeps into the curls of the crown molding.

"I want to stop sitting on my thumbs," I blurt out. "However I can. Please let me."

Naturally, everyone forgot about me.

Dr. Pendleton returns his spectacles to his face and goes back to resembling a spotty bullfrog. "I'll bite, if only for a laugh. How?"

"I don't know, but I've some experience with malicious neighborhood organizations." I glance from Max to Blossom. "I want to help."

"Because you feel guilty?" Jenny supposes shrewdly.

"Or because I grew up surviving the Mafia. Take your pick."

A spark of approval appears in Mavereen's eyes.

"I agreed to research an article," I muse. "Actually, I threw down the gauntlet and spit on it. Who's to say I shouldn't do just that?"

"What sorta article?" Max questions. "You gonna kiss the Portland PD's heinie in print like Overton wants?"

"It seemed from what Mrs. Meader said that you don't know who's been harassing you. What if I start digging? I might not get results, I'm dreadfully aware, but."

Dr. Pendleton expels whiskey haze.

Jenny shoves her writing implement against her brow. "That's not a bad argument. Miss James—"

"Do call me Alice."

"Is here and possesses something of a vested interest. Why shouldn't she pull her own weight?"

Blossom rouses herself enough to chuckle. But whatever sweetly poisoned comment she's concocting, it evaporates when a rap at the door precedes yet another white intruder.

Mavereen kills her cigarette with a neat twist. "Mrs. Vaughan. You find us just a mite preoccupied."

"Oh, I'm so sorry," the visitor apologizes. "I mean, I know. I mean . . . yes, I heard."

"Evelina, *whatever* are you doing here?" Blossom rises with all the poise of an infant gazelle.

Evelina reminds me of a butterfly—petite delicacy and darting movements. It's awfully difficult to imagine her embroidering. Or reading. Nailing any of the sitting-down maneuvers, really, which seems queer since she must be the founder of Mrs. Evelina Vaughan's Weekly Betterment meetings. Her hair is coarse, voluminous, pinned atop her head like an antique Gibson Girl, and an altogether unfair shade of strawberry blond. It's a veritable glowing pile of marmalade locks. She wears a straight-hanging lavender-check dress with a piqué collar. The heart shape of her face makes for a deep widow's peak, her skin is smooth as a blank page, her eyes are a March-sky grey, and there's a glint at the back of them. A fey, feral quality.

"So nice to see you, Mrs. Vaughan." Jenny ceases scribbling, smiling broadly.

"Likewise," calls Max affably.

"Hello, all. Max, please tell me you're all right? Oh, good. That's good. Blossom, I just . . . I couldn't," Mrs. Vaughan says shakily.

Blossom is already halfway across the room.

"You heard all about the police tête-à-tête?" she confirms.

"Yes, Tom told me." Mrs. Vaughan blinks, and suddenly her lip arcs in a snarl worthy of the deepest, darkest woods. "Blossom, when I picture that horrid bully harassing you all—"

"Oh, honey, you're too good to us. What you and I are going to do is picture it over a nice *strong* drink," Blossom proposes. "Come along, we'll order three or four dozen oysters."

"Hold the elevator, would you?" Jenny requests. "I've nearly completed the guest list for Miss Jackson's Benevolent Tea Soiree next month, and it'll only take Mrs. Vaughan three flights up to fix the seating arrangements."

In the wake of Mrs. Vaughan's faltering flutters, Blossom is about as poised as a clock tower again when the three women leave, a palpable relief. Dr. Pendleton walks with great gravitas to a nearby cabinet, selects a cobalt vase without any flowers in it, pours an arm-straining draft from this hidden cache into a tumbler, and exits.

"Saints alive," Mavereen mutters. "*Fine.* We'll parley more when everyone's less shook up. Max, are you all right?"

"Never better."

"You sure enough have a talent for trouble, child."

"Ain't it the truth."

"Please explain . . . whatever else Miss James here wants to know, I ain't got the sense nor the stomach presently. Seeing as she's so itchy to help. Rooster, we're back on duty."

"Never was off it," Rooster concurs.

They depart, shutting the door.

"Well." I exhale.

"How do you like them apples?" Max ruminates, setting his elbows on the table.

"Bit mealy. Care for something to wash them down?"

Max nods, and I head for the cabinet to repeat Dr. Pendleton's procedure. When I deliver the refreshments, I perch on the table in high flapper fashion, sliding off my eyeglasses. Wishing I were in my mixed-lace tea dress, dozens of panels of pure ivory stems and petals twining together. This close, the gash on his head looks dreadful, though he isn't sweating over it.

Second thought, maybe a nurse's uniform, all bleached white with petal-pink lip color.

"Here's how," I say. "Have you been missing me dreadfully?"

We clink as I reflect over my capacity to pose wildly inappropriate questions.

"Aw, sure." Max studies me. "Nice schoolmarm getup."

"You're too kind. Explain your abandonment of the Paragon's population."

"I got a cabin here. Away from the hoi polloi. When I'm in Oregon, I maintain it, oust any possums. Listen to the trees when I get the chance."

"You are a poet, sir."

"Nah. Just a trench boy what likes forests that ain't shooting at him."

"Give a girl a tour sometime?"

He narrows bronze eyes at me, speculative and open—dare I even say hungry?—and I can feel my pulse in my throat.

"Who was that Mrs. Vaughan? She's ever so striking."

Max squints. "Pal of Blossom's. She was born here, heads up just about every charitable concern in town—rights for everyone, grub for everyone, school for everyone. Completely cuckoo. Oh, and married to the Chief of Police, Tom Vaughan, that there's how her ear's so close to the ground."

"My. *Quelque* intrigue. Is he anything like his intrepid staff?"

"Nah, he means well. Washes behind his ears, wouldn't speed up if he saw a stray in the middle of the road."

"A model citizen, then. But wait, I did wonder . . . why did Overton muscle you specifically during the raid?"

A dark smile curls Max's lip. "Once when I was in town, he'd been sampling the contraband and came on too strong to Blossom. Said as he'd pay for a private concert, like, and if she told him no, it weren't no skin offa his nose for it to be free. I told him if he tried anything fresh with my friend, I'd guarantee all of Multnomah County knew he was a nigger lover. It was swell."

The laugh that emerges yanks my stitches. But it's still the niftiest sensation in days. "Your tastes are peculiar, my good man. Now. Deliver unto me the situation, per Mavereen's request."

Max taps at the edge of his tumbler. "Started last year. Pamphlets, auditorium speeches, articles in the 'papes. America first! Over and over till you heard it in your sleep. Figured it for a fluke, seeing as how you could round up all the Negroes in the state and fit 'em at the same Sunday service. But it's sticking, see? They's after the Japanese and Catholics mostly. But the Paragon is conspicuous—chafes at 'em regular. 'Course, they don't outright call for blacks to go home bleeding. It's all raising dough for temperance, baskets of food for poor whites, lady purity. Kris Kringle Kristmas shindigs."

"Marvelous altruism."

"Right up to the dead cats, sister. True enough, we ain't never caught nobody in the act. But it ain't a long walk to figure when white robes start popping up between the pines . . ."

"You've seen them?"

He nods, mouth twitching with disgust. "Sure, plenty often. Sometimes just a coupla good old boys swigging rotgut. Sometimes a regular tent revival."

"Davy's ghosts in the woods," I realize with a shiver.

Max shakes his head fondly. "Yep. Musta overheard one of us some weeks back, way I figure it. Kid could make a fairy tale out of a rock."

"Oh, rocks are easy as anything. There are far less enchanted objects."

He shrugs, conceding.

When staring goes out of style, I ask, "But what do you think of the old bird's idea? Writing an article? Asking around? Snooping, to use the accurate moniker?"

Max pushes to his feet. "It ain't baked, not by half, but then again you just put it in the oven. Worth a try. This shit's got me up nights and no mistake. Anyhow, I'm for the bathhouse, Alice. Ain't no getting actually clean on a cross-country train, and I'm due on the eleven ten sleeper tomorrow. Can you make it back to your bunk?"

Say my name again. And while you're granting favors, please don't go.

"Oh, I'm a regular textbook of health." Trying for a jazzy twirl in languid fingertips first, I slide the glasses back on. "See you on the morrow?"

"S'pose so."

"Topping. Max?"

He stops and his body is angled just so, *that little bit closer*, knee cocked and his cream-and-sugar-coffee face tipped down—I'm not inventing it.

And then it hurts so I can hardly breathe.

"I'll do the best I can to help while you're gone," I vow. "If not for you, I'd have played proverbial taps."

When he leaves, he doesn't say goodbye, but he does brush thumb and forefinger against my chin in an affable fashion and I gaze after him, feeling the prints. Thinking the money in my room could easily pay for eleven-thousand-mile stints with Max if not for the fact that I got my wish.

I'm trapped here, Overton would retaliate somehow if I went missing, and Max would hate me for it.

When I catch my first face full of Portland in blazing daylight, I gape up at it like a salmon, fish mouthed and reeling.

We're standing outside the Paragon Hotel the next morning, Blossom and Davy and Miss Christina and myself, and my eyes swell at the carnival of color. Everything I've ever seen, from Tobacco Club chorus girls to Central Park in July, was in black and white. And now I've fallen headfirst into a box of oil paints.

"The mountains are out!" Blossom rejoices.

"When the clouds break and you can see the peaks," the cook explains. "Too many buildings on this street, but Mount Hood, Mount Adams, Mount Saint Helens . . ."

Blossom waves her fingers like a magician, the bell sleeves of her mustard coat sliding down a switch-thin arm. "Welcome to Portland, Alice James. Now let us make the most of it before the dying of the light. Oh, easy now—you're not long out of bed and this is a marathon, not a sprint."

When Blossom informed me last night after pan-fried trout stuffed with wild mushrooms that if the next day was fine, they were taking Davy to the Elms, I lost no time hitching myself to the wagon. For several reasons. By now I itch to get my bearings; my constitution requires, as it is said, bolstering; I like Blossom in the child-bright way of being surprised someone you admire is letting you share their orange.

And if I quit the Paragon Hotel, I am less likely to make an uninvited guest of myself in Maximilian's bedroom.

We stand at the corner of Northwest Everett and Northwest Broadway. The skies are enormous, flung open and sprawling. A bucket of spilled cerulean. Stately brick and stone buildings tower above us—the Paragon seems small with its fifth-story gable points and its carefully hosed pavement—and pretty iron streetlamps with triple lights blooming from their sturdy metal stems dot our path. A horse-drawn cart sagging under its load of flour sacks passes us, but so do sleek automobiles, Fords and Daimlers with wheel spokes blurring and cloth tops flapping in the crisp wind. Broadway is wide and teeming with locals. Men wearing double-breasted suits in fawn checks and sober pinstripes, carrying copies of *The Oregonian*. Brisk women with bobbed hair, stenographers hunting down coffee and egg salad sandwiches, one meltingly boneless flapper whose lips have likely kissed things of far greater interest than the cigarette she sips from an ivory holder.

Aside from the guests milling at the entrance of the Paragon, and the Japanese boy carrying a lunch delivery, everyone is white. It scrapes against part of my brain I seem to have left on 107th Street.

Miss Christina sets off with Davy by the hand. Blossom follows beside me, her teeth set as if she's keen to crack them.

"Don't think me too forward," I begin. "I'd never be so gauche as to ask what's ailing you, but can I assist?"

"Aren't you a dear," she returns absently. "I've been ill, that's all. Dr. Pendleton and I have it well in hand."

"Awfully unpleasant old coot, that."

"Award-winning prize ass, Alice, but he *did* save your life, mind."

"I hadn't any choice and duly tip my cap. But why in hell would you put up with him?"

"Because you can't chase down a more thoroughgoing black

doctor—he's actually *revoltingly* talented. Graduated top of his class at Chicago Medical School. Nor is there another with his experience, having served in the War and practiced with sterling results at Cook County Hospital before that. He's the tops. That's despite the fact he knocks himself off his own loop starting midday *precisely*. And as you gathered, not being deaf, he doesn't like me any more than he does you, but he yet admires to see my engine restored to tuneful conditions. That's *ever* so sweet, don't you agree? Romantic."

My eyebrows defy gravity.

Laughing, Blossom slaps my arm. "He's not my sort either, honey. The very *idea*. He's also my uncle."

"Your uncle?" I exclaim.

"Oh, *indeed* yes. My late mother's half brother."

"Awfully thick blood you must have, putting up with his . . ."

"Personal quirks? I've hardly any kin left, honey, I can't afford to be particular. He knows me of old, he owns a simply stunning hotel, and when I left San Francisco in nineteen fifteen, he picked up the lost penny and brought me to dwell where he dwelt."

"He must have been so different before serving."

Blossom hoots, clapping. "*Lord*, no, he's been like that ever since the day he graduated from med school! His white professor told him he was the most promising surgeon with the deftest touch he'd ever seen, amazing privilege to have taught him, wasn't his skin simply a *tragic* miscalculation of nature, and then asked Uncle Doddridge to remove a tumor. From the professor's golden retriever."

For several seconds, neither Blossom nor I can breathe.

"I know," she gasps. "It's *crushing*. But isn't it rich?"

"It's giving me gout. Say, I never mentioned last night—your friend Mrs. Vaughan seems a fine specimen."

The expression that twists Blossom's mouth is neither frown nor smile but something soul deep and private. "Evy is the true spirit of Portland. She's its generosity and eccentricity and isolation and passion and rebellion and melancholy and kindness. Of course, it's simply *frightful* trying to pack all that into one person, so she's also hideously uncomfortable."

"Being married to a police chief must be steadying?"

"Yes, it must, mustn't it," says Blossom, and not a word does she say more for fully ten minutes.

What happens later in the day is so deeply stamped on my memory that what led up to it is stilted, like picture flip-books. The gorgeous blue ribbon of the Willamette River, crawling with the stripped corpses of pine forests lashed together on barges. The looming iron hulk of the Broadway Bridge, riverbanks glowing electric green as we cross it in the cool sunshine. The trolley car with its jolly red paint and voltaic hum and us at the back, peering out as we glide along near-silent tracks.

The Elms Amusement Park is bordered by meadowlands, river, and a lake on its eastern side, ferocious brambles disputing every boundary, its white entrance flanked by giant statues of tin soldiers. After days fighting to stay in my warm little cave, I'm ever so giddy to be out of it. Blossom, meanwhile, surreptitiously wipes water from her eyes—whether suffering or wind produces it, I can't say. When she notes my concern, she forces a smile. The gate agent, a sour, fat fellow with ruddy side-whiskers, glowers as he spits a chew into a coffee tin. But he grudgingly passes out tickets after Miss Christina brandishes an extra dollar.

Davy yanks at Blossom's hand, grinning. "First the Barrel of Fun!"

"Why, *just* what I'd have proposed," she agrees.

"Lord, that place gives me the creeps," Miss Christina comments.

The journey is a short one—minutes later, we approach a fun house a little way into the park, looming above the emerald grass and penny candy wrappers. Tattered red flags shudder along the rooftop. The flat facade is black, with grinning skeletons jerking in a graveyard dance. An owl crowned with devil horns presides over the entrance, morbid kohl circling its empty eye sockets, above a plank walkway painted with constellations. It makes the world feel upside down.

"Stay close now, honey," says Blossom, and we plunge into a lightless maw.

Davy laughs.

I can't see, and that shouldn't frighten me. But apparently the old girl is shy of nerve since incurring the wrath of Nicolo Benenati. Trailing fingertips along the corridor, I turn left, right, right again.

Nothing whatsoever save a wall.

"Any point to this place other than elbow bruises, Davy?" I call, aiming for jocular.

No one replies.

Heart skittering like a roach, I try another direction, stumbling into a room draped with fake cobwebs and Spanish moss. In the dim, the plaster headstones look like real marble. The skeletons are arranged in a tableau. One sitting at the edge of his grave with a tin coffee cup, one sleeping with a hat pulled over his eyes. One plunging a knife redundantly into his comrade.

Bit late seeing as the worms are already finished, but good show for technique.

Thinking I see Miss Christina's pleated coat exiting, I follow. A dead end results. Then another. I hate this place with shocking vim.

Davy, you owe me ever so many cookies. Heaps and heaps.

I catch a glimmer of light and quicken my pace.

Mirrors. Everywhere. The kind that fracture me into dozens of Nobodies, every Nobody I've ever tried on, each uglier than the last, each guilty of more shocking crimes, my neutral face transformed into a mob of pale monsters.

Every single one a murderess by proxy, and for what, in the end? For whom?

Bitter, thick liquid pools in my throat. My legs falter, and I slide to the floor with my eyes screwed shut. I don't know how long I stay there, quaking, before I decide that any room is better than this one and flee, smearing my malformed features with damp fingers as I slide along the glass.

Stumbling into broad daylight again, I realize I'm not breathing and gasp. I'm at the back of the fun house. Miss Christina and Blossom stand together, faces pinched, coat hems flapping. They look expectant.

"Oh gracious, honey, did you run into an *actual* ghost?" Blossom questions. "Where's Davy?"

"He's with you," I answer stupidly.

But he isn't. Davy Lee is nowhere to be found.

· *Nine* ·

THEN

Corleone means Lion-Heart.* Korliun *it was named by the Saracens, who founded it and made it a military stronghold in the picturesque thirteenth century. Something of the savage, marauding spirit of the Saracen, always a menace to civilization, hovers about the place—a savagery that has nursed into being a dangerous and powerful arm of the "Black-Hand" Society of Italy.

—WILLIAM J. FLYNN, Chief of the US Secret Service, *The Barrel Mystery*, 1919

The night that the arsonists bled out behind Nicolo's home, I met him in our usual café as he'd ordered. My stomach full of tadpoles and the bruschetta untouched. Harvest festival candles glowed from every alcove, hemorrhaging crimson wax into graphic pools.

"What happened?" I whispered when he appeared.

Nicolo landed opposite, glistening with sweat despite the cold.

"Nothing, *topolina*. All is well."

"Neither of those things are true!"

Releasing a breath like a steam valve opening, he masked his mouth with tented hands.

"They were already dead. Blood everywhere, blood enough to drown in. I dragged them into the alleyway. Then I scrubbed down the yard. Christ, it was such a mess—pray I didn't miss anything in the dark. I'll find my parents, tell them . . . what should I tell them? Nothing, maybe. Wait for morning and word to spread naturally."

"Yes. Don't say anything."

"But, shit, Alicia. How can I do that? Don't you want to find out who was responsible?"

I burned to deliver the dope to my closest friend. But Mr. Salvatici's proposal glued my tongue to my teeth. He hadn't asked for secrecy, not directly. But he expected it.

That was simply how our world worked.

"No." Nicolo lightly slapped his brow. "You're right. If I've someone to thank and can't repay them, that's one kind of trouble. If it had nothing to do with us, that's another. *Grazie a Dio*, and let dead dogs lie in the road. Everything will be all right, Alicia. I promise you."

Nicolo knew how to step around horse shit. But his optimistic nature betrayed him on that occasion. Because the bodies were indeed found the next morning, and the police did in fact uncover bloodstains pooled under a cracked flagstone obscured by weeds. Thus, as his parents were genuinely dumbfounded and had been dining at the ever-crowded Enrico's, Nicolo was arrested for the cold-blooded murder of a pair of Corleonesi who'd trespassed into his rear yard.

I heard the news while fetching eggs. From a knot of men gossiping outside the market, men who never knew I was there until

I dropped the basket. Yolks spilling everywhere. Heedless, I stumbled into the nearest piss-reeking alleyway and raised my forgettable face to empty grey skies.

"If Mr. Salvatici saves Nicolo from hanging, I will join with him." Closing my eyes, I crossed myself for good measure. "For Nicolo. My life is forfeit. I will do everything Mr. Salvatici asks."

Luck and prayer are only two different ways of making bargains. I will give this act if I get this in return. This penny in a fountain. This Hail Mary. I don't know which category that particular plea fell into, since—though heartfelt—it was awfully informal. Not to mention appropriately melodramatic for a fifteen-year-old girl.

But three days and a thousand dread-sodden heartbeats later, Nicolo was released on All Hallows' Eve.

Secretly, I packed my things, hot tears of relief spattering onto chemises and stockings. Tears of apprehension followed. I was about to enter the services of Mr. Salvatici, a man who apparently gave orders to the NYPD. The police in those days were very much as they are now. Canny. Burly. Some kind. Some cruel. But not a single jackal swaggering about in his brass-buttoned coat spoke Italian. So I didn't know how Mr. Salvatici procured Nicolo's freedom, but I did know the bluecoats probably thought themselves well rid of a pest. Court cases often collapsed under the sheer strain of Italian relations swearing on ancestral graves that their kinfolk had never so much as fibbed about taxes.

As for Mr. Salvatici, the idea of life at his hotel was so blank, my mind kept slipping clean off it. And how would I break it to my never-very-alert mother?

Mum, I'm striking out to defeat all of Corleone. Wish me luck?

I was at the Step Right, pondering this very question, when Nicolo burst through the doors. It was the first afternoon that felt like winter, a barbed wire taste in the air presaging hunched shoulders and doubled-up stockings. My friend spent his time in the clink as a punching bag, I noted with a pang of rage. His bright eyes shone from within purpling shadows, and half his knuckles were burst.

"There's the young devil!" a soused Mr. Mangiapane growled from behind the bar. "Sweep the trash out the door, says I."

"Oh, Nicolo," Mum gasped. "Sweet child, what have they done with yer face?"

"Nothing. Just a bit of an adventure, Miz James."

I was off my stool, gripping his wiry forearms. "What son of a bitch hurt you?"

"Easy, easy there, Alicia." He smiled. "This was only their idea of a little fun."

*"Conosco i miei polli,"** I snapped. "Have you seen your parents?"

Mr. and Mrs. Benenati had spent a vociferous forty-eight hours telling anyone who would listen that they had been the subject of a Mafioso threat, yes, but that Nicolo would never hurt anyone, not even the smallest flea, and yes, he cleaned the blood, *naturalemente lo ha fatto,*† but who could blame anyone for doing the same?

"Yeah, they met me at the station house." He searched my face. "Mom sent out for meat, fish, cheese, eggplant. Enough to feed ancient Rome. I'm sore, not starving to death, but she's out of control. I came to ask you to dinner."

"Little Alice isn't going anyplace."

The words were so close to my ear, they tickled. Mr. Mangiapane had emerged from behind the counter. He rubbed a bloated hand over the skeins of hair draped across his scalp.

"Here now, less of that," Mum crooned from her barstool.

"Shut it, woman! I'm putting my foot down." Mangiapane sent

* I know what's true, literally "I know my chickens."
† Of course he did.

a yellow wad of spittle toward my mother. "Nobody at all would be one thing, but *this* Nobody eats my food, sleeps under my roof!"

"Come and have a nice—"

"She's going to work!" Mangiapane roared.

My elbow flared with pain as he dragged me into him, away from Nicolo.

"You thought you could spend your life at this hotel, skulking, and pay for *nothing*?" he spat. "*Mi rompi i coglioni.** I got a top-notch price from a regular, not a bad sort. Healthy fellow. Never fear, *mia dolce*, I'm not a monster—you'll get half."

Crispy Ezio emerged, drying hoary hands with a rag. "What in cockshit is all this bellowing?"

"Let her go," Nicolo ordered. He said it almost calmly. "I'll tell you one time. Not again."

"Get off me, you fat *bastardo*!" I cried. "I'm leaving anyhow."

"The hell you are!"

I've often puzzled over what would have happened if Mr. Mangiapane hadn't been staggeringly drunk. Stupid and loutish as the man was, he liked his own flabby hide as much as the next stupid lout. And throwing me around in front of Nicolo Benenati was as good as waving a red flag in front of a bull.

So quickly I nearly missed it, Nicolo's hands closed around Mr. Mangiapane's throat. Mum screamed. My elbow buzzed as the blood cascaded back. Ezio shouted creative profanity. Nicolo's brows distorted, unrecognizable, spine rippling as he bent our landlord backward over his own bar. It was like watching a snake lunge at a gopher. Savage. Terrible.

Magnificent, I thought, chest swelling.

"Say it again to me," Nicolo hissed. "So I'm clear. You're selling Alicia tonight? To one of your filthy johns?"

---

* "You're breaking my balls."

Our landlord couldn't answer. Or breathe.

"Topolina," Nicolo addressed me, "is that what this *figlio di puttana** just said?"

"Yes. Nicolo, stop, you—"

It may have been the three days in lockup. Too many bruises. Too many growls of *filthy dago* from the worst cops. But Nicolo didn't listen to me.

He bared his teeth and *howled.*

Eventually, Ezio and Mum and I managed to peel him off Mangiapane. But not before our landlord's hysterical yells and the crack of bones splintering brought half a dozen or more Harlemites hurtling through the door. The tableau at the end of the debacle was Mangiapane in a whimpering heap, Mum attempting to mop his leaks with dish towels, Ezio cursing, and an audience of locals muttering dark portents. Nicolo was the only soul looking at me, of course. He stood there panting. His shirt collar rent, his knuckles reopened. One streak of grey light cut over his brow like a sword poised to strike. Everyone fell still as New Year's morning. For a community well used to violence, it was a strange, uncertain hush. It took me a moment to understand why.

Because I was staring straight into the lightning strike, and it was staring at me, and I was looking at love, and everyone else was looking at death. If there had been doubt before, now they all thought he was the murderer of the two Corleonesi. Nicolo swept his gaze over the room. For the first time in his life, he wasn't a magnetic misfit. He had knifed two *cagnolazzi* in cold blood, bribed or bullied his way out of the station house, and nearly murdered my landlord in his own saloon.

A twenty-block radius of Harlem tonight would be talking about Nicolo before the pasta was on the table.

---

* Son of a whore.

We hurried through darkening streets, my tiny sack seized in Nicolo's fist, suppertime vegetal steam from the packed tenements drifting around us like savory fog. My friend muttered continually, which wasn't at all like him.

"What happened at the station house?" I badly wanted to know.

"How long has that waste of skin been after you to turn whore?" he returned with grim fury.

"It's a Raines hotel, Nicolo, are you serious? Since I sprouted titties."

"I'll kill him." His white teeth flashed.

"What would the point be? Anyway, you almost did!"

"I don't know why you stopped me."

"Because you aren't a killer!"

"And you aren't a *puttana*."

"Exactly what else do you think I'm fit for, Nicolo? An heiress, maybe?"

We'd arrived at his door on 106th Street, and Nicolo trotted up the stairs. "Smart of you to pack your bag. You suspected something? That's my girl. You'll stay here with us."

"No, I'm going—Nicolo, wait!"

Listening to me, it seemed, was a lost art where Nicolo was concerned.

The Benenati kitchen burned like a petite sun, its long wooden worktable straining under eggplants, mushrooms, carrots, cheeses, fish staring with mouths agape. Mrs. Benenati, a small woman with steel wool curls, stood at the end of the altar dropping sacrificial eggs into a volcano of flour.

"Alicia! *Bene*, you found her. Come and say hello to me, my lovely girl." Looking up at us as I kissed her cheek, the little matron gasped in fright. "Nicolo! What's happened now?"

"I had a talk with Mr. Mangiapane." The obsidian glitter that had shone so darkly at the Step Right returned, but my friend blinked it away. "When's dinner, Mamma? Christmas?"

"Hush, you rascal, all your aunties and uncles are coming and we'll have a midnight supper celebration when your papa gets back. What's the matter with old Mangiapane? And what's it to do with you?"

"He threatened Alicia, I told him his place."

His mother frowned. Mr. Benenati with his sharp caterpillar mustache and Mrs. Benenati with her stooped posture had always been wonderful to me. Despite my lack of . . . well, anything, really. I'd never questioned why previously. For the first time, I wondered just when Nicolo told them he wanted me. Maybe only me. I ought to have been able to swallow the idea by age fifteen. Instead I thought with vague terror of diapers and drudgery.

Picking up a knife, I started disrobing onions. Already planning my escape route. Grateful that I had one. But first, I wanted to learn what Mrs. Benenati knew.

"Nicolo won't spill what happened at the station house," I said softly as my friend vanished to clean his reopened battle scars. "One of those Corleonesi from the alley was Tommaso Palma, but I don't know about the other. Do you?"

A pleat appeared above Mrs. Benenati's nose as she folded eggs and water into the flour. "He was new to the city, sweet one. But the whole Palma clan takes their orders from the Boss of Bosses—and my Giorgio has refused to cast his hard-earned money to pigs for months now. People look to him! Even when the Family arrived at our door, my son was protected and they met instead with the Angel of Death, by God's grace. And the question of bail? Dismissed! A kind eye is watching out for us."

I recalled Mr. Salvatici, with his machete mouth, and disagreed.

"These Family thugs, Alicia, they are cowards. Counterfeit, arson, gambling, trade, and now our horses. Despicable—I say before heaven that they should all drop dead where they stand."

She wasn't kidding. A new scheme had been hatched by the Family, one cartmen and delivery makers found particularly uncivil. Step one: demand money. Step two: demand money or your horse will be a feast for flies. Step three: execute the horse. I recalled a year previous, Nicolo and I happening upon a Palermo man weeping over the stiffening hulk of his mare. My friend, his affection for animals considered, had leaned on the nearest brick wall and heaved his protest on the litter of cheap black cigar ends.

"I don't see how you stand up to them," I answered, still fishing. "Why doesn't Mr. Benenati pay, like everyone else?"

She bestowed a quick smile. "Nobody, you were sprung from New York soil—the wind in the Old Country never weathered you. But the Benenatis are Neapolitan. We do not lie down and allow Sicilian garbage carts to run us over."

The sound of boots tattooing the stairs struck both of us dumb. I swiveled with the knife in hand, and Mrs. Benenati shouted for Nicolo. He emerged with bandages wrapped over his split fingers just as his friend Nazario wrenched the door nearly off its hinges. Our old companion's face was as grey as the local milk stretched with chalk water.

"Merda," Nicolo breathed.

Nazario's mouth worked, but silently.

"Tell me."

Nazario shook his head, blinking in horror at the uncooked feast. His curls were wild as a briar patch, and he wouldn't look at Mrs. Benenati.

Look at her, I thought, my heart crumbling in my chest.

Look at her so I know that everything will be all right.

An hour later, I fell, flung an arm at the wrought-iron outside Mr. Salvatici's hotel on 110th Street, and missed. Improbably though, I missed the stone steps as well.

"Whoa! Here, miss, just hold on. Breathe in, now. You're not down for the count by a long shot."

The world was awash with stuttering lights. My stomach burned. I tried to blink away the faintness and found there were lean, muscled arms under my knees and rib cage. Next thing I knew, my wrists brushed the furred velvet of a lobby chair and a glass of brandy rested against my lips.

I'd been frightened before. Grief-struck and heartsick too.

Never like this.

"That's the ticket, darlin'."

I forced my eyes open.

The young colored man who'd kept me from falling sat on his haunches. He wore a maroon bellhop uniform with a cap strapped to a neatly shorn head. Maybe Nicolo's age, with a broad, elegant nose, humorous cinnamon eyes with friendly bags beneath, and lips that curled up at their edges even when, as I'd later learn, he wasn't smiling at all. He probably wasn't then. While darker by far than mine, his skin was still lighter than plenty of Sicilians'. It didn't even occur to me to flinch away.

"You had some fright, miss, type to make you drop drawers and run for cover, I'd wager," he teased gently. "Zachariah Lane, at your service. They call me Rye. Welcome to the Hotel Arcadia."

There had always been Negroes in Harlem. But around 1905, some of the streets started dancing in tap steps. Singing the blues. By 1911, the year now in question, the shindig was well and truly in swing. Blacks poured into Harlem from Missouri, Alabama, Texas, Kentucky. True homes in Central Harlem disintegrated—apartments were divided into honeycomb hives, families of six former sharecroppers stuffed into bunk beds. They spilled out, naturally, everyplace. They tipped department-store hats from Lord & Taylor at their sweethearts, got into fisticuffs on rum-swilling Saturday nights. The usual.

The one in front of me was the most magnetic person other than Nicolo I'd ever encountered.

"I have to see Mr. Salvatici," I begged. "Can you tell him Nobody is here?"

"Pardon?" Rye's smile widened in a question.

"Sorry, Alice James." I started to cry, curling into myself. "Or Nobody. Just . . . he can decide."

Rye disappeared. My eyes swam at the orderly bank of lemon oil–polished mailboxes and the wall of keys. A clerk behind the reception desk glared, stroking his chin as if he smelled something amiss. The aroma of slashed entrails enveloped me again and I retched helplessly at the carpet.

I lost consciousness, this time with commitment. When I woke, I rested on a tapestry-printed couch in the finest hotel room I'd ever seen—slipper-soft carpet, a sideboard weighted with glassware, paintings featuring dogs that would have considered the Step Right beneath pissing on.

Mr. Salvatici loomed into view. His shirtsleeves were buttoned without collar or cuffs, as if he'd been interrupted bathing. Damp sable hair fell over eerily pale blue eyes ringed with darker steel. He held up a tiny brown bottle.

"Miss James, I have smelling salts."

The stark reek of ammonia deluged my sinuses.

Please, God, take this day away. If only it were yesterday, and the invitations for tomorrow all canceled.

"That's better." Mr. Salvatici turned to draw up a chair. "My dear young lady, whatever has happened, I'll do all I can to assist."

"They went after Giorgio Benenati again," I heard a voice like mine saying. "His *nemicos** won. He's dead."

I didn't say, *His neck was slashed so deep that when Nicolo pulled him out of the barrel, it flopped, and the only thing attaching his head was a flap of skin.*

I absolutely didn't say, *They took a razor and cut off his nose.*

They took his lips.

His tongue.

His eyelids.

What good were they to anyone save Mr. Benenati?

The two Benenatis and I had followed Nazario to a crack in the world wedged between a poultry warehouse with torn chicken-wire windows and a bleak row of peeling billboards. A weeping charwoman gestured helplessly at a barrel with a leg sticking out. Gore oozed from the cracks between the staves. While Nicolo pulled, his mother screamed, and soon she was surrounded by identical women with dirtied aprons and patched head scarves, all reaching for her like lost souls.

Mr. Salvatici said nothing after I finished. He brought me his jacket when I started to shiver, and I learned he smelled of the cigarettes he smoked and of a subtler, cleaner perfume like starch.

Or money.

"Come with me, Miss James," he directed, rising.

"Why?" I huddled farther into the coat.

His eyes narrowed to match the slit of his lips. There was, strangely, no sternness in it. I could have been watching a lizard sunning itself on a rock.

"Because I want to see that you can."

He offered his arm. We left his hotel room and took a pretty birdcage elevator upward, floors clicking past like so many missed

* Enemies.

chances. When we stopped, to my surprise, we weren't in a hallway but in a small, eerily unmarked room. My escort unlocked the door of this and we stepped out onto the roof.

All Harlem lay spread out before the Hotel Arcadia. To the north, the tall buildings grew stoop-shouldered like old men. To the southwest lay the Park, hugely vacant. In the meadows between tenement buildings, I could see the flickering of maybe a dozen All Hallows' Eve bonfires. The kids would be roasting chestnuts and jacket potatoes as their parents offered hopeful prayers to the constellations above.

Mr. Salvatici placed my hands on the railing. He then went to open a wire-walled dovecote, and I heard muted cooing. A flock of birds burst forth from the enclosure. Mr. Salvatici apparently had a surprising hobby. The gangster tenderly lifted a straggler and returned to the edge where I stood. Other birds swooped up along the ironwork, testing the night with their wings. I'd probably seen Mr. Salvatici's flock wheeling above me dozens of times. Never imagining they belonged to anyone, or that our lives would intersect.

"What happened after the police came?" he asked.

When I stroked the pigeon's trembling head, he passed the docile creature to me, and I cradled it. Its feathers were a pale cream color, mottled with fawn. How he'd known that holding the fragile bird would make me feel more powerful, I couldn't fathom. But I did.

"Nicolo sat there holding Mr. Benenati's body. I finally coaxed him away, but he wouldn't look at me."

"And then?"

"I was frightened. A mob was forming." The pigeon trilled, a mournful sound. "Men talking of stilettos and Old Country grudges and justice for the poor. And other men watching them—rough ones, with brass knuckles."

"Cagnolazzi?"

"Yes."

"You know who they will report any unrest to."

"To the Clutch Hand. Were you the one who sprang Nicolo from jail?"

"Of course."

"Oh, Mr. Salvatici, I can't stand this anymore."

An uneven roaring like a faraway shore met our ears. I tucked the bird against me and leaned over the rail. Turning the corner several blocks south of us, a distant firefly cluster of bobbing lights flared. They could have resembled the hot shower of a holiday sparkler or the beads worked onto a dress I could never afford. But I knew what they were.

Angry men. Either Family, rioting for show, or we slaves, madly rattling our chains.

"Do you want to know what I love about keeping pigeons?" Mr. Salvatici inquired. "Look down there at the rampant disorder. Violence that tends to no purpose. Poverty of the cruelest sort adjacent to waste undreamed of at the Palace of Versailles. But none of it touches my birds. They are sheltered, coddled, cared for the best I can. Which is very well indeed, because I was born to *grow* things. The Clutch Hand is a bottomless glutton, Miss James. What do you know of the man?"

It was the test I'd understood was coming. I took a slow breath.

"When he goes out, no one looks at him because his face is like a skull's. His eyes are the blackest of pits. He only needs to clutch his right hand and the devil comes running to serve him. But most of that is rubbish."

"Why do you say so?"

"Because I listen. At the Step Right. His eyes are black, yes, and his clothes are well tailored, and he's pale, with a ragged mustache. A brown shawl hides why he's really called the Clutch Hand. His right arm is half the length it should be, and in place of five fingers, there's a claw."

"Anything else?"

"His real name is Giuseppe Morello." My voice rose. "And he deserves to bleed to death in a gutter."

Mr. Salvatici's lips angled up like a folding knife. "Will you help me to achieve that?"

I could hear scattered shouts, the tinkle of glass breaking. They were headed past the hotel. When I turned away from Mr. Salvatici, I spied a familiar figure at their head. He was the size of a lost tin soldier.

Nicolo.

"You bet your life I will," I replied.

✦ *Ten* ✦

NOW

Oregon, which bears the negro no ill will and regrets the wrong that has been done to him, is fortunate because it has only an infinitesimally small negro population. We are spared thus one of the problems which many other states have to solve.

—FRANK JENKINS, *Roseburg News-Review*, Roseburg, Oregon, May 23, 1930

We stand before the Elms's ticket booth. Blossom, Miss Christina, and me outside, the red-whiskered agent on his stool behind the counter. Sending streams of chewing tobacco into an empty can of instant Red-E Coffee. The savage blue of the sky has faded to a somber azure.

Davy is still not with us, and the atmosphere thunders with his absence.

"Did you try the Chute the Chutes?" the ticketing man asks, face bland as a cow's.

"Listen to me, you inert *lump* of a human," Blossom snarls. She's been swallowing tears, and by God I believe she's reached full capacity. "As per your earlier *delightfully* salient suggestion, we have indeed searched the Chute the Chutes, every cranny of every precious car poised to slide down that waterfall, to no avail. Our child is still missing."

"Whose child did you say again?" he returns without interest.

Miss Christina replies, "He's an orphan, sir, and we care for him."

"Well, that goes a way toward explaining things, if he didn't care for the situation. Did you work him hard?"

Blossom Fontaine's remarkable face contorts into an expression unlike anything I've ever seen as she whirls around, hiding it. Terror for the foundling she discovered, yes. But hurt and bitter protest spikes the punch into a lethal concoction.

Miss Christina's scrawny frame, so shrunken next to Blossom's elegant angles, balloons in outrage. "You figure every parentless kid for no better than a slave?"

"Wouldn't you know more about that than I would?" Licking his thumb, the agent shifts to count his till.

Blossom's back is turned to me, but her laugh alone could still land her in the hoosegow in seven or eight states. So I intervene.

"Mister . . . what did you say your name was, sir?"

"Did I say?"

Every man needs a hobby. My argument is simply that playing stupid shouldn't be on the menu.

"My name is Miss Alice James, and I'm presently writing an article about your fair city. What, pray, is your handle?"

"Hank."

Hank lapses once more into contemplation of mortality.

Yippeecanoe and fuck you too.

"Hank, a child is missing. It's dreadfully urgent. I'd hate to think the Elms will fare badly in my future publication. Now—"

"How's everybody doing today?" Hank interrupts as a white family of mum and pop and four matching squirts approaches. "'Scuse me, Miss James."

The family antes up to pay. Blossom is too formidable to invite unwarranted touches, but we've taken to each other like the dickens, and her back quivers in distress, so I place a palm against her ribs. When we first arrived, the park was nigh deserted, idle couples playing hooky from their workday trading hot glances and cold lemonades. I think the Paragon's residents planned it so. But now the locals who've taken an early Friday are ambling in, and the sight of every single brat who isn't Davy makes Blossom's throat work desperately and Miss Christina's hand clench.

"Back to it, then," I suggest. The white family's eyes are mottled with questions as they leave. "Hank, the child has been gone for too long."

I don't say *the child has been gone all afternoon*, because I dread with every fiber to know what that means.

Hank deposits fresh tobacco in his face. "Did you try the carousel?"

"Why, yes."

"Did you try the floating bathhouse?"

"Trust in it."

Blossom swallows. It looks like a scream.

"Begging your pardon, I got a few suggestions," Miss Christina announces. It's salt-cured civility, the kind invented for lean winters.

Hank folds his hands together.

"Could your staff help us search?"

"Are you paying them? Or am I?"

"Davy disappeared in the Barrel of Fun. Can we turn the lights on and search it real, real thorough?"

"Is the park closed yet?"

"Then can we at least ask the visitors if they've seen him hereabouts?"

Hank blows his cheeks out, puffing the red cockscomb of his whiskers. "This is the Almighty punishing me for taking your bribe. Forgive me, Lord, for I have surely sinned. I shoulda never let you niggers in here, but I figured, what the hell, they'll lose interest same as they do with every damn thing and shuffle off to the next bit of hoopla. Look, lady, it's not my job to mind your kid. So if you don't get outta my sight, and I mean *now*, I'll send for the cops. We clear?"

If he were addressing a certain set, sending for the cops when a child is missing might strike us as a perfectly dandy notion. We are not the aforementioned set. So we three walk back into the Elms. The trees beyond its border rustle with sharp-toothed creatures, and fairy lights begin to wink to life along the perimeter.

Miss Christina takes Blossom's arm, squeezing ferociously. "What's next? It won't do for us to go to pieces."

Blossom's head falls back on her long neck. "I'm sorry, I'm just picturing that man's corpse with my best pearl hatpin stabbed through his eye."

"Since we're losing daylight," I interject, "might I ask a few questions? As someone who didn't know Davy from Adam?"

"God, *please*," Blossom begs.

I study the crowds as we powwow, searching every passing face. "Eat the nastiest bite first so it's over, Mum used to say. Was Davy ever sick, sick enough for us to think something might have happened to him in one of the dead-end corridors? An attack of some kind? A condition?"

"Not as I ever knew," Miss Christina says immediately.

"No, nor I, but we can't simply *rule it out*, can we?" Blossom demands, stricken. "I mean, we searched with our hands, we went through that building inch by inch. But, God, it's not as if we've a map, and—"

"We'll look there again," Miss Christina soothes, "and we won't wait for closing neither. And we'll start to ask the park guests too. I don't give a damn what that fool told us."

"You'll give a damn if he chucks us out, honey," Blossom says hoarsely.

"Next," I continue, "have you seen any friends of his here, someone he might trust enough to run off with?"

"Davy would trust a grizzly bear if it wore a fireman's hat and offered him an engine ride," Blossom grates.

Miss Christina tugs at her coat collar. "No denying, Davy's an innocent. Even if he was afraid of somebody, that somebody wouldn't have to waste much air explaining it all away."

A towheaded chunk of a child not far from Davy's size tumbles over his own feet and starts up his sirens a few yards from us, and I can feel Blossom's wince. "Do we have any reason to suppose someone threatened Davy specifically?"

Blossom's entire countenance curdles.

"Give the old girl a fair hearing, I beg your honor. Did Davy upset any white kids? Their parents? Specifically, I mean. What about the sprout who gave him a drubbing?"

"I see what you're after, but Davy's *existence* is offensive," Blossom returns coldly. "Trust me when I tell you that none of it *need* make any sense whatsoever. He's a mulatto orphan who lives in the ritziest all-Negro hotel in the venerable state of Oregon. We've been vandalized for *months*. Blacks are being beaten in the streets and city councilmen are wearing dunce caps and bedsheets."

"You think it's motiveless," I supply.

"Oh, Alice," she breathes, shutting her eyes. "I do *not* think it motiveless. I think it ingrained *loathing*. Tell me that loathing isn't a motive, honey. Go on, I'll buy you a bag of penny candy over there if you can manage it with a straight face."

"We'd best be back to searching," Miss Christina frets.

"Just one more thing." I bite my lip. "Davy's an . . . imaginative chappie. Would he ever run off and get a bit topsy-turvy as to the way back?"

"Davy doesn't always mind us as best he should," Miss Christina admits. "He once followed a stray dog he said was trying to tell him something, led him somewhereabouts, ended up nearly a mile away from what we can figure."

My chilled blood warms a fraction.

If Davy is only lost, why then heavens, he must simply be found.

"What transpired? You searched for him, I assume."

Blossom chuckles bitterly. "For all the good it did us. He was returned to the Paragon via the United States Postal Service like the *dearest* of lost packages."

"The mailman brought him back," Miss Christina translates.

"So he could have wandered into the woods nearby?" I prompt.

"Oh God, this is—this is a nightmare. Davy is *out there*!" Blossom cries. "I can't just *stand* here discussing the matter."

She's right. Yes, back to searching.

It's clear from my queries that's just what we should be doing. But by this time sickly sweat paints my brow, my legs tremble, and any trace of the morphine fishbowl around the tunnel through my torso is a blissful memory.

"We could search quicker with more of us," I point out. "And yours very truly is about to keel to starboard, but . . . I think I can make my way back to the hotel alone and give the alarm?"

"Lord, I hoped there was no need to scare them all, but right enough, Miss James," the cook agrees. "Are you sure you can find your way?"

"If I can't, I'll fix a stamp to my head and climb into the nearest mailbox. Blossom?"

She pauses. "Yes, go. Fetch whoever can leave the hotel. And *hurry*."

Miss Christina follows her. A numbness overlays Blossom's usually artful speech, a woolen blanket like laudanum over a toothache. I know the sort of tragedies that bring such tones to people's voices.

I pray that Blossom Fontaine turns out to have no need of hers. Or anyway, I wish so on a likely seeming rosebud, tracing my fingers against it as I exit the park.

Thanks can't express my gratitude, but it's all I have on me. Will an air rifle do presently, or would you prefer a baseball mitt?"

Wednesday Joe Kiona smiles as he sets down a tray containing two bowls of yesterday's sorrel soup and two hot coffees. But a sad gravity tugs at his copper-hued cheeks. We're both of us rather the worse for wear, come to that. I'm sporting a pale green silk set of wide-legged lounge pants with a modest mandarin-style top, and he's switched out his uniform for trousers and a sweater.

It's four o'clock in the morning, and the search party hasn't returned.

Wednesday Joe makes a shy gesture. "Mind if I . . ."

I pat the seat of the chair adjacent. "I'd be offended if you didn't."

"Much obliged, Your Majesty."

The Paragon's dining room is fully as stately as Mr. Salvatici's at the Hotel Arcadia. Eight crystal chandeliers in the shape of huge teardrops mourn over us in the dim. Between the six-foot-high window wells are panels with wall sconces, the wood patterned in byzantine splendor. But the lights are snuffed and Wednesday Joe has left only the electric bulbs in the kitchen and four or five oil lamps shining. I gave the SOS at ten in the evening, when I finally straggled back like a half-dead thing, and then promptly devoted four hours to my bed and Dr. Doddridge Pendleton's drugs.

The two hours I've been awake have been awfully long. Max wasn't here when I arrived back, or at least I didn't spy him settling his affairs before catching the sleeper. He left for his next Pullman stint, without my saying nice knowing you, and even now is smiling at people between here and Chicago, or here and Atlanta, or here and—

Light a goddamn torch and stand in the rain, why don't you.

"Busy night flying solo?" I ask.

"Just orders for tea with something special in it. Extra pillows. Nothing really." Wednesday Joe sighs.

When I emerged around two, it was pouring again, and I discovered that Mavereen had been dispatched so that Rooster could double as guard and night desk clerk, and that Wednesday Joe was seeing to most other needs alongside the maid and porter staff. He wants to be in the woods shoving past bracken, calling out for Davy, squinting at flashes of torchlight.

"This is my fault," he says in a raw tone.

"What?" I exclaim. "Whyever do you say so?"

He shakes his head. "I was seeing to the new window plants yesterday. And I came inside to wash up and still had a spade in my apron pocket."

My heart stings in sympathy. "Oh, but Joe, that means a death in the family, and Davy is fine. Truly, I'm altogether set on it. Did you at least take it back out through the same door?"

"Yeah, of course, and rubbed my rabbit's foot seven times exactly. But what if it wasn't enough?" The teen's voice wobbles.

"It was enough, I'm positive, and it's not like you carried a hoe or a rake in here, is it? Only a wee little spade. There. You know I'm right. Now, tell me how you and your sister came to reside at this veritable paradise. Are you from Portland?"

"Not really." He lifts a spoonful of soup but sets it down untasted. "When Dad was alive, we used to travel from Tacoma to Klamath and everyplace between. Wherever we heard there was some kind of work—fishing, hunting, dishwashing. It was hard to find shelter sometimes, but the food was okay since we could go into the woods for it. Once we heard they needed Indians for an exhibit in Salem and all three of us got paid to wear the costumes the museum put together with feathers and shells and things. That was the best three months ever—all we had to do was stand there and glare, and they let us sleep in the storage loft. Dad could build or fix anything, but he liked boats best. So the War was good for us, when they made so many."

"You're both ever so bright for wildwood children."

Wednesday Joe shrugs. "He couldn't read, but Mom could. It was important to her. So wherever we ended up, he'd find some church lady and pay her to teach us. When the chain snapped and the planks fell, he was finishing raw cut timber to replace merchant marines here in Portland. Left us plenty hungry. We asked just about everyone to hire us and finally ended up at that door." He nods at the kitchen where I likewise arrived, actively dying. "Jenny used to be a maid here, but now she writes for *The Advocate*. She worked real hard every week with Mrs. Evelina Vaughan. Learned good spelling, grammar, that sort of thing. She's smart. Way smarter than me, anyhow."

I don't say *and your mother?* But he sees me staring wistfully into my soup.

"She died having me. She's the one who taught Jenny the tribal stuff—that she's really Ka'ktsama. So I'm just plain Joe, because she didn't have a chance to . . . well. But that's all right."

"Doesn't have to be," I observe.

He hesitates. "I never told Blossom, she'd only take the mickey, but . . . I think you'd understand, maybe. It was on a Saturday it started, her labor, and. And by Sunday she was dead, you see."

"I do see." I draw heat from the coffee mug between my palms. "And am therefore in complete agreement that Wednesday is altogether the jazziest day of the week. I don't think Blossom actually means to make fun, by the by."

"Oh, I know. She's a swell lady. Everyone except for Dr. Pendleton loves her, and that's only because he's kippered most of the time."

"Even your sister?" I ask without inflection.

Wednesday Joe finally tastes the soup, with a bit too much gusto. "Sure. They fight, but who doesn't?"

"They seem to fight more . . . energetically."

"I don't know anything about that."

And now I know that you do.

"What about you, Your Majesty?" he asks, black brows tilting. "Everyone says . . . well . . ."

"Yes, they do, I imagine. And yes, I was."

"Jesus. But that's just awful. Why'd you get shot?"

Colors swirl behind my corneas. *Rye is dancing on the table, his eyes every color as they reflect the gowns of all the chorus girls applauding. His eyes still every color for hours and hours afterward. For too long. Mr. Salvatici is lit from behind with coral dawn as he unlatches the coop door and pulls out a pure white pigeon, sending it soaring. Nicolo Benenati is standing in a lake on a packed earth floor, hay scattered about, and the hay is the wrong color, the entire world is the wrong color.*

"I got shot because I cared about someone. Which begs the question, what should you and I do about Davy?" I trail my spoon through the soup. "Are there any white horses stabled hereabouts?"

His eyes light up. "Actually, there's a pretty big hostelry I know of, and if we bring an apple and wish on—"

Raised voices in the lobby beyond cause our silverware to clatter on the china. When the door bangs open, my hand flies to the throbbing in my side.

"—already repeated half a dozen times just for the sake of my health anyhow, which may I add is decidedly *not* in an ideal state at present!" Blossom cries.

The space between my spine and my belly floods with a queer tingling light.

Blossom Fontaine is giving Maximilian Burton a sizable piece of her mind.

"Aw, that's fair, that there's as reasonable as you done sounded yet!" Max shouts. Apparently his Brooklyn accent stages a coup when he's sore. "Chrissake, I knows you ain't been having no picnic these few months, but why not throw it in my face, like, when everything I's asking you about is aimed at getting Davy back where he belongs?"

Wednesday Joe makes a low sound and flees for the kitchen. Max flings his hat on a table so hard half the breakfast settings fly off, *tinkle-clash.*

Blossom melts into the nearest seat, deposits her finger-curled head in crossed arms, and sobs.

Max winces instantly. Buries his nails in his hair in frustration. Seeing me, he nods, and before I'm stupidly happy over it, I'm baffled.

Oh, the light, I remember. *I'm by one of the only lamps. That must be why he noticed me.*

"Hey, kid." He angles up behind her and drapes capable hands over her heaving shoulders. "Blossom, I ain't none too proud of the last five minutes. But we both meant well by 'em. How's about an armistice?"

She pays him no mind as he rubs circles on her nape with his thumbs, and I can't think of anything to try. I have no right to be here at all. Then the door swings again and Jenny Kiona enters wearing a navy housecoat. Though she doesn't seem to have been part of the search party, she hasn't been sleeping either, for her lustrous eyes are red rimmed and she has plentiful ink stains on her fingers.

"I was coming down to check in with Rooster and heard the most terrible racket. Nothing yet?" she breathes when she sees them. "Oh God. Blossom, no, you have to breathe, dear heart. Blossom? Here, let me."

She slides up a chair and pulls Blossom into the crook of her neck, making low, sweet hushing sounds. My heart cords thrum in aching tune as Jenny strokes her damp cheek, presses her lips against the waves of her hairline. It's not until this has gone on for maybe twenty seconds that I realize Max is purposely not looking at a perfectly typical act of feminine comfort. The question of why they should need privacy has barely entered my grey matter before I've answered it, however.

He isn't my sort, honey, Blossom said about Max.

He's not my sort either, honey. The very idea, Blossom said about Dr. Pendleton.

Jenny came to Blossom's room in the middle of the night and didn't praise her Maker over finding me there. And Jenny is sleek haired, and intelligent, with curves fit to slalom down like Alps. I'm lifetimes too old and several dozen flapper acquaintances too experienced to blush, but I swerve my attention to the vicinity of the cheese cart. In my periphery, I notice Max noticing.

You need to remedy the fact that anytime Max notices you, your entire torso quivers.

"Hush, hush, we'll set it all right," Jenny sings. She turns her attention to Max over Blossom's crown. "So you left off searching?"

Max has already poured four chalice-size glasses of that which is forbidden and sets two in front of them.

"Yep. Searched, kept searching, right up till they tossed us out on our ears."

"The brutes!" Jenny exclaims. "Where are the others?"

"Miss Christina is here, fishing for some shut-eye before breakfast service. Mavereen's camped out in a colored diner across the river till the park reopens. Dr. Pendleton left to join her a few hours back. Sober as a goat, says Rooster."

"What happened exactly?" Jenny asks me. "Earlier. You were there."

The needling pain between my eyes jabs harder. "Yes, though I'm shrouded in darkness myself. Davy was with us when we went into the fun house, and I was separated from the others in a jiffy because they knew better than to take the first dead-end turn. From thenceforth, I made a dreadful ass of myself, I'm afraid. Had the niftiest dizzy spell in the hall of mirrors, found the exit, and *quelque* shame, there's the entire kettle of fish."

"Who was Davy with specifically?"

Max says, "It was Blossom as had him by the mitt. I been grilling her like a regular chump about it, and we ain't gonna mess with her no further, see? He ran off like he always does. Not her fault; next topic."

Jenny rests a smooth cheek against the top of Blossom's head. "I want it all to have been a bad dream."

Max balls a fist. "We done searched everything from the floating bathhouse to the pavilion, which was locked up till I raised all hell, then we spread into the woods after they ousted us. Calling out for him, like. Couldn't see your hand in front of your face to search. Me, I'm gathering the troops. First thing. Then maybe speculating over which heads is asking for knocking. From what they says, I oughta sign that ticket taker up for some dental work."

Blossom rises, combing her fingers through Jenny's waterfall of hair. She downs a swig of liquor a pirate might term *robust.* "Nonsense, Max, you'll lose the last of your trains tomorrow. They'll dock you something simply frightful."

"Yeah, how about that." Max seats himself at my table with more of the strong stuff, his ankles crossed in front of him, and I partake with religious fervor.

"You ridiculous, peacocking *toddler*," Blossom hisses.

"Aw, there's my girl." Max flashes a gallows grin. "That's Second Lieutenant Toddler to you."

"No, honestly, you can't stay." She seems freshly dismayed, and Max exchanges a look with Jenny.

"Why's that, then?"

Blossom's eyes are black and carmine within the sills of her cheekbones, and her voice could finish cement work. "It's really *ever* so simple once it's explained to you, here, I'll do it gratis. You have to get on one of the trains before noon tomorrow or you'll lose your job."

"Eh, good riddance. I'll get another."

"Really?" she questions acidly. "What sort?"

"Dunno, angel, but army veteran generally counts for at least one shade offa my skin tone, and I ain't eager to skedaddle till we bring home the hotel mascot."

Blossom takes a second swallow of whiskey and, hey presto, the drink has vanished. "You can't help."

"How in hell d'ya figure that equation?"

"Because, my sweet, stupid Max, you will not content yourself with mere searching, oh *no.* You will canvass neighborhoods, question white people. You will be as visible as the Rose Parade. You will march that positively *resplendent* ass of yours down to the station house. When they lack the zeal you require, you will antagonize Officer Overton, and he will, allow me to enunciate this clearly, *murder you*."

Max regards the ceiling. "I done got shot at by Germans for the American flag. If it's for Davy? Sign me up."

Blossom's entire gaunt frame has launched in the direction of exploding when Jenny says, "I have an idea."

A tense silence ensues.

"They're a hot commodity. Let's have it," I venture.

"Does it involve ink at all?" Blossom lurches off for more whiskey.

Jenny wisely ignores this. "Anyone else would be going to the cops by now. But the cops—"

"Shake us down for red-eye and attempt to rearrange Maximilian here's handsome features, so please, honey, do me the *exquisite* favor of not suggesting we try the Mounties instead." Swiveling, Blossom reveals a fresh fistful of holy water and quaffs.

"No, I was thinking of the Chief of Police."

Blossom's mouth opens and closes.

Max snaps his fingers with a low whistle.

Jenny leans forward. "Yes, it's a black child gone missing, but Evelina Vaughan has always been on our side naturally, without convincing, and she's your personal friend. Her husband can't very well refuse to help us under those circumstances, can he? What's more, it's a matter of principle."

"Principles. Those and four bits can get you lunch," Blossom replies sweetly.

"You have principles," Jenny snaps. "What, you think you're the only one on earth who does?"

"I—of course not, *no*, I'm being predictably horrid. I'm sorry. Honey, I see your point, I *truly* do, but a troupe of Negroes can't very well hoist umbrellas and march up to the front door of the

Portland Chief of Police without begging to be pummeled by men in quaint medieval caps."

Jenny smirks like a feline with cream on its whiskers. "Miss James over there—"

"Oh, do call me Alice, please."

"Volunteered to help. So she'll go."

Max executes a celebratory kick step from his seated position. "Jenny K., you got a head on your neck, says I."

"Yes!" I exclaim. "What do you want me to ask Mr. Vaughan to do?"

Blossom seems at a genuine loss. I comprehend her fear of authorities, however, and remember her abrupt dismissal of the topic of Tom Vaughan the day previous. She hadn't seemed to harbor any grudge toward the fellow; but I don't harbor any grudge toward great white sharks, and that doesn't connote wanting to palaver with them.

"Call it a woman's intuition, if you please, *Lord* knows I believe in the stuff, but I don't think it's a good idea," she replies, staring into her liquor.

"Is Chief Vaughan crooked?" I ask.

"Gracious, no. He's simply a *model*."

"Of what?"

"Why, decency, of course."

"Do you mean that sarcastically?"

"I mean it in the dictionary sense of the term!" she wails. The pretty sapphire glints to her skin are ashen, and her drink trembles like a plucked guitar string. "Fine, go! Anything for Davy Lee, I know we'd all risk the very *gallows*, I only—the Klan would think nothing of turning this place into a bonfire and toasting marshmallows over it. I want him back, more than my life. But I don't want to see you hurt, Max, Jenny. Alice. Nor anyone else. Now if you *far-too-kind* souls will pardon me, since I'm not crashing through the mud and muck any longer, the dining room is altogether too far away to await news. I'll be in the lobby with Rooster."

"Blossom—" Jenny attempts.

"Try to stop me," Blossom hisses as she sweeps out the etched glass doors.

We sit, listening as the rain plays snare drums against the windows. Max's thoughts have burrowed deep into his skull. Jenny blushes, grimaces in frustration, then says unsteadily, "Max . . ."

"You're too good to ask it, kiddo, because I'd be betraying a confidence." Max squints in sympathy. "Anyway, only folks as know what ails Blossom are Blossom and Dr. Pendleton."

Jenny nods. The *ah, jolly good, so that was the last lifeboat, then* sort of nod. Pulling her robe tighter, she departs.

We are alone.

Max shifts looking, dare I say, sheepish. "Nuts. About, er, Blossom and Jenny."

I try my most innocent moon eyes and he very nearly laughs.

A chorus of cheers for the home team as the batter strikes a single.

"You never quit, do you?" He shakes his head.

"Unto the death knell. Just a moment, though—being a mob flapper is quite the exercise in liberality. Blossom could take up with the Queen of the Netherlands for all I care. But why are you so sanguine over it?"

"Aw, c'mon, lady, I been to Paris. Please. You and me is the only local circle types who've cottoned to it, but I don't have to tell you to keep your lips glued, do I?"

"Her brother most certainly knows," I correct him. "But I won't tell a soul."

One corner of Max's mouth edges upward again.

And the batter steals second.

"No kidding? What're you, then, some kinda spy?"

"Nobody particular."

"I know *that* ain't a full deck."

"March to the rear, sir, you are forward and the hour is late."

"Yeah," he says gravely. "Yeah, it sure is. You're for the Vaughans' come morning?"

"As I live and breathe. I'm no goldbrick."

"I'll write out directions, leave 'em with Rooster at the desk."

"You have my eternal gratitude. Your own plans?"

"Muster some men and be back out there with 'em when dawn breaks." Max goes to retrieve his fallen hat. "We'll find Davy, Alice. I swear to God we'll find him."

He holds the door open for me. As we exit, we face Rooster, hulking and somber, standing at attention behind the check-in counter. We reach the elevator, and Max in lieu of Wednesday Joe operates it.

Blossom remains curled in an armchair, contemplating the empty lobby. Watching like a sea captain's wife searching the shores after a storm.

Eleven

Dangerous forces are insidiously gaining a foothold in Oregon. In the guise of a secret society, parading under the name of the Ku Klux Klan, these forces are endeavoring to usurp the reins of government, are stirring up fanaticism, race hatred, religious prejudice, and all of those evil influences which tend toward factional strife and civil terror.

—GOVERNOR BEN OLCOTT,
Official Proclamation, May 13, 1922

Chief of Police Thomas Vaughan smiles as the maid enters the parlor with a tea tray. She's an ashy-complected girl with teeth that jostle and a center hair part executed with the assistance of either a mathematician or a ruler. Possibly both.

Something has unnerved her—it would cheer me up any amount to learn it isn't me.

"That looks mighty fine, April. Oh, have you eaten, Miss James? It's so early, I can't imagine you have. Should she bring us a bite of something before I have to leave for the station house?"

One might think from reading this that he is archly reminding me of my dawn-crack intrusion and advising me to hoist mainsail. One would miss the bull's-eye. Whatever else is going on, Mr. Vaughan genuinely wants to know the condition of my stomach.

"Oh, really, I couldn't—"

"April, please bring in some of those scones Evy made yesterday."

"Yes, sir. Should I—"

"Enough for two will be fine, thank you."

I regard him, gauging.

He regards me, courteous and distracted.

Something entirely apart from my undisclosed criminal ties is amok.

The Vaughans live in King's Hill, an altogether idyllic neighborhood just to the west of the car-choked city center. You could roll a bowling ball straight down West Burnside and hit it from the Paragon Hotel save for the fact I've discovered that another thing Portlanders are strong for apart from rain and roses is hills. So I took a streetcar in the salmon sunrise, descending onto an avenue lined with fairy-tale trees and thick with bushes exploding in shocking pinks and kingly purples and blinding whites. I nearly couldn't find the house for the flora and the ferns.

"Mr. Vaughan—Oh, should I call you Chief Vaughan?"

"Mr. Vaughan is just fine, Miss James."

"Very well. Again, I beg you'll forgive me, but it's a matter of terrible urgency." I pat my hair primly, ensuring that it's all tucked into the false bun. "You see, I'm writing an article about the colored population of Portland, and residing at the Paragon Hotel to do so."

"Say, isn't that swell." His brows unfurl pleasantly. "A lady reporter. You be careful at the Paragon, Miss James—never know what sort's coming in and out."

Which identically matches the specs of every other hotel on earth, thank you.

"Doesn't Mrs. Vaughan teach a charitable class there?"

"Sure does." He smiles. "My wife is a special lady. I can't keep her out of trouble, but I can keep her well advised. Better safe than sorry is my motto. Parents for orphans, salves for lepers, betterment for blacks—my Evy is fighting the good fight. All I can do is warn her, same as I'm warning you now."

"Why does she hold her weekly class at the Paragon, then, supposing it's subject to occasional rowdiness?"

"My wife has a friend there, a Miss Blossom Fontaine. Artistic type, you know—flamboyant even. But she has a good heart deep down, if you can overlook the rest."

Nobody the stick-assed intellectual frowns skeptically. "Actually, it pains me to say, it's partly about her that I've come."

He pauses as he passes my cup and saucer. Tom Vaughan looks like what would happen if you bred an heiress with a cowboy and ended up with a poster for Colgate's shaving lather. But in a sweet way. He has a flat brow and a narrow chin with a vertical cleft, a wholesome triangular arrangement that probably had its origins in some godforsaken corner of Scandinavia. He's the sort who's never calculated a movement in his life, was born knowing how to cast a fly rod and saddle a pinto. Where Officer Overton's military arrogance invites cringing, Mr. Vaughan's surety makes you think he maybe wouldn't mind taking a look at that shutter that always squeaks.

"Is Miss Fontaine all right?" he asks.

"For the most part. But you see, an orphaned mulatto boy they care for disappeared yesterday at the Elms."

Tom Vaughan clucks in consternation, shifting to pull a notebook and pencil from his jacket. Meanwhile, he keeps glancing at the front foyer like it's a race he has money on.

"His name is Davy Lee," I continue.

"Uh-huh, I believe we've met. Some fund-raiser or other—oh, an ice-cream social for the Bethel AME Church my wife volunteered at. He's in her class too, I believe."

"That's right."

"Cute kid. Odd, but nice manners. Mighty sorry to hear he's missing. What were the circumstances?"

I inform him, in appropriately fussy terms.

"Sounds like you didn't get much help from the Elms staff. Then again, runaways of that age aren't uncommon, so they had a point."

"They hardly seemed to consider the boy a child of God at all."

"It wasn't so bad as that, surely? People are a mite reserved in these parts, Miss James, because so many settlers came here on account of the untouched wilderness in the first place. But you'll find they warm up just as snug as you could wish if you give them some time and space."

They do to you, I imagine.

Pushing my glasses up my nose, I reply, "Possibly. But the hotel employees have been searching these past twenty hours, and I can hardly stand to think that the river might play into this. It's so affecting, Mr. Vaughan. I know Davy's not precisely an exalted citizen, but—"

"I know what you're going to say, Miss James, but you needn't." Mr. Vaughan continues to scribble notes. "Portlanders don't want to import any plantation mentality, slaves and overseers alike, and the low black population helps keep race relations peaceable the way they aren't in other parts of the country. That's swell. But that doesn't mean I treat our Negroes any different from us native citizens. I'm going to put the word out to the whole force, and I'll have a look around the Elms myself. Can't promise miracles, but I take my job mighty seriously. We all do at the Portland Bureau of Police."

Officers Overton and Taffy being blinding examples.

April reappears with an armful of baked goods. Mr. Vaughan glances at the grandfather clock and into the entryway again, a man obviously leaking cheer.

"You want the butter *and* the blackberry jam, Miss James," he informs me as he readies his portion. "You're a stranger in these parts, so. Trust me."

"With pleasure."

"Sir." April twists chapped hands together, then crosses them as if she's been asked to spell something. "Should I—"

"April, we've discussed this." A brittleness beneath his easy charm glints like granite. "You have everything ready?"

"Yes, but—"

"For Pete's sake, girl, of course I won't be leaving for work until all's well. It's probably nothing anyhow. You recall three weeks ago?"

The vertical line of her hair slides up and down.

"Well, that was all pretty silly in the end, wasn't it? Please don't interrupt us again."

April departs. They have a common goal, the pair of them—not a sordid one since they mentioned it in front of me but possibly a secret one. *Quelque* intrigue.

"Sorry—April is the sweetest help we could ask for, but she's a bit of a worrier. Might I ask you something? Why is it you came to my doorstep and not Miss Fontaine herself? She's been to this house any number of times to have tea with Evy."

Hesitating just long enough to bait the hook, I answer, "I don't know if it's my place to say."

"Oh. I guess that means there's a specific reason?"

I fiddle with jam arrangements, an intoxicating aroma of violet berries wafting upward.

"I think that the hotel residents were anxious over being seen in this part of town, Mr. Vaughan." I cast a look over my horn-rims. "They mentioned the rising popularity of the nationally infamous Ku Klux Klan."

Tom Vaughan's handsome face sags in relief. "Well, I'm mighty sorry to hear that, then. I'll head over to the hotel myself and have a word when Miss Fontaine is there. I know what the KKK means in the South, and it makes me sick. But around here, there are hardly any blacks to begin with, you understand. The Klan is a political rallying tool and a charitable club. It's all America first with them—promoting jobs for hardworking Protestants over Orientals and Catholic immigrants, protesting Jew banking, defending motherhood and maidenhood. Fund-raisers, not lynch mobs."

"So they don't wear masks, then?" I question blandly.

He nods his tawny head. "Come to it, yes, they do, Miss James, but that's the culture of the organization. They have their rituals, just like the Masons, the Odd Fellows, the Knights of Columbus. Not meant here in Portland to strike terror into any law-abiding folk, I assure you."

"There have been reports of vandalism against the hotel, however."

"Yes, and my men figure it for some rogue teens, not the conservative businessmen of this peaceful city attacking their neighbors."

"I'll just make that a quote from you, then? For the article?"

"Gladly. I'm sure we'll catch the rascals in the act soon enough."

Staring at the object in my hand, I chew.

It's crumble crust and vanilla, a hint of salt, a kiss of sugar, crisp then pillowy, slathered with fresh butter and crowned with the blood-thick ambrosia Mr. Vaughan referred to as "blackberry jam."

"My God," I say in unvarnished awe.

He smirks good-naturedly. "My wife can cook! There's no denying. You ever had blackberry jam?"

"Never."

"Where are you from, Miss James? Sorry, I neglected to ask."

"Connecticut, and think nothing of it."

"Well, what do you think of the spread we make from the local weed?"

I am so gone on it that I am never putting anything behind my teeth save that which is drowning in blackberry jam ever again.

The front door crashes open.

Evelina Vaughan stands between the entryway and the morning room. She looks much more like herself than she did at the Paragon—her real self, that is, and in a photo flash, I can see what Blossom meant when she said Mrs. Vaughan *was* Portland.

She's its generosity and eccentricity and isolation and passion and rebellion and melancholy and kindness.

The lady of the house is a tearing grand mess. She wears a pair of mud-crusted galoshes, riding pants, and a man's plaid flannel shirt knotted at the waist to fit her. A leather satchel hangs from her shoulder, and the hand hooked around the strap is covered in fine scratches, as if she went ten rounds with a paper blizzard. Her halo of apricot waves is still done up nineteenth-century style but has developed a large population of woodland residents. Leaves, pine needles, flecks of dirt.

I watch Tom Vaughan's heart cracking.

April bursts back in at a run, having heard the door. "Oh, Mrs. Vaughan. Thank heaven you're back. Are you—"

"Please don't take on so, April—we have a guest." Mr. Vaughan stands hastily. "Go and draw some hot water for a bath at once, please. Sweetheart. Did you lose track of time? We've been expecting you since . . . well, we were worried."

Grey irises wide and hectic, she melts into his open arms like a butter curl.

Since last night, I'd judge, from the penciled shadows under her eyes and the layers of dried forest on her galoshes.

"Tom. Dear Tom. I didn't leave a note, did I? You look as if I didn't, and I'm so sorry, please forgive me." Pulling back, she laughs, a happy wind chime sound with a thread of turbulence in it. "I've been—what was it I was doing? Oh yes, that's right, I baked, and then I wrote in my journal, I was very good about it, you can check, and then I had a meeting with the Married Women's Benevolent Society, and when I got home, all the walls were too thick, and you were out late at work, so I went for a walk. But wait, we've company, how lovely. Who's this, Tom?"

"I'm Miss Alice James." Standing, I proffer a businesslike handshake, not in the least surprised she never noticed me at the hotel. "Very pleased to meet you, Mrs. Vaughan."

Her fingers are as cold as her smile is dazzling. "Charmed. Have you business with my husband, or were you waiting for me? I didn't think I had an appointment, but. That's really no guarantee against my having missed one!"

Evelina Vaughan's china complexion is thin with weariness and flushing in—well, I can't call it excitement. But I've seen something similar. The difference on this occasion is that I think it's naturally occurring, like the northern lights firing across a black skyline or iridescent seaweed floating off the prow of a clipper.

Not the same as Rye, chemical every-colored eyes like an oil spill.

Tom Vaughan tilts his wife's chin tenderly back in his direction. "When did you leave the house, Evy?"

"Oh, I couldn't say exactly. After the meeting, and I read for a spell though I don't recall which book. So it can't have been very interesting, can it?" She laughs again. "I had a cup of soup and worked on the invitations for the Crippled Veterans' Picnic next week. I'm sorry about the note, Tom, I'll remember next time. But it was beautiful, the trees all telling me secrets and the wind shushing them. Oh, are those my scones, Miss James? How do you find them?"

Mrs. Vaughan comes to a stop with a questioning smile on her face, dressed for riding without any horse. Her energy could blot out anything—a roaring hearth, a wildfire. She could knock the sun for a loop and not break a sweat.

"Delicious."

I try to say this fastidiously. I manage rapt.

Her husband, poor old sport, is plucking the worst of the great outdoors from her nimbus of hair so sadly and sweetly that I can't look it straight on. "Join me in the other room, Evy?"

"Oh, but we've a guest! And she even likes my baking. I believe we'll have to keep her forever."

"Evy, please come with me."

My cue here is obvious. "I ought to be going anyhow, Mrs. Vaughan."

"No!" She lets her husband pass his arm around her back, nestling in. "I only just met you. I've been rambling for a few hours and probably look a fright, but—"

"Evy, I came home at midnight from the station house," her husband snaps. He softens immediately. "I thought it got dark without your noticing and you stayed with one of the ladies from the meeting, like last time. You've been missing all night again."

She turns in the circle of his body, lips parted in shocked denial. "Oh, no. No, I was only walking. Not that far even, just . . . I can't remember exactly. I'm so sorry about the note, please forgive me."

"It was dark when you left, yes?"

"Yes, but—"

"What time is it now, sweetheart?"

Evelina Vaughan turns to her own bay window and stares at the daylight with about as much enthusiasm as would your average vampire. The almond-shaped grey pools shimmer.

"I didn't mean it."

"I know, Evy."

"I never do, please, I *swear.*"

"Shh, you're all right. Say goodbye to Miss James now, and come along."

"Oh, Miss James." She takes a step, the apologetic hand she lifts as marked as the plaid shirt she wears. "You must forgive the state I'm . . . in, apparently, though I didn't know it. Come back for more scones, would you? When I've had the chance to rest and I'm more myself."

You're more yourself presently than I've ever been in my life.

She's like a tamed deer standing there, balanced on small feet and blinking expectantly, and I've the maddest urge to feed her bits of her own remarkable baked goods.

"I'd love to, if able," I answer.

"Will you tell me your business, though? Here you are in my house and apparently it's just past sunrise, so I'm dying of curiosity you see. I can't abide not being in on secrets, not when we're to be friends as soon as I feel a bit better." She smiles, an open-air expression without a hint of jealousy.

"I've been staying at the Paragon Hotel writing an article, and I regret to tell you that yesterday Davy Lee went missing."

The smile freezes for some two or three seconds before it shatters like a fallen icicle.

"What did you say? You. I've never—You live at the Paragon?"

"Only since very recently," I hasten to explain. "I work for a newspaper, you see, and the hotel is of immense social interest—you tutor there weekly, yes? I actually saw you, when you were last visiting Blossom."

She glances at her husband. The subtle contrast of her deep widow's peak grows starker as she pales. "Yes. I . . . did go to the Paragon. Day before yesterday, after you mentioned there was a raid, Tom. I needed to see everyone was all right. What's this about—"

"How many times do I have to tell you that the aftermath of a police altercation is a mighty poor time to pay social calls?" her husband demands. "Next time you want to see Miss Fontaine, invite her here, for Pete's sake."

"What's happened to Davy Lee?" she insists, silvery eyes darting minnow-like from one to the other of us.

April's ungraceful steps prophesy her appearance. One of her hands is wet. "Mrs. Vaughan, I've drawn your bath. Won't you come up while it's still nice and hot?"

Her mistress's gaze sharpens. "I'll take a bath when I'm ready for one, thank you, April. Tom, you must not keep me behind glass as if I'm some sort of figurine. I know I've lost track again, but—"

"Go on upstairs, sweetheart." He glances at me. "Goodbye, Miss James, and believe that I'll do everything I—"

"Stop it!" Mrs. Vaughan snarls as I edge in feigned mortification toward the foyer. The expression I glimpsed when she spoke of Officer Overton returns, fang-bared and fearless. "Tell me what you know about Davy, Miss James, I'm ever so sorry to be rude, but. Davy's special."

"He disappeared at the Elms yesterday, sweetheart, and we're going to find him." So stating, Mr. Vaughan marches to the front door and holds it open. "Goodbye, Miss James. I'll be in touch, very soon."

Stepping through the portal is the only action this Nobody could possibly take. So I adjust my specs as if embarrassed and exit into the tangled wood. The door isn't shut before Evelina Vaughan begins to shriek, however. I hear her first strangled breaths, and her devoted husband hushing her, and the audible wail, "No, you must let me go if that's true, Blossom needs me! She *needs me*!" before, *sweep-snick*, the voices are silenced and I'm standing on an enchanted street corner.

Wondering what in hell sort of family I was just introduced to.

I've been running myself dreadfully raggedy. I've no sooner shed my simple disguise at the Paragon than I've slithered betwixt the bedsheets again. When I awaken, the rain has returned as if it never left, *splish-plop*, and the day vaulted over its meridian.

3:17 in the afternoon, and Davy Lee could be anywhere.

Or nowhere.

The pang that hits me is unexpected, too sharp for someone familiar with horror. I'm not just worried for a fanciful kiddo I scarcely know, that would be bad enough—I'm on Evelina Vaughan's page to the very letter.

I'm almost sick over Blossom Fontaine.

I check my dressings, dry-swallow a pill, and don a grey-and-blue-check organdy dress with a scoop neck. It's comfortable without being something Nobody the snooty reformist wouldn't be caught cadaverous in. Then I slide on a pair of heeled house slippers and head down the corridor, a strange high flicker of nerves in my throat.

A rustle precedes her when I knock, and she opens the door. Candles glow within, a dozen or more, enough to mean something to a Catholic like me or a sap like her.

Enough for a shrine to the departed.

She wears an onyx silk dressing gown printed with shafts of golden wheat, and her face might as well have been carved from marble like the busts I've seen at the Metropolitan.

Noting my own expression, she says sternly, "Alice, Davy Lee is alive. *Extremely* alive. He is most emphatically not suited for the wooden-box treatment. I found him, remember? We're connected somehow, from the moment I saw his tiny, silly squalling face. I would *know*. Are we clear?"

"As holy water," I vow.

"They are *combing* the woods. The only reason I'm not is that they'd have to drag me around like a sled."

"I know, yes. He'll turn up any old minute. I'm sorry. It's been a long day already."

"And getting longer. Come on in, supposing you don't mind passing the time with an absolute *ghoul*."

"I think you look fine."

"Have a seat anyplace, and never mind the mess. Even pretending that I intend to make up the bed is beyond my capacity."

Her room may be a madhouse, but it's a friendly one. Clothes hanging helter-skelter on the dressing screen and the edge of the vanity, liquor tumblers and silk stockings and lipstick pots scattered about, the candles pin-lighting puddles of domesticity. And curled in the tangled bedclothes, Medea's face, wickedly satisfied by the chaos.

When I look up after perching on the end of the bed, Blossom has already poured drinks. Handing me one, she settles in her vanity chair.

"You've been to the Vaughans', I take it? Did you draw fruit? Do you come bearing simply *bushels* of produce?"

I readily spill. She's attentive but seems to expect poor returns, and I can't blame her. For all that Tom Vaughan was every inch the gentleman, he told me—what, exactly? That his policemen would be on the lookout? It doesn't take a crystal ball to tell me just how valuable that will prove. Then I come to the shoelace I haven't quite unknotted yet.

"When she arrived home, Mrs. Vaughan seemed . . ."

Blossom arches her brows with an unreadable expression. Something paws softly at the back of it other than mere surprise. "*Arrived* home? For heaven's sake, I thought you went at the break of cock's crow."

"Yes, but she'd been out walking. All night long."

I've socked the wind from her. Then the singer produces a guttural groan. "What time was this?"

"I hadn't been there more than half an hour. Obscenely early."

"Oh, God, *no.* The poor creature, I simply must make time to stop in on—Medea, for *shame.*"

The cat abandons its successful effort to chew the toe off a stocking and growls as it slinks behind the dressing screen.

"I've known Evy for some time now, and she's always been something of a tissue upon the winds of extremities." Blossom speaks slowly, gazing at the candlelight. "Mind you, for weeks, even occasionally two months or more, she'll be smooth sailing and cloudless skies. Planning, riding, hiking, inventing a new charity, driving her cook to distraction because she wants to make everything herself."

"Yes, I already had her scones."

"With her blackberry jam?"

"She *made* that?"

"Well, there you are. Yes. Anyhow, up to a quarter of a year goes by at times without incident. Then, *presto.* Evy once stayed awake for two days baking *every* item on the list for a Christmas fund-raiser. Upside-down cakes, almond dominoes, cider jelly pie. It never occurred to her until she arrived with two hired hands to carry it all that the rest of the board had signed up to pitch in."

"What a nightmare that must be."

Blossom bites her lower lip. "She falls into the most *agonizing* state afterward. Like an invalid just come out of a fever with her hair shorn and her muscles wasted—but all this entirely between her ears, of course. I'll have to think of something instantly."

"What do you mean?"

"Oh." She looks bemused, then shakes her head. "To cheer her. Tom's an angel, really, he performs miracles. But it's a concerted effort."

I don't want to broach the subject, but I must, smoothing my fingers over the Chinese silk adorning the end of the bed. "Any dispatches?"

Blossom doesn't wince. But her entire face dedicates itself to preventing it.

"The lines are quiet. No clues forthcoming."

"You said you weren't feeling well. Are you going back out?"

"They don't need the altogether *pitiable* invalid whose fault this entire situation is in the first place."

"No, that's—"

"Entirely, globally, *universally* true," she snaps. She turns to her vanity and begins laying cosmetics out like weapons in an arsenal, and I suppose in a sense they are. "Besides, I have a show tonight."

I blink. "You're performing?"

"Oh, with *gusto*, honey, there's Dr. Pendleton's bills to consider. He's top dollar, don't you know, pride allows for nothing else."

"Piove sul bagnato." I sigh.

"Translation—instantly, please."

"Um, 'Bad situations grow worse.'"

"Alice, it's in Italian, it cannot *possibly* be that dull."

Smiling, I amend, "'It rains on the wet.'"

She grins. It's a heroic effort. I watch as she applies cream, a very dark tincture, a lighter one, a shimmer.

"Your uncle charges you full rates for medical care? *Quelque* churl."

"You said it." Blossom makes a popping sound as she smacks her lipstick into place. "But he has his reasons."

"That's—"

"Don't get steamed up, honey, I can afford him as long as I'm working."

Medea emerges from the dressing area with the satisfied expression of a creature who has performed mischief. Blossom plays a brief *rat-a-tat* on her vanity with a brow pencil and I glance up at her reflection.

"Do you know what I like about you, Alice?" she asks quietly.

"Actually, I'd be much obliged to take the tour," I admit.

"Oh, ever so modest, yes, because you know modesty suits you. Don't take offense, it comes naturally. No, I like you because I have an inkling, just the tiniest phantom of a suspicion, that if you *truly* knew me—the entire instruction manual of my life and my flaws—you still wouldn't hate me."

Astonished, I answer, "I couldn't ever hate you. I've no good reason for knowing that, but it's true all the same."

"And the oddest part is that I've no good reason to believe you, but I do." Something sad twinkles in her eyes, like a jewel box cast to the bottom of the sea. "We go through our lives, so many of us, as fractions of ourselves, with all the other puzzle pieces buried where no one can see them. But there's the paradox, and *do* forgive me for flights metaphorical—we're all of us fractured jigsaws, but we're also the entire picture no matter how far away we walk from what's hidden. I've seen you do it, you understand. You're whatever Alice suits, but you're still Alice always—you can't help it, and neither can I—and deep down you know that to be true. That's why I think you wouldn't hate me."

She looks at me in the mirror, entirely unguarded, and I can't say a word. Chuckling, she shakes her head.

"Don't you mind a cabaret singer getting *tragically* soppy—it's like trying to escape Portland without mud on your shoes. But . . . in any case, please forgive me, honey, if I confess that I'm just the *tiniest* bit overjoyed that you took a bullet."

Laughing, I go to her and wrap my arms around her neck the way I used to do with my friend Sadie. Blossom's head lands in my bosom and instead of regarding intertwined us in the vanity mirror, she cranes her neck to gaze at me upside down.

"Max has a volunteer crew of some twenty, and you're *far* too pasty to be in the woods, forgive the aspersion. If you fall in with my plans, you can pull the background statue stuff and maybe learn something helpful for the Paragon. Come and watch me perform at the Rose's Thorn tonight?"

"Oh, with resounding cheers!" I exclaim.

"You cannot wear *that*," she adds with a mock glare, which is awfully droll on someone whose face is upside down.

"May death come first. I'll be a more suitable Alice, cross my heart."

"You want Maximilian, don't you?" she whispers.

Instead of cringing, I draw my thumbs along her prow-like collarbones. "Dreadfully. Is it obvious?"

"Only to people who love dreams, or who dream about love."

"So, everyone on earth save Officer Overton."

"Indubitably."

"What's the old girl to do?" I sigh.

"What we all do, honey." She reaches a long arm for a brush without breaking the embrace and finishes dusting her cheekbones. "Smash yourself to *smithereens* over him."

Twelve

THEN

Between the law and the Mafia,
the law is not the most to be feared.

—SICILIAN PROVERB

I can't remember going to bed the night Mr. Benenati was slaughtered—the night that would eventually send me to Portland. But I must have wept myself to slumberland, for my lids were sticky when I parted them and my throat was sore.

You fled to Mr. Salvatici last night.

Looking down, I discovered I was still in my street clothes.

You passed the test on the roof. You're at the Hotel Arcadia.

This bedchamber was about as far from a Raines law doss-house as I was from Mr. Mangiapane. The walls were striped in cream and pink, and the table with its brass reading lamp boasted a vase filled with hothouse flowers. Nothing slackerly in the way of comforts, then. Coals still smoldered, and the scuttle was nicely topped up. Curiosity trumped mourning, as it's wont to do in the young, and I padded over to the sky-blue robe folded over the chair-back. Perfect fit.

It's a housecoat, I told myself as the eerie trickle down my back intensified. *They all fit perfectly.*

A wardrobe with a painted trellis-rose pattern loomed tantalizingly. I took a deep breath before baring its secrets.

The rod was positively gasping with clothes. Plain white blouses, high-waisted skirts with sashes, day dresses with the increasingly popular deep V arrowing to the waistline and a panel of lace underneath. Special-occasion gowns in aqua and lavender with perfect three-quarter sleeves. I know now that they weren't decadent. But my fifteen-year-old self figured that since I'd been aiming for a knight's career, landing the princess gig instead wasn't too shabby.

As a matter of fact, I was so jazzed that I wasn't knocked for even half a loop to learn that these likewise fit like they were tailored for me.

The marble bathroom proved another wonderland, the bathtub perched on dainty iron orbs. Lo, verily, hot water gushed out if you turned the handle, and I squeaked like a startled gutter rat.

When two knocks sounded followed by a *click-swish,* I dove for a weapon: a hefty bath brush. But it was only the maid standing in the parlor, a high yellow girl with hair braided into a thick brown coronet. She had a sweet snub nose between deep-set hazel eyes, and seeing her guest en garde with hygienic equipment, she paused. At a loss.

"Should I put this on the table, miss?" she asked, regarding the coffee tray.

"Oh," I said. No one had ever served Nobody before except Crispy Ezio bringing me his last-call specialty, a fried pile of all the edible vegetable ends he'd trimmed. *Fritto misto di verdure* for the insolvent. "Is that for me?"

She blinked. "Actually, I just figured your room would be a swell place for my coffee break."

"Really?"

"Yeah, believe it or not, this is much nicer than the maids' dorms."

Now I knew my leg was being tugged. "What's your name?"

"Sadie."

"Do most of the maids tease the hotel guests?"

"No, but most of the hotel guests are better at it." Sadie surprised a laugh out of me as she set the tray before the lemon-colored settee. "After you've dressed, Mr. Salvatici wants you to have breakfast with him."

"All right. Where?"

"Right through this door." She produced a key from her white apron and gave it to me. "Knock first. That's the Spider's sitting room. You'll keep your side locked, and he will as well, when he's here. Don't worry about noise, the walls here are thick as anything."

"The Spider?"

"It's just a nickname the hotel employees gave him. Well . . . other folks call him that too, down in Hell's Kitchen, from what I gather. I'm meant to ask if the clothes seem like they'll do."

"Do for what?"

"For not being naked."

Sadie's way of expressing herself, I thought with a swell of admiration, *is awfully fine.* Now I'd say that it could have dried up the Hudson and left nary a drop for the fish.

"I think so. I'm Alice James, but you can call me Nobody."

"I know." She smiled as an afterthought, and it felt like a present with a bow. "I hope you're happy here, Miss James. If you ever admire to trade rooms with me, just ask."

Sadie departed. The coffee was as hot and dark as a cast-iron stove, and it did the trick. Though once I was fully awake, I thought of Nicolo and my heart gave a painful squirm.

Mr. Salvatici, I reminded myself. *You're going to help Mr.*

Salvatici purge the Corleonesi from Harlem. The pretty clothes are just . . . that's just how he takes care of his charges.

Like one of his birds.

I found divine soap and thereby set a lifetime record for cleanliness, and when I put on a celery-green dress with a white cotton sash, I looked into the mirror and beheld another creature entirely.

Someone with something to do.

Standing before the portal where my domain ended and Mr. Salvatici's began shouldn't have felt like placing my new boots on the plummeting edge of the world. But it did.

With trembling hand, I freed my side and knocked.

Maybe ten seconds later, I heard a second key in the higher bolt and *voilà*, Mr. Salvatici himself, with black hair slicked and a fountain pen in hand, smiling absently.

"You look much haler, Miss James. I'm glad you're up for a brief *tête-à-tête* along with your eggs."

"What's that mean?"

"Head to head—a conversation."

"Where'd you learn to talk like that?"

"Don't worry, you'll soon be speaking like a sophisticate yourself. Come in, if you please."

The room was as elegant as I remembered—but now I myself suited its richness, my freshly clad ass matched the sofa as it were, so I felt more at ease. Mr. Salvatici pulled a chair out for me in a breakfast nook and lifted a cover to reveal porridge, eggs, bacon, cheese, and sliced autumn apples.

"Do you prefer Alice, Nobody, or Miss James?" he asked cordially.

"I guess whatever you like?"

"Nicknames are familiar and you're going to grow quite familiar with me mounting this great effort of ours, so Nobody it is. If you don't object?"

He took his seat and gestured at mine. Mr. Salvatici was the only man of his age who'd ever looked at me without ogling since I'd approached womanhood, other than Crispy Ezio and Mr. Benenati, of course. So his saying we were going to grow *familiar* didn't carry the weight it could have done.

"What happened last night?" I asked, sitting. "It's embarrassing, but . . ."

He flapped a napkin into his lap. "Help yourself. You grew faint after watching the street brawl break out."

"Shit." I glanced up in dismay. "I mean—"

"I'm an entrepreneur, not a clergyman, my dear young lady."

"But what happened to Nicolo? He was at the front of it all! He—"

"The police broke up the altercation before it grew into a riot, so I imagine he's fine save the profound grief caused by yesterday evening. But that sort of reconnaissance is going to lie with you."

"You mean watching the folk I grew up with?" I spooned scrambled eggs as fluffy and yellow as chicks onto my plate.

"I mean watching anyone. Everyone. When I'm through with you, you'll be as much Anybody as you're Nobody, and thus see through most people's prevarications instantly. You'll need some better schooling—account keeping, dancing and music, basic arts and sciences, the classics. But you already like reading, so that's not a problem."

"How do you know I like to read?"

"I told you." The line of his lips quirked. "When I've visited your mother over these past years, I've mainly done so to watch you. You'll want to change back into your old duds before visiting her and the Benenatis today, but of course you know how to stay inconspicuous."

"Why would you want to teach me something like dancing? I

thought what you liked about me was that I sort of . . . fade into the background."

"Well, there's no point in repeating lessons already learned, is there? I'm not going to teach you how to be invisible, Nobody. I'm going to teach you how to be *unmistakable*."

"Is that . . . is that smart?"

"No. But it's wise." Mr. Salvatici tapped his skull for emphasis. "The most obvious thing in the room is often overlooked."

I wondered as more coffee slid sweetly down my gullet, and snow slipped down my spine, in just what sorts of new places Mr. Salvatici meant for me to be on display? And supposing he was known as the Spider—which seemed an awfully disquieting moniker—how far did this web of his extend?

Well, and I only hope yer happy, nigh giving me fits last night." Mum tried to glare. But as usual, the fire went *fizzle-spit*. She gathered up her blond hair and let it fall as if tossing hay. "On t'other hand, after Mr. Mangiapane lost his shite and poor Nicolo followed suit, I can't hardly blame you."

We sat on a rock on the edge of the Hudson, one reached by stepping across the boulders scattered like a carnage of dominoes. One summer when I was twelve, after Mum was in the dumps thanks to a spectacularly fat lip, I'd brought her to watch the merchant craft floating beneath garlands of freewheeling seagulls. She'd loved it, and we returned every year. One of the only outings that ever reminded me I had a mother—not just a slovenly older-sister type who hogged the quilt starting mid-November.

"About Nicolo." There are fragments of starlight embedded in every hunk of granite along the Hudson River, and my eyes drifted over tiny shards. "What happened last night?"

Mum shrugged. "Bunch of idjits got their faces mashed, is what happened. Poor old Giorgio Benenati, always thumbing his nose at the notion of tribute. Neapolitans. There are some what pay more'n they can afford monthly in protection, and still wouldn't use a Corleonesi handkerchief to polish their boots. Yer da was Neapolitan."

Greed flooded me, and I passed my hand down her arm. "From what part of Naples?"

"Oh, somewhereabouts right on the water. Don't ask fer specifics, my lovely, all the man could gibber in was Italian. Once I sent him out fer more candles and he came back with a bouquet o' daisies and a bottle o' grappa. Well, it served fine."

"Then he would have stood up to the *cagnolazzi*," I told the secretive river, not supposing Mum was paying attention any longer. "If the dog hadn't got him. He'd have given them hell."

"Is that what yer after doing, Alice? Giving the *cagnolazzi* hell?"

I swung my dark eyes to her blue ones, shocked. My mother never asked me direct questions. Statements were her form of suggestive parenting. *Oh, sure enough, Alice polished the liquor bottles* to Mr. Mangiapane, or *Alice ain't a one fer jail cells, so keep yer nose clean* to Nicolo. Telling my story for me served twin purposes: she needn't suffer disappointment, and I'd know what was expected.

"You packed yer things." The breeze put a jig in her hair, and she pulled a wavy tendril away from her lips. "But that were before Mr. Mangiapane said as he were selling you. That means you had a plan already."

"I . . . fine, yes!" I stammered, caught wrong-footed. "But you know what's going to happen if I stay! Not that you care, of course."

"I do," she answered gravely. "I also care whether yer stomach's full. Surely that counts fer something?"

"Yes. But it's not much, is it?" Anger gushed into my throat. "Not that school even counts for girls, but I only ever went because

I liked it, and the rest of the time I just tried not to draw attention. Waiting for something to happen. Anything to happen."

"And it did, didn't it?" Catrin James countered. "I were born with nothing save the cunny 'tween my legs and no imaginings about any other life. My first husband happened, and he up and vanished. Then yer da happened. He was a ray o' sun, but the sun goes down, lovely, and what then? Nights are cold. And there you were, tiny and hungry, and *you* happened, Alice. Didn't take me long to figure out you were sharper than yer old mum. Didn't take me long to figure out you wanted more. Or different. I let you run after it, whatever it was, because fuck if I know any more or different."

The stone scraped under my tensing fingers. I was lucky enough to have a mother—there she was beside me.

So why couldn't I have been born to a mother who acted like one?

Mum rested her chin atop her knee. "You took up with Mr. Salvatici, didn't you?"

"He . . . yes." So many direct and, still more shocking, perceptive questions in a row sent me reeling. "They call him the Spider. He says we should work together. Do you—how well do you know him?"

"Well enough to say I'm not surprised," she admitted. "Little enough to say I never really thought 'twould happen."

"He says he wants me for his ward."

"Aye, legacy's a part of it. He's a lonely feller. But he really wants yer ears, Nobody. And yer sweet little face that folk don't pay mind to until it bites 'em." She smiled sadly at the waves. "What did he tell you about himself?"

This proved surprisingly hard to answer. "Well. He's the boss of a powerful gang, but it's in Hell's Kitchen and he needs eyes in Harlem. He keeps pigeons. It's strange but sort of . . . gentle. He hates the Clutch Hand. Something about building instead of destroying, but like enough he just wants what they all do. More power. More . . ."

"Aye?"

"Girls, maybe." I forced myself to shrug in fine Catrin style. "Maybe he wants to bed me, and that's all."

"He'll never bed you," Mum reported, drinking and then scraping the back of her hand against her mouth. "Never even try."

This was confounding. Plenty of Mum's swains expressed courtly admiration for my developing person.

Catrin James stood, brushing river soot off her skirts. "He'll be good to you. Protect you, even. But he's ambitious. Not the sort of ambition that eats you from the middle and leaves naught save a great hole—that's the Clutch Hand, and you're right as an almanac when you say Mauro Salvatici hates him. I mean the more dangerous kind, the kind what grows instead of erases, the sort o' fellow as sees himself as the king in a storybook. Making a world all his own."

"And you don't mind the danger?" I shielded my eyes to see my mother's face better.

"There's danger everywhere, my lovely. Before he died, yer father talked fer a week of staking a claim out West. Or at least, I think that's what he was on about. I was afeared o' sickness and Indians and begged till I was hoarse to stay. The dog bit his leg two days later. I'll not dissuade you."

Eyes watering, I absorbed this. That Catrin James, rather than uncaring, was maybe only desperately unlucky, and thus resigned to float along like fireplace ash tossed in the gutter. Was that bravery or laziness? Either way, I felt disgusted by it.

"You could try to talk me out of this," I attempted.

"I'd fail. Things happen. We wait for them, and one day they arrive. And Mr. Salvatici has already happened to you."

She left me. I sat there alone, breathing the salty river. I'd been keen on some hearty lamentation and had received a shrug. So I wanted Nicolo. To wipe his tears, run my hands over his tightly corded arms. To hear that he'd rather I stay with him and his mother. I'd say no, of course. Even then I knew how cruel I could be, but I wanted the option, I was positively drunk on options.

Mum was right. If you wait long enough, things happen. And there is no reversing such events. No more than all the love in the world can change the weather.

When I arrived at the Arcadia to change back into my finery and thereby prove to Nicolo my change of circumstances, Rye was holding the door open for a white man who kept making brief bows, as if expressing admiration without actually touching him. He looked like a fat woodpecker—if woodpeckers felt dreadfully awkward around Negroes, which so far as I know is an exclusively human characteristic.

"If it hadn't been my father's, I'd not have minded, but the agony of sentiment—I'll never repay you. Never!"

"Likely not," Rye agreed cheerfully.

It was stated so offhand that the man laughed. "Here's—oh, what the hell, my wife would've noticed and I'd never have heard the end of it. Two bits for your efforts!"

"You're not the first fellow as lost his coat on a night hopping from hotel to hotel like a leapfrog. And I never forget a coat, sir! Watch the corner there, those puddles best be called lakes every year starting September first."

When the chap toddled off, I materialized into view on the bottom steps. Rye's mouth produced an ear-crowding smile, and I felt an unfamiliar sensation tickling at the base of my spine.

"And how are you today, darlin'?"

"Better, I think."

"You sure look it, Miss James."

I almost answered with my rote, *It's Nobody.* Instead my tongue tumbled over itself saying, "It's Alice. I'm going to live here, working for Mr. Salvatici, so."

He was about to reply when I heard from another direction entirely, *"Alice!"*

Unfortunately, this voice was revoltingly familiar—Dario Palma, with a hair thicket sprouting from his open shirt, swinging loose fists the size of melons. Flanked as ever by Doctor Vinnie, the animal-torment specialist, and Cleto the blank-eyed Crow. Doctor Vinnie had his snarling canine, Caesar, at the end of a leather leash thick as a strap; Cleto stood there, collecting flies in his teeth.

"How did you know where I was?" I marveled.

They can't have followed me. No one ever follows me.

"That mouse turd clinging to Nicolo's shoe. Name of Nazario." Dario spat something ripe on the pavement.

Doctor Vinnie's dog licked its floppy chops as its master sneered, "He spilled."

Cleto, who I suspect was raised in a locked root cellar, emphasized expressionlessly, "He spilled all right. Spilled good."

Rye made a curt dip with fingers on his uniform cap. "Afternoon, gents. These friends of yours?"

"No," I stated through my teeth.

"Listen to me, *puttana*," Dario sang. "We need a little favor only you can provide us."

"What's it about?"

"About? This is about our whole neighborhood and its future. We're not going to hurt you—you're Nobody. Remember?" He giggled, the single childlike trait that hadn't yet been bludgeoned out of him. "But if you don't come with us, young Benenati is going up in flames."

The trio walked to the corner. Waited for me with slitted prison-gate eyes. But my friend's name was enough of a bell chime, I didn't need another summons, I was already walking when Rye said in my ear, "You better promise me I don't need to escort you."

"When's your shift over?" I asked.

"Two hours. But—"

"If I'm not back by then, tell Mr. Salvatici."

Shaking his head, he answered, "I don't much like the sound of that."

"It's what the boss wants," I realized.

After joining Dario and his grim circus clowns, we steered toward an alley. Workmen clad in torn coveralls and cloth caps were tearing out the walls of the nearest building and tossing them streetward like so many sacrifices onto a capitalist pyre, making way for the wretched hive the place would become. Once out of sight, Dario ducked his bullish head low.

"You have to talk sense to Nicolo."

"Why would you help him?" I demanded. "You'd as soon kick him in the balls as shake his hand."

"Because he's going to set all Harlem on fire."

"But—"

"Right, a stupid little slut wouldn't understand. I'll lay it out for you. Nicolo Benenati murdered my uncle and the Corleonesi he worked with. Slit their throats like they were lake trout. My uncle Tommaso was pure poison—he used to put his cigarettes out on me if I didn't roll 'em right. He'd killed more than twenty men, here and in the Old Country. Made no difference in the end, though, did it? Fuck Nicolo, that cold-blooded animal. But there had to be consequences, so the Clutch Hand ordered Papa Benenati snuffed."

"Who carried out that order?"

"Fuck me—everyone's saying it was somebody else. Even if I knew, I'd never tell. It should end there, Alice. But it isn't going to, not if Nicolo has his way. It'll be a madhouse. Blood feuds, stilettos in the dark, riots."

"Those are your specialty, not his."

"He's gone crazy, I tell you, the wiry piece of shit. *Chi troppo vuole nulla stringe.*"*

My new employment, not to mention grief for my friend, made me bold. "Why should I listen to a pack of *scurmi fituzzi*?"†

Dario yanked me into his hot, sour breath. My toes left the stones and my head scraped up the masonry. As a child, I'd have kicked him in the cock. But as Nobody, I went limp as a fish.

"He's fucked you by now, hasn't he?" Dario murmured against my neck. "I heard Mr. Mangiapane was trying to get virgin coin for you, but that's a joke. Isn't it? Well, I don't care who's been gutting your sweet little sardine. I could have you right now, and then who are you going to call a *scurmi fituzzi*?"

"Please," I choked.

"Oh. Now you're begging for it?"

"She wants it," Vinnie agreed in his nasal whine.

"Wants it bad," Cleto parroted.

"Stop this!" I pleaded. "I'll do anything you say."

"That's better." More chuckles spilled forth from Dario. "Anything I say? I say you're going to stop him before it's too late, *topolina*."

"Stop *what*? How—"

"I called a meeting and he agreed." Dario Palma bit my earlobe, and it was all I could do to remain a rag doll. "And you'll tell him that his pathetic revolution is over. Then you'll tell him that if he

---

* Literally "He who wants too much, nothing tightens." Proverb against overreaching.

† Rotten mackerels.

refuses, I'm going to shove my cock in your *figa* so far you won't have room in your throat to scream. Now. We're off to the Murder Stable."

"No," I croaked. "God, no, please not—"

He dropped me. When I landed on the mud and brick dust, he chortled, and then I was upright again, being marched as if to my hanging.

We hadn't far to go. The Murder Stable was on East 108th Street. It was a vast livery warren, used to house the draft horses the Clutch Hand employed in his counterfeiting business and produce rackets. It housed over a dozen torture chambers. Its shackles had spikes facing inward. It had drains in the floors like an abattoir. At least sixty men had died there, in so many pieces that their ghosts rose from the stinking floor to spook the mad-eyed mares.

That's not true, though, I thought. *It's a livery where livestock are kept. And men have been held there, yes. Been beaten, yes. Been killed.*

But not today, by Christ.

We turned a corner. A poplar rustled a warning, a stray cat yowled an alarm, but we strode toward the Murder Stable as if the devil were behind us as well as ahead. Then the air stilled, and my frame went rigid.

"Merda," Dario cursed. "It took too long to find you. We're too late."

"Where are the others you invited, Dario?" Vinnie whimpered, dragging his reluctant dog.

"There ought to be others," Cleto confirmed.

*"Vai a dar via il culo!"** Dario snapped.

I reached the entrance. The Murder Stable was as big as a fortress, a hulking island of corrugated metal. Two enormous sheet metal doors gaped open. A broken padlock hung from one of them,

* Literally "Go sell your arse," or go to hell.

and it produced a dry-bones rattle in the gathering dusk. I waited. Hardly breathing.

Then a figure pushed through the darkness like a knife through black cloth, and the men behind me yelled in various tongues, English and Italian and the universal language of terror, and lit out for tamer streets.

Nicolo stood before me, dropping a horse's sawed-off head wearily to the packed earth. His dirty face was lined with tear tracks, and his proud nose looked to have been knocked half off his hatchet-like face.

"Where did those sons of bitches run to? I have something of Morello's to show them!" he snarled. Then his expression changed. "Alicia. It's you."

He walked up to me slowly, and now I could see better. Too much. See the lake of red he'd been wading through as he made tracks as clear as footprints in the sand.

"Did they threaten you?" he asked. It was almost tender.

It wasn't tender—it was mad.

He took my face in his trembling hands, and they were sticky, already crusting. "They'll never threaten you again, *topolina*. They won't threaten any of us."

I remember wondering, as his lips met mine for the first time, whether I was more terrified of a man who would cut a horse's head off because he wanted to, or who would cut a horse's head off despite the fact that the action went against every particle of who he was.

· *Thirteen* ·

NOW

Foreigners and niggers will lower the standard of our community morals, as has been done in those mongrelized communities where the color line is not drawn.

—WILLIAM H. GREEN, "Let's Keep Grant's Pass a White Man's Town," *Southern Oregon Spokesman*, Grant's Pass, Oregon, May 24, 1924

Returning to my room to make ready for the night's reconnaissance, thinking *No lipstick, rouge though, and dancing shoes,* I remember another individual worrying a hole in her head: Miss Christina. Her room is between mine and Blossom's, I know, because once I saw her stoop for a paper scrap edged under her door. Maybe a bill or a request to serve corned beef hash or a torrid love poem.

Can you so much as watch a body pick up litter without wild imaginings?

When I knock, I hardly expect an answer. But the door swings, imperfectly closed, and reveals the tiny chef hunched over on the sofa with another message. She slides it in the pocket of her plain brown dress.

"I'm dreadfully sorry, that wasn't a bit intentional!" I exclaim. "I only meant to—"

"It's all right." Miss Christina's voice is clotted with sorrow. "Come on in, I got a few minutes. The waiters been serving leftover meat loaf sandwiches all afternoon, anyhow. I just needed to—to feel near him."

That's when I remember Blossom saying Davy Lee lived here.

Lives here. Drawing a severe red line through the past tense, I tap a cross on my thigh.

Now I've stepped inside, I witness the fortress of Max's devising where Davy sleeps and feel a terribly warm ache. The bottom half, which boasts an arched entrance, is composed of slender logs standing maybe three feet high. But the top half is crenellated planks, a toy castle, with a neatly swaddled mattress tucked against the back wall and a hole the perfect size for a boy to hoist himself through connecting the levels.

I shake my head. "That right there is the real jazz. I'd have given up hard cider to lay me down in a wooden palace when I was a squirt. And where I grew up, hard cider was required for a cheerful outlook."

"Davy loves it, sure enough." Miss Christina sits, crushing her hands together. "Seeing that fortress empty—it's a terrible hard blow, Miss James."

I seat myself on a chintz armchair. "Any news?"

She shakes her head. "We're none of us trackers—we never grew up in the woods. It's all one to sharecropping and city folk whether we're following branches busted off by a boy or a buck. I been praying to the good Lord some of them volunteers from the South who Max roped in can help us."

"It's awful," I commiserate.

Her eyes are stitched with scarlet needlework that matches the red kerchief she's tied over her hair again. "I keep picturing him. Just a cub, when he first spied that there castle and grinned fit to bust himself open. I done cried all night while I was searching, Miss James. Only way I can look at that bed with a dry cheek is there's nothing left to water it. Now, what's your business?"

"I went to see the Chief of Police."

"Tom Vaughan?" Miss Christina contemplates her interlocking fingers as if they hold some swell miracles. "You consult Blossom over that play?"

"Naturally."

"How's she see it?"

"Long odds. Anyway, it was Jenny's notion. He's pledged to assist."

"Hmm." Miss Christina sighs heavily. "Jenny sure looks up to his missus."

"I'd the pleasure of meeting Mrs. Vaughan at her home—last time I lamped passion like that was in an opera house."

"Davy Lee thinks she painted the sky blue. I like her plenty enough myself—there's no harm in her, mind. Just too much spirit to keep a lid on sometimes."

"That describes her to the veriest *T.* I've never met anyone like her."

She bites her lip. "Maybe she ended up funny coming from the raw land and then the Starr family turning timber wealthy sudden like, but then again maybe she was born feisty. Saw her leaving her church once after the Negro congregation let out. Skies opened up. White and black alike wearing church hats, and did she *laugh.* After that, a wetting from the Almighty didn't seem like such a fuss to me."

"Then you were born here too?"

"Oh, no, ma'am." Miss Christina folds her mouth like she's

sealing an envelope. "No, I got to know Miss Starr on account of her volunteering for every soup kitchen in Portland. Woman's lobster bisque is a dream."

"It couldn't possibly hold a candle to your red fish stew. Supposing she was raised *au naturel*, though, I'm curious—how does she come to be educated enough to teach Weekly Betterment?"

Miss Christina must be relieved at my readiness to switch topics, because the flattery goes over like a lead balloon. "Word is she went away to a girls' school years back after her family struck it rich, a real genuine college. People sure talked. But it worked out just fine. I was one of the chefs when Evelina Starr married Tom Vaughan, and that there was a wedding to beat the band. She's nicely settled now, I hope."

"Can a tempest ever really settle?"

"I'm not the one to say." Standing, the chef twists her back. "Hungry, Miss James? Clam fritters or baked veal in tomato sauce tonight."

"Miss Christina, I don't know that it'll produce any cheer, but Blossom said she was sure that Davy was alive. That she could . . . sense it somehow."

The tiny woman regards me with fathomless wells of loss in her eyes.

"Do you pay mind to that sort of thing?" she asks numbly.

"Oh, as the sun rises," I assure her with hand over heart.

"Well, I wish I did, Miss James. And I'll do my best to try. 'Cause the dearest boy in the world is out there, and if it helps him come on home to us? Hell, I'll believe that Blossom Fontaine can fly."

Disheartened, I exit. A maid passes me in the hall, slender and neat, whose lashes flicker in my direction before she sails away to dust pillowcases and tuck in soaps. Shutting myself in my room, I regard the old girl in the mirror. The corpus appears currently fraught with worry, not to mention battered by sentiment and injury and change.

This will never do.

Not for tonight. I need Nobody the infiltrator, Nobody the mannequin. Flipping my hands, I stretch the interlocking fingers.

And just as Blossom did, I open my cosmetics case and set to work becoming someone else.

We can't see the moon sleeping high above the charcoal-sketched Portland streets. But her cloud-spun quilt glows diffusely. The air below is clear and full of gentle forest lullabies, and the garlands of electric lights hanging like holiday draperies along the avenues are beginning to thin. Several blocks with them, then one without. Two without, then two strung with glass fairy globes.

Three without, the next by contrast shining like the deck of a yacht.

"Oh, I see. We're going to proverbial Brooklyn," I mention.

Blossom laughs, the full-throated one, which makes me smile.

"Well." She clears her throat, surprised at her own mirth. "My regular place of work isn't *precisely* a conventional cabaret—actually, it's the maddest I've yet warbled in, and for a San Francisco girl, you'll agree that's saying something."

"It's the whole alphabet."

"What's the oddest black market affair you've ever graced with your presence in New York?"

Torso twinging, I reflect upon the Maritime Supper Club in the glimmering lap of the East River, sipping a champagne cocktail as a fellow with waxed mustaches ranted about an ambushed rum delivery. He was dead two days later. I remember sporting tails and trousers in the basement-level Cave of the Fallen Angels, smoking a cigarette as a bruiser bragged about having cut off the hand of one of Mr. Salvatici's faro dealers. He didn't last the night.

"The Club Abbey," I reply, citing a frolic with Sadie. "It was in a burned-out church with a bar set up where the pulpit had stood. Literally divine."

We reach the waterfront, businesses giving way to greasy spoons and fading billboards for Kellogg's and Kodak. Both of us are losing the pep in our kick step. I'm about to suggest taking a cab and damn the expense when I remind myself that it's hard enough for a Negro waving a ten-dollar bill to get one in Harlem.

"Here we are," Blossom announces.

"An empty dock?" I question, baffled.

"Oh, honey, it's hardly *empty*."

As we step carefully down pine planks in our dancing shoes, I realize the quay is populated with rowboats—half a dozen of them, helmed by men with nostrils illuminated by their cigars. The nearest slaps gloved hands against his knees, rising.

"Miss Fontaine!" he calls. "Give me the honor tonight—the missus is in a right snit and my bed's been cold these four days running."

"I fear I can do nothing about the temperature of your linens, but if you *promise* not to splash on my gown this time, I shall leap into your dinghy like a fresh-caught trout," she answers.

I laugh, disbelieving. "What's this, then, you perform in a lighthouse?"

"Alice, that would be *patently* absurd. I perform on a sawdust barge."

"Not in that getup! Don't fib, it'll rot your teeth."

Humming, she slides our gloved hands together, and the ferryman helps us into the craft. It shudders happily, waves lapping. Blossom doesn't let go of me when we seat ourselves, and I don't want her to. She exchanges friendly insults with her escort about the effects of Willamette water on tulle as his boat lurches away from the splintering dock. I ought to be horridly fixated on the memory of other waterfront excursions, but instead I note that my companion is shivering as widening wounds in the cloud cover reveal gashes of stars, and hunch closer to her.

"If you might do me the honor of keeping your lips buttoned regarding the exact goings-on at the Rose's Thorn, I'd be *ever* so grateful." She squeezes my hand. "Maximilian is a hoot and a half and well in my inner circle and therefore has come out to watch me at the lung work. The rest suppose I ply my ditties at chophouses, sit in with local ragtime acts. I *do*, of course. But *this* is my source of scratch, and I require an exquisitely steady amount. You'll get nothing but kicks from it, but I'd be the one getting the kicks if the entire Paragon knew where I worked, you take my meaning."

"But that's absurd—they run a speakeasy in the basement."

Blossom shrugs. "The sensibilities within our little family differ. Some know the power of music to gladden the spirit, see Prohibition for the two-faced profiteering scam it is, and even believe in the revered tradition of placing a bet and losing your money. Well and good. Those selfsame individuals are *perfectly* capable of considering bawdy houses hell pits, and the Rose's Thorn does a brisk trade in bodily fluids even if *I* don't work on the second floor."

"Who has your back to the wall?"

"My altogether lovely Mavereen Meader approves of many things. She does *not* approve of others. Look."

She directs my attention to a cluster of lights. The spray and distance combined render them a blur, but we waltz our way across the waves, and soon I see it with exquisite clarity: a sawdust barge.

"Holy Lord, you were serious!" I exclaim. "It's just too grand for words."

"I thought you'd like it." She smiles. "After all, you're *almost* as sick a person as I am."

Squatting in the waters before us, the sawdust barge blazes as brightly as a carnival. On it hunkers a two-story structure strongly resembling the upper half of a paddlewheel cruiser. A few silhouettes lean against the railings, but the lights suggest that the interior of the Rose's Thorn is better populated. With cooks and slingers of firewater, I surmise. Porters sweeping up cigarettes and lost bugle beads. Whores, eyes thick with sleep and crusted mascara, choosing which negligee to wear after they've risen from bed. It's barely eight, though it's considerably darker than Harlem will ever be. We're early so that Blossom can prepare.

"If liking this is sickness, may I never recover," I pledge.

"Sisters in disease, then."

"It's ridiculous, though."

"I *know*. Swear not to say anything unless it's to Max?"

"I'd as soon shave my teeth, I assure you."

When we pull up to the scow, the boatman hands first Blossom and then me up a few broad steps, and we've arrived.

"Best to your wife, and I suggest you pick up a vial of the jasmine scent at the C. Gee Wo Chinese Medicine Company on First Street," Blossom advises him.

"Nah. The way to my old lady's heart is through the butcher shop," he calls as he throws off the line.

"Well, make the ensuing conjugal bliss worth her while, then!" Blossom laughs.

"I always do, Miss Fontaine! Same offer stands for you, supposing you ever find yourself in a dry spell!"

"That would require a stint in Africa," I mutter, amused.

"Yes, he is *decidedly* not my type," she agrees, winking as she turns to enter the double-wide doors.

I follow, curious. Whether she senses that I already know who her type is, that I've found one of her hidden puzzle pieces and pocketed it for safekeeping.

"Welcome to the Rose's Thorn, Alice James," Blossom announces. "The very *finest* pit of iniquity in Portland."

"I'm honored."

"Don't be."

I toss her a smile. We stand on blinding poppy-red carpeting in a very long room lit by four giant chandeliers. The curtains are poison emerald, the effect absurdly Christmas-like. A colored waiter tying his apron hustles past, and the cluster of equally dark musicians on the raised dais pluck out splatters of notes. Between us and the stage are first a wide array of gambling tables where sharps lick their thumbs as they count lucre, then a fan of dining round tops, and finally—polish the skirts and hem the loafers—a simply gorgeous dance floor.

"What a night we have in store! I've heard rumor that the mayor of Vancouver may be in attendance. Take your coats, Miss Fontaine?"

We turn to discover an awfully spherical fellow rubbing white-gloved paws. He's positively nailing the dandy act, violet cravat and a monocle, no less, because why pay the dairyman when you can buy the whole cow. Beneath a set of mustaches that would put a midflight condor to shame, he beams like a sunrise at us.

"May I present Miss Alice James." Blossom shrugs off her cloak, revealing a vivid orange velvet stunner with rectangles of rhinestones bordering the severely straight waist and neckline. "*Don't* corrupt her, Lucius, I'm quite gone on her as she is."

The maître d', for so he must be if the world is as round as he is, dangles his lips over my hand. "Lucius Grint, Miss James, and entirely enchanted to make the acquaintance of any companion of the ravishing Miss Fontaine."

"Oh, I . . . mutual, I'm sure."

Slipping off my coat, I imagine smiling without actually pulling the trigger, ducking my head shyly. I reveal a beige frock done in draping chiffon scallops with tiny silver beads. It's not the least noticeable, especially with my coloring; I might as well have worn dust. The Nobody I am this evening is a wallflower who thinks lipstick makes her look pasty, throws lavish parties for her engaged friends to hide the fact she hates them, ends up worshipping the tile after four champagnes. That sort.

Blossom tugs me, a giraffe leading a gazelle to safety. "I had no *idea*! Your journalistically inclined suffragette was divine, but who on earth is *this*?"

"I told you at the hotel. An Alice who suits."

"Even your gait is different. It's half-fashionable, half-awkward, and *entirely* perfect."

"Just wait till you see my lady daredevil pilot. She's to die for."

The hall we enter is papered in garish toile and smells of river rot. But Blossom's dressing room, when the lights ignite, is charming. A merry menagerie of scarves tossed hither and thither, golden tassels draped over the makeup mirror, and an enormous birdcage containing what appears to be a dozen feather boas. I watch as Blossom pours a set of drinks, kicks hers down the gullet neatly, and hands me the second.

This woman, when it comes to the dingbat juice, is efficiency personified.

"A thousand apologies for abandoning you, but watching me warm up is neither amusing nor advisable." Opening the birdcage, she selects a silver boa and tosses it about her shoulders as she leaves me. "You may do absolutely anything you like in the interim save finishing the scotch."

Soon, I can hear the strains of the band, notes wafting like streamers in the motionless air. I'm excited to see her perform live, haven't been this jazzed over a concert since the Tobacco Club. Blossom said I could make free with the scotch within reason, so I polish off my glass and head for her dressing table.

I have no intention of snooping whatsoever.

It is in fact the furthest thing from my mind. Even though gravity is a constant force, as constant as my deviousness even, avalanches are still random events.

When I pour another drink, a few drips fall on Blossom's vanity, and I wince, because that is alcohol abuse. Fearful it'll run onto the silk skirt, I cast about for a kerchief that doesn't seem to be made of dragonfly wing or fairy dust. She's messy enough to toss accessories about, but too professional to build up any significant layer of sponges or false eyelashes, and there aren't any hand towels in sight.

So I dive, pull the curtain aside, and begin opening drawers.

Here's some old curling tongs. Here's tweezers, a kohl pencil sharpener, a small stack of letters. I don't open the letters, wouldn't dream of it, though I note that the topmost is from her friend Evelina Vaughan, and I think how sweet it is that they correspond as well as call on each other. Here's a pot of facial cream.

Here's a medical pamphlet, apparently excerpted from a larger book by a local physician.

The dressing chamber constricts. It seemed airy enough seconds ago despite the must, and now it's stifling. My hands are steady as I reach for the brochure. But that's only because my life is a veritable Sears Roebuck catalog of ghastly events.

"Christ," I whisper as I read *A Guideline to the Dietary Concerns of Cancer Patients* by Eli Grellet Jones.

> *The question is often asked by a cancer patient, "Doctor, what shall I eat?" Some of our doctors, who have never tired of theorizing about the cause of cancer, have claimed that certain kinds of food caused cancer. For many years pork was supposed to cause this disease. Now it is a well-known fact that the Jews never eat pork; yet I have seen cases of cancer among that class*

of people. . . . It has been claimed that tomatoes cause cancer. . . . In New Jersey tomatoes are eaten in all ways the year round; yet there are many States that have more cancer victims than New Jersey.

Finishing the brochure, I shut my eyes against its contents.

This isn't a puzzle piece I'm meant to know.

And yet. No one ought to face an early grave all by their lonesome.

I'm breathing too hard when I realize I still need something to clean Blossom's counter. My next handle tug unsurprisingly reveals a framed portrait of Davy Lee. He's a few years younger than the vanished boy, dressed in a sailor suit and smirking proudly. The painted backdrop is an ocean horizon with a beautifully pastel-colored city resting on a number of hills. A city that seems familiar, even though I'm certain I've never set peepers on it. Davy's younger face is thinner—so his current baby pudge indicates he's about to shoot up like a New York hotel. Supposing he's allowed, that is, which is positively breaking the hearts of all and sundry.

"Finally," I breathe as I reveal a small face towel.

Twenty minutes that feel like the oceans must have surely swallowed the Alps pass. When Blossom returns, eggplant cheekbones glistening with sweat, I'm as much myself again as Nobody ever is.

"Well, the cords have been warmed," she sighs. "Have you left any scotch? Please, Alice, for humanity, say that a drop remains."

"Plenty of them. How are you feeling?"

"Oh, as well as necessary and not a *bit* more. One doesn't like to overdo that sort of thing."

She powders her nose and fixes a stray hair or two and I can't help it. I barely know the woman. But I've no one else left—so maybe that's the reason my throat works and I tame the spasm with the last of the tipple in my glass.

When we head into the hall, Blossom vanishes backstage. The

place is rapidly filling up with all manner of types. I'm careful to look half-bored and half-expectant. Not someone who requires any social cheering. Swishing a gauzy handful of my muted dress, I find a lone armchair between the gaming tables and the dining room as the band takes their places. It's a small combo—piano, bass, drum kit, saxophone. The scarlet curtain parts to reveal my friend in the footlights. Rhinestones aglitter, wrists loose, coral dress glowing brushfire bright.

Blossom's hip is cocked like a gun. She nods to the gentlemen and I recognize the song almost at once. It suits her, can't help but suit her—"Someday Sweetheart" by John and Reb Spikes.

Someday, sweetheart,
You may be sorry
For what you've done to my poor heart;
And you may regret
Those vows that you've broken,
And the things you did to me
That made us drift apart.

Blossom's singing voice is second soprano. It's nothing like her carefully cultivated speech—here are purrs, growls, slides, floating moments when the only word I can think of is *songbird.* I've had enough tutoring to know where the bread is buttered, musically speaking, and my friend is slathering on the entire churn. I'm about to sally forth for a lap around the periphery when a fellow harrumphs in my ear and I make sure to jump subtly.

"Apologies, Miss James. As Miss Fontaine's special friend, I wanted to be certain you were comfortable. Compliments of the Rose's Thorn!"

Lucius Grint proffers a glass of the bubble goods and I blink.

"Gosh, that's sweet. Thanks ever so."

"The pleasure is mine." His moonlike face changes as he glances back at the entrance. "If you will excuse me? Don't hesitate to call if I can be of the slightest assistance."

I use the upward motion of raising my glass to follow his line of vision and very nearly freeze.

Officer Overton has changed out of his police duds. He's in a light trench open over a slick suit, peering across the room at the performers. At my new friend Blossom.

· *Fourteen* ·

. . . A party of men started in pursuit of the fiend and instituted a search that proved successful this morning. . . . He groveled in the dust, and clasped the knees of his captors crying with all his might for them not to hang him. But the hand of justice had secured too strong a grip on the miscreant and all the pleading in the world would not have saved him from the death he so thoroughly deserved.

—"REGARDING A MOB LYNCHING IN COOS BAY,"
Oregon Journal, Portland, Oregon, September 18, 1902

The first order of business is to vamoose, but one can't decamp from a sawdust barge by slipping out the back. Overton is probably here merely to shake the trees for ripe plums. But Max isn't around to provide muscle, and where Blossom is concerned, the policeman has considerably more on his mind than his hat. Meanwhile, I'm the wrong Nobody. It wouldn't be impossible to play off Alice James the journalist exploring the local habitat. But my hair is unmistakably bobbed—I've put it into a messy halo of fat curls. The hapless debutante's version of glamour, charming but with all the sophistication of a daisy chain.

Draining the champagne, I drift toward the dance floor where three likely looking young swains lean against a railing. I tilt my head just so as one fellow's eyes sweep the room, pretending to blush over catching his gaze.

See me, young fellow, the constabulary has arrived and I've need of your strong arms.

"Say there, stranger!" he calls out. "You look in need of company."

"Oh! Did I—I don't mean to interrupt. Sorry, I'm Alice."

He grins. His chin is dreadfully weak, but his green eyes are kind. "And I'm Gregory, and I've never found a partner this early. Have I got that right?"

"Beg pardon?"

"I mean, would you care to dance?"

"Oh! I'd like that awfully much. You're sure I'm not intruding?"

"Just what is it you figure jazz bands are for, Alice?" But he smiles, and holds a hand out, and we're off to the races.

Just try seeing me while I'm half tucked into a chappie's neck, you unrepentant bastard.

"So what brought you here?" Gregory's voice in my ear is like a faraway radio.

"Um, actually I've an ever-so-slight acquaintance with the singer."

When I lift my jaw, Gregory's has dropped perceptibly. "With Blossom Fontaine?"

"That's right. I must say, she's a marvelous performer, I just never dreamed!"

He whistles. "No kidding. I first saw her in San Francisco, if you can buy that, having dinner with my old man at the Palace Hotel. Never forgot her. I mean, *the* Blossom Fontaine. You couldn't really, could you?"

"Goodness! I should say not." I spin as he leads me. "What was she like back then?"

"The same, but with French songs. The frog stuff doesn't play as well here."

"*Quelque* shame."

"You betcha. A girl like that had to have a powerful reason for quitting San Francisco for this place. Anyway, you can hear it, can't you?"

"Hear what?"

"Why, that she misses something."

I can, I realize as Blossom casts out a cobalt beam of melancholy sound, and I remember what she told me about her pilgrimage.

My true love left. My heart was broken. And what in the wide world was I to do?

Jenny Kiona, I muse, is destined to be a gramophone playing a cracked love song. There will be hisses and scratches aplenty.

Then another notion occurs, and at first I think little enough of it, watch as it whisks by like a bird glimpsed through tall trees. Blossom clearly toured at some point. And she's been to France, all the best black artists have. Meanwhile, she told me she plied the melody trade at the Pied Piper lounge at the Palace Hotel, and that after love exiled her, she took up with her fantastically cantankerous uncle Pendleton. The columns add up.

Still. Something niggles at the grey matter.

"When was it you saw her?" I ask, gently squeezing.

Gregory presses back, friendly. "Gosh. Must have been nineteen eleven maybe? At least ten years ago for sure. Back when I was a kiddo, well before the War."

"Do you know how long she played the Palace Hotel?"

"Nope, but she was real popular. Giant posters, marquee, the works. She really lit up the room."

It takes another few turns on the waxed hardwood, but then it comes to me.

Davy's age. He's six. That is, if he's still alive, as I so fervently hope.

If Blossom left San Francisco, California, for Portland, Oregon, in nineteen fifteen, and it's nineteen twenty-one, why was she in Seattle, Washington, discovering a baby in the lee of a trash bin?

The song ends. I brush a curl from my brow, laugh absently. There's an obvious answer here—but the obvious answer doesn't exactly send a knife through the mustard.

So Blossom Fontaine could have gotten storked by a white suitor, hoisted mainsail, and convalesced in a neutral city, bringing her child back to the Paragon as a foundling. Davy and Blossom don't strongly resemble each other, but that's no proof where mixed races are concerned, and other details even support the theory: Dr. Pendleton could know she'd had a mixed kid out of holy et cetera, and be sore over raising the sprout in his hotel. Then again, despite Davy's harrowing absence, she's been up there for half an hour, serenading for her supper. Not terribly motherly. And I'm not stupid enough to suppose that the obvious answer is always the right one, especially in light of *he isn't my type, honey.* So much is certain: Blossom is clearly dragging her guts around behind her, hollowed out from wanting Davy back.

Because she's his mum? Maybe. Because she found a stray in Seattle? Equally possible. Is she hiding something?

As sure as it's fixing to rain this week.

"Hmm?" I say when I realize I've drifted. "Oh, I . . . came over a bit dizzy. I haven't danced in simply ages."

"You're all right, though?" Gregory asks, frowning.

"Peachy. Didn't mean to alarm."

"Well then, may I buy you a drink? If you're not feeling well, they have lemonade here, or if you're *really* not feeling well, just add a splash of gin, am I right?"

Despite the offense visited on his face by his lack of chin, I like

Gregory. But when my eyes follow his to the bar, I see that Mr. Lucius Grint stands before a seated Officer Overton. The policeman samples a rocks glass, staring at Blossom as if he's about to check the teeth on the mare he's buying. Mr. Grint's hands are spreading as dramatically as his mustaches in supplication.

"Excuse me, but I—I have to congratulate Blossom, that last number was just dandy as anything, and I'll find you when I feel a bit better?"

"Sure, kiddo. Tell her she's the jewel of the West Coast."

I'm at the edge of the stage in under ten seconds. When Blossom glances down to adjust her microphone, she spies me, because I mean her to, and I angle my head.

"Company," I mouth.

Blossom's inky eyes slit to the bar. If she were less self-possessed, she'd arch like a cat hissing.

"The set has been . . . oh, just wonderful, really wonderful," I gush aloud. "Thank you for bringing me. I'm awfully glad you did."

"I'm glad I did too, honey," she answers smoothly, pulling loose fingertips along her forearm. "There's seven songs to go in this set. You get the *most* fun you can out of them, you hear?"

Blossom turns her back, gesturing lazily to her band. A smile tugs at my lips.

Seven songs, eh? Marching orders.

Officer Overton and Mr. Grint are still locked in a conversation that's beginning to look dreadfully taxing to the ringmaster of the Rose's Thorn. But with Overton facing out from the bar that way, eavesdropping is too risky. Meanwhile, seven songs will take at least half an hour.

And there's more than one way of having fun, as Blossom so aptly put it.

I travel the length of the entertainment hall pretending to scan for a particular friend. Silent as a moth's wing, I enter the vestibule where the coats are hung and open my beaded bag, searching. Mr. Grint is occupied. So much the better—it's easier to use this racket on coat-check girls. They're dreadfully sweet. They should come with toothache warnings.

"Can I help you, miss?" says an affable female voice around thirty seconds later.

I'm rooting through my bag like a pig in a pen. "Oh, thank you. I don't . . . I'm such a tiresome little fool. This is positively the worst day of my life."

"Oh, no. What can I do?"

Sniffling audibly, I glance up. She's young, with auburn curls and an open face, and no ring on her left hand. She's perfection.

"I get headaches, you see." Dropping the arm that holds my reticule, I press the other wrist between my eyes. "Beastly ones. And like an idiot, I left home without . . . well, without anything practical. Just my money and my keys and powder. So now I'll have to go home, and I was to meet a fellow here, and now . . . God, I'm sorry. . . . Now I've ruined everything."

"Not yet, you haven't! One of the girls upstairs might have something."

"Do you really think so? I can pay for it. For anything—laudanum or, or maybe a headache powder? I'd be simply the most grateful girl in history."

"Just wait right here."

I intend to.

The instant she's gone, I slide into a forest of coats. Fox furs, woolen overcoats, cape-backed numbers. There may well be another girl working for tips, so I haven't long. But I don't need long. My fingers skip over an ermine shoulder wrap, a duster, a tweed, and *then.*

Straight flush, ace high, and the casino erupts in applause.

There isn't much light in here, but it's definitely Officer Overton's trench coat. The lining tells me that he smoked a cigar on the way here and the stitching and fabric inform me that this isn't some cut-rate factory copy of a gentleman's garment, it's the straight goods. Not more than two years old. So Overton greeted Prohibition's arrival as doth the wandering tribes manna from heaven.

I'd be annoyed about that, but hypocrisy makes me itchy. I move onto the outer pockets: matches, keys, and a few odd coins in the left. Two crumpled receipts for laundering in the right. I'm hemorrhaging time, seconds spilling through my fingers onto the worn carpeting, but then I spear my hand inside the garment, fumbling for the inner pockets, and on the left side, hey presto.

A gun.

That's not part of the uniform for police. But it's all the rage for feds, bootleggers, and the coppers who pay their bills skimming off hard-earned profits from fermented refreshments. It's a Smith & Wesson M&P .38 caliber Special. I sniff the barrel, pop open the cylinder. Clean. Well-oiled. Six virgin bullets.

Fast as fox-trotting, I plunge my hand into the last pocket, which is the right inner. A piece of paper. It's folded in quarters, edges soft as if they've been much handled.

When I open it, I fight the urge to tear it in awfully minute pieces.

Not that the contents surprise me. It's a flyer for a concert here in Portland, dated some years previous. Standing in full-feathered regalia, with her face flung back and her arm outstretched as if she's plucking a star from the sky, is an illustration of Blossom Fontaine, the headliner.

Voices. I start to duck out—but there isn't time. Replacing the revolver, I take two long strides toward a hanger on the opposite wall and snatch my salvation from it, turning to face the music.

"Whatever are you doing in there?" the coat-check sweetheart demands. "Well, never mind, now I've caught you! Nasty trick, sending me off while you pickpocket our—"

"No!" Aghast, I clutch the coat to my bosom. "This is my own coat! I was just terribly desperate once you'd gone, and I wanted to check my pockets. And now I've gone and made you angry—see here's the ticket—oh, I could just kick myself down the stairs, I—"

"All right, all right." She sighs. "Here, I scared up morphine tablets. She wants two bits for them."

I pay four instead and stage a strategic retreat. When I reach the bar, carefully distant from the long arm of the law, I request more of the bubbly goods and take the morphine, because my stitches really are starting to buck the reins.

Taking a deep breath, I look about me.

Ruby-toned light, painting the thickening crowds. *Clinking* of glasses, chattering of socialites, *snap-clack* of gambling chips, the intoxicating *whirr* of the roulette wheel. Blossom at the forefront. Arms wide now, making an ebony cross of herself, telling the rest of us what shattered hopes sound like.

Smile the while you kiss me sad adieu
When the clouds roll by I'll come to you . . .

"May I beg a word, Miss James?"

Since I'm a positive ninny of a Nobody this evening, I startle again, nearly dropping the champagne. Lucius Grint deftly cups my hand. His mustaches twitch like the antennae of a grasshopper, and you could pluck out "Dixie" on his nerves.

"Oh, Mr. Grint!" I make a few pathetically humorous gestures at the flute, ordering it to *stay*. "Isn't Blossom just an absolute peach of a singer?"

"Indeed." He coughs, glancing behind. "She is a highly valued adornment here at the Rose's Thorn, the very jewel in our diadem, and I wonder if I might ask you for a small favor, purely in her own interests? I wonder whether, with my humble apologies, you might await Miss Fontaine in her dressing room." Mr. Grint's snakes of hair writhe in a pond of pomade and sweat. "And then following her present set, escort her away. With great haste."

Gaping at him, I finish my drink with a loud *glug*. "Golly. Sure. But why—"

"Nothing to worry about, Miss James!" he exclaims with a jaw-cracking smile. "An acquaintance of hers arrived, a rather . . . unsavory one. Run along now—you've only around ten minutes to await her. I'll make it up to you in high style on the next occasion you grace us with your presence. If you experience the smallest hint of discomfort on your way out, call for me. At *once*."

No further prodding is necessary; I make tracks.

When I barricade myself in Blossom's dressing room, I realize there's a last precaution to take before we pull any vanishing acts—I'd best partially switch Nobodies. I clutch a filmy grey silk scarf and tuck most of my curls away so the length isn't visible, and I powder over the rouge I'm wearing. I'm very nearly Nobody the sober-faced journalist again when the door opens.

"All through?" I ask.

"I don't think so, Miss James. Though I must say it's a pleasurable surprise to see you here. A very pleasurable surprise."

Instantly, I've whirled with my hands raised. Defensive, indignant, staring down Officer Overton in his pricey suit as he sends the door slamming shut with a decisive *bang*.

"Whatever are you doing in a lady's dressing room, sir?" This Nobody's voice comes out shaky with outrage.

"I think we can safely exempt a Negress who sings degenerate music for her living from the title of 'lady.'"

"Splitting hairs doesn't become a man of the world, Officer."

Overton's dark hair is carefully slicked, his darker eyes

unreadable beneath. He lifts a dainty porcelain figure of a cat resembling Medea. "So this is Miss Fontaine's private sanctuary, is it? I suppose I always expected bigger. She being such a notable performer."

"Surely you don't take an interest in notable colored performers?"

He smiles, recognizing mockery. "Well, I wanted to see her as soon as her set was finished, discuss a few things, but this is quite the unexpected happenstance. I supposed when working on your precious article, you'd stay put, Miss James. You and your typewriter and all those Negroes to fraternize with. Ought to be heaven for a lady journalist who wants to get her hands dirty. But it seems you want to get them even dirtier."

Overton approaches me. He bends, plucks a piece of my beaded frock's skirt and examines the curves of the shells. It's only an excuse to fill my nose with the musk behind his ears and my eyes with the few black hairs that escaped being razored from his whipcord neck.

"I was raised in a Protestant orphanage—with an excellent private education, a thorough knowledge of Holy Scripture, and nothing more other than the uniform on my back," I spit quietly. "I've met men like you. And you can't frighten all of us. In fact, some women find your sort unbearably dull."

He rises with a positively obsidian glare, sharp jaw twitching.

If I can take your mind off Blossom, then hip, hip, hurrah.

"Dull? Now, that's mighty interesting. Dull, you find me?" he hisses.

"As paint."

"In that case, since it's sensation you're after, sensation you'll have—I'll show you just the sort of establishment that darkie slut has landed you in."

Nobody the bluestocking would be frightened, but she'd kick

up a powerful fuss. So I do. Even though it paints my arm in spreading purple watercolors as he hauls me out of the dressing room. Even though I know better, understand that this will stoke his coals. Even though grabbing the railing after he half drags me into a hidden staircase behind a red velvet curtain only serves to bash my shins against the steep steps.

"Shut up, you useless bitch." Overton lets go for long enough to slap me, sending my jaw clanging, before yanking me up again like a child about to be switched. "You want to see where the oh so artistic, so *very* artistic, Blossom Fontaine works? That's fine. Put this in your article—your harpy suffragette friends can read your titillating coon exposé while they frig themselves alone in their pitiful tenements."

If the carnival ride gets any more thrilling, this Nobody is going to shriek her goddamn head off her neck.

Just about now, a weapon about the undercarriage would come in handy—but I never carry one. The cutthroats engaged gunning against Mr. Salvatici hardly ever paid Nobody any mind, thank Christ. But on the few occasions when some goon decided I was worth searching? They ain't never found nuttin', as Harry Chipchase would have said, and I'd slink off and live to write their proverbial obituaries.

But Officer Overton is proving to be Mr. Mangiapane. He is Dario Palma. He likes to hurt people. He is the worst blue button I've ever encountered, and his kind don't bore me.

They liquefy my guts so thoroughly, they made Alice disappear.

As we crest the top of the stairs, I take in the infamous second floor. We're in a hallway papered with cabbage roses that curl away from the walls as if they haven't any awfully keen desire to stay put. Professionals of the mattress stare at us with glass-gleaming eyes—a brunette, a redhead with a daring bob, a black waif, an Oriental with her lips painted a vampirish scarlet. More behind closed doors, from whence thumping sounds emit.

Home, sweet home.

At the sight of Overton, they scatter, and he laughs in delight.

"Help!" I scream. "Someone, *please*, help—"

He claps a hand over my mouth and I can feel my teeth against his salty palm.

"Isn't this what you wanted?" he says in my ear. "Poor, sheltered girl, having to live through books for so long. When you knew you could taste the real thing. It drove you absolutely wild, didn't it?"

I thrash. He wrenches my neck, so I hear rather than see the remaining witnesses *slip-snick* their doors shut.

This lot clearly possesses the usual prostitutes' keen eye for self-preservation.

"No respectable woman would ever spend her time studying niggers, so lucky for you to have met the likes of me, isn't it?" he growls tenderly as he propels us toward a room where we can still see a sliver of lamplight shining. "Because *I know* you're no respectable woman. So I can give you *exactly* what you want."

Officer Overton isn't particularly large. But he's hard as a rope keeping a freighter tethered dockside, and as I try to bite and thrash and shout through my nose, I begin to fight not just my attacker. I'm fighting an instinct born in me a long time ago.

You're not even here, so he can't hurt you. Just be Nobody.

Nobody at all.

He throws me on the bed. The ceiling has a crack, and Portland's habitual weather beads along it like the liquid welling from a knife wound. Overton stands over me, not even bothering to shut the door, his hands are on his belt, and my vision is tunneling. There's an oil lamp here, I can smell it.

If he gets close enough, I can set him on fire.

If he gets close enough, I can kick him where it counts.

If he—

"Step away from her, Officer Overton, or there's going to be a tunnel where your nose used to live."

He turns with his pants undone, a snarl on his lips.

Blossom stands in the doorway. She's breathing hard—from running, not from fear. Her arm trembles the way a pool's surface does when a breeze passes over it. That's not from fear either, though. It's from illness and outrage and aiming the Remington over-under double-barreled derringer she's holding.

"There you are," Overton jeers. Or he attempts to. "It was never any good, you realize, pretending you didn't know your way around the second floor."

"Gracious, certainly, I have plenty of girlfriends up here who like to sit over a hot cocoa at five in the morn." Blossom's tone is as chiseled as her features. "I *am* sorry over any confusion. Now, back away from Miss James. Whatever . . . *tour* of the Rose's Thorn you were treating her to has reached its denouement. Come to that, what was this exactly? A touch of theatrics to really give her the full panorama? What a truly *remarkable* soul you are, I've *always* said so. We'll be going now."

Overton bares his teeth like a hyena. "Supposing I decide she stays? Supposing I decide you both do?"

"But I *really* don't think you will, honey," Blossom purrs. She holds her left hand out and I make my way over to it.

"You watch your sass with me or I'll burn that whole disgusting monkey house of yours to the ground," the policeman grates.

"You watch yours," she replies serenely, "or I'll blow your fucking head off. The river's still exquisitely cold this time of year, but you wouldn't care about that if we did it my way."

She's won—it crackles in the room like a thunderstorm, and I drop her hand.

"Well, in that case, you girls will want to be getting on back to the Paragon Hotel before the weather gets any worse." Overton produces a serrated smirk. "There's some swells already, hefty swells, and I'd hate to see you capsized."

"I really think you would too," Blossom murmurs.

We're almost to the threshold when Overton calls, "Oh, what's this about that half-breed kid going missing? Heard it from the chief himself we were to keep an eagle eye out."

He is, at long last, doing up his pants as he asks this. Taking his leisure about it, adjusting for comfort.

For the first time since leaving Harlem, I wish Mr. Salvatici were here.

Overton coughs, adjusts his cuffs. "I want to be the one to find him, you know. I'd take special care with him."

For a dragging moment, I think Blossom is actually going to shoot the wretch. And I'm fully ready to roll up sleeve and tip him into the waters of forgetfulness with her.

She turns instead and walks away, and I follow.

By the time we make it to the foyer, we're as drained as hourglasses. I'm about to ask someone to send for Mr. Lucius Grint when a gentle hand touches my shoulder.

"Alice?" It's Gregory, lips tightly knotted. "Are you all right?"

"Oh, Gregory, yes, I . . . there was the nastiest argument! I'm sorry to have abandoned you, and when you were so nice."

"Well, never mind, I'm a grown man, aren't I? Have you gone and changed your hair? It already looked swell, but this is nifty too. Miss Fontaine, isn't it? I'm Gregory Churchill."

"Charmed, Mr. Churchill," Blossom manages.

"An argument, huh?" He cocks a pair of elbows and we take them gratefully. "I'll have you in a boat quick as blinking."

The ferries await like patient dogs. As soon as they spy Blossom, there's a general hubbub, but she selects one with her usual aplomb and my dancing partner soon has us handed safely aboard. The fact I'll probably never see him again shouldn't cut so deep. But he's like Max, the cape-in-the-gutter-to-spare-a-lady's-shoes sort, and that makes whatever fragmented Nobody I am want to hunker down for a hot pillow-drenching session.

"Beg pardon, but I saw you in San Francisco once, Miss Fontaine. You were incredible," he says, saluting to shield his vision from the rain. "I never forgot it."

"Oh, how kind," she answers dully. "I never have either, you know."

We're safely back to the western shore, our arms tight around each other and the rain running down our cheeks like fresh tears, before we speak again.

"How did you find me?" I ask.

"Lucius said you'd be in my dressing room." She wipes the precipitation from her throat. "You weren't. My heart, I swear, it *stopped.* Overton was negotiating for me to go upstairs, you see. He does that every few months, threatens to shut the Rose's Thorn down if I don't. Lucius always wriggles out of it—the man is *terribly* nimble for a gopher. Anyhow. When I didn't find you, I knew what had happened. I can't apologize enough."

"You can't apologize once," I object firmly.

"Thank Christ for firearms. I only hope that this will deter him for good."

"If it doesn't, I'll help you. I'll be there with you," I vow.

"Not if I have anything to say about it."

"But why?"

"Because I simply *abhor* waste, Alice," she replies as she pulls herself away from me and continues up the electrically glinting slope alone.

· *Fifteen* ·

THEN

The true, authentic Mafioso almost invariably behaves modestly, speaks with restraint and similarly listens with restraint, and displays great patience; if he is offended in public he does not react at all but kills afterward.

—ANGELO VACCARO, "La mafia,"
in *Rivista d'Italia*, Rome, 1899

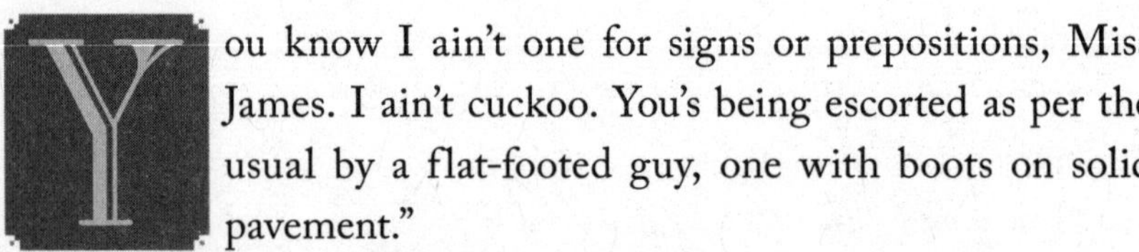

You know I ain't one for signs or prepositions, Miss James. I ain't cuckoo. You's being escorted as per the usual by a flat-footed guy, one with boots on solid pavement."

"Were you any sturdier, you would be a shoehorn," I assured Officer Harry Chipchase. "But why say you?"

"'Cause I's got a real bad feeling about this."

Harry Chipchase had a bad feeling about most aspects of every-day life. Ominous winds. Stock fluctuations. Sunrises.

But this time, I did too. Puffing my breath into my cheeks, I made a hearty show of trying to twist out of Harry Chipchase's grip. My uniformed guardian bellowed into the balmy August night, plentiful *why-I-oughtas* and *I-swear-to-Christs*, and everyone who'd been looking at us ceased, bored. Just a copper and his captive headed to the station house in 1917. And since I was dressed in plain pressed homespun and bellyaching, I probably deserved it.

"Quitcher wiggling or I'll bruise you for reals, kid," Harry complained.

"You won't either. Buck up, Harry old chum, we mustn't succumb to depression."

Harry Chipchase was on the graft, and for a dozen years loyal to Mr. Salvatici, which made him a bosom companion of your humble servant. He had a retired boxer's physique, soft padding with a hard center, and a busted-up nose forever politely suggesting that we turn left. And he was paid extravagantly—mainly to follow me or to plant evidence or better still, to make evidence go away. I found the combination of a regular stick-in-the-mud gifted with the jolliest name on the planet ever so droll.

"Do you want me to cut loose at the station house entrance, give the boys in blue a performance?" I asked. Trying to cheer Harry Chipchase never worked, which made the attempt irresistible. "You can catch me when we're done and lock me up to thundering applause."

Shrugging, Harry's body kept on in a steady line while his nose pleaded we veer off course. "They wouldn't give a mouse turd."

"Then they are Philistines."

"Well, today I ain't in no market for extra excitement."

"Right, then." I heaved a greedy breath. "Nice knowing you!"

Kneeing him in the stomach, I fled, and Harry Chipchase howled in exaggerated pursuit. When I reached the end of the block, I flung myself at a fire escape. The hot breeze tickled the banners of laundry lines, and the puffs of dragon steam from the manholes receded behind me. I hadn't far to go. Just across a rooftop, to prove to dear old Harry I wasn't being tailed by anyone other than him.

When I crested the roof, I paused, catching my breath. Stars above and streetlights below, winking lustily at one another. The great black patch of Central Park. The Hotel Arcadia visible to the south, where Mr. Salvatici forged connections. Sent swift-spiraling birds into the air.

Plotted assassinations.

Jumping down to the pavement in the rear alley, I panicked a trio of chickens and slipped through the back door of the Harlem greasy pasta joint known as Bruno's Café. The floor was littered with dinner service's onion skins and artichoke trimmings, and I didn't bother to nod at the cooks as I donned an apron.

No need. Heaving a tray of steaming silverware, I headed into the restaurant proper.

Bruno's was a big operation, with a rear eating hall and an elegant front dining room for the plush. The saloonkeeper was a strongman type, hulking shoulders balanced precariously on a slim waist.

"I'm the new girl, sir. May I have a rag to polish the flatware?"

Grunting, he nodded. When he returned with the dish towel in hand, I was clutching the bar top.

"Hey, what gives?"

"I'm so sorry, I. Forgive me. I've not eaten since . . ."

He studied my powder-pale cheeks and the violet pencil smudged artfully under my lashes. "Today's bread's not thrown out yet. Sit down at the end here and keep quiet and then tackle the silver."

Muttering humble thanks, I hunched over a plate of thick crusts and a bowl of olive oil. The house pianist finished a melancholy ragtime tune and stood, gathering up his music.

Leaving yours very truly, the bartender, and one table which had long overstayed their welcome. Or so the owner of Bruno's had formally complained to Mr. Salvatici.

Load torpedoes, and take careful aim.

"What a *porca puttana*,"* the cherubic man was bragging. "I fucked her so hard, her grandmother felt it in Florence. And she's been dead these twenty years."

A roar of cheer blasted forth from the restaurant's finest front-window table. Where to start with Sammy the Saint? Baby-faced young sport who flirted outrageously with every holy grandmother and desperate tart who crossed his path. He was also responsible for our Danny "Bones" Ricci's demise, strangled with his own father's belt. Sammy was no saint—he just had awfully long eyelashes.

"You've got a spiderweb in the corner—just there," I whispered to the bullish bartender.

Instead of answering, he poured me a glass of cheap grappa, something that a cleaning woman might be given gratis, and leaned down to polish the waxed countertop.

"You're with the Spider, then?"

I dunked a bit of bread.

"You know about them?" He jerked his neck.

"Plenty."

He lowered his voice further, scrubbing at an imaginary spill. "I need these sons of bitches out of our bar. They stopped paying three long months back. And I've only got half a case of my best Chianti left."

Well, they'll be showing up awfully seldom henceforth.

Within ten minutes, the barking of lewd conversation lulled to a buzz as they patted their bellies. Nearly through, drunk enough to be careless. One said something under his breath and his neighbor shot a look to Sammy.

"Knock over my glass," I ordered the barkeep.

---

* Pig whore.

"Why—"

"Just do it."

As the liquid arced toward my clean apron and I beat a startled retreat, I edged several barstools closer. Not having been able to hear very well previously.

"I ain't never said it was full of holes, Sammy!" one of his collaborators hissed as he refilled the wineglasses. "I said it could be, if it went all over sideways!"

*"Hai un chiodo fisso in testa,"** Sammy the Saint flashed a beatific smile and continued in Italian. "It's risking a little more than we may have previously, true. But it's also blessing our entire organization with the fruits of our courage. Is everything in readiness?"

"Oh, yes, sir. Checked and triple-checked."

"The Clutch Hand wanted five for the job, but I'm keen to hedge our bets," Sammy mused, belching. "I want at least four to arrive for the second set, camp out inside, and another three in the car."

A small chill coursed through me. *Second set* meant a music club. And if he was sending backup in a getaway car, they had more on their mind than watching girls do high kicks.

"We got it taken care of," the thug to his right promised.

"After tomorrow, it'll all be settled," another soothed.

"No, it won't nearly be settled," Sammy replied with knife points in his eyes. "But the account will be closer to even, so say all of Corleone."

Oh holy Mother Mary, I thought as my stomach swooped into my shoes.

The Clutch Hand was, in 1917, a resident of that most infamous vacation retreat, Sing Sing prison. But apparently it didn't matter a soggy bowl of cornflakes that Giuseppe Morello was eating his breakfast with a tin spoon—he was still running his Family

* "You have a nail fixed in your head," or you're stuck on an idea.

from jail. So all of Harlem was still petrified of the *cagnolazzi*. Well, nearly all. Not the Spider, who spelled *incarceration* as *opportunity*. We'd been edging in for long, elegantly mapped years now. A hijacked pallet of San Marzano tomatoes here, a docked Corleonesi-operated freighter exploding there. We weren't as strong as the Family. And we didn't go in for the shaking-down-widows-and-orphans stuff. But we were cunning as foxes, and just about as deadly when it came to snapping rats' necks.

So if the Clutch Hand wanted Sammy the Saint to act, and act tomorrow—I knew exactly whose door was getting knocked on.

Our door. At the grand opening of the Tobacco Club.

Sammy's goons returned to talk of tail and where to come by it. Sliding off the stool, I moved to where the hinged countertop let the bartender exit and rapped my knuckles. He approached instantly. I passed him a pair of greenbacks.

"Hey, hey, that was on me," he said warily.

"No, you just gave me supper. And Sammy the Saint."

"One more drink, then, to the Spider and his crew?"

I waved him off, already yanking my apron strings. This was dreadfully witless of me—terrible luck to refuse a toast like that, simply as dense as any given rock. But I had other, more important things on my mind. The old girl wanted out of the slum duds.

Because by 1917, at age twenty-one, I fancied myself head over heels in love.

Half an hour later I was at the Arcadia—and my escort, Harry Chipchase, had been happy enough over my swift exit that he actually managed half a smile. But I was no longer the respectable and impoverished Nobody at two o'clock that morning. My friend Sadie was hooking me into an ice-blue gown. Its plunging V neckline was edged in copper lace, and more of that blinding substance peeked from beneath the pooling skirt. I loved it unreasonably.

"Ow! Why do you torment me?" I lamented as Sadie yanked another hook and eye into place.

"Torment! There's gratitude. Nobody, this thing is about three miles long. So unless you're fixing to fall on your face, I've got no idea what to do with you."

"Then pour a parched sailor a drink."

"No drinks until you try that plate I brought."

"I ate every scrap of bread remaining at Bruno's."

"Mr. Salvatici's been driving you like one of his Loziers. Eat the damn waffles. And the fried chicken."

By 1917, a combination of dry wit and a head for figures had enabled Sadie to throw off the mantle of maid altogether. Mr. Salvatici primarily employed her as a secretary—and paid her awfully sweet dough too. Sadie had three necessary ingredients for success in Harlem: a heaping helping of brains, amber skin that could mean anything, and an address at the Arcadia. She used all three to live as she pleased, and we were thicker than peanut butter.

"Wait, I'm genuinely curious." I lifted the perplexing plate of grub as she finished my bow. "I'm asking: Is this breakfast?"

"No." Sadie adjusted her own outlandishly spangled costume.

"Then is it dinner?"

"No." Sadie fussed with the black feathers adorning her pretty circlet of braided hair.

"Then how do I eat it?"

"I expected too much, didn't I? When you first arrived, I had to explain what a salad fork was."

"That is just . . . outrageously unfair." Had I known I was shaking a piece of fried chicken at my friend, I sincerely hope that I would have ceased all operations along those lines. "That was years ago! I know how to speak, how to dance, I know long division, and I know how to eat!"

"Oh, good. And you don't look a bit ridiculous waving a chicken leg at me. Take a bite of it. No, *with* the waffle. God, it's like teaching a snake to play tennis."

Obeying, my eyes widened to saucers. "What on *earth*."

She giggled. "Beats just about anything, doesn't it?"

"Whence came this alchemy?"

"Bob serves it up the street at his diner, says he learned it in Philly. But some say it came from the South. Now, Alice: What time is it right now?"

"Just after two in the morning."

"And is this delicious?"

"Of course it is. I'm Italian, not dense."

"And even you being the brightest Italian on the planet isn't going to tell you whether two in the morning is dinnertime or breakfast time, now is it?"

Laughing, I went to my washbasin and rinsed my hands. The Nobody in the glass didn't have her hair bobbed yet. But I could hold my head like a society waif as well as like a charwoman, and—because I was proud that I'd pinned Sammy the Saint—I felt despite our predicament incongruously happy.

"Well, aren't you the cat with feathers in its teeth. What's up, then?" Sadie wondered.

"Sammy the Saint is going to attack our opening night tomorrow."

"And you're *smiling* about that?" she demanded.

"Oh, don't you see, Sadie? I've tipped off Mr. Salvatici with plenty of tidbits before—the alliance of Lupo the Wolf with the Clutch Hand, the mastermind behind the ice protection racket. But this is my biggest discovery yet."

"He'll kill them," she said quietly.

I regarded her in the mirror, but I wasn't really seeing Sadie. I was seeing old Mr. Benenati stuffed into a barrel, his lipless mouth like rows of dominoes. All that had been taken away from us.

Taken away from Nicolo. And thereby, taken Nicolo away from me.

"And I'm glad," I concluded. "Now let's go. You're being dreadfully negligent about pouring me any champagne, and this is a night worth celebrating!"

But that night was only the very beginning of a terribly long ending. Disaster. Not then, and not for years, but catastrophe all the same.

My dear young lady, how fortunate I sent you." Mr. Salvatici passed me another full flute of the genuine French article, quite the sought-after commodity during a War year. "I'd heard inklings that Sammy was itching to strike, but not so soon. Well done indeed."

Champagne was squarely up my proverbial alley. Praise from the Spider even more so. But I was only half listening. Because it was the night before the opening of the Tobacco Club, and its final after-hours dress rehearsal.

Which meant Zachariah Lane was dancing.

Mr. Salvatici's interest in power notwithstanding, the man was completely gone on two things: music and his pigeons. Plenty of other nightclubs had been opening since the advent of ragtime, places from sawdust on the hardwood to crystal on the table. But Mr. Salvatici wanted to bring together the best of Tin Pan Alley, the darkest Memphis blues, the maddest of the moon-addled crooners, the wildest fox-trotters, women wearing Louis heels and ostrich feathers, food and drink and diamonds and dervishes, gents whisking ladies through the grizzly bear and the tango.

Rye outshone them all.

I leaned against the balcony rail, watching my friend the former doorman dance. The band was going full tilt on "The Darktown Strutters' Ball," and he was tapping fast enough to set the stage on fire.

I've got some good news, honey,
An invitation to the Darktown Ball,
It's a very swell affair,
All the "high-browns" will be there,
I'll wear my high silk hat and frock tail coat . . .

"So if you'll excuse me, there are arrangements to be made. I'm calling in a favor from your old childhood friend Nicolo Benenati."

That got my attention.

Rye, with an impossible smile on his face—one beginning to be toxically wide—was just finishing a step so intricate I couldn't even see it. But I turned to the Spider, who had planted himself companionably beside me. He closed the thin seam of his mouth around his champagne glass.

"Whatever for?" I asked.

"He hates the Clutch Hand, and by extension, Sammy the Saint."

"Of course he does. But why wouldn't you use one of your men?"

A pucker formed between Mr. Salvatici's dark brows, a fond but admonishing expression. "Because Benenati is too powerful to keep at arm's length any longer."

He brushed his hand across my hairline, the commonest of his affectionate gestures and one that always soothed me. And Mum had been right. The Spider never looked at me the way my occasional gadabout beaus did. The way I wanted Rye to. Despite everything, in his own unique fashion, I truly think he loved me the whole time.

It's better for me to believe that, and it doesn't do anyone any harm. I'd curl into a shell and never emerge otherwise.

"Ah. Here he is now, right on schedule."

My heart gave a jolt, and not the sort it suffered whenever Rye called me "darlin'." For Nicolo Benenati stood below us, on the spotless new Venetian-tiled floors. Placidly removing thin leather gloves, flanked by his gang's lieutenants: Dario Palma, Cleto the Crow, and Doctor Vinnie.

"I didn't know our Sammy problem would be accelerated in quite this manner, but it's timely that I made contact with him," my guardian said calmly. "Now an introduction will simply become a meeting. Have him join me upstairs, will you?"

I swallowed an intemperate gulp of champagne.

"You can manage him, my dear young lady." He patted my shoulder. "Just don't disappear with this one. He watches you too close."

The song ended, Rye struck a final triumphant pose, and the entire Salvatici outfit erupted in heady applause. The Spider made for the discreet stairs to his office.

And then Nicolo raised his eyes, found mine, and he smiled.

For an instant, nothing had changed. His ax-like profile was chiseled at age twenty-three, his lean physique filled out, his raw charisma undiminished. He was the leader of a sinister brotherhood—one ruled by his own iron fist, universally terrifying, and avoided even by the likes of the Clutch Hand's impressive array of *scurmi fituzzi*, allowed to operate on the outermost edges of what passed for law in our streets. His mother lived quietly above the cigar shop Nazario managed. And I lived avoiding Nicolo, because I could see the death's mask behind his sallowing skin and I was still tied to him in that almost musical way childhood friends are. When you hear the same song on the air whenever you're in the same room, because you share a set of interlocking memories like bass and treble notes on a page.

Then Dario touched his shoulder, and the smile froze, and all that was left was the body of my old friend.

I started down the stairs.

After slaughtering Giuseppe Morello's horse, he'd divided his time between gathering darkness around himself like a cloak, punctuated by rumors of unspeakable violence, and seeking me out. But when he saw I was cared for with Mr. Salvatici, I think he smelled blood on his own hands and stopped trying as ardently. Or maybe murdering *cagnolazzi* and recruiting his vicious pack dogs took precedence. I didn't know. I cared deeply, but not knowing felt safer. I didn't want him kissing me again, didn't want the ghost ring I could see on my left hand whenever he glanced at it. So our meetings eventually were reduced to a quick embrace in the streets as I stammered excuses and he regarded me as if to say, *I know. But I must do this.*

I remember how we used to be, and I know.

Dario and his repellent friends fell away respectfully when I approached. Nothing to do with yours very truly, naturally. But they'd sooner cut off their own noses than offend Nicolo Benenati.

"Alicia."

Nicolo kissed me on either cheek and I wasn't shivering, *I won't disappear, I can manage him.* He smelled of his late father's bitter-orange shaving balm, and of himself, something sharper and searingly familiar.

"Nicolo, it's been months. Isn't that dreadful?"

He studied me. It would have been a fond expression, but tiny muscles in that dear face had petrified. "I ask after you, you know, often. I would know if you weren't well."

"You're a love."

"I miss you, *topolina*."

I miss me too, sometimes. But not as much as I miss you.

"Well, here I am. And Mr. Salvatici wants to see you up in his office."

"I've always meant to thank him, you realize, for taking you away from the Step Right. At the time, I . . . couldn't. Meeting him professionally will be an honor."

I pulled my fingertips down his jacket lapel. "Well, you'd better—"

"Alice!" Sadie appeared at my elbow, breathless. "Beg pardon, but there's a situation developing. It's Rye," she added more quietly.

"Oh Christ," I exhaled. "Nicolo, I'm sorry. I'll see you soon."

"Yes, I never meant to keep the Spider waiting. I know very little about him except that he takes superb care of you." As if on impulse, he kissed my knuckles before turning on his heel.

But it hadn't been impulsive. He'd been thinking about it for a long, lonely time.

"Where is Rye?" I demanded as Sadie pulled me away.

"In his dressing room."

"How bad is it?"

"Worse all the time. But we knew that already."

Rye had been finished performing for about five minutes. Sadie and I rushed backstage, dressing rooms still smelling of whitewash and already redolent of greasepaint and clean sweat. Politely shoving past bejeweled houris and top-hatted crooners. Five minutes might not seem like long enough for a jazz hound to get himself into any serious scrapes.

With Rye, two was more than ample.

"Hey there!" he exclaimed when we tumbled through his door without knocking. "Lord, just the sight of you gals is enough to celebrate, never mind the grand opening tomorrow! Come on and join the party."

Zachariah had been rehearsing relentlessly for weeks now. And he considered his body something akin to a wind-up toy—limp with exhaustion one moment, but hey presto, a little oil, tinker with a cog, and the mechanism could be forced back into action. The remedies on this occasion looked to be one empty pint of liquor and a depleted bottle of Bayer's wildly popular heroin tablets, with a side of their heroin-laced water-soluble cough salts.

"This isn't a party, it's a pharmacy," I attempted.

Rye smiled. It didn't even reach the friendly sacks under his eyes, let alone the irises.

"I'm going for a pot of coffee." Sadie wheeled.

I walked to him, my own heart going rabbit fast, and slid the heroin bottles behind me, sitting on the dressing table.

Out of sight, out of mind. At least for the next ten seconds.

"Isn't the cough any better?" I pressed the backs of my cool fingers to his burning cheek.

"It comes and goes, darlin'."

Sometimes—never for very long, because we can't change affections any more than we can change gravity—I wish I'd given my heart to someone who wanted to live. Because Rye did not. So I walked around with a cavern beneath my ribs, and he with the weight of an unwanted organ in his pocket. It wasn't about lacking affection. His back was one of the frequentest slapped in Harlem and his mother knew how he liked his eggs. Zachariah Lane, I think, was born unable to close his eyes. And when he looked within, he saw garbage. Rye could sail to the moon on someone else's love song, but what he'd been born with couldn't even get him out of bed on some days.

What baffled me was that he didn't find a woman to hit or a dog to kick. Most people like sharing their suffering. Rye kept it all to himself. And if it hurt me that I wasn't enough to make him think life was bearable? Well, that was my own doing. A person doesn't crawl into a seaside cave and then rail at the tide for coming in. I wasn't a virgin in 1917. I'd had flings, fumbles, tears on Sadie's shoulder. But not a soul under the sun had yet afflicted me the way Rye had, and we'd never even kissed.

"Why do you look so sad?" Rye rubbed at his temple. "Pretty girls like you shouldn't look sad, darlin'. Buck up and have a drink."

I poured two and rested my dancing shoes on his knee.

"What are we going to do with you?" I whispered.

"Today? Not a thing. Tomorrow? Let's open this here cabaret and then after we're rich, hop a steamer to an island someplace. Just me, my pal Nobody, and the sand and the deep blue sea."

It was a beautiful picture, and even more beautiful because neither of us believed in it. Rye started tapping his tumbler against my toes, humming "I Ain't Got Nobody," a song he found just dreadfully humorous to regale me with and I found vaguely excruciating.

I would sail away with you, if you asked me, I thought wildly. *There has to be some thing, some place, on this vast fucking planet that would make you feel better.*

I sat there, watching a lovely lie unfold while Rye's breath grew shallower and his speech more off-key. Waiting for Sadie and coffee. Never imagining that the real impediment to our hoisting anchor on the morrow wouldn't be his self-loathing, or even my self-doubt, but that I was going to be awfully preoccupied over getting shot.

· *Sixteen* ·

NOW

Gaping, bullet pated, thick lipped, wooly headed, animal-jawed crowd of niggers, the dregs of broken up plantations, idle and vicious blacks. . . . Greasy, dirty, lousy, they drowsily look down upon the assembled wisdom of a dissevered Union. Sleepily listen to legislators who have given them their freedom and now propose to invest them with the highest privileges of American citizenship.

—"REGARDING THE FOURTEENTH AMENDMENT,"
The Eugene Weekly Democratic Review, Eugene, Oregon,
March 2, 1867

All right. Supposing that good luck comes in threes, and the horse is as white as you say it is, we're going to call forth the dandiest run of serendipity you ever did see."

We're not terribly far from the Paragon Hotel, Wednesday Joe Kiona and me, at Southwest Park Avenue and Southwest Main Street. Still in the heart of downtown. We have a date with a horse—but first, with a tree. Thankfully, this greensward is as lousy with plants as Harlem is with tenements. Tall pines, low boxwoods, swarms of wild lilies hoisting themselves up through the mud.

"You're sure you *found* the first hairpin?" the young chap insists. "You didn't, you know, leave it there to come by the next day?"

"I stepped on it. What do you take me for?"

"Well, I dunno exactly." Wednesday Joe scratches his head under his flat cap. "But seeing as you've been so keen to find Davy, I guess . . . a friend?"

"Heavens, sir, you do me honor."

Spitting into my hand, I proffer it for shaking. He takes it with a manly squeeze. I'm glad of the affirmation, because Blossom and I stirred the pot a bit on our return to the hotel in the after hours, melancholy as drowned cats and almost as wet. We collided with Mavereen arriving home from the trenches, no sign of Davy Lee, her stately bulk seeming to have deflated in search of him.

I won't go into what Blossom looked like at the news that there was no news. Some expressions are so raw, thankfully they defy all description.

Mavereen was heartsick and exhausted and demanding to know what was the matter. Blossom snapped out the truth in suitably vague terms, minus any mention of where events had actually taken place. But following Mavereen shouting over the dangers inherent in pulling a gun on the likes of Officer Overton, and the vitriol Blossom returned over what choice she'd had exactly, Mavereen all but confined us both to quarters. I wouldn't have been surprised if she'd gone for the wooden spoon.

Meanwhile, I still have a headache, my wound nags but I know better than to treat morphine like lollipops, and Wednesday Joe and I had to sneak out through Miss Christina's kitchen.

"Okay, so you found the hairpin and that's definitely lucky," he allows. "Here's a pretty low branch."

"Ideal, my good man. Have you the string?"

Wednesday Joe produces kitchen twine. We step up to the rhododendron tree, a paint spill of pink so berserk you can imagine it staining your fingertips, and tie the pin to a limb.

"Right. That'll make the luck stronger." Joe sends the tiny wire merrily swinging.

"Next step, then." I pull another hairpin from the pocket of my plain grey sack dress, bend it double, and throw it reverently over my left shoulder.

"And that ought to bring a friend." My companion's face pinches. "Wait, how do we know the friend it'll bring will be Davy?"

"We don't. But we're ever so set on it, and that ought to help. Produce the apple and lead us onward."

Wednesday Joe displays a shiny-skinned red apple. We amble across the park in pursuit of the white horse that will bring his small cohort back to us. But I haven't risked Mavereen Meader's wrath just to court kismet, as strong as I am for the stuff. I hunger zestily for information, and I sling my hand over Joe's elbow.

"It seems to me that we're not being terribly good detectives," I suggest. "All hail Lady Luck, but what if we tried a bit of the Sherlock Holmes act to boot? You're familiar, yes?"

"'Course. The one with the hound kept me up like anything. But what do you mean?"

"Just that we've been looking for Davy under every rock, but we don't know *why* he disappeared. Did he lose his way alone or did someone take him or did he wander off with a pal?"

"It's the rottenest. But there's no way to figure, is there?"

"Maybe not, but we can try. In the Dr. Watson yarns, they'd probably start with who the missing person knew best and then simply pepper everyone with questions. Who did Davy know?"

"He was . . . he kind of belonged to everyone."

"Specificity, if you please."

Wednesday Joe frowns. "He lived with Miss Christina. He followed Max like a puppy. Mavereen and Blossom. Dr. Pendleton was always better when he was around Davy. And we played together even though he was younger, 'specially after the white kids roughed him up."

"No foes at the hotel to speak of, then?"

"Well, he didn't like Rooster."

This takes me aback. "Didn't take to or didn't like? They're different, mind."

"'Course they are. Didn't like."

"Whyever might that be?"

"Don't know. Started maybe six months ago. But he'd never tell me why, only that he was mad. I figured maybe Rooster wanted to make Davy stay indoors and they had a scrap about it."

Rooster. He seems a terribly sturdy fellow, in the way night seems darkish. Laconic. Gigantic. His grasp of facts is impeccable, and I think his grasp of boulders would probably lead to the pulverization of the rocks in question. I don't find him personally menacing. Still, young striplings can sense a grub in the fruit from miles away.

"There's not something wrong with Rooster, is there?" Joe inquires, brows slanting.

"Goodness, I hope not, the man could crush a Packard truck. Does he rub you funny?"

"Hell, no. I think Rooster's a real pal. He taught me how to tie my uniform tie when I started working the elevator. And one time . . ." Joe's arm tenses. "One time, a guest at the Paragon who lived in London tried to hail a cab outside. The driver got out, spit on his shoes. There was a real bloody dustup and Rooster pulled three men off the colored fellow and told everyone to scram. But Davy's been gone two days and . . . Christ. It'd be just awful to think Rooster was crooked somehow."

The shadows cast by monsters unseen gather in the overwrought boy's eyes, which is my fault.

"What did the man say to the elevator operator?"

"Dunno," he returns listlessly.

"Hello, I see you have your ups and downs."

"Your Majesty," he says in disbelief, "that is . . ." Stopping, he smiles. "That's the dumbest joke I've ever heard."

"You're entirely welcome. So what about people outside the hotel? Little Davy cavorted with the neighborhood lads before they turned bruisers."

"We both did."

"Anything crummy ever happen?"

He shrugs. "It used to be stupid stuff. Fights over marbles, baseball. But when their parents said not to play with niggers, they started calling us names when we went into stores outside the hotel. Then last month I was trying to practice catch with Davy in the alley and they got us real bad with rotten eggs. That was before they started beating up on anyone."

"Children are unmitigated turds," I announce, knowing from experience.

"I'm used to people throwing things." His eyes are hard and flat. "So's Jenny. Eggs are better than rocks."

"Sound science."

"I like science. I did make a rocket once, at one of Mrs. Vaughan's Weekly Betterment days," he says, brightening. "She's awfully nice. Lots of colored kids come to the hotel from all around just to work with her. And she always seems happy to see us. Not the pretend happy, when an adult would rather just be alone. Really happy. There's the hostelry! I did odd jobs as a groom sometimes before the hotel took us in. Wait till you see—this horse is just about as white as they come."

We cross the street too quickly for my taste, a gap in the line of glistening Model T's making it easy to wing across the cobbles. I can't smell sweet hay and dry manure without conjuring the rotting penny aroma of death. But the old girl gathers herself. The men mucking the stalls pay Wednesday Joe no mind, so I figure he's left fruit offerings at this particular altar before. And the horse really is a picture, snow pale and a regular apple enthusiast.

Not a jolly enough sight to keep me in a stable, however. So I cut the ritual short.

We're back in the dew-dappled world again and I'm loading more verbal ammo to fire at the unsuspecting youth when he gives a loud squawk. Whirling, I encounter an unexpected but not remotely unwelcome sight.

"What you're gonna do now, Mr. Kiona, is deliver the straight dope on what you think you're doing outta the hotel." Maximilian Burton has Wednesday Joe by the ear. "Don't give me any guff about being with Miss James here and that making it kosher. Christ knows she ain't exactly the ideal escort. Well?"

"We had to fix the luck!" Joe protests. "Honest, we're not looking for trouble!"

"Trouble arrived, kid."

"I *know* that, don't I? I'm not allowed to search for Davy, but I've got to try and help! Even Jenny's working, writing all those letters to politicians and pieces for *The Advocate*. You want me to go crazy, or what?"

Sighing, Max releases his catch. "Okay. Yeah, I figured. It's jake, kid, but run along home. That guy what you told to man the elevator? He's chewing gum and buttering up the ladies, and I ain't standing between you and Mavereen when she wakes up."

Wednesday Joe mutters a scrambled farewell as he heads for the hills. Leaving me on a silver-lit downtown street with Max, who regards me as an object of distaste.

No, interest.

No . . . concern?

I can't make sense of the expression. There's no formula. But I'm dying to don coat and turn chemist.

"I need words with the likes of you," he grates.

"Do they include *good morning*?"

"Not here."

"Is there a better morning somewhere else? By all means, let's chase it down."

He quick-marches off, one fist thrust angrily in his pocket while the other swings, and I chase him back into the forested park. I need a machete for this. It's a jungle, so much saturated color that I'm dizzy, and the air has shifted from a soft breath of cloud to a swarm of tiny silver needles. It's too much, the tinsel falling and the sweet dank leaves, and then unexpectedly we break through the thicket.

We're in a tiny circular clearing ringed with yellow rosebushes. They're crowned with scores of tightly packed buds waiting to peel open, spread themselves wide, and burst. A pretty bronze sundial presides in the center of the secluded grove, which is ridiculous. Might as well put a birdbath in the Sahara.

Max and I are about as alone as we've ever been. Considering.

"Blossom woke up asking for you." Max settles hands on hips. "Then she lit off to check on Mrs. Vaughan. I take it you pair was pretty much in the frying pan last night."

Oh.

He's worried about his friend Blossom.

Carry on, old girl, he might be unsentimental about your corpus, but here he stands in front of it, yes?

"And subsequently leaped into the fire, correct. We were at the Rose's Thorn. Blossom asked me to keep it mum from all saving yourself. Not the safest of excursions, I grant. And I'm dreadfully sorry about the firearms business. But if you suppose I intentionally signed up for ravishment by Officer Overton—"

"Cut that shit out," Max snaps.

This is unexpected. "Excuse me?"

"If you think I figure as a girl getting dolled up to paint the town means she deserves a tussle with that pig, you're cracked." Max looks furious. "I done heard about Mavereen, that she was real sore, and she's already sorry. I made sure of that. Ain't a pretty skirt what ever deserved that sorta treatment just by being in the wrong place. I was in France, when plenty of 'em was in the wrong place. So don't kid me about it."

My heart patters rain fast and almost as lightly. "I'll refrain."

"Last night, that there was Overton all over. He's scum."

"Think lower. Less prepossessing."

"But you and Blossom being in his sights and the son of a bitch getting that close, don't make me play some kinda charades as says it sits right with me. It don't."

His concern sizzles, golden thunder sparks flying. Despite the damp, my cheeks flush. Max adjusts his fedora, takes a lap around the useless sundial.

"Look, ain't no way is Mavereen gonna convince Blossom to go in for house arrest." He rubs a palm over his mouth in frustration. "Back when we was in No Man's Land living offa bully beef and rainwater, sometimes a guy would go a few days without any real sleep. Get a little cross-eyed. This here's different. I gotta admit, I'm worn down, Alice. Just the notion of that kid out there . . ." Max stops, wincing.

"I know. Worriment is worse than Jerry fire," I offer softly.

"Damn right it is. But 'scuse my saying so, worriment on this many fronts is just about as much as a fella can stand."

I think of Blossom, and the near-sure fact that Max won't have cause to be anxious over his friend for long, and my breastbone aches. "Blossom held her own. You needn't worry on that account."

"It ain't *just* Blossom."

He steps closer. I'm at the pictures suddenly, or would be if movies could show color, a trick of the rain making the image before me flicker like a celluloid reel.

"Bringing you here, Alice—I didn't have no choice. You was on the way out and I seen that before, more than enough times. But now." He bites his lip, shrugs. "This shit is getting too rough for my taste. S'posing you wants to skip town, I'll put you on the train personal."

This is unacceptable.

"Don't make a girl blush."

"I ain't," he says shrewdly. "I'm making a gun moll think."

"As admiring as I am of my own hide, you'll find I'm just about as loyal as a bad rash. And I'm terribly fond of you all. It isn't in me to leave you in the lurch."

Max scours me with soldierly eyes. "That's real nice. But it ain't regular. So. Wanna get started telling me why?"

"I don't see why I shouldn't," I answer.

Standing there with tiny gem drops decorating our coats, I briefly tell Max about Rye. That there was no protective barrier between him and the world. That when he listened to a ragtime riff, his soul seared on a griddle. That when he saw the Yiddisher kid who'd been blasted by polio begging on the corner of 123rd, her skin the thickness and complexion of eggshells, he tossed her change but never flinched away. That he hated himself more than he ever hated the planet that tormented him. I mention heroin tonic.

Every-colored lights in Rye's eyes. The glimmers of good days remembered but long gone away.

"I don't *leave* people," I conclude. "Or cut my losses and depart simply because times get hard, and I don't pull the butterfly stuff.

I've lost too many old friends. So I'm not terribly anxious to misplace new ones."

Max rubs a hand over his nape. "You're gonna need to spell it out, 'cause I still don't follow. You were pretty strong for this guy?"

"To distraction," I agree. "So what?"

"Nothing to speak of."

"And yet, you're perfectly audible. What?"

He coughs with Brooklyn reticence. "Just that you said as I reminded you of somebody. And here I is, a mixed black sorta fella with a fair amount of music in my bones. And we two been kinda close, proximity wise, ever since I boarded that Pullman coach in Chicago. And I made nice with you. And I ain't blind."

I stand speechless for an instant too long, and he continues.

"How do you figure I remind you of a jazz hound with a taste for forgetfulness?" Max shakes his head. "This guy you see standing here, he *remembers* things. No offense to your boy back home, I seen my share of poppy heads, there's trench rats with chunks missing what suck it down in their orange juice. It happens. Not to the likes of me, though."

A peal of laughter escapes me and I clap my trap shut. Dreadfully keen to snatch it back.

"All right, all right, you ain't soft on me, Jesus," Max protests, raising his palms. "Have it your way. But—"

I catch his hands in mine. "You don't remind me of Rye. At all."

"Then—"

"Blossom does," I explain. "And I adore that about her. The sort of headlong way she has about needing to tell the truth, then regretting it when she sees a lie would have been ever so much kinder. I mean, Rye was kind. He certainly never hung out anyone's foibles to dry in public. But they both . . . it's the seeing too much, I think. She tries to make other people see it with her. And he tried to—to see less of it himself. So I understand her, in a way, and it's easy to love her. Because of Rye."

We both grow more urgently aware that our hands are loosely clasped.

"So I don't remind you of him?" Max repeats.

"No, I assure you. But now it's your turn. You said I remind you of someone and it isn't your white sisters. What are they like, by the way?"

"What are my sisters like?" His eyebrows are battling his hat brim. "They're like the genuine family what my dad lives with, and I'd be real keen to take them out on the town, on accounta they's nice ladies and I've got the scratch for it, but instead they rides the train to Jersey and meets me at a Pullman stop before I get back to Brooklyn. In a nigger coffee joint, pretending to be Salvation Army. You don't really want to know about them. You want to know who I thought of, seeing you."

"I'm . . . terribly sorry, but yes," I admit, blushing. "I'm really very selfish at heart, and you said you didn't like that person. So."

"Me." Max breaks the slack grip, stepping back. "Not at the starting pistol when we was just jawing about jazz, and you was hurt so bad I couldn't help but see it, but. Me."

"How so?" I wonder, shocked.

"Running around getting shot at." He smiles as if tasting something bitter. Takes one of my hands back into his. "I was in a Brooklyn gang, down by the waterfront. Got shot at. Hit, too. Wanted to be a part of something so bad I didn't care what it was I was fighting for. When you done woke up, you sounded like me. Me back then. I hated that guy."

"What changed your circumstances?"

"The army." Max shakes his head. "Figured if I'm already

sporting bullet holes, might as well be for a better reason, you savvy?"

"Better than I can express."

Now he's not two feet away from me, he's barely an inch from me, and I can't breathe for wanting him.

"Who's it you're thinking of, when you think of me, then?" he asks.

"I think if you don't kiss me, this is about to have been an altogether tragic waste of time."

Max does kiss me. His lips make uncomplicated movements, nothing like the jazz we both love, only like the raw ache we both feel. When he starts to pull away, I chase him, and he stops me, putting a hand to my shoulder.

"Nohow is this gonna work." There's a stony certainty in the words. "I got a case on you too, but I'm telling you, Alice. Nothing about this here is ever gonna work."

"What if it worked just once? Or maybe six or seven times?" I whisper.

He laughs, tucking a wisp of hair back under my head scarf. "Aw, for God's sake. Maybe. Not at the Paragon, though. Mavereen gots her standards and she sticks to 'em like glue."

"Another hotel, then?"

He regards me, and I reflect upon the depths of my own stupidity.

"You said you had a cabin." I run my fingers along his shirt buttons and, *wonder of wonders*, he leans into the touch.

"We don't got time for my cabin, not while looking for Davy."

His words aren't harsh, but they bring me back to myself. I'm cavorting with an awfully attractive colored man in a public park in a town being taken over by the KKK. I'm being a sap, in short.

"I never meant to say something so dreadful," I assure him. "If there were any way in the world I might ease your mind just now, what would that be?"

"Wish I could tell you. Maybe if we knew as the Klan didn't have nothing to do with Davy being missing. Maybe if we knew the first thing about this god-awful mess."

I bump my brow against his shoulder. "Yes, it's exhausting. I don't know how Blossom is surviving the strain, to be honest."

I am being honest. But then I do wonder, and wonder slightly more deeply. Blossom is ill. Probably terminally so. But even if she isn't tromping through the thickets, why isn't she interrogating everyone she can think of?

Come to that, why aren't I?

"Back to work, then. C'mon," Max orders, hooking my elbow. "I can't be lamped touching you after we're outta this here shrubbery. But for the meanwhile, I'm keeping it up."

It sounds like a promise, even though it isn't one. When we emerge from said shrubbery, I create a discreet distance whereby he can follow after. Some sort of porter or a servant, it doesn't matter so long as he's beneath me, he isn't legally allowed to be in Oregon at all. Meanwhile, I'm still tasting him, and my lips are flushed and warm. We turn on Southwest Salmon Street. It's a busy thoroughfare, muddying the slender drizzle with bustle and noise. For a little while the mere idea of Max behind me drowns out everything else. But then the cloud relents and it's just air again, and I notice a building that looks much grander than most of the city hereabouts.

"What on earth is this, the courthouse?"

"Might as well be," Max's voice growls. "That there's the Arlington Club. Anybody what thinks they's anybody belongs to that place."

It escapes me for a moment. The association.

But then it hits me square in the kisser.

"I know what I can do!" I exclaim.

"Come again?" Max questions. But for once, I'm paying him no mind.

"I'm the wrong person, though."

"Alice, you better be joshing me, because I ain't in no mood to piece your brains back together."

Mrs. Muriel Snider. From the train. My cabinmate.

Mrs. Snider said that her husband was a member of the Arlington Club.

I glance behind me. "We have to get back to the hotel so I can become who I was on the train. You recall Mrs. Muriel Snider?"

He looks like he's ignoring a pungent smell. "Can't say as I cottoned to her."

"Neither did I, not the smallest thread did I cotton to her, but her husband belongs to the Arlington Club, and if I pump her, I could tell you what the aristocracy think of Davy's disappearance. If they're thinking of it at all, that is. Don't you suppose some of the Arlington Club lot are Klannish, and don't you suppose they chat with their wives?"

I can finally accomplish something other than surviving a bullet wound and whistling "Dixie."

When we arrive back at the Paragon Hotel, we duck into the alley. I pull open the kitchen door, and I'm not halfway inside before I can't help but overhear a conversation.

"It'll pass," says Rooster's rumbling bass.

"But it's so unfair," answers Miss Christina in a voice I've never heard from her before. Plaintive, desperate even.

I push backward and Max pauses, easing the door closed. This provides me with the dual advantage of eavesdropping and gripping Max by the shirtfront even though just now, I can't enjoy it fully. *Quelque* waste.

"Soon enough all this'll pass us by," Rooster intones. "We're the bridge, remember? Just let the water slide on past."

Miss Christina, to my shock, sounds almost tearful. "I'm just considerable tired of waiting."

The inner door *flip-flaps* open. As Miss Christina and Rooster fall silent, Max coughs and kicks the door behind him so it appears we're arriving at the same time. It's inelegant, but I dearly hope the duo in the kitchen doesn't notice that.

"Hello, all," I trill, entering the room. "Are we interrupting? I was just getting a bit of air."

Three Paragon residents view me with positively sprightly skepticism. Miss Christina, whose ropy forearms are tense with frustration—and who I could swear just shoved a letter in her apron. Rooster, whose impressive bulk is as still as a monument. And Mavereen, who just arrived, greying hair wound into a perfect corkscrew beehive despite her lack of sleep—which if I hadn't heard about it from Max would be evidenced by the lines of grief bracketing her full mouth.

"Miss James." Mavereen sighs. "I hope you'll forgive me for that sorry display. Can't say as I approve of Blossom running her head into trouble like that, but it weren't your doing. I'm real glad you're safe."

Safe. If only.

"Thank you."

Rooster checks his watch, turns, and leaves the kitchen. Miss Christina slits her eyes at us before going back to her bubbling pot.

What on earth did we just witness?

"Must've run into Max here when he was getting Wednesday Joe, I reckon," Mavereen continues dryly.

"She did, and I done already told her I'm tired of fetching that boy back where he belongs," Max agrees in admirably irritable style.

"Anyway. 'Scuse the change of subject, but Alice here has an idea she wants to try out, needs to gussy herself up. I'll give you the goods while she changes. Over a drink, I hope to Christ."

"Language, young man," Mavereen scolds, slapping his arm. "You best believe I won't stand for it, you hear?"

"Hey, hey, easy—I ain't fixing to make you sore."

But I suspect he did, seeing as Mavereen in her fresh annoyance has forgotten all about me. I give Miss Christina a friendly smile before departing. Anything more would mean I want her story. Anything less would mean I'm pretending not to have heard it.

Being Nobody, as ever, is the best tack.

Seventeen

As for the mask, 'tis but a symbol, like in comparison to creeds in the different churches. We are ashamed of nothing, neither have we anything to hide for we are proud of the fact that we have nerve enough to express in word and action our true convictions.

—MINUTES FROM THE MEETING OF THE LA GRANDE, OREGON, KU KLUX KLAN, December 12, 1922

"I simply can't tell you how gratified I was to hear from you, dear! I knew that we would see each other again. Everyone says I have the most uncanny sixth sense about these things."

"Oh, I'm sure they do, Mrs. Snider."

Smiling timidly at Mrs. Muriel Snider, I cup my hands around my gold-rimmed teacup. While the Arlington Club jogged my memory, we can't possibly meet there—it excludes blacks, Indians, Orientals, Jews, women, and probably other sorts of folk. Hottentots. The shabbier Norwegians. No, we're at a simply decadent ladies' tearoom across the street from a gorgeous six-story monstrosity called the Pioneer Building. Portlanders, I'm learning, don't slouch when it comes to riding high on the proverbial hog. The linens on our table are pristine, the curtains sage damask, and I could don my rouge and kohl in the reflections from the silver. Not that I'm wearing any.

Mrs. Muriel Snider seems awfully jazzed to see yours truly. Her boxlike, self-satisfied face sports a continuous smile, flushed with camaraderie and steaming Earl Grey.

"It's so good to see you entirely recovered from your riding mishap, Miss James. I quite feared leaving you in the hands of that George from the Pullman car. One really cannot be too careful where the virtue of young single women is concerned, can one?"

I admire to be in Maximilian's hands as thoroughly as humanly possible.

It strikes me, in an uncomfortable wet-slap fashion, that Mrs. Snider is—in her own appalling way—a perfectly nice human being. She wanted to keep a stranger safe from wolves; she wants to outfit a lonesome young working girl with a sweetheart; and it isn't her fault I'm a liquor smuggler.

"Your color is so much better than it was on the train, but you're still thinner than you'd prefer, aren't you? A music teacher's salary—heavens, I can only imagine what it is to live off a hot plate and a coffee pot. Shall I order some more substantial refreshment? You're my guest today, dear, so please don't mind the expense."

Staring into Mrs. Muriel Snider's cubed spud of a face, I'm horrified to discover that I genuinely like her. It's confusing.

"I am a little peckish," I own.

"Wonderful! Waiter, over here, please!" Snapping her fingers, Mrs. Snider secures the immediate and complete attention of a young redhead with ill-conceived fuzz on his upper lip. "A tray of finger sandwiches, *not* soggy this time, and a crab Louis, and perhaps—yes, why not—the steamed razor clams with drawn butter. My dear, whatever is troubling you?" Mrs. Snider adjusts the cuffs of her rust-colored walking suit. "Now, if we are to be friends, we mustn't keep secrets. Is it your poor dear parents being so far from the city?"

Jackpot. A well-intentioned gossip, and one with a memory to boot.

"Oh, my parents are well enough. I mean . . . struggling, but, as I said, I do what I can. It's the living without a husband that truly is beginning to vex me. My roommate is kindness itself, but it would be so easy for some scoundrel to break in and overpower us." I twist my teacup to and fro. "I see such awful things in the news."

"Lord knows it's a sore trial for a young lady to be without a helpmeet, but we'll soon set that straight. As to the news, I never read the papers—Fred tells me current events in a way that won't upset me, he's so wonderfully protective. What do you mean, specifically?"

I hesitate. "I'm just a dreadful muddle when it comes to politics, but there's so much in the headlines regarding the Ku Klux Klan lately. And there's such ugly violence in the South, and it just makes me want to hide under my pillow, truly."

Mrs. Snider clucks, reaching for my hand. "You poor dear. Now, I don't pretend to know everything about politics either, but I do keep abreast through Fred, thinking it my civic duty now women have the vote, and you needn't worry over the KKK in *this* city. *America first*, they say, and. Well, who can argue with that?"

"Only . . . men in masks frighten me so."

"It's merely ritual, Miss James. They want the very best for God-fearing Christians. What with all sorts of disreputable scoundrels flooding in willy-nilly through the railroads and the ports, why, we deserve to have someone stand up for *us* for a change, is what Fred says."

"But I heard that colored establishments had been attacked?"

"Oh, I'm sure only the same pranks as might happen to any public business."

This nail appears to require striking square on the head.

"My roommate subscribes to *The Advocate*—her sweet old nanny was black, you understand, so she likes to follow the Negro problem—and I read a little mulatto boy has disappeared."

"Do you mean young Mr. Davy Lee, from the Paragon Hotel?"

If I weren't a stone-cold bootlegger, I'd positively spray my tea in her placid mug.

"I can't recall exactly," I reply instead. "Did you read about it too?"

"Oh, heavens no, dear, I don't take *The Advocate*." She sniffs. "Though your roommate I'm sure has only the most charitable reasons for doing so. The very idea of Negroes writing and editing their own newspaper, why, it almost gives me hope they might one day rise to our level. I pray so, Miss James, I truly do, for nothing is sadder than languishing in ignorance. I give to every African mission I come across. No, I had cause to visit a friend yesterday. She's acquainted with the boy and was very upset over the news."

My cheeks tingle. "Which friend might that be?"

"Mrs. Evelina Vaughan. Lovely young bride of our very own Chief of Police, Tom Vaughan," Mrs. Snider preens. "Tom and Fred hunt together with Mr. Jack Starr—that would be Evelina's father, the lumber baron. Everyone was thrilled when Evelina and Tom married. It was the wedding of the year, without question. Oh look, here's the food, Miss James. Now eat up! Men like a little shape. I can't imagine what these modern girls are thinking, starving themselves half to death purposely. It's indecent."

A bowl of clams descends, all sea brine and butterfat, followed by sandwiches and a modest mountain of crab Louis. So Evelina Vaughan and Mrs. Snider are acquainted. This isn't much doing as coincidences go, not in a city with a shrunken upper crust. But by God I will sit with Muriel Snider until I drain it as dry as the Eighteenth Amendment.

Because Mrs. Evelina Vaughan interests me. In, as they say, extremis. I wonder whether Blossom met Evelina Vaughan at one of her classier cabarets, or if conversely Mrs. Vaughan's Weekly

Betterment racket caused them to become acquainted. I remind myself to ask her.

"I think I may have met Mrs. Vaughan once, at a sort of fair or fund-raiser or something where I played the piano. Is she very lively, with pale red hair?"

"Why, yes, that's her." Mrs. Snider fussily plucks a clam from its shell with a tiny fork. "Here, take a sandwich, dear."

I dutifully nibble egg salad. "How would the wife of the Chief of Police know a little black boy?"

"Goodness, that's an excellent question. Mrs. Vaughan teaches Weekly Betterment to colored children at the Paragon Hotel. The missing foundling was one of her students."

"Oh! Her husband doesn't mind?"

"Oh no, dear. Tom Vaughan has adored Evelina Starr since they were children." Mrs. Muriel Snider's eyes glow with romance. "They were sweethearts when they were young. If you ask me, they ought to have quite the brood by this time. But little Evelina was always brilliant, and after she finished high school, she wanted to go away to a women's college. Well, there her mother and father were, with plenty of money but scant book learning themselves, and they indulged her. Probably thought it would lend the family distinction, when really, it raised quite a few eyebrows. Now, I'm not *against* educating women, provided it's done properly—only the sort of literature that edifies rather than corrupts, and with an emphasis on a mother's duty to be a wholesome influence on her children. What was I saying? Oh yes, well, in Evelina's case, the poor girl has always been the gentlest creature on the planet, and yet, what's the word . . ."

Incandescent, I think.

"Touched." Mrs. Snider taps her brow. "Her family came into money when she was . . . ten, I believe, which is when I made her acquaintance. Simply the dearest thing! She caught up so quickly with her studies after leaving the rural school that her Portland teachers were astonished. But intelligence comes with a price, you know. Before her teen years, she only seemed a bit fanciful, but so sweet natured we all wrote it off as harmless. Then when she turned—oh, of course, it was her sixteenth birthday, the poor creature! Her parents spared no expense, cakes and frills and a carousel and even a live band for all the young ladies to dance to, and you'll never believe what she did."

"What?" I'd pretend to be riveted, but it's unnecessary—I'm downright glued.

"Why, she wouldn't let the party stop! Flat refused to allow anyone to leave, grew hysterical, and believe it or not, she was up for *days*. Afterward, she was apparently limp as a rag. Similar things would happen quite rarely, thank heaven, and we were all too fond of her to let it affect our opinion. But after she went away to school . . ." Mrs. Snider shakes her head. "She was much too delicate for an education. Stuff enough facts into a girl's head and it's a serious risk you'll do more harm than good. Tom is a saint when she's unbalanced, but I've seen how it hurts him, Miss James."

So have I. It just about smashes him to pieces.

"Oh, please call me Alice."

"Why, with the greatest pleasure, and you must call me Muriel! Goodness, what on earth were we discussing?" Mrs. Snider brushes her napkin over her lips. "Oh! If the KKK had anything to do with that colored boy's disappearance, I'd be shocked. Just *shocked*. They're all churchgoers, and I cannot imagine a good Christian fellow harming a little boy of any color, it's unthinkable."

Not so awfully unthinkable in Arkansas, I reflect sourly.

"But I'll ask Fred about it tonight, dear, to ease your mind, and you ring me up again tomorrow. Take some more crab Louis—you're far too thin and I'm reducing."

I obey meekly, mainly because the crab is mouthwatering. If

Muriel Snider is wrong, and the Klan snatched Davy up and did God knows what with him, matters seem awfully hopeless. But if she's right, and the Klan are about as concerned over Davy as they'd be over an alley cat, then my suggestion to Wednesday Joe this morning takes on new significance.

We must become better detectives.

All right." Mavereen sighs, folding her arms over her ample bosom. "If this Mrs. Snider can't tell us nothing about Davy, well, we can at least be thankful to the Lord we ain't hearing of harm coming to him. And if she can . . ."

"If she can, we'll simply raise a cavalry, arm ourselves against the Klan, and conquer the Rose City—won't *that* be simply easy as winking," Blossom mutters.

We're back in the cozy parlor the unofficial executives of the Paragon use as their boardroom. Mavereen, Blossom, Jenny, Dr. Pendleton, and me. Max is out with the search party, Miss Christina helms her kitchen, and Rooster mans the front desk. Jenny, as ever, is scribbling in a notebook. Dr. Pendleton is the color of wheat flour under his freckles, and sips from a thermos filled with doubtless very fortifying contents. Blossom just returned from her visit to Mrs. Vaughan—which seems not to have produced much in the cheer department, for she sits huddled in a camel cloak, taking up about as much space inside it as your average coat rack.

It's getting to be all I can do not to stare at her with tragedy beaming from the old peepers. So instead I look to Mavereen.

"I'll come straight to you tomorrow with whatever Muriel says. And then I'd very much like to join the search at the Elms, with your permission."

"Honey, out at the Elms it's all blackberry brambles and timber wolves and need I add *colored men*," Blossom drawls. "I realize you've no strong objection to that last item, but you're still stitched up like Raggedy Ann and shouldn't be seen with us, not if we all desire to remain healthy."

I glare at Blossom with vim, fearing that Mavereen might read perfectly correct inferences into this allegation. In fact, one colored chappie in particular occupies my noggin and locked lips with me on this notable spring morn. I'm itching to tell Blossom, my tongue's downright antsy over it. But she's contemplating the intricacies of her manicure.

"The whole sorry pack of you ought to be ashamed," Dr. Pendleton growls. "Who's to say there's going to be a search party tomorrow? Our Davy might be back safe and sound at this hotel five minutes from now."

Blossom winces, tearing, and then rubs her stark brow bone.

"Well, I might not be at the Elms, but I've not let the grass grow under my feet." Jenny sets her pen down. "I'm convinced that this Klannish activity can be curtailed by exposing more whites to our true characters. To that end, I'm writing a series meant to humanize Davy, create sympathy among the greater Portland population. Some whites read *The Advocate*, of course, but most don't, and today I convinced the editors of the *Beaverton Valley Times* and *The Hillsboro Argus* to run a series about Mrs. Vaughan's Weekly Betterment classes. I'm in the perfect position to write it, and I proposed it by letter so they needn't know what color I am. It'll do wonders for our visibility."

"The *Beaverton Times* and *The Hillsboro Argus*," Blossom enunciates with acid annoyance, "are read by pig farmers and dairymen."

Jenny's neck stiffens. "They'll tell their friends, their friends will tell more friends . . ."

"It's a good idea, sugar." Mavereen crinkles her eyes kindly. "The Lord done give everybody their own set of talents, and He blessed you with a powerful pen. Raise it up and fight with it."

"It won't *work*." The whites of Blossom's eyes gleam pearly pale while the irises glitter like jet.

"No. But let the girl have her dreams," Dr. Pendleton concurs.

"This kind of dream is for innocents and simpletons."

Her uncle hoists his thermos. "And never forget, they're not mutually exclusive."

A muscle jumps in Jenny's smooth cheek.

"There's no call for either of you to insult me. If the writing is good enough, bigger papers will pick up the articles, and I plan to make them too good to be ignored."

"Just as you like, honey," Blossom says sweetly. "Make Evelina even more the object of citywide scrutiny than she already is, get called into the offices at some point and then tossed out on your ear, and *don't* let's forget drawing attention to the fact that white people frequent our humble abode, in a clever bid to get it dynamited faster."

"This baggage has the right end of the stick for once," Dr. Pendleton slurs, pushing his comical glasses up his nose.

"Leave off that thermos or you will greatly consternate me, Doddridge!" Mavereen snaps. "And Blossom, there ain't no call to be hurtful. Jenny's pen is sure enough a formidable weapon, but it don't carry half the firepower of that mouth of yours. 'A wholesome tongue is the tree of life.'"

"Oh, isn't this fine, a Sunday school lesson," Blossom shoots back. "It's poking a stick in the hornet's nest, Jenny. Abort the notion, if you please, I've a ghastly headache."

"But it will be beneficial—are you so bitter at me for whatever reason you've conjured up this time that you can't see how?" Jenny cries. "It shows that we value ourselves! It shows that we toil at becoming the finest of citizens. It shows us for what we are—good people who want to work with whites, not keep colored company exclusively."

Blossom slams her hands down on the table. Everyone gapes.

She's a force of nature, but I've never seen her like this, the tendons of her elegant neck rope-tight and the jut of her brow as hostile as the prow of a warship.

"You think that decorum and virtue will make a difference to them. And I am here to tell you, honey, that it will *not*," Blossom states. "You can use the proper cutlery for the length of an entire eight-course dinner. You can wear your modest Sunday best daily, with a five-dollar hat and a pocket Bible in your handbag. You can abstain from liquor and convince dozens of the unwashed poor to sign the temperance pledge. You can cultivate tea roses. You can pawn all your earthly luxuries and spend the money to build an orphanage. You can vote Democrat. You can bow and scrape and mind your place and speak when spoken to and smile when you're slapped. You're still a nigger to them."

Even knowing Blossom's temper as they do, her friends all stare in horror.

"Do you *begin* to understand what I'm telling you?" she seethes. "The way you act doesn't *matter.* The way you smell, dress, talk—none of it matters. You can write articles until your hand falls off, but you're still a nigger, you're a red nigger, and there is nothing to stop the likes of Officer Overton from shooting you in the back and claiming your spine admired to do him mischief. So go on, if you like—try to change the world. I'll be right here cheering for you, honey, *trust* that I will. I'd stand in front of a loaded rifle if it were pointed at you, but don't ask me to stick my neck out over a cause when I'm *terribly* preoccupied with keeping us alive."

Fat tears drop from Jenny's thick lashes. "How can you sit there and say such horrid things?"

"Do you want me to sit here *saying* horrid things, or do you want horrid things to *happen*? Do you even know how *many* horrid things are already—"

"Blossom, shut your trap," Dr. Pendleton growls.

I expect a tirade of Olympic proportions in response to this rebuke. But Blossom simply raises herself to her full height, nods formally to her uncle, and sweeps out of the room.

Cancer, I think helplessly. *Cancer is happening, and none of us can change that.*

Mavereen puts warm arms around a shaking Jenny. Dr. Pendleton tips the thermos fully back and shuffles out of the room. I need to know whether Blossom is all right, so I hurry after him into the lobby. A trio of traveling sales types sign paperwork for Rooster, and a family wearing feather-capped finery stand laughing with hands draped elegantly over their bellies. A silent maid floats past. Blossom is at the elevator summoning Wednesday Joe.

When I arrive at her side, I see that she's already weeping silently and battle a frantic urge to take her hand.

"You needn't bother," she husks. "I'm a monster."

"You're not a monster." My tongue aches with the weight of the word.

The elevator door slides open, and Wednesday Joe's face screws into alarm.

"Jeez, Miss Fontaine, are you—"

"In a hurry," she says as we enter. "Carry us to the fifth floor before one of my admirers catches me sniveling, it's *terribly* poor policy for entertainers. Go on, honey, step on it. I'll be right as Portland rain by tomorrow."

We reach the top floor in record time. She exits, back as straight as one of the local pines, and I pursue. If she wants me, she can have me. If she doesn't, I'll learn about it in no uncertain terms.

She stops before my own door without turning around.

"Alice, if you don't object, and *please* object if you like, I'm not fit company for a Tartar, but I can't face Jenny either, and if she comes looking . . ."

"No, of course, it's fine."

Unlocking my door, I watch as she sits on the bed and unbuckles patent-leather shoes. I kick my flats off and join her. When she's finished, to my short-lived amazement, she curls up like a cat with her head in my lap, breath coming in painful hitches. So I cover her long neck with my hand.

"Merely an experiment. Be not alarmed," she whispers.

"What's the verdict?"

"You're a comfort."

Not that I'd imagined she was pulling the sapphic stuff, but this is a relief, as I've no wish to navigate that particular river. "*Quelque* luck. I enjoy being of use ever so much."

"I know you do, honey. It's *frightfully* endearing."

"Do you want to tell me what in Christ's name that was all about?"

"Not in the slightest degree, but you're the one stuck here with your lap occupied, so consider any other topic fair game."

Pressing a thumb into her spine, I answer, "How was your friend Mrs. Vaughan?"

This brings a fresh gust of precipitation. "Not well. Tom has her confined to barracks, which is both . . . good and absolutely *ghastly*, depending on perspective. She doesn't do well confined."

"When did the two of you meet? I was wondering, when I was having tea with Muriel Snider. They're acquainted."

"When I first moved here, about six months before she became engaged to Tom. Davy was freshly ensconced, the precious boy, and she turned up at our doorstep to suggest the altogether *lunatic* notion of teaching self-improvement lessons to colored children, wanting to use the hotel, and I was strong for her from the start. She's brilliant. And good, which I'll never be."

She doesn't know that I'm aware of her proclivities. But I'm curious whether Blossom's justifiable regard for Mrs. Vaughan has spilled from hail-fellow-well-met into doodling fanciful initials in locked diaries.

"You can be good, I have confidence," I joke. "We'll start you up petting stray puppies and you'll be spoon-feeding lepers in two shakes."

"*Senseless* optimism, honey. My soul is hideous. Dorian Gray would regard it with skepticism."

"That horse you're beating needs burying."

"Touché."

"Is Mrs. Vaughan at least resting more comfortably?"

"She was before I arrived, but as is *very* typical for me, I think I put my foot in it." Rolling to her back, Blossom looks up at me with swimming eyes. "Evy doesn't like seeing me so ill. Neither do I, of course. I'm heinously vain, Alice. Dr. Pendleton and I are working miracles, I promised her we were, it's merely . . . taking a bit longer than I'd like."

Cancer, I reflect, *doesn't generally take much time at all.*

"Of course, to him, whether I live or die is purely a matter of academics—if he didn't possess an unshakable belief in the universality of his Hippocratic obligations, he wouldn't lift a finger for me."

"How is that possible?"

"Because he *detests* me."

"I can't imagine detesting you."

"I'd say that I can imagine it all too well," she replies with a broken smile. "But I don't have to imagine. No one is as skilled at detesting me as I am."

She curls back up, weeping freely now, and I think again with a hemorrhaging heart how much she reminds me of Rye. Beautiful china vases filled to brimming with talent and empathy and humor. Smashing themselves to smithereens at every opportunity.

· *Eighteen* ·

THEN

When a man is marked for death his assassins learn the street which he passes through most frequently on his way home at night. Then an apartment or a stable with the window facing this street is selected. . . . There is a squeeze on the trigger, the roar of the explosion to which Harlem's "Little Italy" is becoming accustomed, and by the time the police enter the building from which the shot was fired there is nothing but a few empty bottles, a table and a chair, and the smell of stale tobacco smoke.

—THE NEW YORK HERALD

January 7, 1917

When I awoke the morning the Tobacco Club was to open, I rubbed at the desert behind my eyelids and reached a sorry conclusion.

Still drunk.

I slithered out of bed.

Unfairly, I was angry. At Zachariah for not caring when I told him how much we all cared. For soaking up my notice when I had so achingly wanted him to notice me. Now I know that I wasn't angry at him; I was furious over my total incapacity to *do something about it*, about whiskey and heroin syrup in particular.

Fresh air was required, to scrub the senses and polish the psyche. So I washed, dressed, and made for the sky. The familiar creak of the rooftop door settled me, as did the velveteen trilling of birds, and the August air for once was as dry and clean as a freshly ironed blouse.

Mr. Salvatici was hard at his monthly cleaning of the dovecote. I didn't feel strong for conversation. But when he spied me, my boss stopped shoveling cedar shavings to deliver a friendly wave.

"Well, as I live and breathe," he greeted me.

"Sounds a lofty goal."

"My dear young lady, you appear fatigued." A twinkle lurked in his deep-set eyes.

"You witness before you an embodied hangover."

"Zachariah Lane was being his unusual self last night, I suppose?"

Mr. Salvatici had rolled in the hay with my own mother and was meticulously gracious around me, so since my original example of male authority had been Mr. Mangiapane, I was strangely open with him about matters conjugal. Rye and I hadn't had any, but that wasn't my fault, was it?

"He's wonderful, isn't he? But . . . I don't think he has a cough anymore."

Mr. Salvatici rubbed his nose with his wrist. "No, but he's a loyal employee and a brilliant performer."

"Plenty of the other nightclubs offer heroin syrup along with cocktails," it occurred to me. "Will the Tobacco Club?"

"I'd never dream of it." Mr. Salvatici dropped more fouled bedding in his barrow. "We are nation builders, and drugs make otherwise thriving populations dependent and miserable. Look no further than the history of the Opium Wars."

I wasn't versed in this topic despite years of lessons in what's probably termed *common knowledge*. But I tended to take my guardian at his word. "Does that mean you don't think much of Rye?"

"He serves a purpose still. Just as everyone must, or they become dispensable."

Remembering my own reconnaissance, I asked, "Did you send Nicolo to take care of Sammy the Saint last night?"

"Oh, no. It'll all take place tonight, at the grand opening. Just as they plan. Well. Not *just* as they plan, eh?"

I assumed he was kidding me. But the clouds scudded by overhead, and the pigeons winked with beady glass eyes, and eventually an icy nail driving into my neck decided that it must be true.

"That's—it's mad. Isn't it? I'm sorry. But for God's sake, why?"

Mr. Salvatici propped the shovel against the barrow and dusted his hands on his work trousers. Reaching into the dovecote, he gently pulled out a fog-colored bird with charcoal stripes on its wings and began to check it over. His thin dash of a mouth drooped at one edge.

"It might appear mad," he admitted, "but since you were lucky and clever enough to provide us with advance warning, we have a far more lucrative opportunity. I'll put my best guards in place inside the club, naturally, and young Mr. Benenati's men will take up sniper positions. When the hit squad rolls to a stop, we'll be ready for them."

"Why not just do away with them quietly, so there's less risk?"

"Because life is a circus. When you risk nothing or little, your audience is entitled to think little or nothing of your efforts, Nobody." Returning the bird to its cage with a fond caress, he chose another, a dear nut-brown creature. "When you risk a great deal, people take notice. Think of your friend Mr. Benenati, for example. If his father had simply vanished, I can't imagine the son and heir would have stood up against the Family. Nor that Harlem would have protested the way it did. But mutilating the owner of a popular local cigar shop? It was dangerous. It garnered a great deal of attention."

"And that's what we want?" I asked faintly.

"We want public awareness that we are capable of solving problems like the one Bruno's Café faced. Think of it like an advertisement."

"Won't people get hurt? I mean, obviously, but. People who've nothing to do with us?"

"I'll do everything I can to prevent it, but this is Harlem. Everyone has something to do with either us or them. We offer an alternative—the organization that builds instead of decimates, feeds instead of drains. People will do practically anything for you, just so long as they believe they're on the right side. And if your Nicolo Benenati is as good as they say he is, I hope only the would-be assassins will come to any harm." He cocked his wolfish head, studying me. "You'll stay here, of course, my dear young lady."

"Yes," I agreed, dazed. "I wanted to be at the opening, but."

"I hate to lose my good luck charm however briefly. But I don't blame you for feeling ill at ease, so I'd prefer you stay safe and snug. The opening will be interrupted anyhow, and you know how notoriety works in this neighborhood. We'll be on the front page of every newspaper and doubly packed the next night, and you'll join me for a steak supper, and we'll celebrate our most public victory to date."

"The police won't be a problem?"

"Of course not. We'll have Harry arrest a few of us, go before the judge with half a dozen witnesses saying we were elsewhere, as usual. Nothing will come of it. The true law of these streets is us, after all."

A muted *pop* sounded, a noise like the sweet push of a cork from a champagne bottle. When I recognized it was the pretty fawn bird's neck snapping, my heart started pounding in thick thuds against my ribs.

"Avian goiter." Mr. Salvatici sighed. He tossed the small body into the pile of shavings in the barrow. "Fatal, and terribly painful. Pity. She was an excellent flyer. I do so hate to see potential wasted, don't you?"

I didn't stop shaking until I arrived back in my room. One might think me awfully dense, and I agree. Of course Mr. Salvatici was a killer—the first night I spoke with him, he'd just knifed two Corleonesi. And of course he lost no sleep dispatching the targets I helped identify. And of course he occasionally had to put down a bird.

Pondering this while hearing the gentle *snap* of the pigeon's spine, however, made my teeth quake.

Mauro Salvatici was a deadly man. And a good guardian. I'd lived with those two truths for years. He trusted me and treated me well, and so it was easy as shelling a peanut to trust him in turn. Now I wondered, seeing as he aimed to make an example of Sammy the Saint in full view of the Tobacco Club, what else he wasn't telling me.

He'd be on the roof for another hour. And he often failed to latch his side of the door. So did I, now we'd lived together for so long.

Church-mouse quiet, even though there was no real need for stealth, I tried the handle.

The door swung open immediately.

Hackles prickling, I sped toward his writing desk—I'd often watched him make journal entries as we sat together over frittata and coffee. The current one rested in plain view.

It took me mere minutes to scan the past two months. The panic drained like a fever ebbing. He was dreadfully annoyed at the Clutch Hand's ability to execute orders from Sing Sing. The construction of the Tobacco Club had run over budget, but he expected to make all back within three months. The political push for Prohibition he found ever so encouraging, because every renegade on the island smelled the same opportunity. He had tremendous confidence in Nicolo Benenati's capacity to murder people.

As did I. Shivering, I replaced the journal and turned to leave.

I hesitated, curious.

It occurred to me that I knew precious little about Mr. Salvatici. He was born in Italy but had a pounding great facility with English because he had gone to a Naples school with a tutor from Boston who admired to master oil painting, and his mother had made the best *burrata* on the planet, according to him. But everything else was shrouded in darkness.

In for a penny, I thought.

Gliding full sail for the bookshelf, I soon found a neat row of older journals. I opened one to a random entry.

> *March 17, 1893. The faro tables at the Rusted Anchor, 44th Street by the river, continue to turn a steadier profit than anyone hoped. I keep after all my associates from home to at least take a job as a dealer even if they refuse to dirty their hands, but many are uncomfortable anyplace outside Little Italy. Learn English, I say. Take some pride in yourself, I insist, to which they answer that our village was so lousy with the Family that simply our arriving in America was enough to count ourselves lucky. It might be enough for them, but when I write to Mamma, I want to tell her I'm king of something, any something. I think of her back home, unable to leave my grandparents as they wither, reading her youngest son's letters. All that distance, all that effort, ought to mean something.*
>
> *More than my most recent entanglement meant, anyhow. I hesitate to speak of that even here, but I ought to have*

forestalled all romantic considerations until after I was established. I never knew temptation could course so strongly through me. But that was no excuse, and I can only plead ignorance of prior experience with infatuation. From henceforth, I must be more calculated.

The first section sounded in character enough to bring a smile to my face. And supposing that my guardian's hometown was riddled with *cagnolazzi*, it explained a great deal of his raison d'être. But as for romance, even infatuation—I'd grown so used to Mr. Salvatici's quiet courtesy toward me that I'd foolishly forgotten he'd the same equipment as any other fellow. I wondered, reading eagerly ahead, who she was, but almost no mention of her was made except to say that the liaison was finished.

August 8, 1894. Saw the local boys over supper in Harlem for the first time in months. Some talk of leaving New York, finding a simpler life in light of the fact the Family begins to thrive here as grandly as they ever did back home. It's demoralizing, watching them turn the other cheek continually. We fought bitterly over the question. Saddening as it is, if they want no part of the empire I mean to build, then I want no part of them.

Meanwhile, I seem to have made as clean an escape from Cupid as possible. I wish her well for all her unsuitability, but great ambitions require great sacrifices. I cannot allow anything or anyone to slow me down.

So this explained why Mr. Salvatici never spoke of her. I could find no further trace for the next two years, as if any ink devoted to her had faded into the white of the page.

An unsettled feeling combined with guilt over reading private diaries caused me to retreat and lock my side of the door, and I fell back against it, limp as an overcooked noodle. My boss's scheme of using Sammy the Saint as a publicity stunt sounded to me like a dandy bet for the local undertakers; I'd as nasty a feeling about it as Harry Chipchase entertained regarding rainbows.

But I'd never openly disagreed with Mr. Salvatici before. And considering the fact I'd always fancifully thought myself in the same category as his beloved birds, that afternoon seemed a dreadfully inauspicious occasion for trying it out.

Following my snooping expedition, I attempted to nap but gave it up, throwing my sleep mask across the room like a tyrannical toddler. I was solidly in the grip of the proverbial willies. At five in the afternoon, the traditional time to begin making poor life decisions, I ordered room service to bring me a pair of bloody marys. Extra mary, light on the tomato stuff. The sunlight through my window bruised to indigo, and my liquid breakfast was nearly through when I realized that Zachariah Lane kicked off the second set leading a group soft-shoe number, right when the firearms were scheduled to start going off.

This alarmed me.

I considered my options. I could send word to Rye not to show up, which would render him, as Mr. Salvatici had put it, "dispensable," but there had been too many graphic avian fatalities that morning to risk such a thing.

And our boss hadn't *commanded* me to stay put, exactly. Had he?

Throwing myself at my closet, I pulled out a scarlet underskirt topped by a black bell-shaped tunic with a riot of poppies blooming on the draped sleeves. A thick red kimono-style waistband finished the effect, which I considered cute as the dickens. Mr. Salvatici was right about hiding in plain sight—wear something striking enough and style is all anyone can see. Meanwhile, this Nobody, I imagined, got snapped for all the fashion rags, had a torrid affair with a British captain who hunted lions, packed elaborate picnics but forgot the silverware. Rotten driver but still took flight lessons. That sort.

The sort Rye would find irresistible.

I cleverly decided I'd arrive just prior to the second set and let Rye escort me home in the aftermath, an idea that seemed fraught with positively long-stemmed romance. Supper involved pink champagne, and by the time I left the Arcadia, young Alice James was about as soused as she'd been the night before.

Never let it be said the old master lacks consistency.

The Tobacco Club was only four blocks away, so I walked. Its marquee blazed angel white, dazzling, and a velvet rope bordered a sumptuous red carpet. Photographers lugging the bulky boxes of their cameras milled about, spit-polished automobiles idled and honked, gents nursed cigars, and women fiddled with diamond bracelets, a hot night at a hot new joint in the hottest burg on the planet.

Somewhere, a car with its plates covered approached, grim as the Reaper. Somewhere, Nicolo Benenati lurked, his hatchet face alert but strangely dead, hunting the hunters.

"Miss James!" Harry Chipchase exclaimed from his post guarding the entrance. "For Pete's sake, whaddaya think you're doing here?"

"Oh, just lending moral support, don't you know."

"Are you nuts or what? Skidoo, kid, skidoo, twenty-three is the number for you."

I tried to laugh as my heart seeped into my stockings. The shine was well off my clever scheme by this time. But I thought of Rye, made quick excuses, and Harry's anxious spluttering faded as I slipped past the doorman.

The Tobacco Club proved packed to the wainscoting with rich

loafers, slick producers, Broadway babies, and horn-rimmed critics. If Mr. Salvatici wanted bigger crowds, I didn't understand where he was going to put them. Bouquets bloomed, matches hissed, smells of prime rib and almond-crusted fish mingled with cigarette smoke and French perfume, and one might suppose I'm yarning this backward, but it's not the fact I got myself keyholed that mattered that night.

It was what happened after the bullets.

The scene roars in my ears, plays in flash-powder fits and starts. Pictures ripped from the headlines. The curtain sweeping aside for the second set and behold—Rye front and center in top hat and tails, flanked by a dozen dazzlingly bejeweled chorus girls. A cool champagne glass in my small hand. Mr. Salvatici's face peering down from our second-tier table, the dash of his mouth quirked worriedly when he spied me.

Percussion that didn't come from the stage.

Rat-a-tat-a-tata-tat-tat.

The crystal I held falling, shattering as people began to shriek.

Sammy the Saint's smooth jowls quaked as he wielded the tommy gun from a half-curtained table. He must have paid someone off royally to have gotten all the way inside, and that someone would be dead by morning. Guests scattered like a firework, a hot metal reek flooding the air. Mr. Salvatici's men returned fire, I glimpsed Nicolo's tomahawk profile cut into view from the wings, and there was Dario Palma, and men were spreading their arms around their lady friends, diving under tables, somersaulting over chairs as the chorus girls shrieked treble clef alarms.

Rat-a-tat-a-tata-tat-tat.

Then a searing stripe painted my upper left arm, and I was contemplating the ceiling.

"Easy there, darlin'. I got you. Jesus Christ, Nobody, this is no time for a siesta. Up now, up, *up*."

It was just like the day I arrived at the Hotel Arcadia, Rye's face blurring, only this time not smiling, not even for show, eyes fearful and every colored, and he lifted me like a rag doll. My body curved in on itself, and there was Mr. Salvatici, lipless mouth curled in a snarl, his revolver gleaming dark as his pomade as its muzzle spasmed, and then a different kind of darkness oozed down my own hair like oil, and Rye was saying something, almost singing it, something I'd have loved to listen to, but he was being a lullaby when I needed a fucking gun, and the last thing I thought of as the world slipped its axis was, *You didn't toast with the barkeep of Bruno's Café when he wanted you to, no wonder everything is being shot quite spectacularly to hell.*

When I woke up, I was in my bed, and Nicolo Benenati was sitting backward in a chair, smoking a cigarette. Watching me.

I gasped, and my arm sizzled like a lightning strike.

"Slowly, *topolina*." Nicolo gripped my wrist. "Just settle into it. They drugged you pretty good after you fainted, but nothing's going to make it easy. Not at first."

Air trickled through my parched throat.

Mr. Salvatici should be here—why isn't he here?

Or Harry or Rye or even Sadie.

"Mr. Salvatici brought in the house doc, knows better than to trust you with any old sawbones who might've been in league with Sammy the Saint. They locked you in, even. But it didn't take much for me to get past the cop. What's his handle? Harry?"

My lips moved. More in the way of trembling than of speech.

"He's taking a nap in the linen cupboard. I wanted to see you, and he took exception. You didn't think I could know you'd been hurt and not see for myself. Did you?"

The old girl wasn't thinking anything except, *Live through this.*

Nicolo shifted to sit on the bed. There were specks of blood on his white collar. More on his cuffs. He frowned, running a single finger along my throat. His active form thrummed and he wore a jackal's famished expression.

"Who was your friend?"

"Which?" I rasped.

"The handsome colored fellow. Leaped down from the stage when you fell."

"Oh. He's . . . he lives here. Used to be a doorman. I'm sorry, I'm all muddled. I should never have gone to the Tobacco Club tonight."

"Why did you?"

"Well, I'm Mr. Salvatici's lucky charm of sorts, and tonight was awfully important. Is he all right? Is everyone all right?"

"Do you mean your dancer friend?" Nicolo put out his cigarette, mechanical as a wind-up toy.

"The fur was well and truly flying, so I mean everybody."

"Your dancer friend is fine," Nicolo reported tonelessly.

I tried my blankest look.

My unwanted companion shrugged. "So are Mr. Salvatici and his men. We had the drop on the Clutch Hand's boys. A society lady got clipped in the leg, a waiter didn't make it, and those Corleonesi are on ice in the club's basement. Coppers didn't do much snooping. It'll be the river for the trash, which is what your boss left to oversee. Sammy the Saint slipped out after he winged you. That was his bullet—the one as passed through your arm. But you're safe, Alicia. I brought him here for you. Can you stand up yet?"

"I . . . think so, but Nicolo . . ."

He courteously offered his hand. Stomach roiling, I took it. My old playmate's palm was dry and smooth and steady. I was wearing a nightgown, and I slid my feet into slippers. Nicolo kept one hand firmly in his and the opposite arm around my waist. I could have been wearing a straitjacket in a nuthouse and felt freer.

"I'd have tried to get to you at the Tobacco Club, but your

friend was quicker. Hell, I'd just seen him dance—quick as blinking. That was probably why you looked at him like that, isn't it? Anyone would look at him, just to catch what he did next."

"Nicolo."

"Alicia. My oldest friend. We're still friends, aren't we?"

"We always will be."

My hallway stretched away from us, pulling itself into a tunnel like a rope of taffy. It must have been the middle of the night. I could have screamed, but Harry Chipchase was apparently down for the count. I could have fought, but I wasn't strong enough.

So I turned into Nobody. Knowing full well that the possum act wasn't very likely to work on a ruthless assassin who also happened to be in love with me.

"Where are we going?"

"To see Sammy."

"No, please." I went all but limp as he propelled me. "My arm hurts. For God's sake, Nicolo—"

"Hush, *topolina*. You're safe, remember? I'm here."

We reached a door at the end of the corridor and he pushed it open.

Sammy the Saint reclined on an oilskin tarp on a hotel bed. Naked, open-eyed. His body was beginning to soften from the slim lines of youth into the rounder curves of excess. A pit had been carved in his breast with something like a hatchet or cleaver. The room reeked of meat not yet started to turn. His jaw had been forced open, and in it rested a lump of gore I supposed faintly was his heart.

The room swam. I know I was sick in the corner, great shaking heaves, and that Nicolo held my hair. Then I folded into a ball with my hands around my knees. I'd never wanted Mr. Salvatici so much in my life, and for some strange reason recalled his argument that I should bet all my chips on his roulette spins.

You find me dangerous, Miss James. Good. I am dangerous. But I am also, you will find, sane. Which compliment cannot be paid to the Clutch Hand.

It couldn't be paid to Nicolo either. Not anymore. I'll never forget his knuckles tilting my chin up gently—satisfied, as if he'd put down a rabid dog for me, and beneath the satisfaction a sick version of the enduring love that had always been there.

"That's what happens to people who hurt you."

"Nicolo. Not this. Clean and tidy, yes, but—"

"No, it had to be this way. I brought Sammy here to make a point to Mr. Salvatici as well as to you. The Clutch Hand was sent a powerful message, but you ended up bleeding. I prefer higher precision. *A fagiolo.** This will show your boss what I think of mistakes."

Nicolo stood up, nodded. He seemed nearly to have forgotten I was there. He adjusted his tie, a bizarre gesture when his collar was seasoned with blood, and regarded the desecrated corpse. I remembered him when he was eleven and I nine, wearing a look like that as he tied tomato stems to stripped branches, and my heart ached more than my arm ever could.

"I had a few words with your dancer friend," he mused. "I thanked him for carrying you out of there so quick. Good night, *topolina*. If anyone else lays a hand on your pretty skin who shouldn't, I'll be there to punish him. Never worry about that. Not so long as I'm around."

---

* Literally "to the bean," meaning to the letter.

· *Nineteen* ·

NOW

Isn't it about time for the Federal government to speak or step out against the many brutal murders, whippings, intimidations and the branding of peaceful, law-abiding citizens by mobs, which are being done in many parts of the country?

—BEATRICE MORROW CANNADY, *The Advocate*,
Portland, Oregon, July 19, 1924

"Oh no, I can hear you perfectly now, Mrs. Snider. Muriel, I mean to say. Forgive me."

"Not at all, dear. No one has a greater bond with our four-footed friends, but Buttons here is the plague of my life. There, that's *quite* enough yapping—you'll let me speak with my friend Alice, won't you, precious?"

The sound like a raven being repeatedly run over by a Daimler continues. Muriel has a point re: plagues. Medea is forever either chewing something expensive or plotting more complex malevolence. It doesn't stop Blossom from slipping her scraps of Miss

Christina's roast chicken and cooing idiotically, but such are the foibles of human nature. I duck farther back into the comfortable cabinet in the Paragon's lobby, nursing a cigarette. People are less likely to remark on a white woman using a colored phone booth supposing it's full of smoke.

"Well, Fred and I had a heart-to-heart, and he thinks you're the sweetest girl, but the KKK are about as sinister as the YMCA." Her voice is thin and metallic through the telephone. "They just wrote a circular to be sent out to women like us who—though naturally ineligible—might encourage upstanding menfolk to apply. Would you like to hear it?"

"I'd be very grateful."

Muriel Snider clears her throat officiously. "'The Knights of the Ku Klux Klan, as a patriotic, fraternal, benevolent order, does not discriminate against a man on account of his religious or political creed so long as it does not antagonize the sacred right guaranteed by our civil government or conflict with Christian ideals and institutions. The Klan asks the support of churchmen everywhere in the great work of uniting into one organization, under one banner, all native-born Protestant Gentile Americans.'"

Those are awfully specific Americans.

"You see? What could be more appropriate, especially with anarchist organizations like this NAACP cropping up? Now. I asked about Davy Lee specifically—oh, think nothing of it, dear—and Fred said it would be the worst sort of paranoia to imagine the Klan had anything to do with the matter. He thinks in all likelihood the poor lad just wandered off and drowned."

"That would be . . . so terribly sad," I manage to say in character.

"Yes, but these things happen, Alice."

"Isn't that a bit callous?"

"Why, my dear, you don't doubt that God's hands are more

capable than ours? Never forget that certain tragedies are beyond mortal control, thanks to our sinner's nature. We must simply abide, and pray for His will to be done."

I've prayed about as often as I've avoided the underside of ladders, with similar results.

She rambles on. "Anyway, what would our Klan want with a harmless little half-breed boy? And if some unhinged ruffian from south of the Mason-Dixon did him any wickedness, wouldn't it have been public?"

Muriel's got the bull firmly by the stabby bits, I realize.

Why wouldn't it have been public, if some crazed backwoods saint was making a point?

"But there is a problem developing, Fred mentioned." Another noxious bark sounds. "Buttons, for heaven's sake, I have had *enough.* Apologies, Alice. Oh, it seems that the child going missing has led to bands of roving Negroes in the woods surrounding the Elms fairgrounds."

I put records on the phonograph for Mr. Salvatici, in the very early days, and accidentally scratched them. Never maliciously, never on purpose. Which is what Muriel Snider sounds like now.

Not malicious. Not on purpose. Ignorant, though, as to how the machine works.

"I think maybe you mean search parties," I supply.

"Well, I hope so, but Fred's associates have wondered. It's all very well to *say* you're a search party, but it isn't as if such people could possibly have any form of identification proving it. Goodness, the very idea gives me the shivers, happening on a pack of colored folk in the forest. But don't fret yourself. Just stay away from the Elms. Simple as that!"

I thank her with appropriate effusion. Stubbing my cigarette out in a pretty brass tray, I ring off. Faintly sick when I imagine the

Paragon's search party coming to any harm over their regard for the life of a small boy.

No good deed goes unpummeled.

Strolling out into the lobby carrying a subtle cloud, I think to find Mavereen and duly report. Muriel's point about public humiliation and terror nags at me something ferocious. I saw Mr. Benenati lipless in a barrel, I saw Sammy the Saint presented like a prize hog with an apple in its teeth.

If the Klan took Davy to strike terror into colored hearts—where's the spit and the sacrificial lamb?

Mavereen Meader isn't present at the front desk. But Rooster is, all bulky baritone and laconic courtesy, checking in a shabby, genteel mother and daughter. Their glances around the Paragon's reception area are furtive, and when Rooster hands over their documents, I catch him heaving a short sigh.

You've unfinished bones to pick with this fellow.

He hangs a room key on its neat brass peg. I remove myself to the shadow of a convenient ficus tree, where I'm less likely to disturb.

"Miss James," he intones without looking at me.

"Mr. . . . Rooster."

The hint of a smile dawns. "I've been called worse."

"Ditto. What ailed that charming pair?"

He settles broadly spaced elbows on the countertop. I've not been alone with him yet, and Rooster is handsome for all his bulk, with a delicate tracework of wrinkles around his eyes and supple lips he pushes outward when cogitating.

"New in town—mother's looking for work. Heard about Davy, heard about the Klan. Word travels fast. We make sure of it."

"Ah. Yes, we had similar methods in Little Italy when someone's insides were about to end up outside."

Another set of guests walk through, these ones a clearly honeymooning pair of lovebirds, and Rooster smiles at them in a surprisingly sentimental way. Two of Mavereen's maids pass us in their usual tidy silence, sharing the weight of a heavy washing bucket.

"I just heard a rumor that the Klan noticed Max's search parties," I state carefully when they're gone.

Rooster shifts, collar digging into his tree-trunk neck.

"That would be lousy," I conclude.

He leans on the front desk, pulling fingers down his square chin.

"So we need to tell Mavereen, she being sovereign ruler. Whereabouts is she?"

"Searching."

"You've not been doing much of that, I notice."

The grandfather clock in the alcove chimes and Rooster pulls out his watch, checks its timekeeping placidly. "Somebody's got to guard this place. I get four hours' shut-eye a night as it is, Miss James. I'll tell her soon as she's back. Meanwhile, best believe I'll keep my ear to the ground."

I'd about ten times rather hide in a wall like a mouse or don eyeglasses and start up the stammering than pull any straightforward stuff. But maybe it's this Nobody's sensible shoes and suffragette pin, maybe it's something in the air other than the rain, but I find myself saying, "Did you get on with Davy?"

Rooster taps his fingers on the ledger. "Davy's a child. What kind of question is that?"

"I heard he was sore at you. Some petty quarrel, I figured, but he seemed like such a happy tyke. What twisted his knickers?"

Rooster's nostrils flare. Given the scale of the man, the act carries weight.

"I don't know where you heard that," he rumbles, "but it's between me and the kid. You're barking up the wrong tree."

"My bark is worse than my bite. What about Miss Christina? Anything amiss with her? She seemed skittish before."

This merits no response.

"Look, I mean no offense, honestly. Did I ever tell you the one about the elevator operator? He sure had his ups and downs."

"No," he answers. "Did I ever tell you about the colored man dangling from a tree? He was just hanging around."

Rooster wins, and I turn to go.

Then I pivot again and find myself saying, "Davy matters to Blossom even if he doesn't matter to you, and the entire lot deserve to know what's going on."

"No," he replies, still not looking at me. "They don't deserve to know what you're asking about, in particular. Especially you don't. And if you dig into Miss Christina's private life, you'll have me to deal with."

No, you're not the most intimidating person I've ever met, I think as I walk away.

He could still flick me out the door like the veriest ant, however. Which makes it strange that my instincts tell me he'll refrain. Rooster just threatened me, that's gospel—but he didn't lie to me, not once. Not about Davy Lee's animosity, nor about the plain fact Miss Christina has indigestion about something. When I spoke to Max about it yesterday, he said in no uncertain terms they were both thoroughly trustworthy, so it must be a private matter and none of our beeswax.

I remember when I assumed people could be trustworthy beyond a doubt. It was ever so nice, like assuming I'd live in New York for the rest of my life.

I head for the hills—which is the elevator and Wednesday Joe. The opening doors prompt a heady sense of relief. Joe doesn't *know* me exactly. But he does in a certain sense understand me, and I step into his vertical chariot with a light foot, considering.

"Where are you headed?" he snaps. The poor lad's eyes are bloodshot again.

"My floor. Where else? Goodness, Joe, you never seemed like the type to tell a bullet to get a move on."

"Sure, be funny about it. See if I care."

When I regard him in blatant dismay, he softens. "Sorry, Your Majesty, but. Going out with you and Max didn't earn me any favors with Mrs. Meader. Here's your floor and you're welcome to it."

This is too abrupt, and the youngster too upset, for me to let it lie.

"Wait! Give the old girl a moment. I'll explain to Mrs. Meader that chasing down a white horse was my—"

"No use. I'm already on duty tonight scrubbing out Miss Christina's stoves. Just . . . leave it alone, Miss James. Leave me alone."

I step backward. He clangs the grate shut.

You don't belong anywhere, Nobody. That's the real secret you've been keeping all along.

Meanwhile, something about this hallway causes my feet to scuff reluctantly.

Ah, yes.

Here I am. Here Davy still isn't. And I've got a knack for hotel locks, a hairpin in my pocket, and I'm standing across from Miss Christina's door when I know she's sweating a fine mist into her soup du jour. Rooster just put me off, and rightfully so. Miss Christina deserves privacy. But, lo and behold, here's a profligate spy, a busybody, and one with a burning urge to find the kidlet whose absence is causing such terrible pain.

The lock takes under ten seconds to vanquish. There's Davy's abandoned castle, which slices a wider ribbon off my heart than it ought to do. There's the settee and the door to the bedroom.

There's her desk, with a pen in a coffee mug. There's a drawer.

The missives I've seen her clutching are stashed on the top left in plain sight. So I open one. The first is a love letter in a masculine hand.

Dear one,

This oppressive atmosphere will not hang over us forever. You seem wearier every day. Know that every opportunity, I send more money. Know that a farm, with all the fresh eggs and beans and strawberries you could ever want, and a stream thick with fish, will be yours. Picture it. Everything I can set my hands on will be yours. I will be yours. You will never have to think of this place again.

Patience will see us through,
Your own

The first thought smacking me on the brow is what an awfully swell suitor this sounds like. Is it Rooster, as I suppose it to be from the intimacy of their interrupted tête-à-tête? Blunt but eloquent? And if it is Rooster, what could possibly be oppressing them? Worse, why should this beautiful hotel be a place anyone admired to forget? Granted, there exist fraught relations between . . .

I stop to think.

Between Blossom and Dr. Pendleton. Between Davy and Rooster. Between Jenny and Blossom. Between Blossom and Mavereen.

The name *Blossom* starts bouncing around my noggin like a racquet ball. So I keep reading.

Dear one,

I understand that you find the money offer unsettling. But we need it. How much we need it you know as well as I do, and even if the arrangement is unusual, it's not as if it'll cause anyone harm. So I've—

"What the *hell* are you doing in here?"

It's against my training to drop the letter. But holy *merde*, how close I come.

"Blossom!" I blink at where she looms like a weirdly elegant stick figure. "I'm . . . well, it looks just horrid, but . . . wait, what are *you* doing in here?"

"Leaving a note for Christina. I heard someone's footsteps, so I thought I'd simply tell her."

Blossom Fontaine approaches me with long strides. She went back to her room after sobbing her lungs out in mine, and now she wears an apple-green gown dotted in complex arrow shapes with bronze bugle beads. One that makes her skin shine peacock violet like polished metal.

Or perhaps that's the rage shining, second thought.

"I don't pretend to be coy around you, Alice," she hisses. "In fact, the only thing I *ever* pretend to be around *anyone* is civil, because I do not give a single shit about civility when civility doesn't serve. What are you doing in Miss Christina's room, if you please?"

Her temper has never been directed at me before. It feels something like a spearpoint, and something like a battering ram.

"I thought I might do good by finding out what's in the letters she's perennially reading. You know the ones, you're her friend. I'm sorry. I'm accustomed to being around people who are altogether full of bull, and if she was hiding something—"

"She *is* hiding something." Blossom snatches the letter away. She smooths it, darts her eyes over it, then slaps it against her lean thigh. "*This* is what she's hiding, Alice. And she never would dream of confiding a word of this wretched business to *you*."

"Oh," I say in an awfully small voice.

I haven't felt mortified for quite a few calendars. And I wasn't troubled by accidentally stumbling upon Blossom's diagnosis. But now—now heat begins to bubble up my neck.

"And it's none of your nosy, meddling, interfering *business*." Blossom scans the note a second time. "How much of my friend's private correspondence did you sample before I arrived? Just this?"

"That was the second, and I barely started it."

"What was in the first?"

"Not much to speak of. She feels oppressed. Something about saving for a farm." Impossibly, I feel like crying. "Please understand, I only meant to—"

"What? Solve some sort of imaginary mystery? Air someone's dirty underthings?"

"No, it's that I can tell when someone's hiding something, and—"

"And you could smell it on her." Blossom steps toward me, a statuesque menace. "Yes, oh I *see*, we've all practically splayed our hearts on a dissecting board for a complete stranger in the past few days and you *liked* that. Didn't you?"

I gape at her. She has me. I'd wanted intimacy and I'd gotten it. And I'd given next to nothing in return.

Blossom smirks. "Gracious, there's the bit that smarts. They're like cough syrup, secrets—no getting enough of them once you've had a taste."

"They're my stock in trade, actually. And I know far too much about cough syrup. I could write an ill-advised novel."

Blossom laughs. Not kindly. She might be good and she might be bad and she might be wrong about which. So many are.

But on this particular afternoon in not-sunny Portland, Oregon, she isn't kind.

"Yes, of course you could write the book on heroin, honey,

you're a criminal I befriended despite the fact Jenny warned me. You lot are practically lining up for respiratory ailments. Ever so posh, perhaps, almost Victorian levels of faked suffering, but also just the tiniest bit *pathetic*, wouldn't you agree?"

"I don't see you leaving any whiskey glasses wet," I snap.

We stare at each other. I in horror that I lost control, even if it was for Rye. She in the identical feeling she'd caused by catching me pawing through love letters. Letters written without any name, letters identifiable only by the swoop of the downstrokes and the flavor of the words chosen, letters I should never have seen. She drinks far too much. We both know it. And now we're sharing the same sensation. Shame.

"Get out." Blossom folds the note, hands visibly humming.

"Blossom, we're both being a bit beastly, and I think—"

"No, you most *certainly* did not think." She raises her eyes. "I have a life here. I have responsibilities, I have family, and yes, I also possess an *absurd* affection for lost pennies, but Alice James, trying to find Davy and smudging your fingers all over my friend Christina's private mail for kicks are different matters entirely."

My dismay at being caught wrong-footed notwithstanding, my brow burns at this. Everyone detests having their motives misconstrued.

"You know as well as I do that's a blue-ribbon whopper," I return, matching her quiet tone. "Davy hasn't been ransomed or made an example of or contacted you. He's just gone. For no reason at all. That bears looking into, don't you suppose?"

Slivers of a second pass when I think I just made Blossom Fontaine cry.

"I don't question your love for Davy," I protest. "But those who live in tin houses shouldn't throw can openers. And I'm ever so sorry I hurt you. You're one of, I—I think you might be my only friend in the world. Please say that—"

"Get out." Blossom crosses her arms around herself, tight as a straitjacket, crushing Miss Christina's letter. "If you decide to dawdle, I'll report this curious event to Mavereen. Get *out.*"

Bowing my head, I approach Blossom as I exit. Her gaunt chest heaves beneath its glittering silk gown, an emerald snake's torso writhing in distress. Then I see up close just how jazzy her choice of sackcloth is this evening.

I hesitate. "Are you performing tonight?"

"Don't stare at me like a simp—of course I am." Blossom inhales hard, but the air around us is acrid with scalding words and burned bridges.

"But—"

"I need the money!" she cries, throwing her arms out as if she's being splayed on a rack. "In case you haven't noticed, and you notice *far* more than is decent, honey, it's what I liked about you, I continue to require medical attention."

"I have money," I remind her instantly. "How much do you need? Just as a loan. I'd be awfully pleased to help."

"I recall instructing you to be elsewhere."

"Listen." I raise a hand to touch her arm but drop it at the flash in her dark irises. "If you won't take my money, then take me with you. You don't even have to speak to me. Last night was so awful, I didn't get the chance to spill everything. That Overton bastard has a gun, not to mention a picture of you in his pocket, and he—"

"Oh, I can handle Overton." Blossom forces a gallows smile. "You've seen me do it, it's better than fully staged Wagner. Now if I were you, I'd vanish in a *pounding* big hurry, honey."

There's nothing to be done. I leave her standing there, with her hand wrapped like a raven's talons around the letter I found. I walk to my room. My heart finding new places to crack for the entire journey, the way even a crumbling ruin can still muster the energy to drop a fresh hail of stones. Locking my door, I spend a moment blinking stupidly.

It's what I liked about you, I hear her spitting.

Liked. Before I read a letter and smashed her trust.

No. One letter and a few bonus sentences. More's the pity, because the latter were terribly interesting.

And it's after reflecting on these aforementioned missives—about a dreamed-of farm, about needed money—that I wonder just who was admiring to pay whom, and what an unusual "arrangement" could mean.

And what could it possibly have to do with Davy? Nothing at all?

These people adore the tyke, and it isn't as if nowadays you can go around selling kids like they're puppies.

It's too wrong to contemplate. But why was Davy angry at Rooster before disappearing? And if Blossom knows all about Miss Christina's secret and wants it left alone, same as Max, what can a white interloper do save to shut up and move along?

My thoughts disintegrate. Curling up on the coverlet, I soak my nest with my sorrows. The tears come bitter and strong and thick.

Liked. So we aren't chums anymore.

She was wonderful. She glowed as bright as anybody, and she even looked for your eyes when she smiled.

Alice's, if she still exists.

Not Nobody's.

And you didn't even get to tell her about kissing Max.

When I awaken, the sky is rotting from purple to black. The comforting rhythm of the rain is absent. But the stars are out—watchful and arrogantly bright.

The short rest revived me. Rising, I wash my face. Don a plain beige pocketed frock with a square collar, wrap up my hair, dab powder under still-swollen eyes. I regard Nobody the spinster suffragette and frown—I'm about as far away from professional journalism as Blossom is from the Woman's Christian Temperance Union. Granted, I've been scribbling all-too-real data and observations in her prop notebook. Whether as proof should Overton ask to see it, or as an aid to my own memory, I can't rightly tell. But I simply cannot commit any of these new aspects to indelible ink.

Miss Christina is hiding something. Rooster had a quarrel with Davy. And Blossom . . .

Blossom needs money. Very, very badly.

All thoughts of slinking away, *slither-swish*, are quashed. There's too much at stake. There's a missing boy and a band of good people and a populace being bullied.

There's Maximilian Burton. And his lips tasted like almonds and rain and clean smoke.

My entire body still glimmers. But now isn't the time; what I need is a heart-to-heart with Jenny Kiona. She'll be happy as a veritable daisy in the field if I confess Blossom and I scrapped, even if I fail to discuss details. And she's closer to Blossom than just about anyone other than Max and Mavereen.

That's the ticket, now join the queue and step onto the carousel.

Fearful of another quarrel, I take the stairs. When I arrive in the nearly deserted lobby, Rooster is reading a newspaper, glancing every third second at the revolving doors. Whatever else can be said about the man, shirking isn't his strong suit. He spies me at once, and I give an apologetic wave.

Rooster finds that he prefers the sight of the printed word.

Then the circular door turns. No—it blasts into orbit, churns dizzily, it makes the jazziest display of revolving that ever a lobby door did, and I flinch in alarm until it spits out Mrs. Evelina Vaughan.

She looks better than when last I saw her—but if it were a race, it would be by a nose. Her pastel features are less hectic, but her cheeks have sunken. Her yellow pleated coat is charming, but the body beneath can't catch its breath. Her apricot waves are piled atop her head, but it looks like she employed two minutes and a fork on the project.

Mrs. Vaughan's eyes gleam like grey pearls. She's crying. Everybody and their maiden aunt seem to be crying these days.

"Oh!" she gasps. "Miss . . . James, was it? Were you at my house? Or did I imagine that?"

I shift into the sober reporter. "I was entirely real, Mrs. Vaughan. But whatever is the matter?"

Rooster bounds from behind the counter. "Mrs. Vaughan. Welcome. Here, sit down—"

"No, I can't, Rooster, there isn't time. Where's Blossom? I need her."

"She's performing tonight," I supply. "Mrs. Vaughan, please won't you sit down? You seem as if you've had a shock."

She touches her palm to her brow, nodding. "Yes, but never mind that, I need to tell her. I got here as fast as I could."

My blood frosts. "I'm . . . an acquaintance of Blossom's. Rooster and I can help you. Tell her what?"

"That the Klan is massing!" Mrs. Vaughan paces in a circle—eyes shut, like a child pretending to be invisible. "I still can't quite think straight, you see, I took something of a spell, and I didn't know what to do, so I have to ask her, she'll know."

"The Klan is *what*?" Rooster growls.

"They're holding a rally, a demonstration, something ghastly, these ridiculous men with their hoods and their nightgowns," she hisses. "My husband caught wind of it. Dear, brave, harmless Tom. I—"

A trio of partygoers, the man with a lady on either arm, return to the hotel, laughing to raise the dead. Rooster ushers us to the side and greets them. They stagger into the elevator.

Rooster returns, resembling the veritable wrath of God.

"I overheard Tom on the telephone at home," Mrs. Vaughan continues, "saying that the Klansmen were gathering, but he rang off before I heard what he planned to do. Then I ran downstairs to ask, but he . . . I haven't felt well, so he wanted me not to trouble myself. And he had to leave! And he'll do all he can to keep the peace, but what if they don't listen? What if—"

"Mrs. Vaughan," Rooster rumbles, "is there a reason you needed Blossom specifically?"

"The Klansmen plan to gather at the Elms."

The lobby floods with chilled silence. Rooster is never spendthrift with words. As for myself, I've forgotten them all.

"They must want to intimidate the search party." Mrs. Vaughan twists her gloves. "Tom suggested so, and after he left, I came here quick as I could. Oh, he'll be furious, but."

My ears buzz as if bullets are singing. I exchange a look with Rooster; he shakes his head. So Mavereen hasn't returned, and the search party doesn't know about Muriel Snider's gossip.

Which means Max doesn't know they're under threat of attack.

Rooster nods decisively. "I'll send Wednesday Joe."

"He's a boy!" I exclaim. "Mavereen assigned him KP for walking a few blocks away—what do you think she'll make of him visiting the Elms?"

"The message needs delivering."

"Then deliver it!"

"I don't leave this hotel when the Klan are running loose." The veins in Rooster's neck strike up a martial drumbeat. "There's three hundred and seventy-two God-fearing souls presently lodging in this building. Who do you want behind that desk when a mob shows up with torches? Me or Joe?"

I bite my lip, willing my pulse to calm.

"I'll go," I announce.

"Yes, fine, yes, but hurry," Mrs. Vaughan begs.

"Like hell you will." Rooster is so angry his teeth are showing.

"Entirely apart from writing my article," I state with clarity, "I've been making every effort to prove I'm not loafing. I went to Mr. and Mrs. Vaughan's house, and I can go to the Elms. These clods would never harm a white woman—it's against everything they stand for. Hail us a taxi, please?"

Steam whistles teakettle bright from Rooster's nose.

"Oh, I can't stand this," Mrs. Vaughan moans. "I'll go by myself, I'll—"

"No, Miss James will take care of it, Mrs. Vaughan," Rooster grinds out. "But she'll see you home on the way. After you, ladies."

We precede Rooster outside the Paragon. I haven't any coat, and the air bites with petite teeth. Mrs. Vaughan takes one look at me and wraps her muffler about my neck, a shawl-like garment printed with violets that does positive wonders.

"I can't possibly—"

"Oh, you certainly can," she husks as Rooster whistles for a taxi. "Just like you can take me with you to the Elms, I've no doubt in my mind. Speaking of my mind, it's rather addled presently, which is why I need an escort, do forgive me for dragging you into this wretched mess, but. I know who you really are, you see."

"I'm Alice James, when have I pretended—"

"Blossom likes you." A secret, sunlit smile dawns. "Actual you. So I like you too."

"I see," I manage.

Liked, I think, impaling my palms with my nails.

"The Elms, driver, quickly!" Mrs. Vaughan calls when we seat ourselves in the sleek little conveyance, and the engine roars into action. "Yes, I know it's closed. Please do hurry!"

The city passes us in stripes of electric garlands and shining glass. It's like being in a river, all shimmer and no permanence. Yours truly is so smashed up over Blossom and so frightened for Max that I'm silent until the delicately wild woman beside me says, "I hear the pair of you have been getting yourselves into trouble."

I turn to Evelina Vaughan in dismay.

"Oh, don't be alarmed—please, you've eaten my scones, you must imagine that we're friends right up until the instant we really are, and then it'll come true." She smiles faintly. "You'd not think it to look at me, but I've spread mayhem with Blossom Fontaine myself. I'm only thankful you're both all right after that horrible Overton beast attacked you. He ought to be in a cage in a zoo, a very faraway zoo."

"Arabia," I suggest.

"Farther than that." Her tone could poison spinning wheels.

"From your lips to God's appointment book, Mrs. Vaughan."

"Amen. And do call me Evelina."

"I'll be Alice henceforth, then."

"You're very sweet. And I'm sorry you saw me like that, earlier, with Tom." She winces. "I don't remember much of it, I never do, but if I've anything to apologize for, you mustn't hesitate but tell me at once so that I can make amends. That's the only way I can cope with the guilt over having such a humiliating condition—instant and profuse apologies."

"You were lovely," I assure her. "Let's talk of something cheerfuller en route to high adventure, my belly's in a dreadful tangle. Did you really pull out the red paintbrushes with Blossom?"

"From time to time. I've never turned up at the Rose's Thorn, it would be unfair to Tom, you understand, as the wife of a Chief of Police. But, yes, we did carry on occasionally before his promotion. I remember her singing some nights, the sort of French songs that make you feel like a flock of sparrows is bursting out of your chest. I really can't do such silly things anymore now I'm something of a public figure, but. She's a dear friend. Oh, do forgive me, Alice, I can't chat any longer. My head aches so."

I pat Evelina's hand. She squeezes mine, then pushes her fists in her coat pockets and lets her head loll on the leather seat.

I huddle in her scarf trying not to think of all the wasted love in the world. Like Blossom's for Evelina. From where I'm sitting, it roars like Niagara Falls.

We don't speak again until after she's paid the driver, insisting, and we step into the chill glow of the Elms's nocturnal illumination. It turns the grounds icicle blue, an awfully eerie landscape but a beautiful one, as if a heartbroken painter had thrown away all his other colors in despair, or you could see "After You've Gone" right in front of you the way I heard Blossom sing it last night.

Evelina Vaughan screams.

The sound is so shrill I nearly stumble, and a hot needle pierces my gut. She seizes my wrist. At first, only gasping, "What is it?" I see nothing—but then she turns me away from the fairgrounds and points at the tree line, silhouetted in sinister spikes against the constellations.

And the enormous cross burning hellishly in the foreground.

Twenty

Silhouetted in the bright glare the marching figures passed in an endless array like silent wraiths, bent upon some solemn mission: ever-silent, ever-moving, a dauntless power, an irresistible force, moving on and on, ever beneath the cross, ever yielding to its glory and magnified by its power.

—"KU KLUX KLAN STAGES MONSTER SPECTACLE IN RECEIVING THEIR CHARTER," *Roseburg News-Review*, Roseburg, Oregon, July 17, 1922

Centuries scrape by as we gape at the monstrous thing.

"I never in my life thought to see one," Evelina breathes. "God, it's madness."

"Blossom calls it loathing," I note.

We stare, holding each other's arms, as the wood dances a devil's jig. Then I recall a body stuffed into a barrel and experience an unholy swell of rage.

"Sod this shit," I declare. "Let's go."

We set off, angling toward the river. The ghosts of figures mill about below their hideous bonfire. Many carry torches. As small as matchsticks at first, then ballooning into grotesque candles. After fifty paces, we spy conical hats painted phoenix orange by firelight, the blurred swish of white robes. After forty more, we hear the occasional raucous laugh. We aren't yet visible ourselves—outside the range of the Elms's haunted illumination, we are ink spilled on darkness. Nevertheless, Evelina pulls my arm.

"Tom isn't here yet," she frets. "Oh, I wanted so for him to be here already, even if I'll be in the hottest water of my life. Peaceful assemblies are one thing and burning crosses are another. He'd be furious, just livid."

"Where is he, then?"

"I don't know. But . . . surely the search party won't come out of the woods at all, if they see a flaming cross?"

"They won't see it. Any black would've lost his last marble to walk toward that thing, but the Klan set it up behind that copse there. The search party will be carrying bright lanterns. They'll be awfully tired. And it's miles of forest on the other side and the river bordering."

"You're saying it's a bottleneck, aren't you?" The grip on my arm tightens. "One they won't spy until it's too late. Can we get around and stop them first?"

We slink like cats. There is no moon, thankfully; hung from that strangely pristine canopy, the moon would serve as well as a great chandelier. So despite my injury and Evelina's exhaustion, after two minutes we've nearly reached the gentler slope where the search party should emerge.

But *nearly* only counts regarding horseshoes and hand grenades.

"You best *believe* she'll be sitting up for me with supper on the table!" an unknown voice calls. A second chuckles, and a third lets out a weary hoot.

Evelina gasps, and I clap a hand over her mouth—gently.

"Evelina," I mouth in her ear, "if you've heard any stories where a white woman shrieking as a gang of blacks approached led to a picnic, discount 'em. It leads to funerals."

She sags in defeat.

"You been married to Gracie for six months and you think she'll still wait up half the night for you?" the voices continue.

"Damn straight! Nursed me through fever sweats just last month."

"Aw, hell, I'd take her nursing if I didn't have to eat her biscuits. Andy, no offense, but does Gracie savvy the difference between flour and cement mix?"

This last voice belongs to Maximilian. A chorus of guffaws heralds a dozen lantern beams crisscrossing like rockets.

One of the lights catches us, snags, momentarily blinds me.

"Saints alive! What on—Mrs. Vaughan, is that you, sugar? And with Miss James?"

Mavereen Meader strides toward us, exclamations surrounding her. Evelina and I wave our arms.

"Quiet, oh, do please keep quiet," Evelina pleads. "We're here to warn you!"

"What kinda warning might that be, Mrs. Vaughan?"

Max appears, tall and calm, and despite the thrill I can't control, I'm dreadfully keen on the notion of his being elsewhere. Argentina has a dandy ring to it.

"The Klan," I report. "Look, over there, they've—"

"You gotta be kidding me," Max growls.

The search party takes in the scene. I can practically smell the quick surge of nerves.

Mavereen groans. "Oh, no, not while our boy ain't yet found. 'The Lord is my light and my salvation; whom shall I fear? The Lord is the strength of my life: of whom shall I be afraid?'"

"Jesus H. Christ," Dr. Pendleton curses in a different sort of prayer. "Just when I think I've seen enough shit for one lifetime."

"Oh, *hell* no," comes another voice.

"Those bastards. Those yellow-bellied bastards."

"Lights out!" Max orders. "Shut 'em down on the double!"

A dozen lanterns are extinguished.

Click-snap. Clink-scrape.

Then we turn, as one crouched animal, toward the cross with the red snakes' tongues flicking upward.

Max's hand, steady and surprisingly warm, smooths down my arm in the darkness, and I can't decide whether to think *yes, yes, do that forever*, or *run and run now.*

"We got no time for chitchat, Alice," he murmurs, "so I'll play it straight, like. I ain't happy to see you here."

"Don't use up all your flattery in one go. Consider a girl's poor heart."

"I'm gonna wring your neck, matter of fact."

"I only hope you get the chance."

"Angels of mercy defend us," Mavereen whispers. "What do we do? Take cover in the woods?"

"Nah." Max spits on the ground. "That'd only bait 'em, see? They'd come in beating the goddamn bushes like we was rabbits."

"She's right. We should run," a voice suggests.

"I didn't run from Jerry and I sure as *hell* ain't gonna run from a pack of hooded clowns. Anyhow, if we ain't running, they can't chase us."

The lights, once tightly grouped, are separating. Drifting and bobbing like malevolent sprites. Shouts reach our ears.

Some of the torches seem to be heading this way.

A soft chorus of swearing erupts.

"Whaddaya say, Doc?" Max questions evenly. "Do we figure this for Mons or Marne?"

"Marne." The glint from Dr. Pendleton's glasses makes him resemble a dreadfully robust beetle. "Skulking away is as good as proof of guilt for these sons of bitches. The aftermath would last a decade. Question is, how to attack?"

"I calculate I know what to do."

Mavereen Meader's natural voice has returned. It's resonant, unafraid, and about as certain as gravity.

"Give Mrs. Vaughan and Miss James here lanterns," she commands. "Quick now, and then light y'all's up again, and we'll meet them halfway. Mrs. Vaughan'll go first, me and Miss James right behind her. It ain't much of a chance, but it's our best. Mrs. Vaughan, you willing to lead this march?"

Evelina Vaughan puts out her hand for a light. "More than willing. It's a brilliant idea, Mrs. Meader."

The quiet that follows is equal parts skeptical and dumbfounded.

"She's right," I realize. "It's our only option. Max, what are you waiting for?"

"Ladies, no disrespect, but—"

"Maximilian, Lord love you for a gentleman, but that ain't wanted just now." Mavereen's tone has turned as steely as her hair. "Let the womenfolk handle this one. I'm your commanding officer sure enough, and these here are my advance guard. Miss James, go on ahead and take Dr. Pendleton's light. Max, hand yours over to Mrs. Vaughan here. I said *hand it over.*"

"You gotta be—"

"Child, you hard of hearing? Pass Mrs. Vaughan your lantern and mind your tongue."

There's no disobeying her. The lanterns hiss to life again, and we three women form a triangular phalanx—Evelina at the forefront, Mavereen on her right, and yours very truly on her left.

"Plumb craziest thing I ever done," Mavereen mutters.

"Likewise," I reply.

Evelina says nothing. She simply starts walking. In awfully fine style, considering everyone is frightened enough to jump clean out of their birthday suits.

The lanterns advance toward the torches and vice versa. I hear an owl mourning a loss, Dr. Pendleton's rasping cough. Max's footfalls are silent. But I pretend that I can feel his warmth as I remember what walking into a death trap feels like. I'd admired to leave those behind—but, then again, I'd admired to bring down all of Corleone, and witness how that worked out.

"Stand and declare yourselves!" shouts a voice like a sawmill.

An unknown energy electrifies Evelina Vaughan. It looks like a firefly taking wing. Small but fearfully mighty. While I'm grateful Blossom isn't here, I wish she could see it.

I'll yarn it to her later. If she'll let me.

"Hello!" Evelina cries. "My, what a display! Are you holding some sort of Klan ritual?"

Despite our peril, I hear Mavereen softly snort.

"Who in hell is that?" a drunken voice yells.

"Mrs. Evelina Vaughan, wife of the Chief of Police. He's on his way!" She shouts still louder, "What luck, I can introduce you to my friends before he arrives!"

It takes very little time for the torches to reach the lanterns. Very little time, for all to change and your world to hang suspended in the balance. The opposing sides stop with twenty or so paces separating us: about fifty people straining against the leash to make around fifteen people bleed. If this idea weren't so absurd, I'd laugh at it. But, very like the notion of paying your protectors to safeguard you against *them*, it's too ridiculous to be remotely amusing.

At least the Mafia weren't so gutless that they hid behind bedsheets.

"Oh, thank goodness, I could hardly see you before—and I still can't see you, what with the hoods and all, can I?" Evelina shields her pupils as if looking into the sun.

"Ma'am," a moonshine-drenched voice questions, "these boys giving you trouble?"

"Come on over here now, and we'll protect you," another offers.

"I beg pardon, but I don't know what you could possibly mean."

"He means to keep you safe, ma'am. Seems to be an awful lot of 'em, and powerful unafraid to roam the woods after sundown," another faceless fellow persists.

"Why ever should they be afraid?" Evelina wonders.

She sounds terribly stupid. But she isn't stupid.

Mavereen's plan is working, and Evelina's bent on nothing whatsoever save time. Thomas Vaughan's time spent in arriving here. Supposing it succeeds, my proverbial cap is off to her. If it doesn't, some of us will be going home in wheelbarrows.

"I can't think of any reason law-abiding citizens should be afraid to comb the woods for a missing person," she adds sweetly.

"Law-abiding. You sure about that?" This new voice is strangely familiar.

"Oh, yes!" Evelina vows. "Absolutely, I was with them—the three of us women were, all searching for the missing boy, and though we didn't find him, thank God no menaces like bears or timber wolves threatened us."

"Look to me like you're right in the middle of a goddamn menace."

The mob hisses its agreement.

"I'm afraid you're mistaken." Evelina smiles. "But how kind of you to worry! I hope that I can tell my husband your meeting the search party like this was only a happy coincidence. Because you see, Tom might be skeptical if he saw the cross lit up this way. And

I think he'd be most . . . disappointed by it. So. Why don't we leave you to your sacred ceremonies?"

"Why don't you just own that you're this fine city's biggest nigger lover, Mrs. Vaughan?"

The stench of tobacco chew wafts in our direction. And I can place him now—it's the ticket booth operator from the day Davy went missing.

Did you try the carousel? Did you try the floating bathhouse?

"You can't talk to Mrs. Vaughan that way!" yells a swaying Klansman. "She's only doing charity for the poor Negroes, same as she does for the Humane Society. Hell, that's why God almighty *made* women."

"Leave off Mrs. Vaughan and see that these darkies answer for the mischief they been hatching."

"She's nothing but a lunatic, you ask me!"

"I'll not have you insulting Tom Vaughan's wife!"

The crunch of a fist meeting teeth rings out among the Klansmen. More swiftly join the fracas, swinging and grappling—which starts off just swell, if you ask me, because only the KKK are getting their faces mashed.

"Stop it!" Evelina cries. "You have wives, you have *children*. For heaven's sake, stop!"

As she shouts, she throws out a hand in protest. Her entire body wants them to cease, and just when I reach to pull her back, one of the hooded men seizes her wrist and—I truly believe through misguided assistance turned drunken accident—throws her savagely to the ground when he keels over.

Max yells and leaps, but the fellows he summoned to search for Davy wrestle him backward as the mob seethes, thank Christ. Mavereen and I dive for Evelina. The Klansmen are still exchanging blows, dragging their soused comrade away as he bellows something about decency and *only meant to help*. Torches come dangerously close to our black friends' faces. Spit flies, and the Negroes stand there silent as their own graves. Mavereen cradles Evelina's head in her lap. No one seems to object to this part—I suppose it must look like a mammy with her ward.

Then Dr. Doddridge B. Pendleton sinks to one knee and takes her pulse. Because he doesn't care what color he's treating. It's his way of flipping the bird to humanity while helping it at the same time, and I hear Max cry, "Don't, Doc!"

An awfully thick silence twines through the pale robes and the licking flames.

"Steady enough, but weak." Dr. Pendleton leans in closer. "Mrs. Vaughan? Can you answer me?"

"Don't you fucking touch her, coon," rasps the Elms's ticket operator.

"That's Dr. Coon to you," Dr. Pendleton volleys back. He's much, much drunker than I supposed. "And my attention belongs to this patient, not some glorified Halloween spook."

For at least three seconds, shocked quiet reigns.

Then the insults start flying. Along with more spittle, and threats, it's like a Gatling gun, and if these idiots weren't shit-assed terrified of what they just did to Portland's marmalade-haired charitable figurehead, they would rip us all in pieces.

"He's a doctor of medicine!" I attempt.

"Sure as I live and breathe, he don't mean her no harm!" Mavereen cries.

"What is going on here?"

Thomas Vaughan approaches at last, with a pair of men behind him. One is Officer Taffy, his florid face goggling in dismay. The other is a tiny white chappie—immaculate posture, meticulously dressed in pinstripes, and approximately the size of Miss Christina.

"See to the crowd, Mr. Snider!" Chief Vaughan shouts as he

breaks into a run with a look of abject terror on his handsome features.

Mavereen quickly places Evelina in his arms. The Klansmen, none too steadily nor willingly, retreat a few yards.

"Sweetheart," Tom Vaughan begs. "Evy, can you hear me?"

"She couldn't hear me, so, no, I don't suppose so." Dr. Pendleton doesn't edge away.

"What the hell happened here?" Chief Vaughan cries. Several pieces of her old-fashioned coiffure have come loose, and he smooths them back. "Which misguided fool is responsible for that cross being on fire?"

"Terrible, just terrible," the dwarfish man Tom Vaughan called Mr. Snider—who can only be Fred Snider, Muriel's one true et cetera—laments. "Where do you lot think we are, Mississippi? Well, we shall chalk it up to high spirits, I suppose, but this is disgraceful!"

"Evy, I'm here," Chief Vaughan keeps saying.

Officer Taffy, who I'd not noticed leaving, returns miraculously hauling a bucket and flings river water at the cross. Which elicits enthusiastic jeers.

"No, no." Mr. Snider waves his hands. "Knock it down and we can smother it. Out of the way!"

"She's only fainted." Dr. Pendleton pulls his glasses off, revealing his densely freckled face. "She'll be fine in a few minutes, I believe."

"Didn't hit her head or nothing, Mr. Vaughan," Max offers. "I done seen it."

"Oh, hello, Mr. Burton." Thomas Vaughan realizes that there are other people besides his wife present. "I'm mighty sorry I wasn't here sooner, wanted to bring one or two men as backup. How did the search progress?"

"Wish as I could say it progressed at—"

Thwack.

Several crashing sounds ring out. I don't know how the brawl started again, but now it's blacks and whites determined to pulverize one another. Which means one misjudged blow, one ripped-away hood, might spell our doom. Fists fly, men with lanterns dropping them to defend themselves against men with torches. Possibly worse.

In the frenzied grapple of bodies tearing at one another, I discern a single yell.

"You *can't*!"

Officer Taffy inserts himself between combatants. His face is crimson, his neck streaming sweat.

"This isn't the law." The hooded men pause in shock. "There's a lady here, and she needs help. She's a good lady. I'll arrest every one of you!"

"Yes, indeed!" snaps Mr. Snider from where he's contemplating how to knock down a flaming cross. "You will not endanger a white woman, and one who also happens to be a pillar of the community! Go! I will make mention of this in my report to the Arlington Club and suggest that your Klavern be severely fined."

Dr. Pendleton settles back on his knees as the ghostly men shake their fists. He checks Mrs. Vaughan's pulse again, uncaring.

"This ain't over," Max observes quietly from behind me.

"No," Mavereen agrees with flat dread in her voice. "This here's the devil's work, and he ain't like to quit till the final trump sounds."

Muttering curses, the specters begin to wander off. Somebody strikes up a tune, and the singing sparks like fire in dry tinder, voices raised in triumphant intoxication.

Over all the U.S.A.
The Fiery Cross we display,

The emblem of Klansmen's domain:
We'll be forever true
To the Red, White, and Blue
And Americans always remain.

Officer Taffy finds the rope used to raise the wretched thing and helps Mr. Snider to pull it down. Evelina stirs, to my enormous relief. Tom Vaughan looks as if Lazarus was just raised from the dead. So the Paragon residents gather at a little distance from the murmuring couple as the search party likewise disperses, the men glancing backward every few paces.

"Mrs. Vaughan came to the hotel to sound the alarm," I say quietly. "She'll be all right, I hope?"

"Of course not. The woman suffers from mental disorder," Dr. Pendleton reports curtly. "But in this case, she can be under no better care than that of her husband. Anyway, I don't have my bag."

"You done touched her, though." Max shakes his head.

Dr. Doddridge Pendleton closes his fists. "I took an oath. It might mean nothing to half the graduates of medical college. But it matters to me, damn it."

"Like it oughta. I just wish there weren't a pack of hoodlums there to watch."

"Mrs. Meader, Dr. Pendleton?" Chief Vaughan calls out. Standing, he lifts his wife, whose face is hidden against his neck. "My car is here, and Officer Taffy has one likewise. I trust him and Mr. Snider to take care of the cross. Would you help me getting Evy home while I drive? I'll drop you at the Paragon after."

"With all my heart," Mavereen answers. "Come along, Doc, and mind your manners. Max, you keep your eyes peeled, sugar, and drive safe. Lord knows what more sorts of ignorant trouble those folks got planned."

So it happens that I find myself slowly walking back to the Elms's entrance with one Maximilian Burton. A brisk breeze dances in the blackberry brambles, pirouetting under clean skies, and as the fear drains out of me, I want to rip off my head scarf and feel the gusts in my hair. I want to strip bare and plunge into the water and emerge frost pale and trembling. I want to climb one of these impossible trees and cling to the top, watching the stars drowning in the river.

I want the fellow on my left to lay me on soft pine needles and play every note of me.

We reach a sandy lot hosting a few scattered vehicles. My hands hang awfully empty where they aren't clutching Max's shirtfront.

Something really has got to be done about this.

"So you have a car?" I query, clearing my throat.

"I got a friend what always lets me borrow his when he's off playing George. Should be in St. Louis just about now."

"Felicitous. What sort?"

"Little Hanson touring jalopy. What, you got an interest in cars?"

"Aspects of them," I breathe.

"Yeah?"

"Yes. They're awfully useful when it comes to getting places."

"What sorta places?" Max cups my elbow as we approach a squat black conveyance with white rims, and my heart leaps like an unbroken horse.

"We can't search for Davy anymore tonight. And by the time Mavereen gets back to the Paragon from the Vaughans' she'll figure everyone for lullaby land."

"What's that to do with the likes of us?"

"You have a cabin," I whisper.

His eyes are charcoal in the dim. But I imagine them as they look in the daylight, golden as a cat's.

"Get in the car," he orders.

I stretch, tracing the muscles of Max's broad chest. The quilt tangled around my feet is threadbare soft, a patchwork of lavender and cornflower squares. It's been months since I've done this, and the space between my legs aches pleasantly. There's a sore spot on my hipbone where Max held me down when I was arching, commanding me to mind my stitches. I imagine it blooming into a spread of purples like his blanket. Outside the cabin—which is military neat, and snug as can be now that Max has lit the fire—the wind is playing "Royal Garden Blues." Or perhaps I'm imagining that, because Max is humming it, floating around the melody as he pulls his fingers through my hair.

"If you can reach my trouser pocket, I got a pack of smokes might not be too smashed up," he suggests.

"Under no circumstances."

"Why's that?"

Leaning up, I say against his mouth, "Because right now you taste like me."

He chuckles. "And you like that?"

"I like it."

"Well, that's good, 'cause I like it too."

"No cigarettes, if you please."

"Aw, I can't refuse a lady."

I touch his eyebrow. "The old girl could get used to this."

A frown flickers across his features. I want to wipe it off with my lips.

"I done told you already, Alice, that ain't what this can be. Nohow."

"Not even sometimes?"

"Not supposing you prefers my neck without a rope around it."

"You're afraid of the Klan?"

"I ain't scared of nothing. But I'm smart."

"Smart enough to know we wouldn't be bothered out here. Twice a month. Twice a week. Two or three times daily. Every other Sunday."

Max brushes his thumb over my mouth.

"I had a wife, and I got kids," he tells me. "Twins, in Brooklyn. They lives with my ma when I'm here. Teddy and Julia Burton."

To say I'm surprised would be a superlative. Of course he has a family. The fellow is positively in prime working order—why shouldn't he? But I still feel my stomach grow a yawning hole, face the all-too-predictable realization, *I'm not the first one to arrive here, and I never even supposed I was.*

"I don't figure like that's gonna flummox you," he continues. "But I said this ain't figuring to work out, and I meant it."

I keep very still.

"What happened?" I ask him. "No, apologies, that's dreadfully blunt, forgive me. But you said . . ."

"Her name was Rosie." Max rubs at his stubble. "Sorry, Alice, but I'm gonna need that smoke."

We light a pair, and he sets an ashtray between us. I settle with my legs over his and my back to the wall. There have been times when I could see dead soldiers in Max's eyes, watched the memory of fallen comrades hardening his pupils.

But that was nothing compared to the way he looks now.

"Like I done mentioned, I was a real stupid kid," he says quietly. "Army was what changed all that. In France, I had a purpose. Respect. Women too, every sorta woman: black, white, brown—all us guys was neck-deep in fleshpots. When I got back stateside, though, that was over. Back to shoeshine boy as a life sentence. Shoulda seen me first time as I was called George. Jesus."

Stroking his foot, I nod.

"Anyhow. There I was, a real man for the first time, and I'd known Rosie since I was a tyke. When I done showed up at church in a pressed uniform, she let on as she'd always felt something, and now I'd made good, she was sure of it—Christ, that woman knew what she wanted. Didn't reckon I could do better. She was gonna make me feel like a king again. No, not a king—just a *man*. I married her a month later, twins was born lickety-split, but the delivery was too much for her. I had a whole future in frontta me, Alice, straight as a goddamn arrow, five, six decades together. Buying a house in Jersey, hollering at grandkids. The two of us feeding 'em too many penny candies. It was gone in a year, and most of that year I was on a Pullman car. When I look at them kids, Rosie's so real it . . . it *crushes* me. When I'm here, or on the rails, she might as well have been a dream."

"I'm so sorry," I whisper, circling his wrist.

He nods. "Saw a lotta fellas die for no reason in No Man's Land. But Rosie died on accountta wanting a family. And there ain't nothing crueler."

"Do the others know?"

"Nah. Apart from Blossom. I don't get no comfort outta being pitied, and Blossom . . . With her, it's different."

"I understand." Pausing, I venture, "Did you love her?"

He shakes his head, eyes shutting. "Wasn't around enough. But I coulda. Another year, maybe two. And that's worse. What a crying waste."

Max sets his cigarette down. He tugs his drawers on and I memorize the lines of his stomach, the V-shaped dusting of hair.

"Coffee," he says. "You wanna cup?"

"With a kick?"

"Like a mule. I got no other way to serve coffee, Alice James."

"You are a gourmet, sir."

"Back in two shakes."

"I'll keep the bed warm for you."

Lovely, Alice. Light a torch in it for him and set the cabin on fire, why don't you?

Max putters around the kitchen, and the purr of the water boiling tickles my ears. It isn't as if I was going to get to keep him. Max lives in-between, in the empty spaces, in the hours spent getting somewhere else. And he'd have to have positively shucked his last oyster to carry on an affair with me in Portland of all places, I don't admire to see him dangling. But I know what Max meant by *crushing*.

Loneliness is a weight, not an empty space, and it's pressing on my chest so I can hardly breathe.

"What in the name of *fuck*?" I hear.

Throwing Max's shirt over my shoulders, I pad barefoot into the other side of the cabin. It's a tiny place, just a living area with a sofa and a low trunk for a table, an armchair adjacent, a braided rug, and a galley kitchen. Max stands with his hands splayed on his hips, breathing awfully hard for a gent fixing liquid breakfast. He stares at a tatty Indian blanket draped over one arm of the couch, spilling onto the overstuffed chair.

"Last night we never done bothered over lights." I've never seen Max this upset, and I've lamped him as he took in a roasting cross.

"Whatever's the matter?"

He stabs a finger at the worn coverlet. "This here blanket and pillow, this is a shit show. Davy Lee always arranges it like this when I brings him up to camp. Pretends as it's a cave. Half the time the kid's a dragon, half the time a bear or a troll, I dunno, there's crazy worlds in that sweet little tyke's head."

"Oh, Max. It must be ever so upsetting to see it, what with him missing."

"No, it ain't." A muscle leaps in Max's jaw. "'Cause I always puts it back, like. I did last time. And I ain't been here since."

He meets my eyes with a haunted expression. "Which means that Davy Lee has."

· *Twenty-One* ·

THEN

The mafia is not a band, nor anything of that sort. It is the resistance which the whole Sicilian people opposes to all kinds of government and authority. It is, how shall I say? A sentiment, a feeling, a sort of wild love of our country, that is a secret, and will do anything. With us, everybody knows what it is, and evil comes to everyone who opposes it—generally death.

—FRANCIS MARION CRAWFORD,
Corleone: A Tale of Sicily, 1896

I stood on the West Harlem waterfront in 1921 wearing steel-toed boots, denim trousers, and a corded sweater that made my neck itch even more than the anxious sweat I'd sprouted. A little artful shading and tucking my hair up in a woolen cap completed the image of your average tidal rat. This male Nobody stood in an unseasonably hot April breeze at ten past nine in the evening, watching the lights of New Jersey's Palisades begin to flicker on, shining electric blessings across the wide river. Down but not out, traded favors to shipping types by keeping his hands soft, collected pornographic playing cards, didn't have a roof but found a bath daily, drank to sleep but not to forget. That sort.

"Bugger," dockyard Nobody muttered. About as strong for the current mission as I would have been for a rotten molar.

In 1921, Mr. Salvatici decided that he needed to examine one Officer Harry Chipchase, see what made the chap's knuckles crack. In fairness, I couldn't blame him. Harry was the best of the harness bulls—I knew this gospel, seeing as I was in closest proximity. But Harry was worried about *everything*. Days that ended in the letter *Y*, the sun, butterflies, walking too close when arresting one of the Nobodies, walking too distant when arresting one of the Nobodies. He muttered grim portents about assignments from shadowing Family men who had the notches of a dozen stiletto murders on their bedposts to whether he'd properly completed my faked arrest paperwork.

In short, he wasn't guilty of anything other than comprehensive disloyalty to the NYPD. But he acted guilty as hell, and *unni cc'è focu, pri lu fumu pari.**

So when Harry was assigned to spirit a hefty amount of pristine counterfeit dinero confiscated from the Clutch Hand out of a police evidence locker—I still remember the childlike glee Mr. Salvatici's paper-thin mouth assumed when he hatched that scheme—and Harry found the safe already plundered by another boy in blue, our boss fell into one of his rare snits. I don't think he really supposed Harry kept the contents of the evidence locker for himself. The perceived defeat rankled, however, and Harry was overdue for the proverbial tune-up. Mr. Salvatici was probably the best-natured

* Sicilian, "Where there's smoke, there's fire."

gangster in human history. But Harry questioned every order with dank pessimism, and I think my guardian wanted to buy himself two or three weeks of peace.

Which is why he hired Nicolo Benenati to interrogate Harry Chipchase in the Hudson riverfront building we referred to as the Cabin. Mr. Salvatici employed Nicolo frequently by 1921—too frequently, in my humble opinion.

"This is killing a mosquito with a cannonade," I had begged that day in the Arcadia's restaurant.

"I've said three times, he's being used for intimidation, not for his . . . particular skills." Mr. Salvatici finished his last mint-and-ricotta ravioli with what looked like fastidiousness but I recognized as pique. "He's under strictest orders not to touch the man. I only want to be sure of Harry."

"Then hire Tommy Toothpick or the Caneri brothers or—"

"Nobody, how many times have I told you that the execution can be more important than the deed itself?" In the act of straightening his tie, Mr. Salvatici brightened. "Oh, of course, the Cabin has any number of spying nooks. You'll go and watch the whole thing."

I could feel the blood departing my cheeks. "That isn't—"

"It's perfect." Mr. Salvatici, having found a way to scratch two aggravating itches with one fingernail, pushed his chair back. "I know you justifiably don't care for Mr. Benenati, my dear young lady, and I make certain not to cause you unnecessary interactions, but he won't catch a glimpse of you and I greatly prefer multiple witnesses during an interrogation. Thank you so very much for mentioning this—I'll be up until midnight, or you can report to me in the morning."

He brushed fond fingers over my hairline, dropped his napkin on the table, and that was that.

Poor Harry had been in the Cabin since around eight,

deposited there with a cozy bag over his head. Nicolo was due to arrive at nine thirty, giving Harry the chance to meditate on his sins. And there I stood at the waterfront, hands stuffed in my pockets, kicking and cursing and this-ing and that-ing.

"Bloody hell," I growled at last, borrowing another phrase from Mum as I plunged toward the waterfront staircase that would take me to the Cabin.

It was a rickety, rotting affair, those stairs—or so they'd been made to appear. In reality, what looked to be a structure that lost its war with salt water in 1899, thereabouts, was elegantly reinforced with camouflaged steel struts and girders. There were gaping holes, certainly. But every half-eroded plank that looked like it would send you plummeting to the rocks below was solid as a fire escape, and I knew them well, so I forced myself to slouch down them in high wharf-lounger style.

When I reached the hidden path along the rocks, I cast a cautious eye about. No company yet. The breeze picked up as I walked, carrying scents of seaweed and the coal from the barges. Skimming my hands along the tall grasses, I tried to reassure myself.

He won't see you.

Because he can't see you.

You'll see him, and that can't do anyone harm.

The Cabin's outline rose before me, sinister but at least familiar. It looked something like an antique operations booth, and something like a forgotten warehouse with iron grids over its windows, and something like an abandoned shipping office. In fact, it looked like so many things, it looked like absolutely nothing. Which was the point.

Bypassing the main door, I headed across the sand-strewn earth for a mass of granite edging the water. Behind this, I brushed grit away to reveal a metal trap, which I unlocked and opened. It yawned blackly, a gateway into the void. But reaching down, I flicked a switch, and muted electric lights sparked to life, revealing a metal ladder running about ten feet into the earth.

Shutting the trap, I swung myself down the rungs. The cool tunnel soothed me after the summerlike fug aboveground. By the time I'd traversed the short distance and started climbing the identical ladder at the other end, I'd convinced myself that Mr. Salvatici knew exactly what he was doing, and that even if no belly laughs came from this dreadfully pointed object lesson, well, no lasting damage would either.

Silently, I pulled myself up into the crawl space. This was now a hands-and-knees affair, and I inched along the floor, which we'd carpeted for both sound and comfort. After two turns that guaranteed no light reached my vantage point from the tunnel hatch, I spied the floor-level ventilation grate in question.

"I ain't done nothing, I tells you! Nothing! You gots to believe me, Mr. Benenati, old Harry Chipchase is just about as loyal as the Pope is to Christ."

Shit, I thought, slithering both faster and more stealthily.

"I want to believe you," came Nicolo's voice. "Truly, Mr. Chipchase. The problem as I see it is that Mr. Salvatici hired me to answer this question definitively, and you haven't yet given me any *reason* to believe you."

When I reached the grate, I dropped my pelvis and settled onto my elbows. Two factors clearly had conspired against me: Nicolo was early, probably having come straight from some other more gruesome errand; and I'd been more frightened than I thought, and overstayed my shilly-shallying interlude.

The room I spied on was simple plaster, lined with a few shelves holding secretarial supplies like paper and a pair of typewriters, and less secretarial tools like a set of gardening shears and the makings of an effective tourniquet. You get the idea. In all my time working against the Clutch Hand, I'd only seen them used to intimidate snitches. My function was to point the finger, and then generally, Mr. Salvatici executed his judgments without an audience—or at least without me. But by 1921, I'd no illusions on the subject however much I admired to forget about it when I lay me down with Wynken, Blynken, and Nod.

I might not hurt the sick bastards who kept the Harlem peasantry shackled to the Family like dogs. But *we* certainly did. And I kept that locked in a very deep drawer, under winter mothballs and girlish regrets.

"What kinda proof you figure suits?" Harry's crooked face gleamed grey with clammy terror. "Wait a sec! There was that job last January—yeah, see, down by Ninety-Eighth and Broad—and did I say peep when I was posted to stake out that loan shark outfit? A goddamn week with my balls the size of marbles and a foot of snow on my noggin, and did I complain?"

My lips quirked despite the ugliness before me: he had complained, and it had been four days, and one light snowfall, but Harry figured the glass for half-empty. And poisoned.

Nicolo wasn't using any of the tired pantomime moves—never learned them, never needed to. None of the circular stalking or cleaning his nails with a shiv for my former pal. He leaned against the wall with his arms loosely crossed, his collar undone, teepee brows slack with disinterest.

"You complain plenty from what I hear, Mr. Chipchase, but that isn't the point." Nicolo pursed his lips at the blank wall. "Point is, Mr. Salvatici doubts your respect for him, and supposing you don't respect him, well then—considering the freedom you're allowed—you could be up to anything. Snitching. Embezzlement. Sabotage. I was hired years back by one of the Jewish operations to take care of a saboteur. His wife noticed her bureau was leaking and found him in a dozen pieces."

Flat as a knife's blade, true as a drunken confession. He didn't even need to look at Harry for the latter to be practically pissing in his socks at the prospect of my old friend carving him like a ham.

Or so I assumed. Wrongly.

"Not respect Mr. Salvatici!" Harry cried, eyes popping. "Christ, Mr. Benenati, I's fucking *terrified* of the guy. Ain't never tried to pull a job for him before warning him as it might not pan out, just to hedge my bets, see? Never fall asleep 'cept I sees him floating in the dark, like. That *face.* Ain't never even thought about working for nobody else on accountta that job as he pulled in nineteen eleven. No disrespect, Mr. Benenati, but when they dumped me here, I knew whereabouts I was at straight off, and seeing you show up instead of Mr. S.? I coulda kissed you right in the snoot."

For the first time in many years, Nicolo and I shared a common expression.

Harry's finally cracked. One too many summer rainstorms and stray-cat sightings.

"Nineteen eleven?" Nicolo repeated in the same steel-plate tone.

Nineteen eleven, my mind echoed.

A luxurious shudder rolled down Harry's spine. "Ten years back. Brand-new to the Force, didn't know a truncheon from a rotten tomato. Coppers was all buzzing over a murder. The real lousy sort, kind what eats at you. Higher-ups working the case was scratching their asses something terrible. You knows how it is in Harlem. I was greener than a grasshopper, dunno the poor lug's moniker what handed in his dinner pail, it never crossed my desk. Hadn't parleyed no Italian back then. But one day I comes up on a pair of crooked bluecoats when the station house was real quiet like, one bragging to his buddy as it was him watched the street for the guy what did it, that he worked for the killer. Cleared the road while he staged the stiff in a barrel. Helped clean the basement where the butchering was done. *Salvatici.* You can bet I remembered *that* name. And not on accountta some dumb mutt blowing hot air neither."

"Why, then?"

"'Cause not a week later, stupid bum washed up on Chelsea piers. Knucklehead blabbed too much, see? And the Spider caught wind of it. So when I was walking the Harlem beat and Mr. S. called me into the Hotel Arcadia sniffing around for a new flatfoot recruit, you can bet I said yes. Harry Chipchase likes his mug to stay *on* his skull, thanks very much."

My first instinct despite the pang of bitter memory was to laugh.

Poor Harry, always was a few pawns shy of a chessboard, and here you're blaming Mr. Salvatici for the murder of Mr. Benenati—and to his son, no less.

Nicolo just stood there, whites of his eyes gleaming like bone shards.

Harry's lips trembled. "Mr. Benenati, youse can see I'm playing straight with you. You want I should make some kinda promise? Pass some kinda test? I'm your guy. Rough me up a little, hell, bring Mr. Salvatici my pinkie, stick a knife in my neck and tell him I croaked loyal to the cause. Just don't turn me over to the boss. I's seen what he can do. Been there personal. Ain't never gonna get my head clean. And ain't never gonna cross him. I protect Nobody, and that's a swell fit—she's a helluva kid, and I'd keep her safe for Mr. S. if it meant a hole straight through my uniform. Honest Injun. Please."

Nicolo's face at last showed sign of recognition when Harry invoked my name. He slowly drew a knife from his pocket. Began cutting Harry's bonds, ignoring my pessimistic friend's gushing thanks. Meanwhile, my mind had gone as smooth and soft as a rose petal.

Go.

Right now.

Fix this hideous mistake before it eats you all alive.

I executed two dodges to make sure I wasn't followed by any lookouts of Nicolo's when I slunk away from the Cabin. By the time I was nearly back to the Arcadia, Nobody the wharf lounger was fighting not to run full tilt for the lobby.

Running means you either need to get to or away from something. Walk.

With your head down.

My eyes floated over cracks in the paving stones, fissures wrought by time and pressure. I skirted a barbecue rib picked as clean as if by vultures, a pyramid of horse shit. It made sense that Harry's allegiance to the Spider was based in misplaced fear. Hell, I ought to have guessed as much sooner, Harry Chipchase meditated on liabilities all the livelong. All I had to do was get to Mr. Salvatici's journals. He'd said he'd be up until midnight, which meant he'd be smoking a cigar in a rooftop armchair, breathing guttering New York streetlights and whispering to his birds. That gave me an hour to find the diary entry proving his innocence before he could catch me rooting through his past. And Nicolo, as insane as he was, was still methodical. He wouldn't come charging into the hotel with guns blazing, he would consider, he would—

"Oh sweet Jesus, and just when I thought my luck had run dry. Hello, darlin'. Sight of you is the best tonic bar none, you know that, don't you? Almost missed you in that getup."

My chin raised at the familiar voice even as my chest compressed, shrinking away from what I was about to see.

Zachariah Lane stood beside the entrance of the Hotel Arcadia. Not waiting for Nobody, I didn't flatter myself. Only waiting for someone. One of his old friends. Maybe me or Sadie or one of the porters. We were all the same to him by then. Friendly shadow shapes, a marginally brighter glow in the deep dark.

But I miswrote that—Rye wasn't *standing* by the stone steps precisely. He was hunched forward, swaying subtly, just drifting in an unseen wind, the body inside the rags he wore nearly as thin as mine.

"Oh, Rye," I breathed.

Where have you been these three months? Have you eaten anything lately? Are you still sleeping in the tent camp under the 116th Street El station, where the soot falls like wicked snow?

I looked for you, you see. I always look for you.

He held his hands up. "Now don't get agitated, darlin'. I've been on the upswing these past few weeks, felt strong as an ox and was fit to hunt down some steady work, and then I took a real bad spell during that rainstorm a few days ago. Couldn't hardly breathe."

"And you need money," I supplied, knowing the script.

"Not for cough syrup, now." Sincerity poured from him like steam from a manhole. He believed every word, and that broke my heart. "I know how you feel about that, Nobody, and I'd never want to bring any grief to your doorstep. So I'd promise never to use *your* money for my medicine. Just a hot meal to clear my head, maybe a bunk for the night."

Where do you keep these separate bank accounts? In your right and left trouser pockets?

Wanting to cry, I fished a crumpled dollar out of my pocket and pressed it into his hand.

"For one of those roast beef sandwiches we like so awfully much at the Empire Diner. And then a good night's sleep."

He smiled, and there in the glow of the Arcadia's gas lamps I glimpsed him realizing. Not that I loved him. But that the sandwich was too far away a dream to touch. He'd walk halfway home and cough whether he needed to or not, and then he'd have to fix it, wouldn't he, for his health's sake, and he'd forget which pocket was which, and he'd detest himself right up until he made it all go away again.

Stepping forward, I kissed him, right above the lids falling shut over pinprick irises and every-colored eyes.

"When you feel better, next week, come see me and we'll visit one of the mixed speakeasies that pours too much and never sweeps their dance floors," I lied.

"Sure enough, darlin'." Rye smiled. It never spread past his lips anymore, hadn't for over a year. "I'll pay you back then—it's a date."

Kissing me on the cheek, he turned to go. Walking straight for the most part, a dancer's sense of balance battling a sucking tide of toxins. And I don't mean cough syrup. I mean the sea of loneliness that surrounded him every day, that he couldn't even begin to battle because he supposed that he deserved it all along.

Nobody the marine vagabond sat at Mr. Salvatici's familiar breakfast table, fingers thrumming with purpose, and flipped through his 1911 journal with full expectation of saving the day. Harry Chipchase, I thought through my haze of grief over Rye, was a good friend and a stalwart bodyguard but not the sharpest nail in the coffin. Mr. Salvatici knifed two *scurmi fituzzi* to *save* Nicolo's family, for God's sake. A few minutes of research and I'd pocket the evidence, find Nicolo, and have this entire farce booed off the stage.

> *October 31, 1911. It is in motion. The thing is done, and what will come of it only time can tell. The Clutch Hand's brutes would have wasted a seminal moment in Harlem, as they are animals and not statesmen—this is the theater of the people, and this sacrifice must prove a call to action. There is such*

spirit in the young fellow that, once the fuse is ignited, he must burst into flame or fizzle, and expire entirely. If the latter, it is a waste of tremendous untapped aptitude for resistance. If the former—well, we shall see.

In either case, it has brought me the girl, which was always my fondest hope. Simple enough to dispatch a pair of enemies who threatened her young love; quite another thing to expose myself in such a way, all to plunge the city into sufficient chaos for her to come running. But come running she did, and oh, the completeness of it. She will barely be missed, and I don't know whether I'm gladder over the comforts I can provide her or the asset she will become, clever wisp of a thing. I will do right by my new ward. I will do more than protect her—I will teach her to protect herself.

What luck that I caught sight of Catrin years ago, and instead of evading her accosted her there in the street. Such decisions often prove disastrous and always irreversible. But now I see my way clear: the Clutch Hand can be thwarted. The opening gambit accomplished, here's to the success of a very long game.

Slumping back in the chair, I sat for a little, staring at the oil painting of a hunting expedition on Mr. Salvatici's wall. I'd always liked it, liked the dogs with their sunset-pink tongues and their glossy brushstroke coats. One had a pheasant in its mouth with its neck at an unnatural angle, a neat red dot through the chest indicating its demise. Too neat, in my experience. The hunter and his prey and the dog bred to deliver it. All in their proper places.

It's an awfully empowering feeling, to be against something. Women against liquor gave the likes of me the vote, for example. It's dandy as hell to rail against poverty or sex or nepotism or vice.

There were two sides, Mr. Salvatici always said. Them: the Clutch Hand no one ever saw, the puppet master, sending his army of Corleonesi to terrorize and destroy at his whim. Us: Mr. Salvatici with his cool gentility, the Spider, directing his shadow ward and his devoted gang to build and bolster and infiltrate. We were the resistance—the freedom fighters—and people paid us for real debaucheries instead of farcical protection, and we robbed from the thieves, and we put down the wild dogs.

Except none of that was true. At least, it held as much water as stories about Giuseppe Morello and his Murder Stable. We were a gang of violent and remorseless criminals, I was no better than an assassin, and Harry Chipchase had been right to be afraid all along.

When I'd stopped shaking, I forced myself to take an interest and start paying attention. The way I'd been trained to do. I flipped back to the entry I should have read the instant it occurred to me to spy on Mr. Salvatici.

Which begs the question—Why didn't I? I want to write that it was because I was loyal or I trusted him or I was too sophisticated to care about the answer. But I can't say any of those things.

I'd always suspected something, but I didn't want to know what it was.

> *October 27, 1911. At last I've made contact with her. After watching for so long, it was a palpable thrill, far more satisfying than knifing a pair of soulless Family men. She is everything I expected from studying her at a distance—pensive and insightful, wary but unbowed. She will fill the single post remaining vacant for this great undertaking: while I cannot anymore under the circumstances risk the danger a theoretical wife of mine would face, Nobody I can keep close, hidden. Safe. Far safer than she would have been in that flesh market. I have the right to a family of a sort, as does every man, having*

left mine behind entirely. The symmetry of it pleases me. I never bothered over divorcing her mother all those years ago, after all.

Quietly, I closed the book. Thinking about a closet full of dresses that fit me perfectly, living quarters I adored on sight. Lessons designed to spark my interest. A chill, dry hand stroking my hairline for comfort and for camaraderie and for no reason at all.

I thought about my mother's opinion regarding Mauro Salvatici's version of ambition versus Giuseppe Morello's, and I shivered with such violence that my head ached.

I mean the more dangerous kind, the kind what grows instead of erases, the sort o' fellow as sees himself as the king in a storybook. Making a world all his own.

Twenty-Two
NOW

Section 6. That if any such free negro or mulatto shall fail to quit the country as required by this act, he or she may be arrested upon a warrant issued by some justice of the peace, and, if guilty upon trial before such justice, shall receive upon his or her bare back not less than twenty nor more than thirty-nine stripes, to be inflicted by the constable of the proper county.

—LEGISLATIVE COMMITTEE OF THE PROVISIONAL GOVERNMENT OF OREGON, Act barring all blacks and mulattoes from the state, June 26, 1844

"Wait, what?" I exclaim. "You suppose that because this blanket is draped in that admittedly curious fashion, Davy is *here*? At your cabin?"

Max snaps back into stoicism. But inwardly, I imagine he's altogether Belgium of 1914.

"Maximilian, the ham is positively absent from that sandwich. What could he be doing here, miles from where he vanished?"

"You wanna make me believe some tramp busted in to make up a pillow fort?"

"But you could have forgotten to set it back," I soothe.

"Nah. I run a tight ship. Either Davy was here or I got an issue with prankster ghosts."

"My God." As I allow myself to believe him, more questions arise, a domino effect of uncertainties. "Who has a key to this place?"

"Just me, since everybody as comes up here, I bring myself. That don't mean I carry it on the road, though. Hangs it on a rack in my room at the Paragon."

"Oh, my Lord." Even though I questioned the possibility of an inside job, facing evidence of such is mortifying. "Someone could easily have copied it. They'd never fear you catching them—you're out there clacking away for days on end."

"I can't wrap my brains around it. It's like family at that hotel."

"And how could he possibly have gotten here from the Elms? And if he did, then what happened next? Davy could still be in the area," I realize. "We've been carrying on like rabbits, and he's been—what, hiding from us? Hurt or lost?"

Another possibility materializes, one we both see but don't speak: freshly spaded earth under the bracken, a loamy and far-too-small hole dug deep enough for the rain not to wash it away.

"Shit." Max brushes his hands over his head in distress.

I pull his shirt around me tighter, if only for the comfort of its smell. "Max, I'm fantastically good at this. Allow me to pose some questions?"

"Hell, I'll try anything. I love that kid, and there's burning crosses involved."

"Who from the Paragon has ever visited here?"

The space between his pale eyes folds into a thoughtful groove. "Davy, plenty. And Blossom with Davy. Dr. Pendleton twice, when the hooch got real bad and I figured as he needed some peace and trees. Davy with Wednesday Joe maybe a dozen times. Fishing, shooting arrows, showing 'em how to track. That's it."

"Very good. Now, how many people have ready access to the keys behind the front desk? Supposing they didn't just take a hairpin to your door, of course."

Max whistles, glancing up as he reflects. "Rooster and Mav, rotating night clerks. Anybody else would hafta time it out careful."

The inkling of an idea has already dripped into the old girl's cranium. It's still just speckles, mind. But they're present, and they give me chills.

"All right, here's the kicker, and I ask that you give this due consideration before considering fisticuffs. Which of the Paragon's inner circle has *not* been out searching for Davy Lee?"

Max's eyes widen.

"I know!" I throw my hands up pleadingly. "Just think it over. Wednesday Joe is too young to fault for not beating the bracken—he wanted to, terribly. You and Mavereen have been frantic. But something dreadfully fishy must be going on, if what you say is true. Blossom I could chalk up to illness and Rooster to duty and Miss Christina to work. But none of them have been taking a comb to the undergrowth, and . . . and shouldn't we ask why?"

Rocking on his heels, Maximilian gives a defeated shrug. I can't blame him. These are his friends.

It took me years to question my friends, though, and look where it got me.

Max sighs. "I'll search the woods. It's plenty light enough now. And you go through the cabin for whatever else you can find. Food scraps. Crayon or pencil shavings—the squirt loves to draw. A goddamn shoelace. Anything to confirm what I been saying. All right?"

I make a quick salute. "I know what I am about, sir. Trust in me."

Max looks at me, really looks for the first time since he told me about his lost wife. "I do, you know. Kinda figure that makes me nuts, but. I do."

Blinking, I accept this statement. It makes me feel considerably more like whoever Alice James is becoming these days.

"Go forth, handsome swain. Search the mouseholes and neglect not the birds' nests."

The door shuts, and I'm alone.

First I toss my wrinkled chemise and frock back on lest Max prove lucky enough to return with a little boy in tow. Then I start flinging open cupboards and growing intimate with nightstands. There's a simple larder of nonperishables like tinned fish, powdered milk, coffee, rice, some flapjack flour. A small shelf of books, mostly travel and guides to fishing or carpentry, the rest in French and therefore Greek to me. The straightest row of folded socks a woman could ever wish for. A phonograph with a predictably large and thorough collection of ragtime, blues, jazz, and classical, doubtless purchased in dozens of cities. A photo of him in uniform that leaves me flushed for minutes, not on display but neatly hidden under a set of sheet music catalogs.

Nothing whatsoever of use to us.

So I start doing what I used to when looking for Rye's heroin syrup, after he'd sworn to discontinue the medication and instead started wedging the stuff in loafers and sugar bowls: I snoop. Salt cellars, laundry hampers, cleaning products.

When hark ye: I reach into an empty vase on the mantelpiece and encounter a slip of paper within.

I unroll it. It feels quite new. The handwriting is crisp and clean, the language terse enough to make me suspect it deliberately cryptic, lest somebody—or Nobody—stumble upon the thing.

To Those Concerned,

The exchange has been made, and all is satisfactory. First payment safely in receipt. Subsequent installments may be delivered to the same address.

I remain,
At Your Service

Minutes pass as I stare at words I shouldn't be seeing. This note, then, must have been left by whoever brought Davy here. And was to be retrieved later by someone with access, when Max was flying over rail ties. But who?

And far more important, why? Is this a ransom note? What in God's name are payment installments? Can this be some sort of blackmail? Or worse yet, the twisted indenture of a child?

My skin goes cold.

Miss Christina has secrets. Oppressive ones. And an *arrangement.*

Blossom needs money. Badly. And wasn't jazzed over finding me prying.

And neither of them having been out searching for Davy since that first night, I remind myself.

Impossible.

It's an instant rejection. Both women were with me that afternoon at the Elms. Yes, it ought to be further evidence damning them, but the opposite is true—they were destroyed when Davy disappeared.

I have to quit the cabin or else perform the Alpine summit routine on its walls. So I steal one of Maximilian's cigarettes and occupy the front porch. The morning air is misty, rich with soil and conifer, clearing my head even as it obscures the trees. I still have Evelina Vaughan's scarf and I snug into it, wondering how she fares. Then my hackles rise again.

Evelina Vaughan.

Rigid with the force of my discovery, I think back upon several small clues. Others less smallish than they are perfectly gargantuan. It's another twenty minutes before Maximilian arrives back, boots crunching through the fallen debris, and by then I've calmed. He greets me with his slumped shoulders already rising in apology, and I can see he has nothing to tell.

He can see that I do, however, and his steps quicken.

"What's the story?"

I pass him the note. As he reads it, he exclaims, "For Christ's sake, Alice—you done found this in my cabin? Where?"

I deliver.

"But what's it mean?"

"It means," I say grimly as I stub out my cigarette, "that—although I don't know quite what—I'm afraid that something perfectly ghastly is going on."

As we navigate winding roads in the car, I tell Max everything else. About Wednesday Joe's spilling to me that Davy didn't get on with Rooster, about reading Miss Christina's letters and being given a firm friendship court-martial by Blossom Fontaine. Max is sore that I broke in too, and treats me to the range of Brooklyn vocabulary. But in light of our new discovery, he peters out, up tapping his thumb against the steering wheel.

"It just don't figure that either of them dames woulda hurt Davy," he insists. "Blossom found the tyke behind a garbage bin, and Miss Christina practically raised him."

"Your biographical details are ever so fine."

"Well, then what the hell?" he bursts out. "Whadda we do?"

"Again, I don't know," I admit. "But I'm in a tearing grand hurry to speak to Miss Christina privately."

Max splutters, and it is, dare I confess this, adorable. “Why not me? Why you, a broad what she barely knows?”

“Because I am a broad what she barely knows.” Wearied and anxious, I lean an elbow against the automobile’s window. “And it is sometimes easier to tell a fellow broad something—especially a strange broad—than your honorable gentleman friends.”

After arguing for ten minutes, as we reach the city proper in the diffuse morning sun, Max caves. Because he knows I’m right.

This early, it’s as easy to slip off timber as to tell whereabouts Miss Christina will be: the kitchen. So after Max drops me in front of the Paragon like the chauffer he’s pretending to be, I hightail it thence. Rooster stands at the front desk, looking bone-tired.

He studies his watch, and I carry on.

The kitchen basks in the smells of butter and garlic and tomatoes, and the reason must be that Miss Christina’s cioppino is a featured luncheon today. She is alone. Her lithe arms make the smallest strain, and then *pop*. The oyster is shucked. She doesn’t look up, but that’s no surprise when I enter a room. Her lean face is tense under the folds of her kerchief.

“Miss Christina?”

The oyster spasms out of her fingers.

“I’m sorry, I didn’t mean to startle you.” I walk to the other side of the wide worktable.

“No, you’re fine, Miss James,” she says hoarsely. “Hearing about all that business last night, crosses and lynch mobs? It’s got me spooked. Are you after a cup of—”

“You know what happened to Davy Lee, I think?”

Miss Christina slowly rises from where she retrieved the fallen oyster and leans to throw it away. It’s terrible how her already taut frame petrifies. She doesn’t turn around.

“Can’t guess at what you’re talking about, Miss James. If you’ll excuse—”

"You searched for Davy the first night. You made a terribly good show of it, but you never went back. And it certainly isn't as if you have more duties than Mavereen Meader. Either you were in on it from the start, or you learned something. And—"

Miss Christina has me by the forearm. Panicked people, yours truly ought to have reminded herself, are dreadfully quick. These are chef's hands—I can feel my veins splitting.

"Not here," she hisses.

"But—"

"*Hush* you."

That one does the trick.

Miss Christina drags me off. I follow, because yes, I'm desperately curious, but also because no, I have never sensed a murderess in her. If survival is your business, you grow ever so apt at recognizing when someone is about to kill you. I frankly don't think Miss Christina capable, for all her prancing around rooms full of knives.

Blossom could, though, I think. I learned that when Officer Overton tried to force himself on me. *If Blossom loved you, she could fillet anybody who hurt you like the veriest mud-sucking catfish.*

Our destination turns out to be dry storage—potato sacks, hanging braids of peppers, bags of flour. Dust motes glint in the faint electric light. As my shoes scuff against a gritty cement floor, Miss Christina whirls me around to face her, and I barely keep from squealing.

"All right, Miss James. You go on now and say what you want from me."

A small tug suggests she set my arm free. She complies.

"I only want a general line on the Davy Lee situation. I'm on your side, as long as it's a reasonable angle."

"What's reasonable to the likes of you, Miss James?"

"Well, yes, that's fair." I rub at my arm. "I can promise that if you pour out to me, I'll never tattle any of it, supposing that's possible."

"And if it isn't?"

"Then that would be because a child's life is at stake, wouldn't it?"

Miss Christina starts crying. She grips the support of the nearest pantry shelf, and it's about all I can do to continue.

"Do you know where Davy is?"

She shakes her head, flinching.

"But you do know where he was taken?"

"No!" Hearing how loud she was, she pushes her wrist against her teeth and unnecessarily hushes me with her other trembling hand. "I wish to holy Lord I did."

"You were there!" I urge. "The day he went missing, you were there, surely you have some ink—"

"Miss James, I was there sure enough. But I don't know what other cause you got to frighten me like this. I only want Davy back, I swear."

The heat in her tone makes me hesitate. I settle on delivering the least informative, most alarming words.

"You stopped searching for him after one night. And I've accidentally—forgive the horrific bluntness—watched you slip letters in your pocket too quickly to suppose they were circulars for beef shanks. We live on the same floor. Again quite by accident, I happened upon you arguing with Rooster, and—"

"God save me," she gasps. "I'll never live in a hotel again, never as long as I live. Only where there's land. Space enough to keep people away."

"Away from your secrets?"

She nods.

"Is yours to do with Maximilian's cabin?" I risk, betting on her connection to Rooster and his access to keys.

She stares in shock. "How could you know anything about that?"

"Max went up and searched the place. Turns out sometime in the awfully recent past, Davy was staying there. After he was . . . taken."

"No." Her voice is low with horror.

"Ask Max if you admire to. Or would you rather I tell him that you arranged to have Davy Lee kidnapped? I'll just see if I can call for—"

"It was Blossom," she sobs, clutching at her own throat as if to bottle up the words.

I can't unhear it, can't even be surprised.

I wish I could be both, though. More than anything I've wanted since leaving New York.

"She made me. No, that's not . . . it was Blossom, though. Only please say that Davy's all right. You've all been trying to track him, and me in my kitchen chopping lettuce while at the end of my wits. If what you say is true about the cabin, then it's for certain—Blossom's your woman. She loves him, though. I don't understand."

Whatever scanty material remains in my stomach turns black, simmering with dread. I liked Blossom. Even loved her, probably, in the headlong way new friends sometimes have. I probably still do.

"Tell me," I request.

She nods. Miss Christina and I take seats on a pair of sweet potato sacks, and she yarns me a tale.

"First off, I'm not *Miss* Christina. I'm Mrs. Christina Charles of Washington, DC."

Once, far from Oregon in a land called Florida, a girl dreamed of the culinary arts. From stew to steak, she proved herself, studying under master chefs, and ending up cooking at a very fine house, serving a very fine family, under a very fine head butler by the name of Anton Charles.

"Anton was . . ." Miss Christina's frame seems, impossibly, to shrink. "He was handsome, no mistake, and always kind when he wanted something. Giving out a half day off, bottles of wine. I was younger then, prettier."

"He took notice of your charms, and you took the bait?"

"Never figured it for bait—I thought it was love. And he was already working for the same folks as me, so that neither of us would have to up and quit and get hired someplace as a pair. When he bought a ring and I said yes, our boss agreed quick as anything."

This portion of the account contains no tears. Only blinks about as grainy as the Sahara must be.

"Anton was better downstairs than upstairs." She twists her apron between her fingers. "There was all the usual, mind. Long sleeves in high summer. Noses I had to go about explaining, yes, bloody again, yes, I've tried poultices. The time when I finally ran away, though, I'd been putting up a real fight, and he said if I didn't settle down and let him whup me, then he'd whup my closest friend Sarah belowstairs for stealing spoons. It wasn't common anymore to whup servants back then, but if the butler was powerful enough, he could get away with it. Who'd the boss believe, anyway?"

"What a horrid circumstance."

"The devil was in me that time, and I kept scratching and biting and carrying on." Now the tears come, hot and fast. "I couldn't believe he'd really do it. But he did, he whupped her awful, and on top of that, he fired her without a reference to get back at me. I never saw her again."

It proves impossible not to reach out a tentative hand. She takes it, takes several seconds, and wipes her eyes with her sleeve.

"I got as far away as I could," she continues.

"That has a familiar ring."

"When I first applied here, I used my real name. And when I explained what happened, I asked Mavereen if I could be Miss

Christina hereabouts, no last name, since anything that called Anton to mind was a powerful woe, even the "Mrs." She said yes, and made a fuss over me. But then about five years ago, Rooster got hired, and I . . . I fell for him. He fell right back. I been yearning to marry that man for so long, it's put years on me."

"Well, whyever don't you, then? Surely—"

"She won't let us!" Miss Christina stifles another sob. "Says in God's eyes, I'm yet married, Miss James. Unless I get a divorce, or find out Anton's dead. Says if we were caught fornicating, we'd be cut loose."

I'm about to ask how she could ever know such a thing when I think back—to Blossom's cautions about debauches, to real warnings I half took for jokes.

The maids.

Mavereen's eyes. Everywhere, throughout the Paragon Hotel. Who knew when one would be walking down a hallway, starched and alert? Who knew what they could hear from outside a thin door?

How does a body dare to dirty bedsheets when you know exactly who'll be washing them?

"But that's cruel. And absurd," I say slowly.

"She's not cruel. But the Bible's real important to her. More important than me and Rooster, that's certain. Maybe . . . maybe more important than anything."

Still holding her hand, I rub at the back lightly. This puts Blossom's aversion to discussing the Rose's Thorn in a different, dare I say blinding, light.

Mavereen Meader approves of many things, I hear her saying. *She does* not *approve of others.*

"All right," I continue. "Mavereen won't allow any of the marital whoopee; meanwhile you're dangling in each other's sight like carrots every day. I take it the problem is money?"

Staring at a garden she never expects to have, she nods. "Took me eight months scrubbing floors before I found this place. Rooster was lifting crates at the docks. And we want a farm so I can cook for us, sell produce and milk and eggs, maybe even start a grocery. He sends a little every month to an older couple keen to go live with their daughter. They've arranged he'll get the money back if another buyer comes along. We'll never pay them in time."

"You might. So I take it Blossom approached you with some sort of offer?"

Miss Christina shuts her eyes in despair. "She wanted Rooster to let her into Max's room so she could copy his cabin key, about six months back. Said she needed it so she could leave a present there for him and gave us twenty whole dollars to keep quiet. Twenty dollars for practically nothing. We thought it queer, but were glad of the extra savings. And we trust her. She said she knew we needed it. When Davy went missing, I recollected that she'd asked me to dress him in his hiking boots—which that walk didn't warrant, but I didn't fuss about. Then I remembered it was funny she'd paid us so much when we'd have done it for free. So I asked Max if he'd gotten any surprise gifts in the last six months and he didn't know what I was on about. Then I went to see Blossom, and."

"What did she say?"

She grimaces. "You know how she is. Said how dare I ask, and that I was crazy. That she just lost the key and forgot the notion. And that anyhow, we were paid plenty handsome to do it, so anybody we blabbed to would blame us."

"And?" I question, hearing worse stuck at the back of her throat.

Miss Christina now stares numbly ahead, chewing her knuckle. "And that if we ratted, she'd tell Mavereen that Rooster and I were having an affair. We aren't. We write letters."

I recall how frantic Blossom was when Max announced he was staying to search for Davy Lee. She'd timed the whole thing perfectly except for underestimating him. She'd wanted that cabin for her own purposes.

It's really ever *so simple once it's explained to you, here, I'll do it gratis. You have to get on one of the trains before noon tomorrow or you'll lose your job.*

Miss Christina and I sit there in the barely lit quiet. I was queasy enough before—but if Blossom paid Rooster and Miss Christina twenty entire dollars to copy a friend's key, she's about as guilty as Judas with a puckered kissy face and a jingling pocket. I feel like I'm about to be ill.

"By the by, did Davy and Rooster have a quarrel? Wednesday Joe confided something of the kind to me."

Miss Christina huffs a humorless chuckle. "I was fool enough to tell Davy that Rooster wanted to marry me and that we were saving to buy some land and till it. That boy's all heart, the precious critter. Cried for days at the thought of me leaving, since he rightly supposed he'd be staying put. Blamed the whole thing on Rooster. I been working on him slow, but . . ."

I fall mute. This is a disaster of Noachian proportions.

"What you going to do?" Miss Christina asks tremulously.

"Might I ask you one more question?"

"If it'll help."

"You've worked her wedding, rolled up your sleeves at many a soup kitchen with her, taken Davy to her Weekly Betterment classes. Do you know where Miss Evelina Starr went to college?"

She frowns. "No, I reckon I don't. But it was around San Francisco. Why?"

A strike for the bowler, and the pins clatter to the floor.

And all thanks to the French language, no less.

Blossom informed me that she met Evelina Vaughan here in Portland shortly after her arrival. Evelina, when asked about cutting a rug with her bosom mate, mentioned that Blossom used to sing French heartbreakers in cabarets, and that she missed hearing them.

But my new dancing pal Gregory, at the Rose's Thorn, said he saw Blossom in San Francisco performing the same numbers—and that here, she never sang any more French love songs. Which goes right in line with why Blossom claimed to have quit San Francisco in the first place.

My true love left. My heart was broken. And what in the wide world was I to do?

There was even the picture of a younger Davy I found in Blossom's backstage vanity—a fine young sprout, standing before a pastel city that seemed fairy-tale lovely and oddly familiar. It was San Francisco exactly as Blossom described it to me. God knows where she had the picture taken. But *quelque* sentimentality.

So. The way the deck stacks to my eye, Blossom and Evelina met when the latter was in school and cutting every caper her pretty head could dream up. She was fraternizing with blacks for the first time, did the horizontal number with some fine fellow. Maybe a dancer, maybe a jazz hound, a painter, God knows, point is that the session had staying power. She was pregnant and alone, but with a friend. A friend who loved her. Unrequitedly, but none the less madly for lack of reward.

What could Evelina do? She couldn't very well return to Portland with a mulatto baby, or stay at college with her belly button making swift tracks from her spine. Clever, madcap Evelina and lovesick, fierce-hearted Blossom hatched a doozy of a scheme, though in its way a classic: take the show on the road. They went to Seattle together. Evelina popped out a wee one, delivered him to Blossom, very likely *not* behind a trash bin, and they reunited in Portland because Evelina's family and Blossom's uncle resided there. And in a final stroke of genius, the veriest coup of the gras, the friends invented Mrs. Evelina Vaughan's Weekly Betterment program. Davy was safe with Blossom, Evelina could see her son, Blossom could see Evelina, and no one the wiser.

Blue ribbons to all parties. But what went so horrendously wrong? I ask again, the knot in my stomach now the size of Rooster's fist.

"You look awful, Miss James." Miss Christina presses my hand and releases it. "Please tell me what's going on?"

Miss Christina is in the proverbial soup, same as Blossom, thanks to the twenty bucks. And Blossom—no matter what happened—is going to need allies, not enemies, especially not enemies who are by rights old friends. So I decide to give the full field report.

"What's going on is that Blossom is trying to fight trouble with trouble, which I'm dreadfully afraid only leads to more trouble."

"If you can't talk plainer than that, don't bother."

My voice drops lower. "I think Mrs. Vaughan is Davy Lee's mother. I also think that she's being blackmailed or threatened or somehow extorted. By whom, I don't know. And I think that Blossom would do anything—absolutely anything—to protect Evelina Vaughan. Even if it meant somehow sending Davy away."

Miss Christina gapes at me. She's about to protest this outrageous claim when we are interrupted by one of the most harrowing screams I have ever heard.

Top five, easily.

We fly up the stairs like bats, reach the kitchen as one and, finding it still empty, burst panting into the Paragon's lobby.

The first thing we see is Jenny Kiona fresh out of the elevator. Two hands clapped over her mouth, her lustrous black eyes shimmering holes. Rooster is charging out from behind the desk but stops, dumbstruck. A dozen early-morning hotel patrons are all frozen into pillars of salt.

Miss Christina and I turn our heads, and I gasp for the first time in a very long while.

"Help me, please!" Lucius Grint of the Rose's Thorn begs. His spherical face is paste white, sweat dripping from the scattered ends of his combed-over coiffure. "She refused to go to the colored hospital, she said she needed a doctor at her hotel because she has a special condition. I bribed a cabdriver outrageously and got here as quick as I could."

He has an arm around Blossom Fontaine, who is barely standing despite that aid. Her face is a pulp—sweet lips cracked, one eye swollen shut, a split on her rectangular brow, and her posture announces at least one cracked rib enters the picture. She's wearing a man's overcoat I presume belongs to Mr. Grint, since it hangs ludicrously short on her. Which is the reason I can see through the gap that her ball gown has been viciously ripped on the vertical.

"Good morning, everyone," she rasps. There's blood caking her teeth. "Oh, *don't* look like that, I beg. You should see the other fellow."

Then she collapses into the maître d's arms.

Twenty-Three

That she may serve well, the Negro woman must first learn to believe in herself and her race—ridding herself always of any false notions of racial or self-inferiority. We must admit that this is often hard to do, hampered as she is by her sex in what we sometimes term a man's world and by her race in a white man's world. But it can be done. . . . The time demands real women.

—BEATRICE MORROW CANNADY, "Negro Womanhood as a Power in the Development of the Race and the Nation," speech delivered June 28, 1928

It must be for only an instant we stand there, the elegant room shrunken to the size of a single terribly thin woman. It feels like millennia. Then the lobby of the Paragon blasts back into its rightful proportions, exploding into action. Women fanning themselves, men firing off questions.

"What's happened to the poor dear?"

"Lord have mercy!"

"Somebody call the police!"

"No calls, please, thank you, ladies and gentlemen!" Rooster booms. "We locals know which folks in the department to contact."

He darts back behind the counter, snatching up a room key. "Excuse us! Wednesday Joe, get back in that elevator and keep it running, you hear?"

Wednesday Joe, stark terror on his young face, obeys.

"Oh God, oh no," Miss Christina moans. "I'll boil water. And towels, I'll get clean towels."

She dashes back into the kitchen. The crowd's energy crackles with unease as the guests start to mutter and exclaim. Rooster gathers Blossom up and heads for the stairs, a small but fearfully furious squadron of allies in his wake. And I see his plan—with the elevator running, the stairs will be much emptier. When we reach the second-story landing, he stops.

"Jenny, fetch Mavereen and Max. Then find someone to man the front desk." Rooster's suave voice is jagged with anger.

Jenny pauses with one hand stretched toward Blossom.

"Jenny," Rooster repeats. "I know, sweetheart. But *go.* Now."

Sobbing in dry hitches, she rushes out of the stairwell.

We continue, surprising a respectable middle-aged woman who shrinks backward. Rooster's pace is hard to match, and I fall behind as my belly starts to pierce. When we reach Blossom's room on the fifth floor, Rooster unlocks the door despite his limp cargo, and we crowd behind him as he lays her on the coverlet. Medea hisses, scurrying behind the changing screen.

I sit by the singer's head and check her pulse. "I think she's only fainted. Rooster, why in God's name didn't you tell Jenny to call Dr. Pendleton first?"

"He isn't here." Rooster is at the window, staring out like a wolf that's just heard a twig snap underfoot.

"You can't be serious!" Mr. Grint squeaks. "Then I ought to have taken her to the colored clinic, special condition be damned! Where the devil is he?"

"Had a private house call from a colored patient. He gets them every so often, when the other black doctors are stuck. Always takes them."

"Of course he does," I lament, decidedly *not* panicking. But, oh, how I admire to—because I know who did this to her, and what he was after, and if he got it, then the entire population of the Paragon including myself will carve Overton apart and fricassee the pieces. "Dr. Pendleton took oaths, yes, sacred oaths. Blossom, can you hear me?"

"Could anyone have followed you?" When I glance up, I see that Rooster is checking a Beretta Model 1915, and my heart sings hallelujah.

"What?" Lucius Grint is staring at his cabaret star in open dismay. "No, no, we were in a car from the dockside and then walked through the door. She had finished her set and I thought she'd gone upstairs to have a morning pick-me-up with her friends. When I was doing final check, I found her like this."

"It wasn't your fault," I tell him.

"Yes, it was. I should have been there to help her sooner." Lucius Grint, as is the case with most speakeasy proprietors, is inured to brouhahas, fracases, and melees. So his distress means he genuinely cares. "But I think I can promise that no one followed us."

"Good," Rooster concludes. "Because if they did, they'll need a wooden coat."

Beneath my fingertips, which are skimming the few bits of her face that aren't smashed, Blossom shivers. Her eyelids flicker, wincing.

"She's coming 'round," I report.

"Oh, thank God." Mr. Grint smooths a hand over his squiggling hair follicles. "It's Blossom's room, so there must be—should I fetch her—"

"The spirits are in that perfume diffuser." I point, then stroke

Blossom's cheek again. "Blossom, you're in your room. You're going to be just fine, the fittest of the fiddles, all right?"

Her single operative eye opens. I worry that she'll slap me away. Instead she whispers, "Why, Alice James. You find me just . . . the *tiniest* bit indisposed."

I laugh, more from strain than relief. Lucius Grint toddles over with liquid fortification. Placing it to her lips, I lift her head.

"I'd best be downstairs. I don't like to leave you without a weapon." Rooster tucks his gun away, addressing Blossom. "Can we give Miss James yours?"

"It was removed from my person," Blossom reports in a tone dry enough to drain the Atlantic.

"Oh! Here, I insist. I always keep it fully loaded. One never knows, working on a saloon barge."

Lucius Grint displays in his damp palm a 7.65 millimeter Mauser Model 14 pocket pistol. I place it on the side table.

"I like you," I tell Mr. Grint. "I like you awfully well. I want you to consider yourself kissed on either cheek."

"I'll do so immediately, Miss James."

Rooster nods. "Let's leave the ladies to the nursing. Blossom, you need me for anything at all, I am your man."

The gents make their exit.

"Blossom," I say, and find myself too choked to continue.

"Oh, Alice." Tears seep from the edges of her eyelids.

"You gave Officer Overton what for, didn't you?"

"He looks like he met a gorilla and took its banana."

"I told you I'd be there if he ever tried to hurt you, I—"

"Hush, honey, I stormed off in a terrible tantrum."

I'm dripping something indecorous on Blossom's ruined dress. "I'll kill him personally, without middlemen."

"You'll probably have to get in line."

"What's the worst of the damage? Miss Christina is boiling water. But for now, I could—"

"No, it's just some bumps and scrapes. I've had worse."

I regard her, eyes brimming, and she tries to smile.

"No, Alice, he did not," she states firmly. "He tried. He failed in his efforts."

"Are you telling me the truth?" My voice breaks badly.

"Why, what a complimentary fallacy, to think I'd be good enough to spare your feelings on the subject."

"You are good," I insist senselessly, despite the still nebulous dark deeds I know she's been about.

"Of all the lunatics in all the world, you may be my favorite. Second favorite," she amends. "But, no, I am decidedly *not* good, and, yes, I am telling the truth."

"What happened?"

"He made use of that gun you mentioned. Oh, I was so miffed at you I couldn't see straight, Alice, and then I wasn't thinking about *anything* save patching it up. I was *that* sick over us. He snuck into the club and went straight to my dressing room. Pointed that shooter, made me give him my gun, frog-marched me upstairs, and told me it was death or dishonor. *Well.* Turned out he wanted both hands free, and he set the gun down, and I simply flew at him. I'm stronger than I look, and there was a tussle. After I'd caught him in the undercarriage, I grabbed his sidearm, and I *really* ought to have put a hole in the creature, but stopped short of actual murder and told him never to set foot in the Rose's Thorn again or I'd tell everyone in Portland a nigger woman beat him in a fight. *That* seemed to open sesame. He slunk off. But he'd knocked me halfway to China, and Lucius found me, and the rest you know."

I'm sniffling something awful. "I'm sorry you had to do any of that alone."

"What, kick the ever-loving shit out of Overton? I wanted the privilege *entirely* to myself, honey."

A soft knock sounds, and I pick up the gun.

"Come in."

Miss Christina enters first, her arms full of towels and a steaming bowl. Mavereen follows, pulling a miniature ice cart. She raises her head. When she spies Blossom, she makes a sound as if struck in the gut.

"Mav, honey, it looks terrible, but it isn't." Blossom, struggling mightily, sits up. "Now, I am going behind that screen to attire myself in something other than what now only qualifies as a *very* pretty dishrag."

"Land's sake, sugar, we'll fix you up right here," Mavereen protests, stricken.

"Nonsense. I'm a heinously proud person, and—"

"Blossom Fontaine, you lay yourself back down this instant. Where's your nightdress, sugar? We can just slip—"

"No."

Everyone stops. Including Mavereen, who sets her hands on her hips with a look equal parts motherly and horrified.

"Bless you, I deserved that. Blossom, sweet precious girl, being hurt this way ain't nothing to be ashamed of, it's a thing to be survived." Tears spill down her broad cheeks. "Now, you lie back down and—"

"I wasn't raped," Blossom says testily.

Oh, I realize.

It's a tumor.

The cancer is a tumor, and we'll see it, and everyone at the Paragon will treat her like the walking dead for the rest of her ever-so-brief life. They won't let her sing or drink or carouse or do anything she loves ever again.

She'll be in hell until the day she dies.

"Not that word, now. We don't need to talk about that kind of iniquity in here, in our *home*." Mavereen makes prayer hands, convinced Blossom is lying.

"Mavereen, he wasn't trying to hurt me or ruin me or seduce me or take advantage of me. Officer Overton was trying to *rape* me." Blossom staggers to her feet, using the hand I throw out to catch her as a crutch. "But I prevented him."

"Blossom," Miss Christina pleads despite the ugliness between them, "you've got to let us help you."

Blossom's face, or the fraction that's capable, melts. "Christina, I'm warmed to the very *cockles* of my soul that you admire to, but let's get down to brass tacks. Where in holy hell is my beloved uncle?"

We exchange the sort of looks one probably found in the trenches whenever a loud whistling sound streaked across the sky.

"Dr. Pendleton isn't here," Miss Christina says.

"Of course he's here, he's always here." Blossom is walking toward her dressing screen and, since it's terribly difficult to wriggle out of a tornado, I'm helping her along.

"Blossom, you've every right to hysterics right now, but that don't mean it's the time for them." Mavereen stands before us, immovable, with her bulk like an empress and her spiraling slate hair like a crown. "Doddridge had a house call."

"He *what*?" Blossom exclaims.

"So you need to be a good strong girl and let us tend to your—"

"Get out," Blossom hisses.

Mavereen's hand flies to her breast and Miss Christina drops the cloth she's holding.

"All right," Mavereen answers, low yet loving. "I need you to heed me, Blossom Fontaine. Your mamma ain't here, rest her, but *we* are here. We're your family now, sugar. Ain't nohow we're leaving with you in this sorry state."

"Please, I'll give you anything you ask. Just—"

"Ladies, I can be of help here," I find myself announcing.

They regard me with befuddlement—save Blossom, who wears a look of such forlorn hope that it sears my skin.

"It's . . . it's ever so awkward, but I know what's going on, and Blossom is right. When I was waiting in her dressing room the other day, I needed something to wipe a spill, and like a ninny I opened one of her drawers and saw a pamphlet there."

Blossom's eyes blow sky wide. Instantly, they narrow to furious points, so I whip up the pace.

"And it seems—well, we all know that Blossom's been ailing lately, but—it seems that Dr. Pendleton is performing some dreadfully experimental measures. She'll be entirely herself again soon! The halest horse in the paddock, Mrs. Meader, but the treatment is, how shall I put this—"

"Modern," Miss Christina pipes in out of the blue.

I regard the woman with adoration. Blossom, meanwhile, marvels at us as if we've stockings on our ears and chopsticks up our nostrils.

Miss Christina retrieves the dropped cloth. "Dr. Pendleton was three sheets to the wind one night, talking funny, sketching it out on a page so he could do better by Blossom. Looked just plain terrible to me."

"Embarrassing as anything," I add.

"Painful!" Blossom chirps at last. "God, *ever* so painful."

"And supposing I had to take that cure," Miss Christina continues.

"Heaven forbid," I insert.

"Then you'd never want anyone save your physician—and a *family* physician at that—to see the Frankenstein's patchwork he has made of you," Blossom finishes, her free hand over her heart.

Mavereen seems not to know where to look any longer—back, left, or upside down.

Miss Christina places the soaked cloth in my grip. "Mav, let's go and wait for Dr. Pendleton. Blossom just faced the unspeakable, and it wouldn't be Christian to humiliate her twice in one day."

A tearful Mavereen brushes her hand over Blossom's finger curls. "You want me to send your friend Jenny over? She was that worked up, poor lamb, I told her to keep to her room, but would she be any comfort?"

"Ah, no. That was, as ever, wisdom," Blossom manages.

"I'll be praying all this while for you, you hear me?"

"Like angels' trumps." Blossom wilts in relief. "I'll be *quite* myself again after Alice and Dr. Pendleton have worked their charms."

Slow with grief, Mavereen exits. As Miss Christina follows, glancing behind, I fling her a silent *thank you.*

She nods as she closes the door.

"Oh my God," Blossom groans.

"Lie down before you break that swan's neck of yours," I command, backing her onto the bed.

"But I need to—"

"I'm not going on an Easter egg hunt for your cancer, Blossom."

Bringing the washing materials, I sit on the bed, pressing a damp cloth to the cut on her brow. She hisses.

"Hello, you," I greet her.

"Hello, you," she whispers.

Cleaning her face seems necessary, since everyone is strung dreadfully high. Dab, rinse, wring. I'm of two minds just now. Do I care about Davy Lee? Well, naturally. But in this particular tableau, she is my friend Blossom, and I am her friend Alice. After a while, she's breathing evenly, and she's staring at me.

"So you tried out the gumshoe act in my dressing room too? Because I *certainly* don't want to feel left out."

"I didn't dream of it." I finish wiping her brow. "Scout's honor. Better yet, honor among thieves. I spilled a few drops of the good stuff on your counter and didn't want to wipe it up with French silk. I needed a cloth. So."

"So," she repeats, her eyes lost someplace I've never visited.

I tackle the streaks from her split lip. Her face is nearly clean, and that makes me feel immeasurably lighter, for all that she's still battered to hamburger.

"You found the dietary pamphlet," she supposes.

"Yes, and never breathed a word of it to a living."

She gives a meaningful cough. "That cleverly vague excuse you gave Mavereen regarding the torturous, embarrassing, excruciating, altogether *soul*-crushing modern treatment for my sort?"

"Oh, Blossom!" I drop the cloth, kiss the top of her head, the tip of her nose, the undamaged eyelash. "I didn't know. Christ, I could kick myself from here to Canada except that it worked."

"It even had the virtue of being true."

Lips at her hairline, I say, "There's nothing virtuous about it. Please tell me the rest of it's true too—that you're going to be climbing Mount Rainier ten years from now."

"Probably not."

She taps at my knee and I swiftly meet her gaze.

"I couldn't tell that you knew. I . . . hadn't realized it could be like that. Thank you."

Lifting one shoulder, I think of every-colored eyes and muscles wasting to nothing more than paint for their bones. "It's not my first rodeo with serious conditions. You remind me of him, actually."

"Really?" Her nose wrinkles. "Then was he the most sophisticated and cultured gent in all New York?"

"Of course he was."

"Naturally. Did you adore him?"

"To mortification."

"Oh, honey. Did he meet a tragic and glorious hero's demise?"

"Haven't the faintest. He may still be alive, actually. If he is, it won't be for long."

She tucks the uninjured part of her lip between her teeth.

"Don't be sorry," I interject, although I still am. Every day. "He will doubtless perish as he lived, beloved of all the world save one. The mirror played wretched tricks with the fellow, if you understand me."

"Yes, I do."

"There. *Voilà*. Now that you are ravishing again, I suggest that I help you to your dressing screen and I pour us two very immodest drinks. What say you?"

"I say I'm throwing you a *parade*."

I leave her gripping her wall of painted herons. Then I wrap a generous scoopful of the ice in a dry towel, pour libations, and steel myself for what unfortunately must—supposing I can manage it before Dr. Pendleton returns—be accomplished now.

Bite the bullet and pull the trigger, old girl.

When my friend emerges in a floral red, gold, and sapphire kimono-style robe, my resolve goes the way of the punctured balloon. Because she looks improved, even smiles faintly. We ensconce ourselves quite cozily on the bed again. Blossom on her side facing me, accepting the ice and applying it to her brow. I sitting up with my knees tucked, casting about for a way to do this gently.

"Should I ask Miss Christina to bring you some chow?"

She adjusts a pillow. "I can't countenance any other humans presently."

"In that case. Not to appear to wish to, um, change the subject, but . . ."

"Anything!" she cries, almost laughing. "Christ on a tricycle, *anything* else, I am *literally* dying and had simply the dreadfullest morning, may we speak of taxation reform?"

"How perfectly ghastly. No." I smirk into my grog. "How should I best put this?"

"Oh my *God*," Blossom breathes. "You didn't? You *did*."

"Yes, well, you see last night—never mind last night as a general concept, when taken by averages we should chuck it right out, there's much to tell you, but last night, I did manage to seduce a certain second lieutenant."

I grin at her. It's shockingly easy. I care for her that much, you see.

Blossom's dark eye glows as wickedly as her cat's.

"Tell me everything there is to know about Maximilian in the sack, sparing no detail. Commence."

I do—well, I do in sketch form. I answer *yes*, and *oh God*, *yes*, and *actually*, and Blossom tries not to cackle, and fails.

"And so you see before you," I conclude with some pathos, "a woman in the thrall of a man possessing a set of twins, two medals of valor, and a work address that changes time zones."

Blossom clucks, but her eyes are dancing.

"What?"

"You had him, though," she drawls in finest Blossom style, "and it was *luxurious*."

"Ugh," I moan, remembering. "It was the veriest."

Setting aside the ice, she plays with my fingers. "I'm so *glad*. Two of my favorite lost pennies together. Gorgeous."

Capturing her hand, I let it be known I intend to keep it, to which she makes no objection.

"I haven't informed you yet where we indulged in this tête-à-tête."

She blinks. "Do tell."

"It was Maximilian's cabin."

Of course she knows the instant I say the words. The spark in her gaze turns from sunlight to steel.

"There was convincing evidence Davy had been there."

She tries, bless her, to look surprised. But all she can do is heave a single devastated sob into the pillow.

I curl toward her. "Shh, it's me. We'll work it out between us. Tell me every little thing and I'll fix it with you. Oh, here, I've a jazzy notion, I'll tell you the bits I already know and save you the trouble."

I yarn her fairy tales about a chef and a doorman who wish for a farm more than anything, and so unlock a door they had no business touching. About a glittering city by a great bay, and a wild creature who went to live there, and a beautiful woman who never thereafter could sing French love songs, they hurt her so. About a foundling who may never have been lost, and a sinister force threatening a once happy kingdom—or anyhow, as happy as it could be.

Blossom shakes, face half hidden. But she doesn't contradict me.

"Then I found the ransom note," I conclude. "Blossom, this must be nightmarish, but I have to know where he's been taken and who's been persecuting Mrs. Vaughan."

Her head rises. "Ransom note?"

"Blossom, I've seen you with Evelina, you'd throw yourself on a spit for her and baste yourself with butter. The only reason you could possibly be involved—the key, the cabin—is because you love her, and I know that he's her son. The note said repeated installments. If someone is blackmailing her, or otherwise threatening her—who would do such a horrid thing as frighten a mother by way of her child? And in such a hideous way that you would ever dream of agreeing? The boy's father, maybe?"

Blossom produces a ghastly laugh.

"The boy's *father*?" she repeats.

"Yes."

"I'm his father."

Have you ever looked at a picture in a penny arcade in high summer, with salt in your hair and sand on your toes, and been asked, is this an evil witch or a beautiful princess? Is this a face, or is it a vase of flowers? And you're in a tearing great rush to get it right, because you think there's only one answer. So you choose the first one you see, and you're so strong for it that you can't see the other. But it's there the whole time. And if you squint the peepers, hey presto, the whole image changes, and you wonder why you couldn't see it before.

"Oh my God," I breathe. "Of course you are."

It's a dumb response—I'll not haggle over that. It rouses the Blossom I know and love though, which is awfully fine.

"Of *course* I am?" she snaps.

Then she—my brain can't think of her any other way, the same as if you see the princess first, it's so taxing to find the witch—forces herself to a sitting position.

"Whoa there!" I exclaim.

"Of course I am," she repeats. "I tell you this secret, this simply monstrous secret, Alice James, the one that has *ruined* my *life*, the one I've never voluntarily told a human soul other than a lover, and you don't have the decency to be *surprised*?"

"Well, when you put it that way."

Blossom throws her head back and this laugh—the one I gladly join in—is a pure middle finger in the face of the universe. Then she collapses onto the bedclothes and it turns sharp and irregular. She covers her spectacularly bruised face with her hands.

"Oh God, what have I done?"

"Hey—"

"Decades!" she snarls at the ceiling. "I have been *perfect*, I have been *immaculate*, and now it's not enough I'm dying, oh no, I also have to be neck-deep in *shit*. Only Evy and dear old Uncle Doddridge hereabouts could have spoken a word against me."

"What about Jenny?"

"Oh, I'd never tell her, we only—"

She clamps her jaw tight with a snap. It would be amusing, if this were the time to be amused.

"What *are* you?" she cries. "Must you know *everything*?"

"Nobody special."

"Oh, no, nobody special, you're just the one who made me crack finally, who utterly decimated my perfect record of devotion to my one simple rule, which is *never tell anyone*."

"I think . . . I've seen people crack before, in several sorts of ways. But I don't think that's what this was. Cracking. By all means blow the penalty whistle if I'm out of bounds, but I think this was spilling?"

"Spilling," she repeats incredulously. "And why would I do that?"

"Two reasons. In the first place, because you said that you thought if I knew you, really knew you, that I wouldn't hate you."

The bristling is replaced by fear. "Do you?"

"No."

She considers this, finds it truth. "That's . . . astonishing. And good."

"Yes, rather."

"What's the second reason?"

This time I fold her hand in both of mine. "You spilled so you wouldn't crack."

Tears swim, but don't overflow.

"Blossom, will you please tell me where Davy is? Everyone's going bananas, and they can have the boat, hell they can have the whole jungle, but you don't want to do this to Max and Mavereen and Miss Christina, do you?"

"Not to any of them. But they're going to have to remain in ignorance."

"Blossom, for Christ's sake, where is your son?"

"At a boarding school for promising Negro youth in Chicago."

She barely has the final syllable out before she's weeping so hard she can't breathe, and I manage to snatch her up, and even before she has the chance to do halfway decent work soaking my frock, the words pour forth.

"We had to, we *had* to," she gasps. "I can hardly bear it, Alice, I want to jump off the roof, save only for Evy. We had to. This *city*. We thought it would be different, when we decided to be near family. Being used to San Francisco, we thought—we were so wrong. But we're as trapped here as if there were actual *chains* on our legs. Evy's family. My uncle. The husband she married so she'd be able to live near me and Davy—though I like Tom, very much. He loves her the way I do, and she loves him so sweetly. But I'm dying, Alice, and Evy's mind is . . ."

This isn't crying, this is heartbreak like a fault line splitting.

"What if I die next week? What if she were so grieved, she claimed Davy was hers and was disgraced? What if she let every goddamn cat out of the bag? Her spells are worse and worse now. A dying father who isn't even a father and a troubled mother, all in a city that *hates* mixed children. And then the Klan came, and oh, we were *terrified*, because if anyone found out, we'd all be lynched and Davy with us and so we put every cent of my savings and some of Evy's family money together to save him, we only want to *save him*, Alice, but I'll never see my baby boy again, never, and it hurts *so much.*"

With my hand on her hair and my arm 'round her back, we stay like that.

I can't say *I'm sorry.*

I can't say *that isn't fair.*

Words don't suffice.

When her grief quiets—I won't say ebbs, or lessens, because how could it—by some awfully clever maneuvering I manage to reach our glasses, and we huddle in the sort of stillness that follows a storm at sea.

"Medea, *for God's sake!*"

The cat, perched on Blossom's vanity with a feather from one of her hair ornaments in its mouth, yowls and slips to the carpet.

"I was wondering something," I venture.

"What?"

"Less specifically, I was wondering positively *everything*. So I thought perhaps it might help if, while you're so stretched and limber and warmed up to the spilling, it might help for you to tell me about it."

She looks hesitant. "As a way to . . . what, pass the time other than whiskey and two-handed whist?"

"No. Because it matters to me."

Blossom looks uncharacteristically pensive.

"I've never in my life tried it before. But . . . I am an *intensely* professional performer, so. Once upon a time, it is."

· *Twenty-Four* ·

THEN

The affection of gangsters for their own offspring, and even for all children, birds and animals, although perhaps not always the touching and splendid sentiment which the romanticists would have us believe, nevertheless is often real enough.

—STANLEY WALKER, *The Night Club Era*, 1933

When I opened the door, *snick-whoosh*, to the Hotel Arcadia's rooftop, a pair of comfortable armchairs were set out with a table between them and a set of crystal stemware, as if Mr. Salvatici expected me, and from the left-hand perch snaked a thin coil from his cigar. The pigeons were snug in their nests, ruffling feathers as their dreams bade them, and their contentment ought to have soothed me.

I was limp with dread. So I made myself ever so small inside, shook out my shoulders, and sidled up to take my place.

"Ah, there you are!" Mr. Salvatici flashed his sketched-on smile and reached to pop the bottle of champagne resting in the silver bucket at his feet. "Look here, Nobody—an apology gift. I was out of sorts earlier and never should have subjected you to the sight of Mr. Benenati, no matter that he couldn't physically intimidate you. Forgive me. I trust that all's well with Harry and we can now put this entire incident behind us?"

"Actually, Harry needs close attention." I sat down as the flutes filled, careful to make the husk in my voice sound like fatigue. "If you don't watch your back around him, you'll end up with a robe on it. He admires to make you a crown out of tinfoil and anoint your heirs with frankincense."

"Steadfast?"

"You could set your watch by his whisker growth."

"Well, here's to old associates proven trustworthy, then."

We clinked. Gaze fixed to the tiny sea of golden froth in my glass, I wondered where Nicolo was. At a Bronx warehouse, buying enough dynamite to level this place? At Sing Sing, throwing his lot in with the Boss of Bosses now that he knew who had really slaughtered his father? At home, cleaning his tommy gun?

"My dear young lady," the Spider questioned gently, "did Nicolo Benenati frighten you somehow?"

"Why do you ask?"

"Because you carry a rabbit's foot when you know you'll encounter him, and you're stroking your thumb over it inside your left trouser pocket."

It was true. I had the French tonic raised contemplatively before my nose, and my other hand trying to squeeze some luck, any luck, out of a chunk of taxidermied bunny. Draining the bubbles, I stuck my arm out for more.

"That bad, was it?" Mr. Salvatici sighed. "It's a damnable thing, how efficient that boy is, and how depraved at the same time."

"If he's depraved, you made him that way."

"I beg your pardon?"

"You killed his father."

This pronouncement tore a hole in me so wide that my fear poured right out to pool around our ankles.

There. You've said it.

Mr. Salvatici had never hurt me, and he wouldn't start now.

With legs like jelly, I went to the dovecote and unlatched it, selecting a misty grey bird with the sweetest white bars over her wings. I cradled her as I carried her back. Sat down and watched her fluff herself awake. It was as if I'd set off a bomb and there we sat with a thin high shriek in our ears, watching shrapnel fall like confetti.

"I've been reading your journals," I continued, eyes on the pigeon. "I'm dreadfully sorry, but I needed to know, and. You're not my father, are you? My stepfather. You're my stepfather. In a way."

Mr. Salvatici winced minutely, just a crinkle at the edges of his pale eyes. Topping up our drinks, he went to the railing, taking in the glow and stink and glory of Harlem below us, all the lives he played with while his birds wheeled untouched over the melee.

"You needn't be frightened, Nobody," he said softly. "As the man who taught you how to dig for secrets, I can't be surprised over your unearthing mine, not when I was so careless over them. I suppose . . . I almost wanted you to. That's cowardly, but I saw no reason to upset you if you were contented. This way, you had the choice whether to learn about me or no."

Car horns blared in the distance, and the gentle bird nuzzled my hand. I'd sat here with Mr. Salvatici more times than I could recall, and now in the very center of our ever-so-peaceful oasis all I could see was how he looked the night I staggered into his hotel for the first time—fresh from his bath, half dressed, with kindly old Mr. Benenati's blood staining the water cherry pink in the next room.

"I met Catrin on the ship from Europe." The Spider turned to face me, resting his lean body against the wrought iron. "I don't suppose, knowing her, that she ever told you anything about me? The past is a foreign country, so far as Catrin is concerned. I was in second class, and your mother was in steerage, but I caught a glimpse of her on the promenade just after a vicious squall that had everyone prostrate in their bunks—supposing they'd bought bunks—and the air was sparkling that morning, electric. She'd snuck onto the deck and was staring out over the waves, and there was . . . a calm about her, and a beauty, unlike anything I'd ever seen."

Nodding, I brushed my index finger over the pigeon's quavering head. Mum was nothing if not beautiful. And calm.

"The ship's captain married us. I was poor, and she was poorer. But I was also enchanted, and afraid, and alone, and she was . . . amenable?"

"Things happen to people."

"I'm sorry?"

"Mum says things happen to people." I focused on the pleasantly rough avian feet gripping my hand. "You happened to her, so she said yes. Like later, you happened to me."

Smiling, Mr. Salvatici shook his head. "Catrin to the letter. And therein lay the problem, you see. I very quickly realized that I'd foolishly tied myself to a woman content to drift wherever life took her. Did you know that she won her berth to America in a card game, in a bawdy house where she plied her trade in Cardiff? Oh, yes. She held that ticket, mulled it over, and decided, why not? I thought she would steady me, ravenous striver that I was, but soon after I'd married her, it was clear that we would become a misery to each other. We parted ways a week after landing in New York."

"You mean you left her."

"My dear young lady, she didn't need me." Mr. Salvatici's high brow furrowed sympathetically. "Not before she met me, and not after."

He was right. She'd never really needed anyone.

Not even her daughter.

"Then she met my father," I continued with a catch in my voice. "And he called her *bella*, and I think she may have loved him because she's never told me his name, and I was born. And then you came back."

"I'd been working like a fiend—forming connections in Hell's Kitchen, watching the Corleonesi spread like an infection." He propped his elbow against his wrist. "Growing powerful enough to make a difference. When I considered branching uptown to Little Italy, I started taking long walks—just soaking it in, the Raines law hotels and tenements and street vendors. One day I saw Catrin again, and. Couldn't look away. We'd never suit each other, but instead of evading her, I planted myself in her path. When your mother nearly ran into me, she set her hands on her hips, laughed, and invited me back to the Step Right."

This brought the specter of a smile to my face.

Of course she did.

"Which is where I learned about you," he added.

Swallowing, I let the pigeon pass from one of my hands to the other, back and forth. I thought of the day I was shot at the Tobacco Club, of my guardian's words just before he killed the little brown bird.

People will do practically anything for you, just so long as they believe they're on the right side.

"You were ferocious when I first saw you," he said wistfully. "Screaming at one of Catrin's johns to give you back your favorite handkerchief. As you grew older, you grew less visible, but never less alive. And you were always watching."

"And you felt alone."

"Yes."

"So you took me."

"Not precisely," he corrected, sipping his drink.

"You killed three people." My knuckles were crushed against my mouth, the pigeon cupped against my chest. "No, it was four. You killed Nicolo, that day. The person he was died."

"It's natural for you to think so." Mr. Salvatici inclined his head. "I admit, I didn't expect the results to prove so drastic. Rebellion, open defiance? Rage, even? I hoped for that. Did I expect this . . . twisted mechanism of a person to be born? No."

"How could you," I whispered. "No—don't answer that. You were telling a story."

The dash of his lips tilted.

"You wanted a world where people fought back against the unspeakable, so you did something unspeakable to make them fight."

He lifted one shoulder. "When my father's torso was slit from his breastbone to his cock by the Family, and he was left to rot in our vineyard, it was the crows' screeching that led us to him. He'd been crawling for the house with his entrails in one hand. I'm happy to tell you he didn't get very far. The event became a source of . . . motivation for me. As far as the Benenati family is concerned, I admit I needed a catalyst. But I am sorry all the same, my dear young lady."

We were silent for a spell. Just the bird nipping my sweater, and the delicate scrolled rail, and the memory of Harry Chipchase begging that Nicolo kill him rather than leave him to the mercy of my guardian.

Just don't turn me over to the boss. I's seen what he can do.

Mr. Salvatici cleared his throat. "The Veuve Clicquot was a conciliatory gesture, but it was also a celebratory one. While you were at the Cabin, I traced the missing counterfeit. It was stolen by a police captain with a certain enthusiasm for gambling, and luckily for us he indulges at our faro palace on a Hundred and Tenth. When he showed up far more flush than usual, I was notified—oh, he's quite all right, I simply removed it from his keeping and elicited a promise to think of us fondly in future, considering what we know about him. He hadn't spent much yet. There's approximately fifty thousand dollars in *immaculate* bills in my bedroom safe. I'm quite admiring of the craftsmanship. The cops only seized it in the first place as part of a liquor raid."

"Congratulations."

"Don't sound like that."

"Why not?"

"All right, forgive me, you're . . . tired, overwhelmed. Perhaps even bitter. But because I want you to invest it."

Raising my eyes in astonishment, I sat dumbstruck as the bird flapped out of my hands and landed on a metal curl beside my guardian.

"In a saloon, a casino, a racetrack, anything that interests you. Nobody, it's never been formalized, but you are my heir." His blue eyes were nearly imploring. "We can . . . make it official if you like, you can consider that later, but—"

Footsteps clanging up the stairs made us pause, and the pigeon fluttered to the peak of the dovecote. Mr. Salvatici's hand strayed toward his gun.

I waited too long, I thought desperately. *And now—*

Sadie burst onto the roof, dressed to go out in a creamy velvet shift, with seed pearls worked into her coronet of hair. Panting, she rested one hand against the doorframe. It held a slip of paper.

"Nobody!" she called. "Heaven's sake, the hotel's been looking for you this past half hour. A street kid delivered this, said it was an emergency."

I had it in my hands seconds later, as Mr. Salvatici went to coax his anxious pigeon from its roost. When I'd read it, a moan escaped me, the sort that all wounded creatures make without intending to.

No, please. Please not that.

"Nobody, what's the matter?" Sadie exclaimed, touching my arm.

Latching the cage, Mr. Salvatici thrust out a hand. "Let me see that."

"No." Faltering, I crushed it in my fist and shoved it in my pocket with the rabbit's foot. "No, this . . . this is my trouble."

My heart pulsed in syncopated beats, champagne starbursts clouding my vision.

Anything but that.

"My dear young lady—"

"He knows," I gasped, coming back to myself. "Oh, God. Mr. Salvatici—I ought to have told you that first, but he, Harry Chipchase, learned what really happened to Mr. Benenati long ago from another crooked cop, and so now Nicolo knows too."

"He what?" Mr. Salvatici exclaimed.

"You have to prepare, ready yourself for whatever he means to do. I'm so sorry, but I have to go."

"Go where? And how could—"

"Harry spilled and Nicolo believed him. I'm—I'm helping to fix it. I'll see you in the morning."

"Nobody? Nobody!" Mr. Salvatici shouted. "Come back!"

I was halfway down the stairs when I heard him cry, *"Alice!"* I stopped to close my eyes against the pain of it.

And then kept running.

The door of the Murder Stable groaned, the dangling chain scraping the stones as if clawing to get away. Water dripped from the rooftop cistern. A horse snuffled, shifting uneasily. My feet were silent on the loose wisps of straw, and I shouldn't have been able to see them, it ought to have been black as pitch in there, but a world away down the aisle of that sickening corrugated barn, an entire city block distant, a lamp shone, illuminating one thin upright shadow and a shapeless mass beside it.

Nobody the saltwater stray had disappeared with my cap. So it was only me, whoever that was, crossing that monstrous distance to find Nicolo standing in an empty stall with a long knife in his hand, and Rye bound helpless and shaking to a chair.

"Darlin', you run!" he croaked. It wasn't panic making Rye tremble—he'd been after a fix-up, and been interrupted. "Right this second. Get—"

The back of Nicolo's free hand met Rye's cheek in an explosion, sent his head dropping limply to his breast, and I leaped forward. Stopped when I found the knife aimed at my eye.

"I knew that would get your attention." Nicolo's familiar face sliced toward me, the profile of a sleek, carnivorous bird. "Actually, I thought you'd arrive sooner—but no, I see you ran all the way; it must have taken them a little while to find you. That's all right. You're here now."

"Nicolo." My voice quavered. I dropped every pretense from false defiance to blank passivity. "What are we doing here?"

"I sent for you."

Squeezing my fist around the message in my pocket, I nodded.

Your dancer friend lost his way. Come to the Murder Stable alone and unarmed, and we'll see whether we can get him safe home.

"I never carry a weapon," I said.

"Just being careful. You might have decided to start tonight."

"Nicolo, for God's sake, why would I do that?"

"Because you and your precious Spider *butchered my father* and then stuffed him in a barrel!" he roared.

The knife flashed golden in the sallow light. I flinched away.

"Oh, Nicolo, I didn't know!" I cried. "We all loved your father, I just found out tonight, I swear to you."

"Tonight?" The snarl on his face belonged on a wounded panther. "Why tonight, the same night I did? Why—oh," he realized. "You were there, is that it? At the Cabin. When I was giving Harry the third degree. You were spying for Salvatici, weren't you? For the man who destroyed my family. And now you're trying to mop up his mess for him. Nobody the cobweb. Nobody the dust on the shelf. Nobody my little fucking mouse."

He inched closer, and I took a step back.

"I'm still your *topolina*. Nicolo—"

"Two Corleonesi filleted behind my house. Then my father is slaughtered, he is mutilated, Alicia, in public, and do you come stay with my mother and me, or even, God forbid, go back to the Step Right? No. You take up with a complete stranger, fall in with him entirely, I never see you anymore, you were thick as thieves from the beginning, and you expect me to believe you knew *nothing* about what he did? When you went to live with him the *day* my father died?"

"Yes, before tonight I—"

"Do you know why we're here, Alicia?"

"No. But I want to leave, Nicolo, we should—"

"This is where I had to talk to you. This is where it makes sense. There were a couple of the Clutch Hand's *scurmi fituzzi* slinking around when I arrived, but you can bet I sent them running with their tails between their legs." Nicolo's eyes slid to his knife blade. "Here's where I kissed you. Once. You remember that, *topolina*?"

"Of course I do."

"But never again, did I?" He pushed his hand through thick black hair, grimacing. "Just the one time. Keeping you safe. That's all I was thinking about, when I . . . with the horse. You and my mother. I had to get stronger, Alicia, I had to be more dangerous than them, and *this*?" he shouted. The knife swung, full of thwarted spite, in the unconscious Rye's direction. "This pathetic *garbage sack* of a man, oh, I'll admit he was something to look at once, quick too, I could forgive him for touching you since he saved you from a shootout, but you kissed him in front of the Hotel Arcadia, I was heading there to confront you before I stuff Mauro Salvatici in a fucking barrel, and you . . . you kissed him."

"Nicolo, please, I—"

"Stop saying my name like you used to! Christ." Nicolo was shattering, all the icy edges crackling with fissures, and he didn't listen to me anymore, so all I could do was watch. "I am going to kill your guardian, Alicia, but before I do that, tell me whether I need to kill this colored boy too."

"No! He's never hurt you, never touched me, we're only—"

"He might have carried you out of the Tobacco Club, but I brought you Sammy the Saint, didn't I?"

"Yes. I never—"

"You think I'm some kind of ogre, don't you?" Nicolo spat onto the flat of his weapon, polishing it with his sleeve. "You didn't like my gift. That's a shame—I worked so hard on it too. What can your dancer friend give you now?"

"Just let him go."

"I *loved you*." He choked, covering his mouth with his wrist. "I still do. You knew who really sliced Dad up, and I still do. But you want this skeleton, this scarecrow?"

"No."

"When you kissed him, what did he taste like? Pavement? You want me to start sleeping rough, develop a taste for Bayer?"

"Stop it!"

"You must miss him, not living at the hotel anymore. Was he easier to sleep with that way?"

"No, it's just, he was the star of the Tobacco Club, he was special, and Mr. Salvatici—"

The knife was under my nose. I fogged it as I breathed old blood and clean manure.

In and out. In and out.

"Still working for him, then." Nicolo's furious expression chilled to one of utter contempt. "Jesus. And you want to try to keep selling me the line you didn't know about my father? You're the Spider's girl to the last. Say that name again and I will slit your throat so fast you won't even know you're dead."

"Step away from her before I plugs you square in the skull, you hear?"

We turned, eyes blown wide in the dim.

Harry Chipchase advanced, a Smith & Wesson with which I was very familiar raised high. His outline was vague and his cock-eyed nose lost in shadow. But it was Harry all right, from vulgar grammar to shuffling stride.

Nicolo hissed, edging backward.

"Hey, kid, everything kosher with you?" Harry called.

"As pickles," I managed. "We were just—"

"I said to come alone, Alicia," Nicolo grated. "But you can't even do me that tiny courtesy?"

"But I didn't bring anyone. Tell him, Harry!"

"Same as you knew nothing about my father's death."

Harry was only thirty feet away by now, and drawing closer. "That's right. She didn't know nothing. Let her be. And put that toothpick of yours on the ground."

"You might've at least brought your guardian in the flesh," Nicolo observed. "Him I could have carved up with pleasure, but it's none of this fool's goddamn business."

"Alice is always my business." Harry's voice scraped, but his hand was steady. "And it ain't just on accountta I works for the same boss. Me and Alice is chums, *capisce*?"

"Yes. I remember what that was like."

"So on my way to make nice to Mr. S., I sees her running through the lobby of the Hotel Arcadia in one of her getups, and Alice never runs, so whaddya think old Harry Chipchase does? I follows her, that's what. Respectful like. Not meaning no disruption to her business, giving her privacy, but listening real careful. And I's about through with liking what I hear. No offense, Mr. Benenati, but you don't drop that shiv on the double, you's gonna make a real mess of this here floor."

Face a portrait of rage, Nicolo tossed the knife to the stones. I dove, and when the warm wood was safe in my grasp, whirled back toward the only illuminated stall. Rye was beginning to moan, and I ducked behind him, cutting loose hands with palms bruising violet from the tightness of the knots, ankles bound so cruelly they were bleeding.

"Now your lead spitter."

"You do not want to take my gun," Nicolo informed him.

Harry shot a slug into the ceiling. The horses, in a terrifying testament to what regularly went on in their living quarters, merely snuffled as splinters fell.

"You're a dead man," Nicolo stated simply as he pulled out a Colt 1903 semiautomatic .32 caliber and slid it toward the bluecoat. *"Cui scerri cerca, scerri trova."**

"Better than what Mr. Salvatici would do to me if I let Nobody get busted up."

"No, it won't be."

Crouching to sling one of Rye's arms over my shoulder, I called to Harry, "I think I can walk with him. What do we do?"

"Youse two get on the good foot, and I'll cool down Mr. Benenati here." Harry looked at me, appraising whether I could truly manage Rye. "Then we meets back—"

---

* Sicilian, "Who looks for a quarrel, finds a quarrel."

It took only that long.

Three seconds of attention on me and Nicolo had whipped out an FN Vest Pocket shooter. He didn't aim it at Harry, though. Because Nicolo, my dearest, my brightest young love, had lost his mind.

He aimed it at Rye and fired.

Rye was already half draped over me. I did move, though. Between Harry flicking his eyes to me and Nicolo pointing his backup heater at Zachariah Lane, I pushed in close, and the bullet ripped its merry way through yours very truly, who made not a sound as I fell into the hay.

That was dreadfully stupid, I thought first.

But at least now he knows, I understood as I stared up into Rye's fully awake and horrified face.

"For *him*?" I heard Nicolo screaming. "For that *pezzo di merda*?* You keep my father's murder a secret and now you make me do this to you?"

Harry, I saw through spasming eyelashes, was already taking the second gun away from my disintegrating friend. He threw it yards off into the murk of the corridor.

"Fucking shoot me," Nicolo howled. "Bastard, go on and pull the trigger!"

"Can't oblige youse, mister, the Spider hires you too much. I needs his say-so."

"If you don't bleed out from that, I will finish it," Nicolo spat at me. "Or somebody else will. I sent word to Dario. Cleto the Crow. In case the Spider was too cunning, they know, Alicia, they all know, and if anything happens to me, they will *tear you apart.*"

Gasping, battling the deluge of pain, I watched Harry shove his gun muzzle against the back of Nicolo's head. Still snarling a

---

* Piece of shit.

mixture of threats and dares to put an end to him, Nicolo had no choice but to let Harry muscle him into one of the stalls. Plenty had bars that went all the way to the ceiling, because they weren't for horses, were they, and the plank Harry slammed into place could have done awfully serviceable work locking a castle gate.

Harry's crooked face was stricken when he knelt beside me. Lifting my sweater without ceremony, he looked at the twin pocks pumping hot blood onto my trousers.

Then he twisted the sweater into a bunch, pressed down, and I shrieked so loud even the jaded horses took notice.

"Easy, kid. Settle down now."

I quieted, panting at the ceiling in disbelief over how dreadfully poorly my day had gone.

"That's right. I gots you."

He pulled me up, propelling me toward the entrance. A city block distant. A lifetime. A ruined existence, an unraveled future.

When we reached the threshold, I staggered but didn't fall, and turned to face him with my life crumbling to ashes around me.

"I's gonna miss you, kid," Harry said, planting a wet kiss on my brow. "Now, run."

"Harry—"

"Run, kid!"

"But I—"

"Damn it, Nobody, hitch a ride to the moon. You're dead to this town now, you hear?" Harry pulled a hand down his jowls. "I swear to you, I'll find a body somewheres. Trust me, kid. You died today. Now, *run*."

It was the only time during our friendship I ever knew Harry to be optimistic—running was impossible. I staggered westward, my sweater clutched against my torso. The first time I was shot, the shock of it tipped me straight into dreamland. This time, though, I couldn't be bothered to faint.

Nobody was coming to my rescue. So I walked.

I stepped through the front door of the Hotel Arcadia, and a maid screamed at the sight of me.

My vision flickered out. I blinked it back on again.

In my room, I drank three swigs of whiskey and felt ever so much better.

I cleaned myself with soap and a wet rag, and during that hygienic lark decided screaming was absolutely the done thing for metropolitan hotels, and tried it myself. Twice.

Thick bandages were located and cotton wadded and my torso wrapped like the veriest mummy.

I packed a large carpetbag and a valise with an array of clothing and arranged for a porter to drive me to Grand Central Station.

More whiskey followed.

I retrieved the fifty thousand dollars in impeccable counterfeit bills from Mr. Salvatici's safe. Being familiar with the combination, and instructed to invest the funds as I saw fit.

The porter arrived to hoist my luggage and ferry me to midtown Manhattan.

At the station, I purchased a cross-country ticket.

And then I boarded a train.

Twenty-Five

NOW

Illicit relationships between the races have not gone on without causing many a troubled conscience. Nor has a difference in color always deadened the feelings of the human heart. In spite of laws and color lines, human nature, wherever found, is profoundly alike.

—RAY STANNARD BAKER,
Following the Color Line, 1908

There are Nabiscos and Fig Newtons in Blossom's vanity, plenty of water and whiskey, and after a lightning sprint to my room for licorice and medicine, there's the makings of a nifty picnic on her coverlet.

"God, *thank* you." Blossom chases down four Bayer tablets—aspirin, not heroin—with water and a cookie.

"Best I can do until Dr. Pendleton arrives," I say ruefully. "Should I be stanching a wound, by the way?"

"It's really just a *whopping* amount of bruising." It pains her to speak, but she'd be climbing out of her own ears if she weren't. "It was the conk to the melon that had me so out of commission earlier. But there's something about opening your soul with a scalpel that does wonders for drowsiness."

"Speaking of which. What did you do before you moved to San Francisco?" I select a licorice. "You toured, I can tell that much."

"Oh, *very* good, honey," she approves. "Yes, I was with a little Negress company, singing and dancing from Des Moines to Baltimore. Theater was in the blood, you know. Mum was a costumer, did laundering and repair work for the white companies and original design for the black ones back in Chicago, everything from vaudeville to parade floats. That was Daisy Howard—dear Uncle Doddridge's half sister. Dad was a stage carpenter, Mr. Solomon Howard, and they met when he was building the set for a colored production of *La Cenerentola*."

She pauses.

"What is it?" I break into the package of Fig Newtons.

"Aren't you going to ask?"

"Ask what?"

Blossom gives me a look so withering, I turn briefly into a raisin.

"All right, fine, yes! And you were?"

"Young Mr. Henry Howard, rascal at birth."

She tips her whiskey glass at me. We clink.

"And were you always . . ."

"As you see me?" She rubs at the back of her neck. "Yes. My parents had the *sweetest* stories of me raiding my mother's costume collections—and like many artistic types, they really thought nothing of it. The shiny colorful fripperies were *there*, of course I played with them. By the time I was around ten, yes, they *vehemently* suggested that I curb the feathers. They were probably desperately worried I might end up an invert, and they'd have to have fireside chats with me about confirmed bachelorhood. Then puberty arrived and wonder of wonders! I *adored* girls. I chased them. I befriended them. I did all the usual things you're not meant to do with them. No, liking girls not the problem."

"What was the problem?"

Blossom stares into her scotch. "The problem was I *was* one. I suppose I sound rampantly insane, but the person on the other side of the looking glass wasn't *me*. It was a boy I knew named Henry. What do you see when you peacock?"

"Nobody."

"No, but really."

"Really. You've seen me as two people other than this one, I've concocted too many more to count, and I suppose this one is . . . the least effort." My chest feels heavy. "Sometimes I even dream I'm those other Nobodies. The girls who don't exist except when I'm their skin."

Blossom stares, rapt. "You are *fascinating*."

"You were saying," I retort.

"I was saying Blossom Fontaine was who I *was*, but she wasn't what I looked like. When my parents died in a motorcar accident when I was sixteen, I was so berserk with grief that I decided to get rid of myself altogether. The circumstances made it shockingly easy. I was already a performer. I'd been playing dress-up since practically birth. Everything I needed was in Mum's stock, I auditioned there in Chicago as Blossom Fontaine, and when I got a touring gig, I left. *C'est tout.* At first I was simply the shyest, *dearest* virgin in the dressing room, but after I learned taping and how to shape my pectorals from other odd individuals, that wasn't such a problem either."

"Did you ever miss yourself?"

Blossom sighs. "I never knew him very well. Do you miss Alice?"

"Sometimes," I whisper.

"You needn't, you know," she says softly. "I suspect she's sitting right here."

I swallow, picking crumbs off Blossom's bed. "You've been to Paris, you said. Was that simply everything? Divine music wafting up from the cobbles and gold-plated baguettes?"

"Ah, *oui, bien sûr.* I'd gotten as far as New York City and was performing at a simply *atrocious* nightclub, the sort where people who are decadent go when they want to pretend they're not being decadent. But the set I'd put together was entirely French, and one night a Gallic fellow came in who took an interest. No, not *that* sort of interest—he couldn't have weighted a loafer down with a lead shoehorn. But he did take me to Paris," she recollects dreamily. "I had everything there. Even the diamonds came with a side of fresh butter. It was a Cinderella romance without the sex."

"That's the awfullest fib I've ever heard!" I laugh. "Max says French women are welcoming to all sorts."

Blossom makes a gallant effort at a smirk. "Then I am *ever* so gratified to learn that Maximilian and I share our opinion of Parisian women, which is something the dear boy could never tell me himself."

Chin on hand, I question, "How many?"

"What an unthinkably invasive question, Alice James."

"How long were you there?"

"Six months."

"Three?"

"Oh, *honey*," she reproves.

Grinning, I double the figure. "Six?"

"Eleven. If you count the one I decided to bed without taking any of my kit off, just to see if I could make her happy. I made her *very* happy, Alice. Twice. Yes, I count her."

"So shall she be counted. But whyever would you leave?"

Her smile evaporates. "I did say I've had worse beatings than this one."

"You were attacked?" I exclaim.

"Three drunk *boulevardiers* wanting a taste of blood sport. This sort of thing happens in Paris too. New York. San Francisco twice, I lived there longest. And now Portland. You don't suppose creatures like me always pass unnoticed, do you? I'm *astonishingly* proficient, but. Still."

Aghast, I can only say, "You made every one of them bleed for it, though."

"Oh, not in Paris. Christ, I was a mess. After recovering enough, I decided to cut out for a place that was actually *mine*, and that meant returning to America. Must've lived in some half a dozen cities before arriving in San Francisco, and, Alice, the moment I arrived, I was *gone* on the place."

I refluff my pillow. "Candy-colored houses and salt winds and Bohemians, and you sang at the Pied Piper Bar at the Palace Hotel."

Blossom points a finger at me slyly. "You have the memory of a woman up to no good whatsoever, you know."

"I do," I admit ruefully.

"When I stepped off the train at the Third and Townsend Depot, I'd never seen anything like it. It's just a quaint Mission-style terminal, but the *people*. Mexicans touting street food, Orientals carting barrels of produce, white lunatics dragging tin cans, and everyone in the most *lawless* hodgepodge." She smiles. "Once I'd hiked from China Basin to downtown, standing in Union Square with *ridiculously* cold gusts in my face even though the sun was shining like anything, I made up my mind. It was perfect. I don't pretend it's utopia—blacks mostly work in the shipyard over at Bay View, but it was proudly, *frankly* mad. I felt ever so cozy."

"So you set up shop?"

"Yes, on Drumm Street in the thick of it all. They'd never have let me get away with that, it's as crawling with racists as any place, but they adore Europeans and I made out as if I were fresh off the boat from Paris."

"And you polished the pipes and burst into song."

"Yes, first at smaller venues, and then at the Pied Piper."

"To great acclaim, I suppose."

When she falls silent, I realize that I must look like a nitwit waiting for the moment in the film when the ethereal woman walks into the bar, a day or so before she becomes the heroine, and these are decidedly not the circumstances.

"You don't have to tell me any of this. Lord, I'm a dolt. Skip to—"

"I didn't meet Evy at the Pied Piper," she corrects me. "Evy could never have gotten *into* the Pied Piper, this was before Prohibition, mind, fresh-faced young ladies didn't do that sort of thing. I met her on the street while she was losing her hat."

"Oh?"

Blossom gathers up the ice pack. "San Francisco is nothing but hills, yes? *Mountainous* things. Anyhow, the wind whips 'round them like anything, and I was walking down one while Evy was walking up, and this small hurricane tore her hat off, and there was this *hair.*"

Since I yen to smile, I stop preventing myself.

"And as she was watching the hat fly off into oblivion, she laughed, and I don't know if you've heard her laugh, but *Jesus.*"

My smile grows.

"And I said, 'Oh, what a shame,' and she said, 'Never mind, I lost my umbrella yesterday and I think it was pining. It wouldn't do to keep them apart.'"

Pouring more whiskey seems sage. "You were taken with her."

"Alice, I was *broken,*" Blossom groans.

"After two sentences."

"Gracious no, honey, after the hat came off."

"And you knew it would only get worse."

"Which was why I *had* to pencil down where I was staying so she could write to me, and she insists that she never supposed that was madness, a black songstress foisting her address on a young white woman studying the humanities. She was at Sacred Heart Academy in Menlo Park, which is *miles* from the city, Alice—she was only on that street because she had wandered completely fearlessly away from her tour group. And I was only there because I had broken the heel on my favorite pair of boots and was coming back from the cobbler. It still frightens me how easily I might not have met her."

The grief she now suffers seems not to play into this equation. As if it hadn't occurred to her they were connected.

"So you were correspondents first?"

"We were the authors of unrepentant *reams*, honey." Blossom's lashes fall closed. "I was twenty-eight, but we may as well have been schoolgirls passing notes. A letter a day, I think, during the really ripping periods. Once I wrote her twice and forced myself to delay posting the second. She would write to me about Sacred Heart, the nuns, recipes she was tinkering with, but the *poetry*, the sheer brilliant *nonsense*. I would carry them everywhere, walking into street signs. As for me, I couldn't hear a joke or learn a ditty or think a thought without telling her about it. Then summer break came, and I was given the shock of my entire life, bar none."

"Sounds awfully promising."

"One afternoon there came a knock at my door," Blossom says with a thrill in her voice, "and who is standing there upon my opening it but my friend Evelina Starr with a suitcase?"

Evelina had, it seems, many times written of her dear new friend to her parents back in Portland. Some details were factual—that Blossom was from Chicago and a few years older and recently returned from a six-month lark in France. Other details possessed less basis in science. Blossom's name, for example, was Bernice Plank—one that Blossom claims Evy invented specifically to bedevil her—and this spinster Blossom lived with her own mother and father when she wasn't touring the Continent or praying for orphans. Evelina planned to pass the summer with the Plank family. Wouldn't that be nice?

As for the color of Bernice Plank's skin, Evelina didn't see any reason for mentioning it.

"She marched into my apartment, set her case down, and threw her arms around my neck," Blossom says with a faint smile that speaks more than any brighter expression. "I'd met her once on a public street, *once*, but we'd written so much that it was like she was mine, and I admired to know what that felt like. I didn't say no. I could have, but. I loved her."

The pair lived together for two months. Evy experienced one nervous attack, but since she had already described the condition, no one was surprised. The rest passed in a sort of frenzied tranquillity. Blossom smuggled Evelina some dozens of times into the Pied Piper disguised as a mute Englishman aesthete who wore his remarkable hair in a long queue (which in San Francisco apparently passes without comment). They could also go anywhere Blossom might be assumed to be Evy's hired companion—so they explored galleries and museums, attended female rights lectures, walked through the parks arm in arm.

They were fiercely, quietly happy. Evelina cooked elaborate suppers while Blossom strummed the guitar. When the fall term approached, however, the inevitable happened.

"We'd been drinking champagne at home, and she kissed me," Blossom says quietly. "It broke my heart. I'd thought we could last out the summer, at *least* I would have that one summer. Of course, I had to tell her. I thought just saying it would be the death of me."

"What did she answer?"

Blossom sets the ice down and regards me full in the face. "She said she already knew my late mother's shoe size, my favorite color, which operas I detest, and that taking my arm made me happier than any small gesture ought to do. She was relieved there were more things to know about me."

"I like your Evy," I manage to say after this pronouncement. "She seems to actually deserve you."

Evelina Starr never went back to college. She invented incapacitating but harmless illnesses, both her own and in the ever-widening Plank family. Her parents, who'd been mystified over this college notion in the first place, were as lax as they'd ever been. They sent her plentiful money and occasionally cured venison. Then Evy discovered that, despite all the couple's precautions, accidents could happen.

"I was out of my *mind* when she told me," Blossom groans. "Can you conceive a *less* suitable couple? But Evelina said she wanted to know whether it looked like me, and that was more important than anything."

"He does a bit, but what was confounding after I worked out who his mother was is how much he looks like *her*." When Blossom's head droops, I swiftly continue, "So you whisked Evy off to Seattle and waited for your son and heir to be born—where, exactly?"

"Well, we knew what it would look like when it arrived, didn't we, so we chose the route absolutely *every* pair fantasizes over when expecting their first child, and said she was raped."

Blossom resided in their apartment as Evelina's personal maid for most of her pregnancy. The latter was still baking cookies up till the day she packed her valise. During the final few weeks, Evy lived in a home for abused women. And when Davy arrived healthy and squirming like anything, the nuns tried to take him away.

"Evy was absolutely *brilliant*," Blossom gushes, eyes alight again. "You could have put a *live bear* between her and Davy and she still wouldn't have left that ghastly antiseptic-smelling hell without him. She staged a screaming fit, told them she had powerful parents, the entire circus. She's phenomenal."

Remembering a slight woman agreeing to walk toward a burning cross, I say, "She's top-drawer on a *very* tall bureau."

"Yes. The fact that she also happens to love me is . . . perennially astonishing. So to wrap up the saga of our exodus, we moved here within weeks of each other, as soon as Davy was old enough, and the first person Evelina looked up was Tom," Blossom concludes without a trace of spite. "That was my notion. I *needed* to know she was loved even if it wasn't by me, and he's marvelous. We do . . . respect that commitment, by the way. It was enough for me to see her so often. Write to her again. Know she was safe, and be with my son."

"And Jenny?"

"Oh, Lord. Jenny likes to kiss me when I'm drunk and try to convince me the world can be improved. She thinks I'm the *height* of the tragically unattainable. Little does she know, eh? I simply dote on the girl when she's not driving me to distraction. And that's all three acts, Alice."

"But wait," I protest. "What happened at the Elms?"

After reaching the Elms, Blossom and Davy were to run straight through the maze and thereby scare the newcomer and Miss Christina, which Davy found awfully droll. Upon emerging out the other side, Davy's mother was waiting, ready to put his hiking boots to use. Evelina walked her son across the fairgrounds, got into her car, and drove them to Max's cabin with the aid of a map drawn by Blossom. She parked on the barely cleared lumber road just as Max and I'd done, and they walked the five minutes' distance up to the house. There the two played and ate and talked, pretending to have an altogether marvelous adventure, until the gentleman arrived in the dead of night to take him to Chicago.

Then Evelina ceased to be at peace with this stratagem. Her agitation grew and her memory lessened. She was supposed to leave Blossom a simple "all went as planned" symbol hidden in the vase, because they had decided it would be wise not to see each other in person for a few weeks. But she despaired when she couldn't recall what it was meant to look like. The boarding school escort was forced to pen as cryptic a note as he could devise before he made farewells and apologies, gunned the engine, and whisked the now-bawling child off to make their train.

"Oh, I should never have put her in such a position; it was bound to light her fuse and *boom*," Blossom says with ripe disgust. "I'm Portland's prize idiot. She couldn't find her own car, wandered in the woods for hours. She could have—I can't even *think* about it without wanting to be sick."

Remembering Evelina looking like Titania had just been mugged, I sympathize.

"So Davy left, and you went on as well as you could. Then last night, Overton caught up with you. Blossom . . ." Running a hand down her arm, I hesitate. "That story you yarned me about wrestling the six-shooter away from the bad sheriff . . . he still had his gun when he ripped your dress, didn't he?"

Blossom's lip quivers. "Yes."

"Then he . . . found out, and *then* he beat you. Didn't he?"

This time, she can only nod. I brush her cheek with my lips, and she presses into me.

"You'll be better in the most lickety of splits, and back to simply raking in the ducats," I vow. "But I still think it's rotten for Dr. Pendleton to charge his own flesh and blood."

"His own flesh and blood wears dresses and lip rouge." She smooths moisture away from her lashes. "When I first turned up at his hotel like this, I think he'd have preferred a call from Kaiser Wilhelm."

"Lucky that he's able to treat you, though."

"Honey, if this is *lucky*, Christ save me from further serendipity."

I shouldn't ask. But I do.

"When you said the treatment, for your sort of cancer, was—"

"Thrillingly modern and basically torture?"

I wince for her, since she refuses to. "Sorry, I don't mean to pry. But—"

"I have prostate cancer. Simple enough, it involves appointments with my beloved uncle and a catheter full of radium."

At my expression, Blossom smiles wryly. "Fussing doesn't become you, Alice James. Anyway, I honestly think it hurts him more than it does me, which is *stupendous*. Hell, it might even work, who am I to doubt the machinations of the Almighty? Saving my life might give the old Coot a giggle."

"Here's to cosmic jokes, then."

I clear away the remains of our rudimentary feast. The sun is high, a rare crystalline yellow, and by the time I've closed the curtains and given a trilling Medea some beef jerky Blossom keeps for emergency feline sustenance, I'm numb with exhaustion. Fetching the gun, I cozy up to Blossom with her head on my shoulder.

"Get forty winks, and I'll watch the door."

"Alice, honey, you look like you built a pyramid single-handed. I recognize the danger, but must you stand guard?"

"You don't, actually." I sigh. "That's the fiddly bit."

I tell her. About flaming crosses mainly, and Tom Vaughan's decency, and that yes, Evelina may have fainted, but that it was more like a catnap. Blossom is frenzied at first. But after I revisit the flaming-cross business in vivider terms, she allows herself to be corralled on the condition that the instant Dr. Pendleton proclaims her hale, she will check in on her beloved with yours truly as escort.

Minutes later, she is sound asleep. And I left to ponder how much you would have to love someone to give them up entirely, and whether there will still be flaming crosses in the unknowable world fifteen years from now, when Davy Lee steps out to make it his own.

When I startle awake, the gun has slipped from my slack hand to the coverlet. Blossom shifted and now lies huddled in her kimono with her back to me.

The light is wrong.

I go to push the curtains open. Where before the warm wash of morning flooded the globe, now the sole remaining luster is a military navy, marching toward full darkness. No one knocked all that while.

Something is rotten, and it isn't Medea's disposition.

Turning up a lamp, I confirm that we are deep in the proverbial manure—nine twenty-five p.m. Blossom opens her eyes, both of them this time.

"Was I dreaming, or have I been pummeled *very* thoroughly?" she croaks.

"You were tenderized, yes. And it seems, I regret to report, that it is nighttime."

Blossom sits up, blinking in dismay. "No one came?"

"Not unless it was the Tooth Fairy, no. I'm going to consult with our man Rooster. You keep the gun. When I've—"

"Alice, going down there alone is a *frightful* notion."

"I don't see what other choice we—"

Rap, rap, rap.

I have the gun aimed at the door before the knock finishes, I feel that strongly on the subject.

"Who is it?" Blossom calls, sounding much stronger for the shut-eye.

"It's Mavereen."

"Oh, thank God." I set the gun on Blossom's vanity.

The door swings open and Mrs. Mavereen Meader enters.

She holds herself stiffly, easy dignity replaced with girders and plaster. And though she doesn't look different, she *feels* years older. Her ornate beehive hair is perfectly set, hands folded, and she is giving me positively terminal fidgets.

"Why, Mav, whatever's the matter?" Blossom exclaims.

"They done arrested Officer Overton," she announces in a dead tone.

Blossom barks a disbelieving laugh. "*Arrested* him? Who did the arresting who wasn't scared shitless he'd get them back—the canine trackers? Please. Even dogs have more sense."

"Rooster done told Max what happened to you, and Max headed straight to the Vaughan residence," she continues. "Gave Tom Vaughan an earful, did our Maximilian. He said as Overton been worrying us something fearsome, and that pestering you was the last straw, and we wouldn't stand for no more. The chief listened, and he listened good. Seems there was a nurse with Mrs. Vaughan by then, so he went with Max to scare up his star thug."

"I don't know that I'd call Overton a thug—it's insulting to thugs across the continental United States." Blossom studies her hands. "Is, is Evelina . . . Alice says she fainted. Is she all right?"

"She ain't fixing to climb any mountains, but Mrs. Vaughan'll keep."

"Good." Pure joy floods Blossom's face, only to be ruthlessly tamped down. "You said that Overton is actually *detained behind bars*?"

"Max and the chief went out hunting." Mavereen stares at a spot on the wall, and I don't like that, not a particle. "Officer Taffy pointed them in the right direction. They done found Overton nursing rotgut at a speakeasy, busted up like he'd been in a fight. When they searched him, they scared up two guns—his, and that toy shooter you like so well. Max swore a blue streak that firearm was stolen when Overton attacked you. The chief believed him. He stuck Overton in the lockup till he gets the whole sorry mess figured."

"You look less than thrilled," I observe.

"Of *course* she does!" Blossom scoffs. "Even supposing they proved Overton roughed me up and swiped my gun, a court of law would never *convict* him. The second his shoes strike free soil, he'll be back to plaguing us. I'm so sorry, Mavereen."

"That's as may be. But Officer Overton came up with a real interesting reason why he took your revolver." Mavereen's eyes are as warm as granite. "Says you attacked him first and he fought you off—and that we'd all best take care around you."

"Whatever for?" Blossom whispers.

"On account of you being an abomination."

The very walls around us breathe secrets and dread. Mavereen's tone hasn't shifted, remains both lilting and about as inarguable as tides.

By some miracle, Blossom conjures up a laugh. "Well, I do on occasion put syrup on my bacon, and once in nineteen seventeen I wore chartreuse, but surely *abomination* goes too far?"

"What on earth does that even mean?" I add. "Pathetic attempt to deflect attention, if you ask me."

"Glad you bring it up, because I ain't nohow asking you, Miss James," Mavereen states. "Matter of fact, you been nothing but a thorn in my side, and I'll thank you to hush now. I'm addressing the person in that bed, in my hotel, who been going by the name of Blossom Fontaine. Because Officer Overton claims that person's a man, a man what assaulted him in a drunken state of undress. *Ask,* he said. *Check,* he said. He said he took your gun because you're a mighty queer character, and we house good Christian souls here—men, women, and children, and I ain't fixing to add no other sort apart from them three. So I'm asking. And if I don't get me a straight answer, you better believe either I check or you walk straight on out of here. Are you a woman born?"

Once in Harlem, I found a baby bird on the pavement that had fallen from its nest but tragically survived the landing, blinking up at the blue sky with wondering, wounded eyes. Blossom looks similar.

At length, she shrugs, because that is what people like Blossom do when the walls are blazing.

"It took me some practice, I'll admit," she purrs. "But now I've got the knack, I'm *ever* so much better at it than most of you, don't you agree?"

Mavereen's nostrils flare. "You'll pack your things, and you'll be out by morning."

"Mrs. Meader!" I cry. "She's injured, she's sick, you can't possibly—she's your friend!"

"Yes, whatever happened to 'your Mavereen,' not to mention the word *family*?" Blossom stands with an effort.

"You done lied to us," the matriarch announces, and it would be like hearing Moses give one of the more rousing numbers except for the pain. "Every day. To our faces, behind our backs, laughing while we held you in our hearts and called you our own. You lied to *children*. Davy—"

"Leave Davy Lee out of this, or I'll make you sorrier than you have ever been in your *life*," Blossom snarls.

"That suits me just fine. I'll not argue over that precious child of God with the likes of you. What's your real name, anyhow?" Mavereen wants to know.

"Blossom Fontaine."

"You know right well what I mean—the name your sainted mother gave you afore you made it no better than mud."

"Blossom Fontaine."

"I ain't asking again."

"*Outstanding.* I would prefer to take up residence in Officer Overton's cell than to *ever* tell you the name on my birth certificate." Blossom's hands form skeletal weapons.

"Bless your heart. I don't suppose we'll be acquainted long enough for it to matter much, after all. Miss James, I figure it's time you were on your way too. I know I can't force a white woman to do nothing. But I can sure make you hanker after a change of address."

"Gladly," I cry, "if you're the sort of household to learn something private from an utter bastard and then—"

"Save your breath, Alice," Blossom dismisses. "I'm nothing but a freak to her now."

"I won't tolerate your perversion breeding iniquity under this roof!" Mavereen's voice cracks, and *there*, there's the loss of her friend, despite her fury. "You ain't a freak—God loves the afflicted and the downtrodden. Freaks got no choice save to be what they are. You're something considerable worse—you're a deliberate, calculated sinner."

She turns to go.

"And to me, you're still just a nigger," Blossom spits cordially at her back. "So we're even."

Mavereen pivots, teeth bared.

"Oh, I don't want to argue anymore, honey, I'm simply *expiring* with fatigue. Would you tell my darling uncle I need to see him *now*, supposing he's not already so lit he's sleeping in his bathtub?"

"You can't see Dr. Pendleton," Mavereen reports, eyes misting glassy and blank.

"The fuck I can't. I might be your tenant, but he's *my* uncle, not to mention the owner of the Paragon, and he took a *sacred oath*, I'm not aware if he's mentioned that to you, send him up before I rip your goddamn head off."

"You ain't never going to see him again."

"You can't exile me from my own uncle, you delusional *tyrant*!" Blossom cries. "Hand him over or—"

"The KKK done hanged him."

Blossom descends straight to the edge of her bed, legs giving way. There's a buzzing like a thousand hornets in my ears.

"Dr. Pendleton touched Mrs. Vaughan last night when she fell. Well, folks who burn crosses don't care for that sort of mixing." Mavereen's delivery is hollow but matter-of-fact, and even as I watch the white sparks of fury dance in her eyes, I recognize a voice that knows the inevitability of atrocity. "Somebody done wrote a false note calling for help from a colored doctor—he went, and the neighbors told us three masked men packed him into a car. Nobody knows who. Ain't nobody going to find out neither. Just hush it, and hush it, and bury it deep. They stripped him bare, and cut off his balls, and they hanged him from a tree by the river. And nobody is going to pay for it but us. 'Keep me, O Lord, from the hands of the wicked; preserve me from the violent man; who has purposed to overthrow my goings.'"

Mavereen resumes her path toward the door. When she reaches it, she turns back to say brokenly, "Don't think I won't miss my friend Blossom. I'll always recollect her fondly, for all she weren't never real. I got sad work to be about, Miss James. Mister."

We sit there, motionless. Her footfalls fade away. Then Blossom snatches up the empty ice bucket just in time to be sick in it. I rush to her side.

"Are you all right? Here, let me—"

"Waste of time." Blossom's skin glows slick. "You're nursing a dead woman. Man. It doesn't matter any longer."

"Of course it does, and you're nothing of the kind. What—"

"The Klan just managed to kill two niggers with one stone. How wonderfully efficient of them. Oh, *poor* Doddridge, I can't bear to think on it, but though I'll go slower, they've ended me just the same."

"What in the name of—"

"We weren't nearly finished with the treatments." Delicately, she sets the bucket on the floor. "Now we never will be. You had better go, honey."

"I won't leave you like this!"

"We both need to pack."

"But—"

"Please leave, Alice." She hugs herself in a familiar gesture, turns to the window. "If Officer Overton was shouting that bit of gossip through a megaphone, and Mavereen warns the rest like I suppose she intends, then it's really just as well."

"What is?"

"That I'll be dead soon enough," she answers, "and won't have to pretend to be Henry for very long."

Twenty-Six

A moratorium on race prejudice would mean that 13 millions of colored people in America would become politically free from disenfranchisement; physically free from lynching; mentally free from ignorance and socially free from assault.

—BEATRICE MORROW CANNADY, *The Advocate*, Portland, Oregon, October 3, 1931

The Paragon Hotel on the morning I leave it feels like a living creature. The dear old kid hums with awakening guests stretching their arms and smacking their lips in anticipation of coffee. An awfully lucky few will know nothing; most will wonder as they yawn why they feel heavier inside. And a few will recall instantly that a colored war veteran was mutilated and hanged, and will blink for long seconds at the ceiling before rising. Wondering when their own time comes, whether they'll drift up to heaven from their warm beds or from the cool rustling of strange tree branches.

Rap, rap, rap.

"Come in," I hear, and I turn the knob.

Entering, I survey Jenny Kiona's room. My bags are packed, but

I've business to settle first, on several fronts. The chamber is girlish and dreadfully brainy at the same time. A pink throw lazes at the end of the bed, a row of simply darling miniature porcelain animals from a Chinese apothecary shop grace her mantel, and a bunch of wild daisies beam at me from a cheap vase. But there are also shelves aplenty here, and the amount of books wedged into them would knock a librarian for a loop. I remember her brother telling me that Jenny started life as one of Mavereen's silent, stalking maids and hand it to the girl with due gusto: Wednesday Joe might be the sort to avoid walking under ladders, but Jenny is the type to climb them.

"What are you doing here?" she rasps.

"I'm sorry. You must feel awfully unwell, everyone does, but I need to speak with you before I hoist skirts and vamoose."

Jenny sits at a secondhand desk that's wide enough for a Wall Street tycoon and scratched enough it could have gone ten rounds with Medea. Papers are strewn over it in a way that's incomprehensible yet apparently organized, because she's shuffling rapidly through them with crimson eyes, her plump lips locked like a bank vault. Her sable hair hasn't been brushed, just wound into a roll with a pencil speared through it.

"You look different," she comments. "Is this who you actually are?"

Intriguing query. Sometime around six in the morning, I changed into a loose peach crepe blouse with powder-blue scrollwork stitching and a belted waist, and a kicky blue skirt, and I brushed my hair and added a few fat curls around the face, and rouged my cheeks and lips but left my eyes alone.

You put all this on because it suits you. It may even be what you look like.

Who can say?

"I don't know. I admire to do some research on the subject. Any tips?"

"You aren't the faintest bit interested in research or journalism." Jenny blows her nose and then applies the kerchief to the wet pools she's trying to see out of. "The whole thing was a horrible joke."

"Jokes can sometimes serve a purpose. What are you working on so early?"

"Dr. Doddridge Pendleton's obituary for *The Advocate*, with an accompanying piece about lynching." Her chin juts, daring me to mock her. "Go on—tell me it's useless, tell me it's childish to even try to make people aware. Say it."

"The way Blossom would have done? I wish I could make a dandier advocate in her absence, but the truth is, I think you're a jolly good scout. As to whether one article and one obituary will make any difference, I'll right merrily admit that I don't know. One might not help, but twenty might. Two hundred. And you've got an awful lot of words left up your arm."

Jenny regards me afresh. "You're—you just called her, I mean, you said *her*," she stammers miserably.

I twitch my shoulder. "I'm a terribly old dog. New tricks are as algebra to the poodle."

"Mavereen says she lied to us all. And we were close, we were . . . we were very good friends, and I feel such a fool," she whispers.

Blossom, of course, was right: Mavereen lost no time in baring all to the inner sanctum. I heard this from Miss Christina, who came to my door with a haggard face after dinner service, wondering what if anything this shocking news could have to do with Davy Lee.

I told her I didn't know. We may never know: Blossom was about as forthcoming as a spare tire. Miss Christina left with her face in the apron she still wore, mourning the little boy she was beginning to suspect was lost to her forever.

"You're not exactly expiring to hear what I think, but here it is anyhow," I say with care. "Blossom isn't your usual breed of *Homo sapiens*. She doesn't pierce any mustard with Mavereen, she does with me, and wherever you land on the question is your own affair. But I think you just preached gospel—you were very good friends, and if Blossom had first shaken your hand in a three-piece getup and a bowler, why, I don't know but whether that might not have been a bigger whopper than this one."

"Maybe. It's all so tangled. But I hated to see what—how she looked when she left." Jenny's sweet mouth wobbles. "It was horrid."

Blossom departed about an hour ago. Dressed in a quiet grey suit with a button-up, a striped tie, and a hat pulled low over her bloodied, unadorned face. Because she is an awfully recognizable personage hereabouts, and now the news is spreading like wildfire, and Henry might not be noticed at all. Jenny stood with tears running down her cheeks, unable to move. Wednesday Joe hugged the singer tight, confused but uncaring. Rooster nodded soberly. Miss Christina shook her hand, very hard. Max, carrying both a hatbox containing Medea and a trunk full of necessaries, played George for her with his head high.

I watched all this from where we parted ways outside the elevator.

Mavereen was nowhere to be seen.

Jenny scratches heartbroken circles on her notepaper. Since there's nothing I can do for her save what I came to accomplish, I approach the desk.

"Here." I drop my scratch pad before her, all my very real observations, though minus any hint of scandal. "You're right: journalism isn't my strong suit. How awfully fortuitous it happens to be yours. I hope you can read shorthand."

Jenny looks up incredulously. "Of course I can. But . . . you're abandoning your notes about the Paragon? Like your time here meant nothing?"

"Actually, I'm abandoning it like it meant a terribly important something, deserving of a professional eye. Go on and look, they're real details. In case Overton ever checked them. An article about the importance of the Paragon Hotel is a swell notion, says yours truly. Finish Dr. Pendleton's obituary and then introduce your nose to a new grindstone."

"Wait!" she calls after me, standing. "I don't argue that this whole business of the Klan and the Paragon needs telling, but there's no finishing it. Overton could walk at any moment, there isn't a single lead regarding the lynching, and we still haven't found Davy Lee."

"Maybe that's the story," I posit. "That we need to do better at solving things."

"I . . . yes, I suppose that could be. Miss James—"

"Alice."

"Where will you go now you're leaving the Paragon?"

"Oh, don't think me secretive, but I haven't decided yet." Tapping my cranium, I smile. "I'm looking for someplace specific for a change. None of this flinging myself at burgs willy-nilly like a bird crashing into a windowpane."

"When you find the place . . . will you send me your address so I can show you the article?" she inquires, chilly but sincere.

"That would tickle me entirely senseless."

"All right, then." She seats herself, flips through a few pages of my notebook. "Thank you. Goodbye, Miss James, and good luck."

I leave her scribbling. Blossom is probably correct—Jenny can't change the world. But I wonder what a thousand Jennies, sitting at a thousand typewriters and punching millions upon millions of letters into straight columns, all those separate words in newspapers across the nation marching as one great force, might accomplish if given the means and the time.

After fetching my coat and bags, it's with a profound sense of loss that I lock the door of my room. I don't want anyone else to live there. I know all has been warped past straightening, but I still feel ever so sore picturing a spotty young secretary or a bull-shouldered ironsmith asleep in what I came to consider my bed.

When the elevator door rattles open, Wednesday Joe regards me with haunted eyes. Stepping in as he busies himself, I say gently, "I'm awfully sorry it came to this, old pal."

He stops manipulating levers. Slumps into the corner with an unsteady chin, tugging at his uniform collar.

"First Davy, then Dr. Pendleton and Blossom. It's not fair, Your Majesty."

"Not by any standard, no."

"What's going to happen to my sister?" he forces out.

This sends us off the proverbial rails. "Beg pardon?"

"The luck." The sweet laddie's shoulders shake. "It's a mean streak, a real bad one, and what if Jenny's next? Ma died having me, from Sunday luck. I couldn't protect Dad no matter what charms I left in his pockets every night. And now we're in the middle of a hex, and what if it takes my sister? I'll be alone."

Wrapping myself around the youth, I thank my stars I already anticipated what he'd consider a nifty parting gift. Fishing in my skirt pocket with my other arm still tight around his shoulders, I thrust a snub of lead under his nose.

"Make your sister carry this around. Unless you're heading into a sticky situation, in which case you can borrow it. Remember me when you use this, please, for I seem to have grown ever so fond of you."

Wednesday Joe steps back. He holds a flattened bullet, edges irregular and metal gleaming, and his eyes seem to reach for it.

"Don't tell me this bullet has hit somebody," he says reverently.

"Joe 'the Coffin Maker' Castano. The bullet struck the wall of the cellar where he was ambushed. I picked it up and cleaned it, of course. I'm no rube."

"But anybody who carries it can't die a sudden death!" he

exclaims. "I dunno if I can keep this, Miss James. I'm grateful, but what'll protect you?"

"I've got plenty of other talismans. Use it in good health."

Wednesday Joe squeezes me tight before firing up the elevator and slipping the bullet in his pocket. "I'll never forget this, Miss James."

"Neither will I, Joe." I watch as the floors whir past, gravity taking me ever closer to the ground, and thence to the street, and after that the wide, uncharted world. "Neither will I."

Bags in hand, I enter the lobby. The usual morning crowd bustles about, but the poisonous news has sickened their smiles and leached the color from their smart metropolitan clothes. Miss Christina is sharing a quiet word with Rooster behind the counter, both looking as if they were shouldering all of Portland's mountains.

Mavereen remains hidden. Picturing her in what is doubtless an avalanche of mourning, I calculate just how much her world has shrunk in the past week, and forgive her for that. I don't plan on forgiving her for what she did to Blossom. But as for not slicing my farewell cake, she's well and truly acquitted.

"I'm off," I say from my usual cover by the ficus tree. "Thank you for . . . thank you. Please know that I'm forever sorry I couldn't accomplish more."

"Was never your business to set right, Miss James," Rooster answers, not unkindly. He engulfs my hand, shaking it. "Safe travels."

Miss Christina, who wears black under her apron now, presses me furtively and releases me. "It's too much for a body to bear, crashing from one grief straight through to another like this. You were a nuisance, Miss James, but you were a comfort too, and you ought to know it. Please take care." She pauses, chin quivering. "If you ever find out any more about . . ."

"You would be my first confidant," I assure her. "Trust in it. But

I do believe, Miss Christina, that some of your other trials are destined to end sooner rather than later. There's been enough suffering. The tide has to turn."

She shakes her head. "I can't see my way past violence and misery just now, Miss James. But I'm sure enough gonna try."

As I turn away, I wonder whether the five thousand dollars in untraceable counterfeit cash I slid in an envelope under her bedroom door will lift her spirits. The information she imparted to me was as manna to the Israelites, and lo, did I in turn shower her with greenbacks. Well—paper indistinguishable from greenbacks.

Anyway, it's better than a kick in the pants.

When I've pushed the spinning glass round and the Paragon Hotel spits me out, I turn to look back at it. Its dozens of windows with its hundreds of guests, all of them hiding something. All of them fighting for something. All of them frightened of something. That's the kicker about hotels—they aren't homes, they're more like the paragon of waiting rooms. Unless you're part of the inner circle of this one, and you burrow underneath one another's surfaces, air the cupboards, lift the drapes, and everyone is unhappy, and everyone is searching, and everyone is both cruel and kind.

The bedroom that April the nervous housemaid shows me into is just about the charmingest I've ever seen. Wide windows, lace-edged curtains, the walls papered in lilac sprays. There's a table with a pair of overstuffed armchairs flanking it, and a writing desk with sparrow-claw feet. Like the rest of the house, the outdoor vista is blocked by nature, but here the dripping trees seem like friendly sentinels, and a dainty chandelier sends crystal shards of light scattering in all directions.

"She's not to be excited, Mr. Vaughan says, and so does the doctor," April frets.

"I won't excite her," I vow. "I'll calm her like anything. Please leave us, and thank you for allowing me to see her."

Evelina Vaughan is nestled in a bed all done up in white and lavender, which matches both her complexion and the circles under her eyes. Her hair is down, and *gosh* and *golly* don't cover it. I'd paint her if I had any brushes or talent.

She cranes to see me. "Is that you, Alice?"

"None other." Sitting at the edge of the bed, I take her hand.

"Tom told me," she says quietly. Her eyelids are edged azalea pink. "What Overton . . . what he did to Blossom, and why he said he did it, and. I don't know where to start, Alice."

"You needn't start anywhere, actually. It was such an awfully unmitigated disaster, Blossom spilled all. So you just rest your head."

It's not a lie, but it omits key aspects of the chronology. I imagine Evelina would prefer to think that Blossom unburdened her bosom to me after the cat had already checked out of the bag, so I let her.

"Oh, Alice," she laments. "And to think I wasn't there. I said I always would be, whenever she needed me, and I wasn't, and—"

"Believe it or not, so did I, which means I know this sort of rumination isn't going to help." I lightly clap her hand, encouraging. "You would've if you could've, but you couldn't so you didn't."

"Is she all right? Please say that she'll be all right."

"She's just scratched and scraped, more worried about your adventures than hers. You were awfully busy staring down the KKK, and a girl can't be everyplace at once. Blossom wouldn't want you to make yourself sick over it and neither would Tom."

"Tom!" she exclaims with a strained laugh. "Tom, sweet Tom, dear Tom. And Blossom, fighting off Overton all by her lonesome. And poor Dr. Pendleton. It's my fault, you know. Fainting of all things under those circumstances, God. It isn't as if I meant to, but

I'm a horrid little idiot, and now Dr. Pendleton is dead, and Blossom . . ."

I'm getting to be expert at the crying-lady wrangling by this point. But that doesn't mean it hurts any less. I stroke her hair off her brow until the weeping thins out.

"Blossom admired to be here more than anything to see that you were all right, actually, but she didn't want to run afoul of Tom. He's at the station house?"

"Yes," Evy whispers in an odd tone. "At the station house."

My bag rests at my feet, and I pull a sheaf of papers from it. "That's just as well. I know there likely isn't a good place to hide these, but you're going to need to ferret one out. Blossom's tasked me with giving you all of Davy's boarding school paperwork. Obviously it's more of a hat trick for you to correspond with the faculty, but she has duplicates and will keep helping."

"For as long as she can." Evy's grey eyes melt into mercury. "It's admittedly . . . off the topic of your visit, but. I don't know how anyone can be expected to stand this, Alice."

"Neither do I." I set the papers on her nightstand. "One foot in front of the other, I suppose. At least, I haven't any other brilliant ideas."

"No. No, I don't expect you to."

"Blossom also wants you to know that she'll write the instant she gets to wherever she's going."

"That's how we started, you know." Evy's memory reads love letters that I can't see. "Clever as she is in person, have you any idea how clever she is in writing? It's. She's uncanny. She knew just how to make me laugh, simply by putting the alphabet in the right order."

"She said much the same of you. And if Tom objects to her corresponding, she can address them under a false name to Wednesday Joe and he says he'll deliver them during Weekly Betterment."

"Oh. I hadn't thought of Weekly Betterment, but I don't

suppose I can quit, can I?" she muses exhaustedly. "Please don't think me a hateful hypocrite, Alice, but as much joy as I got out of the cause itself, it paled in comparison to holding Davy, watching how his tiny hands grew, putting my nose in his hair."

"That's the least hypocritical thing I've ever heard. You're trying to do what's best for him, and in my opinion it's goddamn heroic. Evelina, please don't answer this if you don't like to, but do you . . . as Mrs. Vaughan . . ."

"Do I mean to have children with my husband?" She worries at the edge of the coverlet with listless fingers. "Davy took up so much of my mind before, I took precautions. Now? I rather like the idea, but I don't know how useful a mother I'll be in five years. Ten. It would be wonderful to have more children. Tom would be so happy. But right now I only want to see Blossom and Davy again, and—" Evelina thumps her fist against her breastbone. "It's like a hole. It'll always be there, yawning open."

"Unfortunately, I know the feeling. But just think of students like Jenny Kiona—ones who have something to show for it."

"Yes," she sighs. "I wonder if Tom will object to my going to the Paragon after all that's happened. He supposes I never knew about Blossom's true nature, that was easy enough to pretend, I was so genuinely horrified. I did the same the morning Davy went missing—the feelings were real, I just. Pretended they were for another reason. And he was far from hateful over Blossom. He only thought it strange, and sad, and wondered if there might be treatment for her. Oh! She must be headed somewhere she can continue the radium cure. Yes, of course. She'll write me soon, I know she will, and if Tom objects, well, I'll just talk him 'round, won't I, I can't be expected to hear from her once a *week*."

Blossom figures finding a new doctor is about as likely as electing a black Portland mayor. But I see no reason to upset Evelina further.

"In light of how topsy-turvy everything is, once a week would be grossly inadequate." Rising, I bend to kiss her cheek. "Mavereen says no one will ever be charged with Dr. Pendleton's death, and maddening as it is, I can hardly disagree with her. And what with Blossom displaced, and Overton bound to be set free any second—I had a tasseled dress once with fewer loose ends."

Evelina regards me with a quicksilver light in her eyes. It startles me. I'd nearly forgot she's a wood nymph, with a host of spirits and spells at her disposal.

"Officer Overton won't be set free, Alice."

I set a blank envelope on the nightstand, another parting gesture. "But Blossom said a policeman being arrested for assaulting a black woman—well, man in this case, which makes it worse—would never lead to a conviction."

"Oh, well. She's right. It wouldn't. He'll rot in jail all the same."

"How?"

Evelina snugs closer into her pillow, a fire-haired witch with vengeance on her mind. "I mentioned before that Tom's at the station house. When he told me what happened, I was—well, you can probably guess I was so hot I could hardly breathe, and I thought the same thing, that nothing would come of it, so I told Tom that Officer Overton attacked me too."

"He—you *what*?" I stammer.

"Oh, I'm fine, Alice, he'd never do anything so stupid, but Tom doesn't know that." Evelina smiles, and I think she could give Cleopatra tips. "I was already crying over Blossom being hurt, so I just kept right on crying and I said I went to find Tom at headquarters once, during one of my spells, and that Overton took advantage of my confusion. Touched my breasts, kissed me. I said I'd been too ashamed to tell him before, since I'm meant to be ever so careful when I feel a rush of nerves coming on, but that I'd got it into my head I needed him right that instant, and afterward thought he'd be furious. Dear Tom. He fixed me a drink, and stroked my hair. He says that Overton will be locked away for ever so long, and he'll speak with the judge personally. He's filling out the police report now. Sweet, loyal Tom."

I laugh harder than I've laughed at anything since I arrived in this wonderful, terrible town of roses and rainfall. Then Evelina grins at me, the Cheshire smirk of a woman who took about six seconds figuring out how to destroy the man who assaulted her lover, and I laugh even harder. Only yesterday, I reached the conclusion that Miss Christina could never hurt me, but that Blossom would readily snap a neck in a good cause.

Evelina would too, I discover. Jail will be a lucky break for Officer Overton. She wouldn't blink over crushing his windpipe with her bare hands.

"It must sound ever so odd coming from a near stranger, but I'll miss you," I tell her.

"Oh, not odd at all, you're lovely, but surely I'll see you soon?"

"Mrs. Meader set me adrift along with your beloved. I'm for the Israelites-in-the-desert routine."

"Alice!" she exclaims in dismay. "And here I never even thought to ask whether you were harmed in all this wretched business. Forgive me. Where can I visit you, then?"

"I'm leaving Portland, actually."

She sits up fully, hair cascading around her shoulders. "No. Oh, I wish you weren't! Please write, you must promise that you will. Where are you going? And why?"

"There's important business I have to settle. And of course I'll write—I'm sure my prose isn't much doing compared to Blossom's, but I'll write all the same."

Now Evy understands this is to be a more permanent goodbye than she'd imagined, she insists on embracing me in a warm cloud of moonlight and moss. It lingers on my blouse as I depart. I wonder what her reaction will be to the ten thousand bogus dollars I left her, with instructions that it should go to Davy's schooling. Around thirty-five thousand still resides in my bag, minus expenses, which is simply staggeringly important, because I know precisely—God willing and the Creek don't rise—what I'm going to do with it.

It will be, supposing I pull it off, exquisite. The jazziest expenditure in the history of ill-gotten gains.

The platform at Union Station is alive with the bustling crush of busy train departures, farewells and admonitions and rustling newspapers humming in my ears. A little towheaded chappie in a sailor suit wants to know whether there will be ice cream on the journey. His mother shushes him, which is unfortunate, because I admired to know her answer.

Any second now, Nobody, and do try not to make a profounder idiot of yourself than you already have.

"Hey there, Miss James. Ain't this a swell surprise."

A smile lights my face as I pivot. I amend the Cinderella-at-the ball routine for a calmer expression. But sweet berobed Jesus, does Maximilian look fine. Wearied in body and soul, yes. Awfully plentiful lines etched around his honey-colored eyes, his Pullman uniform pressed in haste. Still.

I could, as Blossom puts it, eat him with a spoon.

"Five more minutes and the southbound express oughta pull in. Carry your bag for you?"

"That would be just fine, George."

"Watch yourself there, miss." His hand lingers scandalously long over mine as he grips the handle of my valise. "They're still sore at me about the last few days. I had to pull in some favors so's I could work this here train, and I ain't gunning to get kicked off it 'cause I had words with a passenger."

"Blossom seemed to think you'd be drummed straight out of the Pullman racket."

"Nah, they love me. On accountta my looks, I figure."

"Surely not."

"Aw, nuts. My charm?"

"Doubtful."

"'Cause I bathe regular?"

"Now you're on the trolley." Under my breath, I add, "By the way, I'm ever so glad Blossom told you. Secrets are a particular area of specialty, but this one—I don't know if I could've kept it buttoned that Davy was safe, not where you're concerned."

Max grimaces, but there's no anger in it, only sorrow. "Us two had a real long chat last night while he was packing. I ain't gonna pretend to understand it. But if there's one thing I knows for certain, he loves that kid. And Mavereen did what she figured she had to, but . . . I don't gotta like losing friends that way."

A whistle sounds in the distance, and the crowd shuffles its feet. "Where did you take her?"

"Boarding house not too far from the docks I knows from before I found the Paragon. Pretty clean, mostly day laborers. Communal bachelor dining hall, cheap grub, but plenty of it—stew and taters and biscuits. Medea should take care of the mouse situation."

"Blossom will detest it," I say with quiet certainty.

"Yeah. But it ain't like he'll be there for long."

She won't be. But it hurts all the same, the way sometimes large griefs engulf, send you blessedly reeling, while smaller ones rankle maddeningly. I've been shot twice, and that was unpleasant—but I've also had the chicken pox, and was just about ready to walk into traffic over it.

I glance back at the station I first met when I was dying. Not expecting to see it again for quite some time, if ever, I breathe in tall trees and pure skies. A family of six pack themselves onto the southbound express, squalling and hushing, before Max and I hoist anchor and head for the same entrance. A smartly coiffed young gal and her porter. Two people whose worlds are only meant to intersect in moments like these ones. Trying not to look as if anything electric is passing between us, sparks as real and as glittering in our heads as the fire soon to be thrown from the great iron wheels of our locomotive.

Later, in the deepest dark, after he's seen to all his duties and then some, Max skips out on shut-eye and pays a visit to the single-person first-class compartment I've booked. It's an indulgence. And a gamble. He sells me a few more jazz records, at a steep discount, bartered for my door being locked and his tongue on my hip and my laugh quiet in his ear as he times his movements to the clatter and roar of the train.

Afterward, Max captures what remains of the curls framing my face in loose fingers. "You still ain't answered one thing, and I gotta admit to curiosity."

I push my hand up his shoulder, admiring. "Well, go on and interrogate a girl. It isn't as if I can escape you."

He shakes his head, pretending not to be amused. "You reminds me of me. And Blossom reminds you of your friend what liked the poppy juice. And I reminds you of somebody else. So who?"

We can't risk a light, so I pull the curtain aside to see him better. It seems decadent, only a glass pane between our naked selves and the headlong rush of countryside, and even though I don't suppose evergreens fret much over human relations, I feel exposed.

I *want* to feel exposed.

"You remind me of my friend Nicolo, the way he was when we were kids," I tell Max as he studies what Alice James looks like lit all in silver. "Life was hard, but he didn't hate anyone else for it. He was strong and good. It was awfully hard to be good in Harlem. And he loved me. I wasn't ready for that—I was too young. Then the wrong people died, and parts of Nicolo died with them. So. I missed him, you see, I missed the Nicolo I did love back, the one before he changed, and you—you went to war, and you still manage to be strong and good, and I don't know how anybody admires to do that. But you remind me of him, before. And I think it's ever so miraculous, you know, that you've seen the wrong people die too, and it didn't change you."

"I ain't as special as all that, Alice." Max's face darkens, and he shifts his weight to the side. "You gotta understand. . . . Last night, after we found out Dr. Pendleton done got strung up, I was crazy. Wanted to wreck that whole city, set it on fire. I went down to take care of his body myself, but they already cut it down, them coloreds as got there first, and took him to the station house. There I was—empty hands, aching to use 'em." His lips tighten grimly. "If it hadn't been for Blossom's situation, and me needing to have words over it, ain't no telling what I mighta done."

"You'll miss his funeral, escorting me like this," I realize with a pang.

"I don't want no part of that sham funeral," Max growls. "Doc was a soldier, and you think they'll bury him like a hero? I'd carry him to Paris if I could, throw my own goddamn parade. There's times I wish I'd never left. At least in France it was clear what sorta man you were—the kind what kept marching, or the kind what fell, and you was all on one side and at least could figure out who was gonna shoot at you. Christ. See? That there's crazy talk, Alice. Ain't the notion of a sane fellow to want to be back at the front."

"Actually, I think it's eminently sensible." I fall away from him, study as the line of cars curves around a bend, watching a great steam snake ferrying me to another unfamiliar new home. "It taught you precisely who you are. Who doesn't admire to know that?"

The moon has risen, slender and delicate. Seeming awfully small. But that's the trick about the moon. You might only be able to lamp a bit of it, like I do then. But that doesn't mean the rest of the moon isn't there. Only that it's waiting for the right time to be visible. Showing sharp white sickles of itself until suddenly it's flooding wheat fields and coastlines, shocking everyone over how much was hidden all that while.

EPILOGUE

It is breaking down the color line. It is destroying the psychology of caste. It is disseminating joy to the most humble and the most high. It is the dynamic agent of social equality.

—CHANDLER OWEN, "The Black and Tan Cabaret—America's Most Democratic Institution," *The Messenger*, August 1922

Stretching, I shuffle back through the pages I've written over these last months. You've asked me any number of times what I'm working on and whether it has to be so secretive, and I laugh, and ask who's the shameless busybody now. But the truth is that I don't think I could have shown it to you in what you call puzzle pieces. I wanted the entire portrait of how it happened. The unbutchered cow. The whole shebang.

Fond as I am of the current vernacular, I need to say plainly: I don't like everything I've written here. But it's as close as I can come to the truth.

Now, I'm awfully anxious you're going to find this gift silly. But you aren't feeling very well, and when you aren't feeling very well, you like being told stories. So did I, when a mere stripling. Most of us, misfits and fits alike, hanker after a yarn when the chicken soup isn't quite up to snuff. And ever since we turned roomies, it's essential to keep you in the goodest possible cheer. When you're sulking, you hog the whiskey and depress the cat. Don't try to deny it.

Considering the stakes involved, I'm awfully glad you like it here. San José is prosperous but quaint. Gun ready but peaceable. Not shy on sunshine, not strong for overcoats. I can't wait to pal around with you here—if they dole out more of these blue skies, we'll be spoiled for anyplace else. But in the meanwhile, we do more of the staying put than the gadding about, and supposing I'm not careful, I'll trip and fall in love with our cozy little rented corner of the world. I like our palm tree. I admire our gravel drive. I adore our bungalow, even though it's withering around its edges. I love that they let us abide here together because I'm budgeting, ostensibly, and you're my devoted but ailing maid, theoretically.

Best of all, I like Dr. Ishimaru. Leaving you in Portland while I went off in search of good weather and a better physician was a dreadful wrench. But he makes up for it, what with the way his nose crinkles, and his marvelous facility with radium, and the way he nods to himself as if doing sums in his head.

But we have copious moola left over for jazzier prospects. I've half a mind to buy this place. I've half a mind to take us to Paris instead. I've never heard rust squeak as the gateway of a palace opened, never walked along a garden hedge trimmed with a straight razor. And now I've met you, I think I'd rather you showed it to me than going there as a solo act. I know you feel guilty over the moths flying out of your wallet just now. But it isn't your fault Dr. Pendleton left the Paragon Hotel to the administrator of a veterans' charity, and it isn't San José's fault they're not strong for watching virtuoso vocalists wheezing.

Anyway—for now, we live on the cul-de-sac, with the orange-peel sunsets and the smell of eucalyptus trees. Halfway between the best amaro I've ever tasted and a pneumonia poultice. Wonderfully strange.

As strange as living someplace other than a hotel for the first time in my life. But things happen, as my mum says, and you happened to me, and then there was no undoing of you. So I admire to help you understand why you thought that if I truly knew you, I wouldn't hate you.

Because you were right about that. And sometimes you half suspect you were wrong after all, when you're cross and hate me, or when you're sick and hate the treatment, or when you're sad and hate yourself, but you weren't, so here.

Here.

This is the reason. I wrote it all down. And I could never hate you.

You just coughed, loud as a rooster crowing, and it made me smile. You feel better, I know you feel better. I just finished your get-well gift, after all—tomorrow morning I'll write a prologue, a bit of an introduction, a letter of sorts, and then *c'est tout*. And none too soon, because Evelina is going to visit her alma mater in Menlo Park to run a massive charity drive next week, and before she pays us a call, I admire for you to perk up a touch.

Yes, I know all about you. But now we're even. And I don't think you're a monster any more than I think I'm Nobody anymore. You taught me that. Even though you didn't realize you were doing it.

So here's to the saps and the sinners. To survival of the fittest and the terribly unfit. To the paragon of animals in all our many forms. To you, friend Blossom, every piece of you. It mystifies you sometimes, that I can still say that after you've railed at me for half an hour or woken up in a haze of Scotch and sorrows. But I can't change it any more than I can stop liking the color violet. I do like it. Awfully much. You're just going to have to accept the fact.

Let's mourn only for our losses. And never for the things we haven't lost quite yet. We already have an entire language that would be dead if you were.

Let's make it last.

Historical Note

I grew up in Longview, Washington—about an hour's drive north of Portland, Oregon, through lushly forested countryside—but I was born in San José, California, into a thriving multiracial community. Children only notice things by contrast, so at such a young age, I didn't realize that my birthplace and my parents' social circle comprised such a broad color spectrum. But when we moved to the Pacific Northwest (I was six), I famously asked my mom where "all the tan people" had disappeared to; I couldn't seem to spot any. She admitted to me that they didn't appear to live hereabouts. Longview, it seemed, was preternaturally pale save for a smattering of taquerias and a Thai restaurant run by a wonderful Cambodian family. The event that really drove this point home, however, was when my bronzed California complexion and I sat down in a church pew at Vacation Bible School, and the kid next to me stared in unvarnished horror into my very, very dark brown eyes.

"Eeeeeeew," he said with conviction. "I don't want to sit next to a *Japanese girl.*"

Granted, I was only six, but I was old enough to know three things. First off, that I wasn't Japanese. Second, that anyone who was in fact Japanese must have been having a tough go of it. And third, that something was seriously amok with racial perceptions in my new town.

The first Oregon settlers envisioned an unspoiled paradise free from strife, crime, and poverty—and from racial diversity. As early as 1844, prior to statehood, the Legislative Committee thought it prudent to pass a provision sentencing any blacks who refused to leave the territory to a flogging every six months until they found the environment inhospitable enough to vamoose. Oregon's founding ideal was that of an all-white utopia. When it came time to write a constitution, it forbade blacks from living or working in the state. And it would be easy to just cluck ruefully at the fact that Oregon was the only state among the fifty ever to explicitly deny blacks the right to live and work there if the effects of such sweeping intolerance weren't still being felt. Oregon was also one of only six states that refused to ratify the Fifteenth Amendment (which guaranteed people of color the right to vote) when it passed in 1870. Thankfully, they quickly saw the error of their ways and ratified blacks' voting rights on February 24, 1959, a mere eighty-nine years later. According to a July 2016 article in *The Atlantic* titled "The Racist History of Portland, the Whitest City in America," at the time of its publication, Portland was 72.2 percent white and only 6.3 percent African American. I grew up thereabouts and, while I can't claim to have counted heads, I can attest this is accurate. And that statistic is the direct result of oppressive policy and culture, not of random accident; during the 1920s, when *The Paragon Hotel* takes place, Oregon boasted the biggest Ku Klux Klan organization west of the Mississippi River.

Americans enjoy pretending that the KKK has always been a predominantly Southern problem, breeding only where slavery once thrived. Nothing could be further from the truth. In 1924, a Dartmouth sociologist named John Moffatt Mecklin wrote in *The Ku-Klux Klan: A Study of the American Mind*, "The Klan draws its members chiefly from the descendants of the old American stock living in the villages and small towns of those sections of the country where this old stock has been least disturbed by immigration, on the one hand, and the disruptive effect of industrialism, on the other." The principle holds true to this day; of the people I know who are mistrustful of all Muslims, for example, most of them have never met one.

This rampant national paranoia all too often led to violence, and Dr. Doddridge Pendleton's fate in this novel is based on two real accounts. In the first place, in 1902, a black man named Alonso Tucker who was shot while trying to escape a lynch mob accusing him of rape in Marshfield, Oregon (now Coos Bay), died while being dragged to the scene of the crime, and his body was hanged by the neck from a bridge. In the second, in 1924, another black Marshfield citizen by the name of Timothy Pettis was murdered and tossed into the bay. It was only after the black community insisted on a second autopsy that the public learned the testicles had been stripped from Pettis's body. Such atrocities are often glossed over as "unthinkable" aberrations, when their roots can be traced all too clearly. Following World War One, America experienced rapid societal shifts, as well as a recession and plentiful race and labor riots, and the Klan reacted by entrenching themselves implacably against feminism, Catholicism, Judaism, and "racial amalgamation"—proving once again that, when in doubt, it's much easier to be *against* something than it is to be *for* something else.

The Paragon Hotel is, in every particular, patterned after Portland's historic Golden West Hotel, a haven for people of color from 1906 to 1931. The descriptions herein are as accurate as I could make them, from the dining room's decor to the ground floor's business directory, and while it hasn't been a hotel for many decades, you can still visit the Golden West Building at 707 NW

Everett Street. An African American businessman named William D. Allen saw the urgent need for housing to serve the employees of the transcontinental railroad following the completion of Union Station in 1896, and his hotel became not merely a successful investment, but a center of the black community until it was finally felled by the Great Depression. The first hotel in Portland to accommodate colored guests, the only hotel open to traveling railroad porters, cooks, and waiters, and by far the preferred lodgings for famous black politicians and entertainers passing through town, the Golden West was one of the strongest cornerstones of African American society in the entire state. Naturally, people being people, it also housed a gambling den in the basement.

One of the themes I thought worth exploring was the ways in which communities—white and black—deal with racial violence and oppression. Alice James finds herself weirdly adapted to battling the KKK after surviving the Mafia, and in some minor ways the Italian American and African American experiences possessed common ground. Both communities were forced to live outside what was considered the respectable Manhattan city limits, in dire poverty, in Harlem. Both were ostracized for assumed moral inferiority, Italians because they were Catholic, and blacks simply due to their skin color. They lived in close quarters, surprisingly harmoniously, for some decades. But in other aspects, the two populations' stories could not have differed more widely. Italians were immigrants by choice, never by indenture. African Americans faced a system that had enslaved them and continued to terrorize them, day in and day out, without respite. And while blacks were being persecuted by the KKK and myriad other forms of racist oppression, Italians found themselves in the bizarre position of being bullied by their own people. The prejudices of their Old World carried over into the New—the Mob almost exclusively, both as a means of playing to their strengths and avoiding the ire of white law enforcement, preyed upon their fellow Italians.

HISTORICAL NOTE

The New York Mafia, even in its earliest incarnation, was a terrifying organization despised for its ruthlessness and cunning. It had already perfected its techniques in the Old Country: destroy all perceived enemies, strike horror into the hearts of commoners, and above all, work closely enough with politicians and landlords to get away with it. The average Italian American at the turn of the century would have had no recourse among the NYPD's three-quarters Irish ranks when threatened by the Family. Many of the events in this book are set in motion due to the gruesome murder of a local Italian shopkeeper; the real victim of the so-called Barrel Mystery was Benedetto Madonia, a vendor of Morello's counterfeit currency, and he had arrived in America only the week before. A stiletto was thrust above his Adam's apple, a slash with another knife nearly severed his head, and, after dumping the corpse into a barrel, Boss of Bosses Giuseppe Morello—known due to his deformity as the "Clutch Hand"—left the body to be found on a public street with its limbs dangling over the rim. Such techniques were far from subtle, but they were effective. His cruel syndicate would blossom into the Genovese crime family, the oldest of the Five Families of New York. Aspects of Mr. Salvatici's character—the sinister but kindly man who becomes Alice's guardian—were borrowed from the historical mobster Owney Madden: founder of the world-renowned Cotton Club, avid pigeon fancier, passionate philanthropist, and vicious cutthroat.

A very great deal has been written about Prohibition, and much of that generalized, but it seems fair to conclude that its enforcers owned a talent for extortion. Positions as dry agents, particularly in New York, were passed out to men with no interest in the teetotaler cause itself but instead a keen affection for lining their pocketbooks. All one required to land a job defending the Volstead Act at a local level was to possess the right political connections. The Bureau of Prohibition thus swiftly earned its reputation as a corrupt body employing a small army of thugs, based on scandals ranging from widespread bribery to an agent who shot a cabdriver point-blank in the back of his head during a shady liquor deal gone fatally awry. The general public, even those in favor of dry laws, could not condone such tactics, and therefore scofflaws and rumrunners became populist heroes in the eyes of many. Otherwise upstanding citizens turn a blind eye to liquor consumption in this novel because much of the country felt that way, even when they realized that liquor could be dangerously addictive. At the same time, while Bayer stopped marketing heroin as a drug in 1913, addiction to its popular cough suppressant had already soared, and cocaine was still readily available in tablet form until the Jones-Miller Act of 1922 finally limited its manufacture.

"Nobody" Alice James and the other female star of this tale, Blossom Fontaine, are creatures of fiction. But the women of the Prohibition Era empowered themselves more rapidly than their foremothers might have dreamed possible. The Nineteenth Amendment, guaranteeing women the right to vote, was ratified on August 18, 1920. Once alcohol became illegal for everyone, the playing field was in many senses leveled, and hitherto "respectable" women found themselves quitting their drawing rooms in favor of speakeasies. And the binary roles of mother and maiden, so desperately defended by the Klan, began to crumble. Being female no longer depended so entirely upon virginity, or on a ring on one's finger; strength, style, wit, grace, and charm began to be prized beyond technicalities of reproductive status. In his September 1925 article for *The New Republic,* "Flapper Jane," Bruce Bliven wrote of modern women, "They don't mean to have any more unwanted children. They don't intend to be debarred from any profession or occupation they choose to enter. They clearly mean . . . that in the great game of sexual selection they shall no longer be forced to play the role, simulated or real, of helpless quarry." I therefore set out to make Alice and Blossom anything but helpless, in honor of those daring females who decided to bob their hair, find employment, pour themselves a drink, and change the world.

· *Acknowledgments* ·

This is the most difficult book I have ever written. It began with the mental image of a critically wounded gun moll fleeing Harlem and the Mob, ending up in Portland fighting the Klan, and emerged as you see it. May it serve the reader well! But between those brackets were about two and a half years, maybe a hundred thousand deleted words, plentiful tears, and enough liquor to floor Ernest Hemingway.

Thank you to the Key West Literary Society for giving me a month-long writer's residency during the balmy month of February 2016. During that time, I wrote copious words, met chickens, reclined on beaches doing research, made friends with holy vagrants, quaffed beers with colleagues, and threw out my entire first draft. There's a first time for everything! When I went into hysterics about having wasted my residency to my husband, he said, "But how long would it have taken you to throw it out if you *hadn't* been in Key West?" I'm grateful to Arlo, Nancy, Mark, Ian, Carla, Miles . . . I could go on endlessly.

During the research process for this novel, I tackled the history of Prohibition, the Family, the Klan, Portland, Harlem, and the vernacular of the early twenties. As you can imagine, this was a piece of cake. When I had torn out most of my hair and decided I could never learn enough about Portland history for the world to feel real, I went on hands and knees to a librarian, seeking help. There's a first time for everything! To Emily-Jane Dawson and the Multnomah County Library, bless you and bless your advice and bless your microfilm department. So many historians' work was invaluable, but thanks especially to Carl Abbott, with whom I corresponded, and to publications by the likes of Elizabeth McLagan, Kimberly Mangun, Ellen NicKenzie Lawson, David A. Horowitz, Kenneth T. Jackson, Michael A. Lerner, Finn J. D. John, Stanley Walker, and Mike Dash.

When I was two-thirds finished with the book you're holding in your hands, I had a meltdown over whether it was entirely guano, so I showed an incomplete draft to my editor. There's a first time for everything! Kerri

Kolen, we've been together for three books now, and I'll never cease to be in awe of your work ethic, graciousness, brilliance, and caring. You told me I could do it, and I didn't believe you, but look—I did. This novel is here because of you. Thank you. Thank you also to the absolutely lovely Sara Minnich for your passion, meticulousness, and for championing my new baby like—well, a champion. Hey Katie McKee, Alexis Welby, Ivan Held, and about a dozen others, did you know you are full metal badasses? 'Cause it's truth.

After that, when my manuscript was due and it was still dropped-spaghetti levels of hot mess, I went sobbing to my agent about it. There's a first time for everything! My people at William Morris Endeavor are all the veriest feline pajamas, as Alice would say, and at the top of that list is Erin Malone. If we are on the subject of cats and nightwear, she is absolutely the Coco Cody Silk Shirt Pajama Set by Olivia von Halle (Google it). But seriously: she *takes care of me*, she makes me better, and I adore her. Thank you also to Tracy Fisher, Anna DeRoy, and all the other tireless kitty jammies at WME.

Throughout this process, when I was weary and angry and about as cheerful as Mitch McConnell at an LGBTQ rally, my friends were always there for me. And *not* for the first time either! Thank you to every author, neighbor, actor, saloon keeper, and Sherlockian who kept me afloat. Also I want to acknowledge that first, I'm grateful for the eternal devoted support of my family; and second, thanks Mom and Dad for moving to the Pacific Northwest—it gave me lifelong friends, endless creative space, an affinity for blackberries, my matchless husband, my brilliant high school English teacher Jim LeMonds and therefore this career, and so much more. Bethy, thank you for your faith in every version of me, and for ruthlessly shutting me down every time I even mentioned giving up on this book, and for the encouragement that always comes straight from the left side of your chest. Gabriel, you watched this process turn me into a headless chicken, to put it kindly, and you stapled my noggin back on hundreds of times. Every day your strength and courage astonish me. You are my rock.

To my readers, as ever: I'm forever grateful. I think of you all as people who, to quote Blossom, love dreams or dream about love. Thank you for taking this journey.